DEATH OF A PROMISE

SHARON ROWSE

THREE CEDARS PRESS

Death of a Promise
A Barbara O'Grady Mystery
By Sharon Rowse

Book cover designed by Sharon Rowse & Three Cedars Press
Published by Three Cedars Press
www.threecedarspress.com

ISBN: 978-1-988037-17-2

ALSO BY SHARON ROWSE

The Barbara O'Grady Series: (in order)

Death of a Secret

Death of a Threat

Death of a Promise

Death of a Shadow

Death of a Lie

Death of a Dream

Death of a Chance

The John Granville & Emily Turner Historical Mystery Series: (in order)

The Silk Train Murder

The Lost Mine Murders

The Missing Heir Murders

The Terminal City Murders

The Cannery Row Murders

The Hidden City Murders

The Dockside Murders

*For details on these and upcoming books or to sign up for her mailing list, visit
Sharon's website at: www.sharonrowse.com*

For my readers

CHAPTER ONE

The phone rang and I jumped, scattering half a scoop of dark Italian roast across the worn beige carpet that my landlord insists is just fine. Dammit, after a day like today, I needed coffee.

And they'd just vacuumed that carpet. Knowing our cleaning service, I'd be lucky if it was vacuumed again this century. This had better be good, I thought as I reached for the phone. "O'Grady Investigations."

"Barbara, I need your help," my best friend said.

Oh, no. "Andrea, the last time you asked for my help, I ended up chasing a killer."

"You caught him, didn't you?"

I sighed, and clamped the phone to my ear with my shoulder as I tried to scoop up coffee beans. I needed that coffee. Now. "That's not the point."

"That's exactly the point. It's why I called."

"Since I doubt you're involved in another murder…"

"But I am," she interrupted.

I dropped the coffee beans again. "You're what?"

"Calm down, Barbara. I don't mean I'm involved in a murder…"

"Good thing!"

"But Kathleen is."

I gave up on the spilled beans and reached for my pre-ground coffee stash. Andrea was talking about another murder case. This was now officially a coffee emergency.

"Kathleen?" I said warily. I knew I'd regret asking, but I had to know.

"Kathleen Marshall. One of my temps."

Andrea always looks out for her temps, but this was ridiculous. "If this Kathleen has involved herself in a murder investigation, it has nothing to do with you."

"I feel responsible. If I hadn't sent her on that job, none of this would have happened."

Before I could reply the jack-hammering started up. I was getting a little tired of never-ending noise and dust from the luxury condos being built along the water, not to mention the mess construction vehicles were making of downtown traffic. Plus it was raining again. All this and no coffee.

I slammed the window shut, and switched on the coffee maker. Listened to that wonderful gurgle that said help was on the way. "What job?"

"I sent her to fill in as a secretary at Vancouver University – in the PR department."

That sounded innocuous enough. "So?"

"So she found it so stressful that she went to Hornby Island to recuperate."

"And this involves you how?"

"There was a murder on the island and now she's worried she's a suspect. If she hadn't put so much of herself into the job I sent her on, she wouldn't be."

I fought back a sudden desire to laugh. Hysteria, probably. "Wouldn't be what, under investigation or worried?"

"Not funny, Barbara."

"Andrea, this isn't your problem."

"It is. It's the responsible thing."

"No, it isn't. It's your usual over-protective response to your employees."

"Well, she is my employee, and I'm worried about her. I want to hire you to help her."

Here we go again. I shifted the phone to my other ear, did my best to sidestep. "You're kidding, right?"

"No, I'm not."

"You do not want to hire me to help your temp," I said. Knowing it was useless.

"Barbara, she's frantic," Andrea said. "She needs help."

Andrea knows me too well. I tried again. "Then hire a lawyer for her."

"She says she doesn't need a lawyer."

"Then she doesn't need a PI, either."

"It's you she wants."

Me? I didn't remember ever meeting a Kathleen Marshall. How did she even know who I was? Oh no. "Andrea, you didn't. Tell me you didn't tell her how I 'saved' you."

"Well, you did."

I stared at the rain sliding down the window. I did not want to be involved in another murder case. Especially not one connected to Andrea.

The last one had been quite traumatic enough, thank you. I don't think I'll ever forget how it felt knowing Andrea's future lay in my ability to track down a killer—one I couldn't find. I never wanted to feel that helpless again. "If she really is a suspect, she needs a lawyer. Not a P. I."

"You could at least listen to the details," my persistent friend said.

"Are the police involved?"

"Yes, of course."

"Then it's being handled. You don't need me. Unless your temp actually committed the murder—she didn't, did she?" I asked, suddenly aware of another possible pitfall.

"Kathleen is one of my best people. She's absolutely reliable."

I couldn't stop the grin. "That's nice. But did she kill somebody?"

"No, she did not! Barbara, you're not helping here."

"Just keeping my facts straight." I said, glad she couldn't see my face. Andrea always says my sense of humor has no sense of timing. She might be right, at that. "So, she's not guilty, the police are working on the case—Why exactly did you want my help?"

I've known Andrea too long to expect to get out of it that easily, but it was worth a try.

"Kathleen is a suspect, a strong suspect. You have to help her. She says she won't trust anyone else."

Oh great. Then my mind caught up with the other part of Andrea's remark. "Kathleen is a strong suspect? I thought you said she didn't kill anyone."

"She didn't! But—but she knew the guy who was murdered."

"She knew him? How well?"

"I think they'd dated. But not recently."

It only needed that. This case was sounding flakier by the second. I wanted no part of it.

But if Andrea really was worried, I'd end up trying to fix things for her. Just like always.

First I'd have to listen to every tiny detail. Then I might have a hope of convincing her there was nothing to worry about.

I looked at the client reports strewn across my desk. It was going to take me hours to finalize them, but then I'd officially be between cases. It had been a slow winter. And I really hate paperwork.

Suddenly talking to Andrea's temp didn't sound like such a bad idea.

And I had to admit I was a little curious about the situation Kathleen had got herself into. "This is getting complicated for a phone call," I said.

There was a relieved sigh from Andrea. "That's what I've been trying to tell you. Kathleen and I need to meet with you. She needs some advice."

"I still say she needs a lawyer."

Dead silence answered me. When Andrea gets into her mother hen mode, dissuading her is like trying to stare down a bulldozer. From a tricycle.

"Okay, I can take a couple of hours now. Where do you want to meet?"

"Brady's?"

Brady's is a chic little lounge with a terrific view of the harbor and the mountains. It's one of my favorite places to go for a watch-the-sun-set drink.

Even on a bleak day like today I could watch the play of light and dark in the water and sky for hours, assuming I had hours. Though I don't paint much anymore, I suspect I'll always have a painter's eye.

But Brady's doesn't leap to mind as a place to talk about murder. On the other hand, it should be pretty empty this time of day, and the service is fast and discreet.

The place is also close to Andrea's office and not far from mine, with decent parking. Well, decent for Vancouver, which means convenient but pricey. It's when they start charging by the half hour that you know you're being taken.

And if I was going to be consulted on murder, I needed something a little stronger than coffee.

"Brady's is good," I said. And switched off the coffee maker.

———

HALF AN HOUR LATER, the three of us were seated at a black marble table at Brady's. We had window seats with a view of a gray windswept stretch of water meeting an even grayer sky. The North Shore mountains were lost behind heavy clouds, and only one rusted black freighter lay at anchor, where usually seven or eight are moored. Rain lashed against the wall-to-ceiling windows, making me glad of the fire that blazed in the limestone fireplace taking up most of the far wall.

Andrea introduced us.

"Kathleen Marshall, Barbara O'Grady."

Kathleen didn't look like a woman capable of murdering her ex-lover. Even Andrea, soft blond curls, angel-smile and all, looked like she had more passion in her.

Kathleen was in her early thirties or thereabouts, a tall, thin blond with a horsy face and pouty lips. Her hair hung lank around a pale face, and her eyes looked glazed.

Grief? Or something else?

Andrea ordered a soda water with lime. Kathleen ordered a double Scotch. I'd expected her to order something sweet and trendy—maybe there was more to her than showed on the surface. I was tempted to join her, but I had reports to finish. Plus I was working, sort of.

I ordered a glass of Merlot.

We made polite chit chat until the drinks arrived. Then I looked from Andrea to Kathleen. "One of you fill me in. What's going on?"

"Andrea sent me on a job at VU about six weeks ago," Kathleen said. "It was a tough one, and after it finished I needed a break. So I booked into an inn on Hornby Island."

Taking a long weekend on one of the Gulf Islands located between the BC mainland and Vancouver Island is most Vancouverites' version of the perfect getaway, and Hornby has always been my favorite.

It takes three ferries to get from Vancouver to Hornby, so it isn't as touristy as Saltspring or Galliano. I love the unspoiled quality of the island, but with my schedule, I seldom find time for a long weekend away.

The price of having one's own business, I thought, feeling a touch of envy for Kathleen's freedom. "You ever been there before?"

She shook her head.

"What made you choose it?"

"One of my co-workers, said it was quiet, with top-notch service. Just what the doctor ordered."

Right about now that sounded wonderful.

I wasn't exactly having one of my better weeks, even before Andrea's call. Nick was out of town—I hadn't heard from him for three days—my insurance was due at the end of the month and it had been raining since Monday.

Plus the last three cases I'd worked had been insurance surveillance. Which are boring at the best of times and deadly in the rain.

There was nothing I'd have liked better than going to Hornby and leaving it all behind. If it weren't for those pesky bills.

"So you arrived when?" I asked Kathleen.

"Friday morning. The job ended Thursday."

"Okay. And the death happened when?"

"Sunday morning." She paused, looked down at her hands, which were gripping the glass until her knuckles showed white. Loosening her grip, she continued, "We—we found him dead. He was late for breakfast."

Yeah, dying will do that to you. "What time was this?"

"After eight, nearly eight-thirty."

"And who was he?"

"He?" She seemed to be having trouble focusing.

"The dead guy."

Kathleen's face went white and she downed her Scotch.

I'd temporarily forgotten she had a history with the dead man. Andrea patted Kathleen's shoulder and grimaced at me.

Well, at least Kathleen's distress seemed genuine. That was slightly reassuring, given the doubts I had about what I'd heard so far. Not reassuring enough to take her on as a client, though. "I'm sorry. Can you tell me his name?"

"Bill. Bill Rampage."

"And where did Bill live?"

"Vancouver. He is—was a consultant."

Ah. A business shark. "Andrea tells me you'd dated?"

She nodded, and signaled the waiter for another drink. "Yes. Yes, we did."

"For how long?"

"Four months. But it seemed longer. Bill…" She stopped and for a moment I thought she couldn't go on.

Then she took a deep breath and finished, "Bill was a wonderful man. Warm and caring. I don't think he ever met a soul he didn't like. And they all loved him. I can't believe he's—he's—" She stopped, put her napkin to her lips.

Andrea made soothing noises. Kathleen gave her a weak smile.

I gave her a moment, and drank some of my Merlot. Which was excellent. I prefer red wines anyway, but on a day like this red wine and a real fire are essential for keeping the bleak grayness out there, where it belongs.

"When was it you dated?" I asked Kathleen when she seemed to have recovered a little.

"Two, no three years ago." She dabbed at her eyes with a tissue and gulped down half of the drink the waiter had just presented her with.

Four months, three years ago, and she was still missing him. She must have really cared about the guy. "Did you know he'd be on Hornby?"

"No," she said, but her eyes flickered.

Something wrong here. She was lying to me, and I wasn't sure why. "You'd seen him since you split up?"

"Oh yes. Bill and I were friends."

"When had you seen him last? Before Hornby, I mean?"

"I can't remember exactly."

"But the two of you made independent arrangements and happened to arrive at the same place."

"Yes."

Uh huh. I believe her, and her story wasn't making sense. What did she hope to gain by lying to me?

But then, why did any of my clients lie? And most of them did—I'd accepted that a long time ago. Not happily, mind you, but I'd decided life is better when I can pay my bills on time.

"And was Bill alone on Hornby?"

"Not initially. But by Sunday."

"He arrived with someone?"

"Sure, some blonde. But she got upset, left on Saturday."

"And what was she upset about?"

"I don't know. Me, I think," she said, downing the last of her scotch and signaling for another.

I took a slow sip of my wine, so I wouldn't start yelling at her. "Let me get this straight. The dead man's girlfriend left because of you."

"Yes," she agreed, sounding calmer than I felt. Probably it was the scotch. Especially if she'd been drinking before she'd arrived, as I'd begun to suspect.

Nothing like a little alcohol to undermine logic and dull a healthy sense of panic.

"Are the police calling it murder?"

She nodded.

"And you're a suspect?"

"I think so, anyway."

"You think so?" How could she not know?

"Well, they haven't said so directly, but they asked an awful lot of questions. And they didn't seem to believe me when I said I hadn't known Bill would be there."

This was sounding worse for her by the minute. I kept my voice level with an effort. "Why did they think you knew Bill would be there?"

"I don't know."

Right. I looked at Andrea. Her face said she didn't know what to think. She wasn't the only one.

I turned back to Kathleen. "Has there been an arrest?"

"No. But I've been told not to leave town," she said, smiling at the cute blond guy who'd just brought her drink.

That didn't mean she was a suspect. Maybe Kathleen was misinterpreting the police reaction to the case. "And when did this all happen?"

"Last weekend."

Today was Thursday. "Last Sunday?"

She nodded.

"And you haven't heard anything else from them?"

"No," she said absently. She seemed to be trying to flirt with the waiter.

That was good news, but Kathleen's current behavior wasn't. I looked at Andrea, who read my expression accurately, because she jumped in.

"Kathleen," she said, her voice sharp. Kathleen looked at her. "Barbara needs to know what you've heard from the police."

"Nothing at all." And she smiled sloppily at Andrea and then at me before turning to look for the waiter again.

"So why did you call me?" I asked Andrea, speaking across Kathleen, who was ignoring us.

Giving Kathleen a look that was half anger and half compassion, Andrea shrugged. "I was worried about Kathleen and it seemed like a good idea?"

"Yeah, right. Look, you don't need me on this case. I'm not even sure Kathleen's a viable suspect. And Hornby's a small island. There can't be that many suspects. Anything I could do the police can do better."

Andrea gave me a direct look. "But what if Kathleen is a suspect, Barb? We both know innocence is no guarantee. And I know Kathleen hasn't made a good impression, but I've never seen her like this before."

She wasn't kidding Kathleen hadn't made a good impression. Aside from the fact that she'd been lying to us, she couldn't hold her alcohol.

It's funny—or maybe sad, I'm not sure—I automatically think less of people who don't drink well. The influence of my father, I guess, who could always hold his liquor. Just not his temper. "From what I've heard, Kathleen may need a good lawyer, but she doesn't need me."

"She thinks she does. And she won't talk to a lawyer."

"Why not?"

Andrea shrugged. "That you'd have to ask her."

We both looked at Kathleen, who was now gazing raptly into the bottom of her nearly empty glass. "Of course, right now there's no point in asking her anything," Andrea said.

"She'd do better talking to Claire."

Claire Chan is the lawyer who'd represented Andrea when she was arrested for the murder of her tenant last fall. I wished I hadn't mentioned her when I saw Andrea's face. Every time I mention Claire, Andrea remembers being arrested. And then she remembers that I was the one who tracked down the real killer and cleared her name.

"Kathleen won't talk to a lawyer," Andrea repeated. "I've tried to change her mind, but she's convinced she wants you."

She paused, took a sip of her soda. "She thinks she needs someone to find the murderer. After all, you caught Jake's killer," she added, as if it were an afterthought.

And look how much fun that was. "Oh no, you don't. I only got involved then because it was you."

"And you saved me from a life behind bars. I don't know why you're so upset. It wasn't as if you actually had to confront a killer or anything. And this time it's for one of my employees. And for my peace of mind."

Easy for her to say. She wasn't the one who had everyone's expectations on her shoulders while her best friend rotted in jail.

"I have a business to run, Andrea, bills to pay." Which meant invoices to send out, dammit. I hate paperwork. And I especially hate it when there are no new cases waiting when the paperwork is done.

"I realize that. I'll pay for your time, at your standard rate. For the time you spend with Kathleen, and any other time you might put in. And look at it this way. If you're right, and you find out Kathleen isn't a suspect, your job is done."

Andrea was worried enough to put money on the line. This was serious. "And if she is?"

"You said she probably wasn't."

"Just trying for a little clarity."

Plus I needed to know exactly what she wanted me to commit to. With Andrea, it's never a wise idea to proceed on assumptions.

Andrea shrugged. "Think how it would reflect on my agency if it gets around that I'm hiring suspected killers."

"So you want her name cleared. As long as you don't share Kathleen's delusion that I'm going to be tracking down killers."

"Look, Barbara, I won't leave one of my employees in a jam because of a job I was paying her to do. I'd never be able to sleep at night."

Andrea's temporary help agency is literally the best in town, for two reasons. One is that she provides top-notch people who can actually do the job they're hired to do, which is a lot rarer than you'd think. The second is that Andrea really cares about her people, and they know it.

But even for Andrea, this was carrying loyalty too far. Not that she'd see that, of course. "Even if the employee doesn't seem interested in helping herself?"

She glanced at Kathleen. "Even then."

I sighed. In the twenty-three years I've known her, I've never managed to get Andrea to see the logic of a situation once she gets that tone in her voice.

She thought Kathleen was in trouble, she felt responsible for the situation Kathleen was in, and she'd worry about it until it was resolved. Barbara to the rescue, as my younger sister would say. So much for my getting out of investigating this one.

Well, what would it hurt to talk to Kathleen again, find out what she was lying about? It wasn't as if I had another case.

Wouldn't be today, though, I thought, looking over at Kathleen, who was now face down on the table. At first I thought she was in tears, but then I heard the gentle snores.

Taking out my card, I handed it to Andrea. "Have her call me," I said. "And you owe me one."

She grinned at me. "I knew I could count on you, Barbara."

Uh huh. That's what got me in trouble the last time.

CHAPTER TWO

So how had Bill Rampage died? And what wasn't Kathleen telling me?

As I drove back to my office, the windshield wipers swished rapidly in an odd counterpoint to my growing annoyance with this case. Kathleen had given me few details to work with. Aside from a rather nice glass of Merlot, the entire meeting had been a waste of time.

Back in my office, I glared at the disaster of paperwork I'd left behind. With a quick sweep, I cleared all of it off my desk, plopping the resultant pile on top of a handy filing cabinet.

Pulling off the top report, I sat down and finalized it. While the invoice printed, I rewarded myself by picking up the phone and calling Andrea.

I was surprised when she answered on the first ring. I'd half expected her still to be ministering to Kathleen. "So, what did you do with Super Secretary?"

A long sigh was my answer. "Poured her into a cab. Honestly, she's not usually like that, Barbara."

"I hope not, cause if that's your best employee, your agency's in deep trouble."

"Funny, Barbara. Very funny. Why are you calling?"

"I need some details on the murder, and I don't think I'm going to get much out of Kathleen for a while."

That got a reluctant laugh. "No, probably not. Did you see her trying to flirt with that waiter? If I didn't know better, I'd swear it was Kathleen's evil twin."

"That's it. Kathleen's evil twin is the murderer, and your so wonderful employee did nothing."

"Barbara, you've solved another case. I'm so impressed."

"Does this mean you're not hiring me?"

"Not likely."

"Figures."

"Never mind complaining. What did you want to know?"

I grimaced at the coffee beans still spread across the carpet. I still had to do something about those. "Any details you have on how Rampage died."

"Why don't you call Nick and ask him? He's supposed to be some hotshot police detective, isn't he? I'm sure he could find out for you."

Nick and I had met a few months ago on a case when I wasn't sure which side he was on—even then it was hard to keep him at arm's length. When he turned out to be one of the good guys, I gave up trying. And we're great together.

This much heat this fast, though, I figure we'll burn ourselves out before too long, though. It's not exactly a relationship, but I'm enjoying the hell out of it while it lasts.

"You are still seeing Nick, aren't you? You haven't managed to find an excuse to dump him, too?" Andrea was asking.

"What do you mean, too? And yes, I'm still seeing him."

Andrea ignored my question. "So ask him," she said.

I would have, except that he was undercover on a case of his own. I couldn't even get hold of him, which I found frustrating, but I wasn't about to admit that to Andrea.

She'd make way too much of it, like she always does.

I've never figured out why Andrea's so determined to find the right guy for me. It's not like she's in a committed relationship, after all. And I'm not the type for a long-term relationship—too much trouble. Which Andrea should have figured out by now, given my track record.

"He's out of town," I said. Close enough.

"Does this mean the romance is in trouble?"

"It means he's out of town."

"You don't sound too happy about it."

I wasn't, but I wasn't ready to admit I missed Nick, even to myself. I definitely wasn't about to admit it to Andrea. "He'll call me when he's back."

"So when do I get to meet this Superman of yours?"

"He's not a Superman, and I don't know. Soon, maybe."

"You've been dating him, what? Four months now? Any man that can stay in the running with you for that long is a Superman in my books."

"Three months." And four days. Something else I wasn't planning on sharing with Andrea. "You make it sound like I'm too critical or something."

"No, just gun-shy. Jayson has a lot to answer for."

I wasn't touching that one. Not that I agreed with her—my relationship with Jayson was more than four years ago now—but if I said anything, we'd end up arguing in circles.

Why do best friends always think they know you better than you know yourself? And then insist on sharing that knowledge with you? Time for a change of subject.

"Did Kathleen tell you anything about how Bill Rampage died?" I asked her. Again.

"No. Just that they were staying at someplace called the Sunshine Inn, on Hornby."

I hate places with cutesy names. Probably because my ex-flower child mother loves them. "Thanks, Andrea. I'll be in touch."

"And I still want to meet Nick," she said. "You can't hide your world from him forever."

And she hung up.

———

I SAT in silence for a moment, thinking about Andrea's last remark. I wasn't hiding Nick from everyone, I just enjoyed being with him. I didn't want to mess with it. And Andrea might not see herself as a disruptive element, but even she'd agree that my family was one.

I grinned at the thought and punched in the number for my other official source, my old buddy Jerry. Of the Vancouver Police.

"Hawald."

"Jerry, it's Barbara. Do you have a minute?"

"Is this official?"

"Yes."

He sighed. "Tell me it's not another murder, O'Grady."

"My client is barely a suspect. I'm trying to clear her name."

"Yeah, right. I've heard that before. Okay, you've got ten."

"Do you know anything about a murder that happened on Hornby Island? Local guy named Rampage."

"Nope, can't help you there, O'Grady. Not our jurisdiction."

"Come on, Jerry. The local RCMP would check with you guys, as a courtesy if nothing else."

He grunted. "They contacted us, but that's about it. I don't know where the investigation's at."

Well, if he was going to be difficult, I had a secret weapon. It helps when you've known someone since you were both seven. "Rocky Road ice cream?"

"The good stuff?"

"Aren't you concerned about the state of your arteries?"

"Not when it comes to ice cream. Deal?"

"Depends what you've got."

He chuckled. "Not a lot. But I want the good stuff anyway."

"Okay, okay. You've got it. But under protest."

"The local RCMP made some inquiries after the body was discovered. We're not handling the case, but they'll keep us advised."

"You don't know if they're near making an arrest?"

"Nope."

"Do you know how he died?"

"Sorry, O'Grady."

"Sorry you don't know, or sorry, you can't tell me?"

All I heard was the patter of raindrops against the window and the swish of tires on wet pavement in the street below. Okay, he knew but couldn't tell me. "Who has the case? I'll give him a call."

"I don't think you'll get very far."

"It won't hurt to try."

"Your funeral. Talk to Sgt. Brad Bramwell in Nanaimo."

"Thanks, Jerry. What about the victim, Rampage? Know anything about him?"

"Not officially, no."

"Not officially? Do you know something unofficial?"

"The man liked the ladies, and he liked to live high. One DUI charge, no conviction."

"Good lawyer?"

"You bet. Craig."

Ah. Ian Craig had made a small fortune defending well-heeled clients from their own folly. Still, it was food for thought. Bill Rampage's background would bear looking into. "Thanks, Jer."

"And my ice cream?"

Ice cream on a cold, wet April day. I shuddered. I'm one of the few women I know that only likes ice cream on really hot days. Sit by myself after a messy breakup and eat a whole carton of ice cream? No thanks. Give me chocolate any day. "On its way."

"I've heard that before."

"You don't believe me?"

"I've been let down before."

"I'm wounded."

"And I'm waiting for my ice cream."

"I'll send it by courier. Satisfied?"

He laughed. "Sure you will. Keep your nose clean, O'Grady."

"Yeah, yeah. See ya, Jerry."

I hung up, then grinned to myself and picked up the phone

again. I wished I'd be there to see Jerry trying to explain a courier delivery of ice cream to his buddies. The best part was, once word got around, he'd be lucky to get more than a couple of spoonfuls.

That detail taken care of, I looked at the name Jerry had given me. If I called Brad Bramwell, asking questions about an ongoing investigation, I'd be lucky to get the victim's name, never mind any details. The police don't like private investigators messing in their murder investigations. Not that I blame them. I don't much like it either.

Given Jerry's reaction, I suspected that Sgt. Bramwell was more close-mouthed than some. Maybe I'd hold off, see what sense I could get out of a sober Kathleen. I shrugged, turned off the computer.

It was still possible that there was no case for me to worry about.

CHAPTER THREE

Fifteen minutes later I was propping up the bar at Guido's with a glass of good burgundy of one hand and a menu in the other. I surveyed the busy main room of my neighborhood restaurant, nodded to a couple of the other regulars.

All the booths along the walls were full, and red-checked curtains were drawn against a wet and windy night. A fake fire blazed in the raw stone fireplace across from the bar, and most of the barstools were taken. The room felt warm and welcoming, smelling of baking bread and roasting garlic. I'd have to shout to be heard over the din.

Now this was more like it. Even if I had taken on another of Andrea's impossible cases. Even if Kathleen was a strange one, and even if I was missing Nick. For about the third time that day I wondered how Nick was making out on his latest investigation, the one he couldn't tell me about.

I ordered another glass of burgundy and a plate of calamari and turned my thoughts to Kathleen's case. It had been nearly five days since the murder and so far no one had been arrested. Either the police had no clear suspect, or they wanted to be very sure of the one they had.

At least Kathleen hadn't been found with the murder weapon in her purse. That was the risk in having a lying client—not knowing how wide the lies spread. Kathleen's lies seemed mostly about her relationship with the victim.

Since he'd been the one murdered, I didn't find that terribly reassuring.

Guido brought my calamari himself, putting the heaped plate on the counter in front of me with a flourish. *"Ciao, bella,"* he greeted me, giving me a hearty kiss on each cheek. "Tonight, my calamari is perfect. It will make that sad look fly away from your face."

"Thanks, Guido. It smells wonderful." And it did, but it looked even better than it smelled, if that was possible. Piles of rings breaded golden brown, the pale green of tzatziki sauce and the bright yellow of the lemon slices had me torn between reaching for a fork or a paintbrush.

The fork won out, but I grinned, imagining the look on Guido's face if I told him I wanted to paint his calamari instead of eat it. He'd probably never let me through the doors again. Guido has an Italian's respect for art, but food is his first love.

"So, how is it?"

"Just a sec." I picked up a perfectly round piece, swirled it through the creamy tzatziki and took a bite, closing my eyes to savor the rich garlicky taste. "Mmmm. You've outdone yourself. It's great."

He nodded in agreement and bustled off. How, after all, could anything at Guido's be less than great? And while Guido might be a bit of an egomaniac, he's not only a great cook, he's a dear.

Dinner at Guido's can cheer me up no matter what I'm dealing with. Even clients who've had intimate relationships with men who have subsequently been murdered.

I chewed on a piece of squid, thinking about Kathleen. For a woman who thought she was in imminent danger of being charged with murder, she was doing a pathetic job of clearing herself. Of course, I had only her word that she was a suspect.

She could be intent on having me investigate the murder for some reason of her own.

I swirled another morsel of calamari through the tzatziki and popped it in my mouth. It's amazing how good food helps my thought processes. It's a very good thing I run every day. And that I inherited my mother's metabolism.

————

"BARBARA O'GRADY! It is you, isn't it? What are you doing here, so lost in thought?"

I nearly dropped my fork at the cheery voice from right behind me. I swiveled the bar stool to see a laughing face framed in long dark hair and a pair of twinkling eyes.

"Shelley? Shelley Campagnaro. I don't believe it. How long has it been?"

"It's me, but it's Masters now," she said, waving a finger emblazoned with a couple of very large diamonds at me as she slid into the seat beside mine. "And it's been way too long."

I caught Guido's eye and pointed at my glass, then held up two fingers. He beamed.

Guido's always pleased to see me with other people. Social himself, I suspect he thinks I spend too much time alone. I suspect he may be right, but that's what happens when you're a P. I. Surveillance is a solitary sport. And I grew out of wild parties a couple of years after university.

"That's right, I'd heard you got married. You still drink red?" Shelley's a friend from university days, and at that point cheap reds were about all any of us could afford. Judging by her silk tunic and pants, to say nothing of that ring, she could afford better these days.

"Of course."

"Good thing," I said as Guido placed a glass in front of her.

"Now, that's service." And lifting the glass, she asked, "What shall we drink to?"

"Old friends?"

"Sounds good. To you, Barbara. It's so good to see you again."

We clinked glasses, drank. "It's good to see you, too. What brings you back? Last I heard, you were settled in Seattle."

"Still am. I'm here for a show, at the Courtland Gallery."

"The Courtland, no less? I'm impressed. A one-woman show?"

"No, it's myself and two other women. A bit of a retrospective."

"That's terrific," I said warmly, beating back a spear of envy. I'd always liked Shelley, and I was happy for her.

Still, it was hard to hear about someone else's success in a field I'd once expected to be mine. Even though I hadn't finished a painting in over a year.

"Thanks," said Shelley. "You know, I used to dream about us doing shows together one day. You were good."

"Well, thanks. Same goes."

"Do you still paint?"

"Now and again. My current career keeps me pretty busy."

"It must. I couldn't believe it when Sara told me you'd become an investigator. However did you get into that? And don't you miss your art?"

"Whoa. Slow down," I said, laughing. "Same old Shelley, I see. I'll tell you, but it's a long story. Do you want some calamari?"

Guido had thoughtfully provided an extra fork and another napkin when he brought Shelley's wine.

"Sure, thanks. But only if you'll tell me your story." She picked up the fork as she spoke.

"If you insist." I paused for another sip of wine, prolonging the suspense. Shelley's always hated having to wait.

She knew what I was doing and shook a finger at me. Which didn't stop her spearing another golden ring of calamari with her other hand.

———

SHELLEY HAS ALWAYS loved good food as much as I do, which was another of the bonds between us. Looking at her now, it seemed impossible we'd lost touch so thoroughly, despite the ten plus years. "You know I was doing temp work?"

She nodded. "Me too. It paid the bills."

"Exactly. One job was a security company, offered me full time work. The money was good, my career wasn't going anywhere, so I took it. I told myself I'd still have time to paint, but without worrying about paying the bills."

She made an expressive face.

"Yeah, pretty much, but I found the work fascinating. When they offered to train me as an investigator, I couldn't see a reason to turn it down."

"And your art?"

I knew she wouldn't let it go so easily. And my painting wasn't something I could easily lie about, not to Shelley. Not when she'd pursued the dream I'd abandoned.

So I told the truth. Sort of.

"I couldn't do justice to both, so I focused on investigating. It's a career that is going somewhere. I've had my own firm for a while now, and things are pretty good."

"Do you paint at all?"

"Once in a while. When I've got some free time and the mood strikes."

Shelley just looked at me, then shook her head slowly. "I don't buy it, Barbara. You're an artist, and that doesn't go away. I have no doubt you're a good investigator. In fact, it kind of makes sense. You were always the one who had to solve everyone else's problems. But giving up your art makes no sense."

She paused, tilted her head slightly sideways as she looked me up and down. "You're no quitter. It's not like you to give up on something that matters to you. Okay, who was he?"

"He who?"

"Never mind he who. The guy who undermined your confidence in yourself as an artist, that's who!"

I reached for my wine and took a long swallow. Had Shelley known Jayson? No, I met him after she'd left town. And he hadn't made me give up my art. I'd come to accept I'd never be quite good enough.

Of course, Jayson had never hesitated to give a little friendly criticism, point out areas that needed improvement. But he hadn't had that much influence on me. Had he?

Shelley looked at me shrewdly. "I see I was right. Don't bother to deny it."

"Have some more calamari."

"You can't deny yourself forever, Barbara. I learned that the hard way." She paused, took a tiny sip of wine. "My husband's one of the best plastic surgeons in Washington State, but he's a busy man. He needs a wife who'll care take for him. I tried to be that wife, but it meant that painting came second and after a while I couldn't live that way. I was withering, becoming a nagging, impatient witch. To put it politely."

She paused again, took another minuscule sip. What had happened to the Shelley I knew, the one that savored life in great laughing gulps?

"I was lucky," she said. "I figured out what was happening before it got too late, and we managed to find a compromise. Now we've got a housekeeper who lives in and takes care of both of us, and we each have our careers. But when there's something so central, so core to who you are, you can't ignore it. Can you?"

I shrugged. I should have known better.

"Barbara O'Grady! You can't deny yourself and shrug off your God-given talent like that. It isn't healthy. You'll wind up paying for it."

Shelley was always a bit of a crusader. Unfortunately for my peace of mind.

I didn't want to rehash my career choices, especially with someone whose painting career had clearly taken off. As if sensing something of how I felt, Shelley gave me a searching look when I asked about her latest works, but accepted the change of topic.

"I've moved away from abstract—you'll remember I was pretty focused on abstracts for a while?" At my nod, she continued "Now I'm doing representative work that's almost photographic in detail, but the perspective shifts—I can't describe it. You'll have to see it."

"Sounds good. How long is the show on?"

"Till mid-June. But the opening is tomorrow night. Why don't you come?"

"Well," I stalled, not sure how I felt about seeing her success in that kind of public situation.

"Oh, come on. If you've got a date, just bring him along. The more crowded it is, the bigger success the media will report."

"True. Fine, I'll be there," I said, making a sudden decision.

"And bring someone?"

"He's out of town," I said before I thought about it. I'm not sure Nick is my 'someone', but my subconscious seems to be clear on the matter.

"Well, I'm glad there's someone. Unless—is he an artist, too?"

"Not exactly. He's a cop."

"A cop? So not the guy that put you off art?" she said. "Good."

Interesting conclusion she'd drawn. I wanted to argue with her, but I couldn't, not with these unexpected doubts about the role Jayson had played yammering at the edges of my mind.

Andrea had talked about Jayson putting me off relationships often enough, but I'd avoided thinking about him and my career. I really didn't want to think about it now, or remember his cutting remarks, but Shelley's words wouldn't be banished. Maybe because she was an artist too.

Shelley didn't notice my hesitation. She was busy rummaging in her suitcase-sized leather shoulder bag. They used to be imitation leather, but other than that it looked exactly like the bags she's been carrying forever.

And she could never find what she was looking for back then either, I remembered with a grin. It was good to know some things never changed.

Before I had time to change expression, Shelley was facing me again, a triumphant look on her face. "Found it," she exclaimed, handing me a very elaborate invitation. "And take that look off your face. I always end up finding what I'm looking for."

Even the line was the same.

I couldn't help it, I burst out laughing, and Shelley, bless her, laughed right along with me. "Thanks, Shell," I said, taking the card from her. "Very impressive. They're doing you proud."

She nodded, and beamed. "Sometimes I can't quite believe it," she confessed. "Remember when it was our dream to show at these little chi-chi galleries?"

I nodded. I remembered only too well.

And sitting here, eating, drinking, laughing and talking art with Shelley felt so familiar, it suddenly felt utterly wrong not to be sharing that dream with her. "And now you are. I'm glad we ran into each other. I wouldn't miss your opening for the world."

Shelley reached over and gave me a hug, nearly managing to spill my wine in the process. "Barbara, you put up a good front, but we all know that underneath that cynicism you're as much a dreamer as any of us."

Before I could respond, always assuming I could think of a response, she glanced at her watch and gave a small shriek. "I'm late. Blake's going to kill me. I'm always making him wait, and I promised faithfully that this time I'd be on time."

And she was gone in a swirl of cloak and admonitions not to miss her show.

CHAPTER FOUR

The following morning came way too early. I hadn't slept well, had lain listening to the rain for what seemed hours, then been caught up in disconnected dreams that left me feeling empty. By the time I'd gone for my run and made it into the office, it was well after nine.

Luckily I had no appointments that morning. Of course, no appointments meant no new revenue, which was worrisome. Putting on a pot of French Roast, I sat down to deal with the rest of those invoices.

My eye fell on the invitation to Shelley's opening, which I'd propped against my phone as a reminder, not that I was likely to forget. I'd decided to go. Shelley seemed to want me there, but though I was curious to see how her style had evolved, I wasn't looking exactly looking forward to it.

Before I had a chance to talk myself out of going, the phone rang. "O'Grady Investigations. Barbara O'Grady speaking."

It didn't surprise me to hear Kathleen's voice. "We should meet," she said in a subdued voice.

I suspected she was suffering from a killer hangover, which served her right. "I agree."

"Shall we say Brady's?"

And let her near the Scotch again? Not a chance. "Sorry, I can't fit it into my schedule. Why don't you come to my office. Say around eleven?"

"Yes, I can do that. How do I get there?"

I gave her directions, and rang off.

———

COMPLETING reports and finalizing invoices always seems to take forever. I was surprised when I looked up and it was quarter to eleven. Stretching mightily, I put on another pot of coffee, then stood at the window watching the city darken under thick black clouds while I waited for the gentle bubbling sound.

It had stopped raining earlier, but it looked like we were in for another deluge. No wonder travel agents are always so busy this time of year. Despite an incredible week of warmth and sunshine in March, it felt as if it had been wet, cold and gray forever.

Kathleen announced her presence with a rap on my door.

"Come in."

She strode in and gave me a firm handshake. There was no sign of the woman who had been downing Scotch the previous day. Her makeup was perfect, her hair up in a French twist. She was wearing a trim navy suit and tiny diamond earrings and carrying a furled navy umbrella.

This must be Kathleen's business persona. No wonder Andrea had been so surprised yesterday, if this was the Kathleen she was used to dealing with.

Kathleen seated herself across the desk from me and folded her hands together. "What would you like me to tell you?"

I like a client who gets straight to the point, but in this particular client it made me uneasy. Who was the real Kathleen? "Care for some coffee?"

"No, thank you."

I got up to get my own cup. As I did so, I noticed her eyes were very busily checking out every detail of my vintage oak desk and dented filing cabinets. I remember from my own long ago days as a temp how much an office can tell you about the business that's conducted there.

Long-term temps seem to develop a sixth sense when it comes to the work environment. I'd once walked out of a temp assignment because everything about the setup screamed sleazy.

I wondered what conclusions Kathleen was drawing as she looked at my office and tried to see it through her eyes. It wasn't fancy. I'd had neither the time nor the money for frills, but it was organized and it was professional.

And it was mine. Maybe it didn't look like Howe Street, but I was proud of the accomplishments it symbolized, battered furniture and all.

Sitting down again, I looked directly at Kathleen. "You've temped in a lot of different offices. What was your first impression of the Sunshine Inn as a workplace?"

She looked taken aback for a moment, and slightly guilty, as if she felt caught out. Then she relaxed, and smiled at me. "You're good. Andrea told me you were."

She paused, bit her lip. "It was very clean, nicely decorated, had a welcoming feel to it. Warm. You could tell they know their stuff."

"Had Bill Rampage been there before?"

"Yes, several times."

"But you hadn't?"

"No."

I made a note. "So, why don't you start by giving me the details of the death. Was it murder?"

"The police seemed pretty sure it was."

"Okay. Tell me why."

"Well, we found him on Sunday morning. About eight-fifteen, if that matters?"

I looked up from the notes I was making, nodded. "I need as much detail as you can remember."

"Fine." This must be the efficient woman Andrea knew. She

took a deep breath. "He… he was half in and half out of his bed, his face was splotchy red, the bedclothes were twisted around him and he'd been… he'd been sick. Everywhere. I still can't get the smell out of my mind."

"Poison?"

She nodded. "That seemed to be what the police thought."

Her description matched the little I knew of cyanide poisoning, but death by poisoning is not exactly a specialty of mine. At least it meant that the murderer wasn't likely to be violent. Just deadly.

"Did they say what kind of poison?" I asked.

"No. They said nothing, just secured the scene and set about interviewing everyone."

"Other than yourself and the victim, how many people were there?"

"Well, besides Bill and me there were four other guests, the innkeeper and his wife, and two, no three staff. I think most of the staff were part-time."

"And did you know any of the other guests?"

"Just—just to say good morning to. It was Bill who…" Kathleen put her hand to her mouth and gave a half-sob. Then, as she composed herself, "Sorry."

"Are you all right?"

She nodded. "I want to get this over with."

I could understand that. "Sure. You were saying something about Bill?"

"Everyone loved him."

Someone didn't. "Do you know who found the body?"

"I did."

Oh, great. "You went up to his room?"

"Yes. We'd arranged to meet for breakfast. He was late."

"You knew which room he was in?"

She nodded. "It was next to mine."

Of course it was. This just kept getting better. "When did you arrange to meet for breakfast?"

"The previous evening."

"And was this before or after his girlfriend left?"

"After."

It seemed Bill didn't waste any time. "And the girlfriend's name?"

"He introduced her as Terri. No last name."

"You'd never met her before?"

"No."

Her eyes flickered. She was lying again. I was getting tired of it.

I picked up a pencil, tapped the eraser end against the desk. "Had you ever seen them together before?"

"Not really."

Tap. Tap. "Not really?"

She flushed slightly. "I'd see them walking together sometimes. On the Seawall."

Vancouver's Seawall, ringing Stanley Park in the heart of the West End, is one of our claims to fame. It's the perfect place to stroll on a sunny weekend afternoon. Even in the rain, with the wind throwing up whitecaps, the Seawall is spectacular, and you can run into almost anyone there.

If Kathleen had seen Bill and Terri more than once, though, it probably meant they, and she, were locals. "Do you live in the West End?"

"No. But Bill did."

Hmmm. He lived there but she didn't. Unless you know someone's schedule, you have to walk the Seawall a lot to run into someone more than occasionally. "So he must have walked the Seawall regularly?"

"Yes, I think he did."

"And you?"

"I—I try to walk it most weekends. And sunny evenings."

Which mostly meant the summer. I wondered why the question had thrown her. "And where do you live?"

"Kerrisdale."

Kerrisdale was a twenty-minute drive from the West End, thirty or more in rush hour. A long way to go for a relaxing walk on the

Seawall, especially when the equally appealing shoreline walks at Jericho, Kits Beach or Granville Island were only ten minutes away from her.

So what made the Seawall so attractive to her? Bill Rampage, maybe? "Back to Hornby. Did Bill seem to know anyone else there?"

"No. But he is…" she paused, cleared her throat, "was gregarious. He loved people, chatted away to them. It made it hard to tell who he really cared about."

Strong undercurrents there. Just how over was this relationship of theirs? "Is there anything unusual you noticed about any of them, or their reactions to Bill's death?"

"What do you mean?"

"Someone who's hiding something can act out of character, or inappropriately to the situation. Did you notice anything like that?"

She twisted her hands together. "No. No, not really. Everyone was shocked, and upset. One woman had hysterics. But it was an awful time."

"Do you know the name of the woman who had hysterics?"

"Lois something. But she's old. Surely you don't suspect her?"

"At the moment I don't suspect anyone. I'm gathering facts."

"Oh. Does this mean that you'll help me?"

"I'm not convinced yet that you need help, at least not my help. I can give you the name of a good lawyer."

Kathleen's face was set. "Andrea told me what you did for her. I need someone like you on my side."

I wasn't sure I wanted to be on her side. "Why are you so sure you're a suspect?"

"I think I'm a suspect because—because there were so few of us there. And being an island does limit the pool of suspects."

Hornby wasn't exactly an inaccessible island. But she did have a point. Unfortunately for my peace of mind.

"Tell me about your relationship with the deceased." I said. I deliberately didn't use Bill Rampage's name. I wanted her off balance.

Which didn't work.

"So you will take the case?" she asked instead of answering my question.

I wasn't ready to go that far, but there was something about Kathleen's situation that intrigued me. Maybe it was because she was so full of contradictions. Maybe it was just that nothing she'd explained about her relationship with Bill made sense.

I never could resist a good relationship mystery, as long as it wasn't my own. And my office wasn't exactly overflowing with other clients. "Probably."

"Probably?"

"If you answer all my questions. And after I've talked to Andrea again. She's the one who's paying my bills."

"No, I'll pay them."

I looked at her. Her chin was thrust forward and there was a glint in her eyes. "Are you sure you can afford me?"

She smiled slightly. "I can afford you."

"You haven't even asked what I charge."

"I can afford you."

Now I was really confused. This woman worked for Andrea as a temp, which ordinarily means money is tight. Yet now she was sounding exactly like my—admittedly few—wealthy clients whenever I dared mention money. Almost offended that I'd feel the need to bring it up. "Fine."

"So you'll take my case?"

"I'll decide after you've answered my questions."

"What did you want to know?"

"Your relationship?" I reminded her.

"With Bill? Oh. Well, we dated for six months or so."

"When was this?"

"Two, nearly three years ago."

"And what does dated mean?"

Her hands tightened in her lap. "Are you asking for steamy details? How often we made love? What his favorite position was?"

I raised an eyebrow. She'd immediately jumped to their sex life. Interesting.

Did that indicate a hang-up on her part, or simply the focus of their relationship? "No, I'm asking how often you saw each other. If you lived together."

Her color rose. "Oh. We saw each other three or four times a week, sometimes more. We weren't living together, but we spent a lot of time at each other's places."

"Overnight?"

"Obviously. If you must ask."

"I must. And how…."

"He was a terrific lover, if that's what you were going to ask next."

Way too much information. "It wasn't. How did the relationship end?"

She looked down, fiddled with her purse strap. "It was a mutual decision."

I'll just bet it was. "Because?"

"We—we just didn't suit."

"Too different?"

"Something like that."

I wished I could ask Bill the same question. I'd love to hear his answer. "And had you seen him since? I mean before that weekend?"

She nodded, smiled a private little smile. "Yes. I ran into him frequently. For a big city, Vancouver can be a very small town."

We were back to the Seawall again. And I noticed that she said she ran into him, not that they ran into each other. "Was it awkward, seeing him with someone else?"

"Of course not."

Now that I didn't believe. "Tell me why you'd planned to meet for breakfast."

Her face flushed. "For companionship. For old time's sake."

"Really? So you'd parted on good terms."

A shrug, eyes averted. "Of course. I told you it was a mutual decision."

Something was wrong here, and it came up every time I pushed her about their relationship. What was she hiding? "Are you sure he didn't move on? Find someone else?"

"No," she said, her voice rising sharply. "How could you even suggest such a thing?"

Andrea's poised employee was disintegrating into the woman I'd met the day before.

What would happen if I pushed a little harder? "Because the man had something of a reputation with the ladies."

"Bill wasn't like that! I know some people saw him that way, but they were wrong. That wasn't Bill. Not the real Bill."

Uh oh. It seemed like Jerry's information had been good. I wasn't liking the sound of this. "And you knew the real Bill Rampage?"

She nodded.

"After dating for six months?"

She met my skeptical gaze with a defiant look. "After six weeks. The carefree dilettante was a mask he wore for the world. To me he was a warm and caring man with an enormous heart and a gift for loving."

"And yet you broke up. You were too different?"

She paused, running her fingers along the strap of her purse as though debating adjusting it. "I might not have been quite honest about that."

"If you want me to work for you, you have to be honest with me." Didn't work for most of my clients, but it was worth a shot.

"See, Bill wasn't ready for our relationship just then. He wanted to be, it was right for the man he really is, but he needed more time."

"More time?" Was that like needing space? Kathleen wasn't some naïve eighteen year-old. Surely she hadn't fallen for that old chestnut?

She nodded. "He'd committed to me on a soul level, but he

needed some distance. I told him I'd wait until he was ready, and he just held me. It was a beautiful moment."

Apparently she had fallen for it. "But you didn't know he was going to Hornby Island."

"Well…"

"Truth, Kathleen."

"Then yes. Of course I knew."

Oh great. She'd been following the guy around. Did the police know?

I had a feeling I didn't want to know the answer to my next question, but I asked it anyway. "How did you know he'd be there?"

"I'd made it a point to know where he'd be. I didn't want him forgetting me while he explored his distance. I might love him, but I'm not stupid."

That was debatable. And this was not sounding good for my would-be client. "So you followed him there?"

"Yes. But it wasn't like you're making it sound."

I was tapping my pencil on the desk again. "No? Then how was it?"

"We enjoyed each other's company."

"Even though he was there with another woman?"

"I see what you're thinking, but it wasn't like that. Bill and I— well, I knew the other women were temporary. They weren't important, just Bill making sure I was The One. And it was important to both of us to keep our connection alive. And that meant spending time together. Whether he was with another woman or not." And she gave me a defiant look.

That was the most cock-eyed explanation for infidelity I'd ever heard. Either this woman was desperate, or she was delusional. Or both. "So that was why Terri left?"

"She couldn't handle it when Bill enjoyed my company more than hers. He was mine, and for a change, she was smart enough to see it."

"For a change?"

"Most of the women Bill chooses—I mean, that he chose," she

swallowed hard. "They were pretty stupid. They really thought they had a chance with him."

Uh huh. I wondered if Kathleen ever listened to herself. Or maybe it was Bill she'd been listening to.

Still, she didn't sound like she'd wanted the man to die. "But you have no idea who might have wanted Bill dead?"

"No, I don't. But whoever they are, they are going to pay. They took my love away from me. That's why I need to hire you, to find them and make them pay for what they've done."

———

AS SOON AS KATHLEEN LEFT, I picked up the phone and called Andrea.

"Trusted Temps, Andrea speaking."

"Your prize employee is seriously odd."

"Barbara? Did you just talk to Kathleen?"

"Uh huh."

"And why are you calling her odd?"

"Because she was pursuing Bill Rampage."

"She was what?"

"Pursuing him. Or rather, making sure he didn't forget her while still giving him the space he'd asked for."

"You're kidding me, right? This is Kathleen we're talking about? My poised, efficient temp?"

I sat back in my vintage leather chair, grinning as I pictured her expression. "That's the one."

She sighed. "Relationships do us in every time. Do you think she killed him?"

"I don't know yet, though I doubt it. But I think I've agreed to work for her. At least you won't be paying my fees."

"No, I'll pay your bills until you clear her name."

I'd leave Andrea and Kathleen to sort that one out between them. As long as somebody paid me, I was good. "If I can."

She groaned softly. "If you can. But I really don't think Kathleen could have killed anyone."

"Had you ever seen her belt back drinks the way she did the other day?"

"No."

I twisted the phone cord, let it spring back. "So there's a lot you don't know about her."

"I guess."

"For one thing, she apparently doesn't handle stress well."

"Being accused of murder is not ordinary stress. I should know."

"Andrea, you were arrested. So far the only one who has told us Kathleen is a suspect is Kathleen herself."

"True."

"You don't sound very happy about it."

"I like Kathleen."

Good that someone did. "If you're still insisting I take this case, you should let Kathleen pay my bills."

"I don't think she can afford you."

"I suggested that to her. She sounded offended that I'd even asked."

"She did?"

"She did."

"Oh." A silence. "I'll think about it."

I suspected I'd regret taking the case, but I'd be happier if Kathleen and not Andrea was paying me. Then the more Kathleen lied, the longer it would take me to solve, and the higher her bill. "You do that. By the way, I found out how Rampage died."

"How?"

"He was poisoned."

"Ouch." She was silent for a moment. "Barbara, I'm almost sorry for bringing you into this."

"Sure, you say that now. Never mind, at some point I'll have to head over to Hornby. And I plan on ordering the most elaborate meal the Sunshine Inn can provide. On Kathleen. Or you. Whatever."

"Send me the bill. I have a feeling you'll have earned it."

Unfortunately, I had that same feeling.

I put on a pot of Costa Rican coffee, flipped on the computer and began going through my notes. Kathleen had pursued Bill Rampage to Hornby Island, booked the room next to his, chased off his girlfriend, then found him dead. It wasn't looking good for her.

Except I was beginning to think she really had loved him. In her own unique way. And she hadn't been arrested—not yet, at least. And she really did seem to want retribution for whoever had killed her former lover.

There might still be some hope for my client's innocence. Or not.

I sat and glared at my computer for a minute. Stared out the window, at dark skies and the persistent, drenching rain the earlier clouds had prophesied. No inspiration there.

The person I really wanted to talk to was Nick, but I had an uneasy feeling that had more to do with personal reasons than professional ones. Besides, he was out of town on some hush-hush assignment, and I didn't have his number. Which I was finding increasingly annoying. I've never been good at sitting and waiting for the phone to ring.

I'd have to settle for the local RCMP officer, Bob Bramwell. Assuming he'd talk to me, that is.

I dialed the number Jerry had given me, waited on hold for far too long. Finally I was put through. "Sergeant Bramwell, this is Barbara O'Grady. I'm a P. I. In Vancouver…"

"Barbara O'Grady," he said. "It's an honor."

He was kidding, right? "Oh?"

"You're the one who cracked the Stewart case."

I was proud of that case, and I can't say that about many of my cases. "I'm surprised you've heard about it."

"My father is a lawyer, retired now, but he values justice. He trained with Maria Stewart, always said she was the most promising student of their year. We both watched the conviction of her murderer with a great deal of interest. My father was beyond pleased that bastard paid for his actions, even twenty-five years later. I made a point of finding out who'd tracked him down."

"Oh, well thanks," I said, feeling awkward.

"So, what can I do for you, Ms. O'Grady?"

"Oh, please, call me Barbara."

"Barbara, then. I'm Brad. And I'm guessing you want information in regard to the Rampage case."

The jack hammering started again. I rubbed my temples where the unrelenting pounding was creating an echo. And I'd forgotten my Excedrin. "How did you know?"

"Only case we have right now with ties to Vancouver."

"What can you tell me about that investigation?"

"Not a lot, I'm afraid. It's an ongoing investigation. What's your interest in this one?"

"My client was at the Inn, knew the victim," I said. No point dancing around it.

"Kathleen Marshall."

Something tightened in my chest when he identified her right away. She was obviously a 'person of interest' to them, if not an outright suspect.

I'd been hoping it was all in her head, and I could clear Kathleen's name with one phone call. "I can't confirm that, client confidentiality and all. But can you tell me if you're close to making an arrest?"

"And I can't confirm that, I'm afraid. At this point, there isn't much I can tell you. I wish there was."

He sounded like he meant it, too. It made a nice change from the usual response I got from Jerry, who doesn't want me anywhere near his cases. "Can you tell me anything about how Rampage died?"

"He appeared to have been poisoned. We're waiting on lab test results, but that's all I can tell you."

I was surprised he'd told me that much. Though, except for the lab tests, it was no more than Kathleen had told me. "Fair enough. Would you have any objection if I came up and had a look around?"

"Be my guest. In fact, if you're heading through town, look me up. I'd like to meet you."

The most direct route from Vancouver to Hornby Island was by ferry to Nanaimo, then straight up the Island Highway—eventually leading to more ferries and Hornby Island."Will do. And thank you."

"I'm afraid I wasn't much help."

"It's okay, I understand," I said, and rung off.

It looked like I needed to pay a visit to the Sunshine Inn. I turned on my computer, logged onto the Web and checked out schedules for both ferries. Because I'd be island hopping, I'd have to catch a seven a.m. sailing from Horseshoe Bay.

I shrugged. Needs must when the devil drives, or so my father used to say. And my father was a man who knew a lot about being devil-driven, though he never admitted what whiskey did to him, or to his family, until it was far too late. 'A drop of the Irish', he'd say with his twisting grin, and pour out another glass.

The coffee maker burbled at me, breaking the memory before it turned painful. I poured a cup, sat down and thought about the next step.

Schedule a trip to Hornby? I decided instead to do a little digging into the victim's background. If my client was the obvious suspect, wasn't it logical that I should be looking at the less obvious ones?

Especially given that the obvious suspect was paying my bills. Not to mention her relationship to Andrea. And speaking of Andrea—I picked up the phone.

"Barbara? Again?" Andrea said. "I do have an agency to run, you know."

"Very funny. Besides, you were the one who wanted to hire me. You have to expect some fallout from talking me into this stupid case."

"Ah, so it's payback time."

"No, that's still coming."

"Oh, good. Something to look forward to. Because things really are hectic here today."

"You can run that place with one hand, and you know it."

I could hear Andrea smile. "Thanks for the vote of confidence. So what's up?"

"Tell me what you know about Bill Rampage."

"The guy who was murdered? Well, he—hold on." Andrea's voice broke off and I could hear a murmur of voices in the background. There was a rustling sound as she covered the receiver with one hand, and I listened to the silence for a bit, sipping my coffee and thinking about next steps.

Before I'd come up with anything, Andrea's voice came back on the line, apologetic but hurried. "Sorry, Barbara. I've got a crisis here. I'll have to call you back."

"You know where I am," I began, then heard the click. She hadn't even waited for my response. Must be a real crisis. So much for finding out about Rampage.

CHAPTER FIVE

Turning on the computer, I focused on completing the paperwork on a couple of earlier cases. I lost all track of time, and the light was already fading when the phone rang.

"O'Grady Investigations. Barbara O'Grady speaking," I answered, expecting to hear Andrea's voice. But it was my sister.

"I'm worried about Mom," Susanna said.

I'd hate to count the number of conversations she's begun with those very words. I love my sister, but we don't exactly have the same outlook on life. "What is it this time?"

"She's starting sky diving lessons. Next week. And I hold you responsible."

Uh huh. "Well, good for her."

"Good for her? Barbara, what are you thinking? Do you know how many people are injured jumping out of planes every year? And that's not even counting the ones who are killed."

I was pretty sure I didn't want to know, especially if I thought about my mother being one of those people.

But my mother was a mature, competent adult. It was her risk to take, wasn't it? "I'm sure it's small compared to the number of people who actually go sky diving. It is regulated, you know."

"Barbara, this is our mother we're talking about. She has no business jumping out of planes. How would I explain to my sons that their grandmother got killed jumping from ten thousand feet?"

Trust Susanna to bring her kids into this. "Well, at the moment she's not actually jumping. She's taking lessons."

"Lessons so that she can go and jump. You have to talk her out of it."

I grimaced at the tall ficus tree currently dropping leaves in the corner by the window, made a mental note to water it. Soon. "Why?"

"Because she could be killed."

"She could be killed crossing the street. And this is something she's always wanted to do."

"I don't care what she wants to do. She can't go jumping out of planes at her age."

"Why not?"

"Because she can't, Barbara. Her bones are fragile. They'll break on impact. And it'll be all your fault."

"How can it be my fault if she's doing what she wants to do? And what makes you think her bones are fragile, anyway?"

"She's nearly sixty-two. Her bones have to be fragile."

"No, they don't. Susanna, she told me it was the one thing she'd always wanted to do. And now she's doing it. I'd say that outweighs a little risk, wouldn't you?"

"No, I wouldn't. Barbara, you have to talk her out of it. You have to fix this."

"Why?"

"Because you're the one that put the idea into her head. So she'll listen to you."

I hadn't exactly put it into her head, just encouraged her to do a little dreaming. How was I to know my increasingly conservative mother had always dreamed of skydiving?

But no way was I going to talk her out of it. Not when she'd finally decided to do something she considered important, instead of feeling vaguely sorry for herself that her life never turned out as she expected it to.

I thought about explaining that to Susanna, realized it was a waste of time. My sister needs my mother to be the woman she's always seemed to be, the woman she's emulated her whole life. How ironic that now I'm the one who's cheering her on, when I'm the one she always clashed with.

"Susanna, Mother's more likely to listen to you. You're the one whose life she can relate to. You have the husband, the kids, the house, just like she did," I said instead.

"That's exactly why she won't talk to me. She knows I don't approve of what's she's doing. And I'm a reminder of the wonderful example she set for us, which has to be making her feel guilty now. Plus she doesn't want to worry me."

Maybe Susanna saw more than I gave her credit for. Of course she was the good example. I was the bad example—single, self-employed, not even a steady boyfriend in sight. Spare me. "Oh, and worrying me isn't an issue?"

"You can handle it. You're the independent one, the big detective, you can handle anything. Besides, you're the eldest."

"Give me a break!" Sometimes I don't know why I even bother arguing with Susanna.

Sensing my resignation, Susanna closed in for the kill. "She relies on you, Barbara. And I really think she's putting herself in danger."

"Fine, I'll talk to her." And tell her how proud of her I was. It wasn't an emotion I was used to feeling about my mother. And it wasn't something I could begin to explain to Susanna.

The phone rang again. "What?"

"I'd have called you back sooner if I could," Andrea said.

"Oh, sorry. I thought you were Susanna."

"Oh no. What does she want you to do now?"

"Talk my mother out of sky diving lessons."

"What? You're kidding me."

"Nope."

"Your mother is taking sky diving lessons?"

"Uh huh."

"So what are you going to do?"

"Egg her on."

"But Barbara…"

I grinned at the shock in her voice. "Finally she's doing something she wants to do, instead of waiting for someone else to do it for her. And you want me to talk her out of it?"

"When you put it that way, I guess not. When are you going to tell Susanna that you support your mother?"

"I'm hoping never."

"Somehow I don't think that strategy is going to work."

"You think?"

Andrea laughed. "Okay, what was it you wanted to know?"

"What do you know about Bill Rampage?"

"Not a lot, but hang on a sec. "

I could hear keys clicking.

"He works—worked for a firm called Willis and Murphy. He was a business consultant and facilitation specialist."

"Which means what?"

Andrea sighed theatrically. "Oh, come on, Barbara. You know what a facilitator is."

"One of the less useful members of our society."

"You're hopeless."

"No, just clear eyed. And glad to be out of the business world."

"You're in business."

I thought about all those offices I'd temped in—the backbiting, the gossip, the petty bureaucracy—and shuddered. Much as I hated finalizing reports and preparing invoices, they spelled freedom to me. "Sure. But as long as I have no employees, I don't have to deal with anything except my bottom line."

"Which means you work too hard."

"I can live with that. Besides, look who's talking."

"Sure, but I'm not an artist."

"Neither am I."

"You are." Her voice was irritated and I could picture her looking like an angry kitten. It isn't easy for a short, fluffy blond to look angry. Or professional. But that never stops Andrea.

Every now and then Andrea brings up my abandoned painting career. I don't know why she can't accept that I don't paint anymore. Well, not seriously, anyway.

I've accepted it, and it was a dream I dreamed for a lot of years before I finally faced reality. "We've had this conversation before."

"And we'll have it again, as long as you persist in denying your talent."

"It's a very minor talent."

"And you're blind."

I knew my own abilities, and I was not having this conversation. "Do you know anything else about Bill Rampage?"

"Trying to distract me?"

"No, just to do my job. You do remember Kathleen? The woman you begged me to help?"

"Fine, but this conversation is not over."

The conversation was so over. "About Bill Rampage?"

More keys clicking. "We've placed a couple of temps at Willis and Murphy in the last several years. Let me ask around, see what I can find out."

"Thanks. I'd like to talk to someone at the firm, too."

"Why?"

"Well, a facilitator deals with conflict. He's supposed to resolve it, but it's always possible someone was carrying a grudge against Bill Rampage."

"Don't you think murder is an extreme response to a grudge?"

"Doesn't matter what I think. I need to investigate the possibility. Do you have a contact at Willis and Murphy?"

"Tad Murphy. He's one of the partners."

"Think he'd see me?"

"Probably not without an appointment. They're a very successful firm."

"I always did like a challenge."

"Oh no. Every time you say that, you piss someone off. You won't use my name, will you?"

"Not unless I have to," I said, and hung up before she could protest.

———

THE DOWNTOWN OFFICES of Willis and Murphy weren't as bad as I'd expected, though the receptionist cast a disdainful eye over my dripping Gore-Tex jacket—which does yeoman duty three seasons out of four. I guess it didn't suit her idea of appropriate attire. When I peeled off the Gore-Tex to reveal a well-cut black jacket and slacks with a cream sweater, her expression warmed considerably.

"May I help you?"

"I'd like to see Mr. Murphy."

"And your name?"

"Barbara O'Grady. I don't have an appointment."

The receptionist, a streaky blond with a high maintenance "I've just rolled out of bed" hairstyle, looked shocked. "Mr. Murphy's schedule is always very full. I'm afraid you'll need to make an appointment. In advance."

"The matter is urgent," I said in lowered tones. "In regard to the death of one of his employees."

"Are you—are you talking about Bill Rampage?"

At my nod, her eyes got misty, but she picked up the phone and held a brief conversation. Turning back to me, she said, "Mr. Murphy will see you. If you will wait for a few moments?"

So wait I did, admiring the understated Asian style of my surroundings, walls paneled in cream silk, low, black-lacquered coffee table, two clean-lined black leather couches. My black and cream fit in nicely, even if I didn't.

I wondered who their decorator had been. He or she had clearly known good art when they saw it. There were several very nice pieces, including one of Jayson's smaller early works, when he was still painting recognizable subjects. Early or not, that piece must have cost them an arm and at least one leg, maybe two.

My musing was interrupted by the entrance of a petite, dark-haired woman who looked like she'd spent too much of her life frowning.

"Ms. O'Grady?" Without waiting for an answer, she turned and went back the way she'd come, an abrupt, "This way please," drifting over her shoulder.

I followed, wondering how many paying clients she'd managed to scare off.

We ended up in an over-marbled anteroom, leading into an enormous office furnished with heavy dark furniture. "Go right in," my small guide said. "He's waiting for you."

Being self-employed, I sometimes forget how strange office life can be. People with even a little power will use it to remind those lower on the power scale how much lower they are. I'd obviously been judged and placed at the bottom of that scale. I hoped it wasn't a reflection of how helpful Mr. Murphy was going to be.

I needn't have worried. Plumply ensconced in his early forties, Tad Murphy had a jovial round face and a toothy grin. He beamed at me, as thought there was nothing he'd rather be doing than chatting with me. I was immediately suspicious. I'd barged in, interrupting his day, wanting to talk about murder, and he was pleased to see me?

"So, Ms. O'Grady. What can I do for you?" he asked as I sat down opposite his massive desk.

"I'm a private investigator. I've been hired to look into the facts surrounding Mr. Rampage's death."

Murphy's face changed from welcoming to sorrowing in a flash. I suddenly wished I could sketch him, see who he was behind his mask. I discovered early on that sketches of a person often show me the self that lurks below the surface, though I'd never fully been able to capture that truth in paint. I wanted to know what lay beneath Murphys's surface grief.

"It's a great loss to all of us, as I'm sure you can imagine," he was saying. "One of the brightest lights of our firm, and a personal friend. His death was so sudden, and in such terrible circumstances. Even now I can hardly talk about it."

All of this was said in rich resonant tones, which I'm sure he practiced, and it was said with nary a quiver or a break.

I disliked him immediately. I can't stand a phony, and Murphy was a fake from his too expensive shoes to his too white teeth.

"It's because of the circumstances that I'm here," I said, keeping my tone neutral with an effort. "I'm interested in knowing about Mr. Rampage's clients, especially those in the last six months."

"I'm afraid that information is confidential."

"I understand that. Without giving me names, or specific details, can you give me a sense of the kinds of situations he would have been dealing with? Would tensions have been running high in these cases, for instance?"

"I'm afraid I can't give you that kind of information. This is a reputable firm and Bill was a professional, Ms. O'Grady. He could handle any circumstances that came his way, without fallout."

"So you aren't aware of any employee or group of employees that might have held a grudge against Mr. Rampage?" I couldn't resist needling him, if only in hopes of seeing that facade deflate. I knew I was getting to him, too, when he started to drum his fingers on the polished surface of his desk.

He caught himself right away, and stopped the motion. I could almost feel the effort it cost him. "Absolutely not."

"Well, someone killed him."

"I have no idea why Bill was killed, I only know it had nothing to do with this firm."

"Did Mr. Rampage have enemies?"

"Bill was the nicest guy you'd ever want to meet. Salt of the earth."

Sure he was. And you didn't answer the question. "So you aren't aware of anyone who might have had a grudge against him?"

"No, of course not. He was a great guy."

Somehow I wasn't finding this assessment of Rampage's character compelling. It might have been the rehearsed smoothness of Murphy's tone. "And what about in his personal life?"

"I don't know anything about Bill's personal life."

"I thought you said you were friends."

"Well, yes, but I meant we were friendly colleagues. Bill was a great guy, but I don't socialize with my employees."

What an idiot. "Did he know anyone on Hornby?"

"Not that I know of."

"Was he worried about anything? Did he have any personal concerns?"

"Not that I was aware of. I'd have tried to help him out if there had been anything. This is a very close firm."

Of course it was. "Anything that might have affected his work?"

"As I said, Bill was a professional, Ms. O'Grady."

Yes, but presumably he was human, too. Though I could see why he might not have shown that side of himself to this man. "Can you think of anything else that might be helpful?"

"I wish I could, Ms. O'Grady."

Sure he did. I gave him my card anyway, just in case.

On the way out, I stopped by the reception station on a hunch. Something about the way the blond had looked when she'd said Bill Rampage's name was tugging at me. Only now it was a different blond receptionist, and this one said she'd just started, had never met Bill Rampage. Making a mental note to find out what the first one hadn't said, I left.

———

BACK IN MY OWN OFFICE, I looked at my well-aged filing cabinets and desk with something like affection. I'm all in favor of success, but not Murphy's form of success.

If I ever get caught in that ego trap where all that matters is surface appearance, I hope someone will call me on it.

The phone rang, as though confirming the thought, and it was Andrea. That fit. Any time I require ego deflating, Andrea is the one to perform it. In fact, I think she makes it her mission in life to ensure I never have any ego to speak of.

Except when it comes to painting, of course. I've never figured out that aberration.

"Barbara, I found out something else about Bill Rampage."

Of course, she does have her uses. "What?"

"He had a name for liking the ladies."

Jerry had already told me as much, as had Kathleen, in her own way, but it was useful to have another confirmation. "Anyone in particular?"

"I gather he wasn't. Particular, that is."

Ah. "Anyone I can talk to?"

"Sure. Another of my temps. Dianne is her name. Dianne Klassen. She worked at Willis and Murphy. At the moment, she's working at Vancouver University, in the Fine Arts Department." She gave me the number.

"She's willing to talk to me?"

"Happy to."

"Not too happy with our Mr. Rampage then?"

"Willing to talk about him, anyway."

"Okay. I'll give her a call. Thanks, Andrea."

"You're welcome. So, have you talked to your mother yet?"

I'd been avoiding it, as I'm sure Andrea guessed. "No time."

"Hmmm. Heard back from Susanna?"

"Not yet." Thankfully.

"Don't sound so relieved."

I grinned. "Stop needling me. You know my sister."

"True enough. Well, good luck, that's all I can say. And keep me apprised on Kathleen's case, won't you?"

"Count on it. Oh, and Andrea? Thanks for everything."

"You're welcome," she said, sounding puzzled. But then, she hadn't just spent an hour with a man who would benefit greatly from having an Andrea in his life.

After we hung up, I sat and thought about the relationships in my life. Andrea. Nick. Jerry. Susanna. My mother. Especially the latter two.

Growing up, Susanna always seemed to be my mother's pride and joy. I was the disappointment, the one who was always too loud, too late, too messy. The one who wanted to be an artist, not a wife. Not something my mother understood.

Lately, though things have been looking up. My mother is changing her own life, and we seem to have a rapport, however tenuous. So now, of course, my younger sister and I are at outs. She's trying to guilt me into fixing my mother's life, I'm trying to avoid telling her what I think of her life. I sighed.

I love Susanna dearly, and I truly wouldn't want her life, but sometimes compared to her I feel like a colossal failure.

She's living our mother's dream for us both— she's been a happy homemaker for more than a decade and her kids seem to be thriving. Me? I failed as an artist, I'm on my second career, my business barely survives from month to month and I'm not too thrilled with how my latest investigation is going.

Susanna's been married forever—I've blown every relationship I'd ever been involved in. Except the one with Nick, and that isn't even a relationship.

But might it be becoming one?

Shaking my head at the direction my thoughts were taking, I gulped down the last mouthful of coffee. Looking back at my desk, I found Shelley's invitation staring back at me. I checked the stated time, glanced at my watch.

I had less than two hours. Part of me wanted to skip the event entirely, but I had promised Shelley I'd be there. And there's no point in arriving at a gallery opening late. Not if you have any interest in looking at the art itself.

CHAPTER SIX

A little over two hours later, I was walking towards Granville Street and the Courtland Gallery. I'd showered and changed into my version of a little black dress—short and clingy enough to flatter the few curves running has left me with, exposing enough pale skin to look dressy. A pair of heels—black, of course—a deep red necklace, my gold hoops, a spritz of Nu and I felt sophisticated, sexy and ready to face Shelley's success.

It had finally stopped raining and the clouds had moved on, so it was cold and clear. I wore my long sleek raincoat, also black, rather than the usual Gore-Tex.

Vancouverites wear Gore-Tex almost everywhere—I'm told that more of the stuff is sold along the coast that includes BC, Washington and Oregon than anywhere else in the world. No surprise—living in a rainforest we'd all grow mold if we wore anything else. For an occasion like this, though, navy Gore-Tex wasn't going to cut it.

As I strolled towards Granville Street, Vancouver was decked in its evening lights. The sky was the deep gray-blue of a spring twilight and the street lamps glowed against it. The air was crisp and almost frosty, with a hint of ocean underneath. Between the buildings I caught glimpses of the ski runs along Grouse Mountain, their lights twinkling in the still air like a chain of rhinestones. I love the fact that those lights are lit all year. I think it's my favorite feature of the city's night skyline.

The gallery was brightly lit, and the sound of voices all talking at once spilled out onto the street. This was a place to see and be seen, the social cachet so high you could almost taste it. I found myself standing in a small cluster of people just inside the Courtland Gallery's door.

A smiling woman in a clinging black halter dress had taken my invitation while a tuxedoed waiter handed me a glass of champagne. Taking a sip of crisp, sharp bubbles, I looked for Shelley. There was no sign of her. Even this early the crowd filled the spacious main room of the gallery. Finding one person was going to be a challenge.

For Shelley's sake I was pleased at the turnout—it argued for the show being a hit. Personally I was a bit disappointed. I'd not get much chance to appreciate Shelley's work tonight. Still, I might as well get some sense of it.

Draping my coat over my arm, I veered towards one wall. I was maneuvering slowly along, peering over shoulders at the canvases hanging there, beautifully framed and lit, when a familiar voice came from behind me.

"Hello, stranger," he said.

Just the last man I wanted to see. It had been awhile, but not long enough.

I turned to face him. "Jayson. What a surprise to see you here."

He smiled that smile. My heart didn't melt. My stomach didn't turn to jelly.

This was good. There was a time when being in Jayson's presence was enough to send my good judgment flying. And it had lasted a ridiculously long time.

Jayson was holding out his right hand, so I raised mine to meet it. To my embarrassment, instead of shaking my hand he lifted it to his lips and pressed a lingering kiss to the backs of my fingers. "*Cara,*" he said softly.

His old pet name for me. All I felt was annoyed.

And a little amused at his pretensions. Did he really think I'd fall for that, after all this time, after the way he dumped me? "Don't call me that, Jayson. It's not as if you're even remotely Italian."

He grinned again, that imp of mischief dancing in his dark eyes. Before he could annoy me further, another familiar and more welcome voice came from behind me.

"Barbara, you made it! I'm so glad."

"But introduce me to this lovely lady," said Jayson in his smoothest tones before I could do more than smile at Shelley.

"Shelley, this is Jayson Ho. Jayson, Shelley Masters."

Jayson took Shelley's hand, holding it a little too long. Shelley looked from Jayson to me, turned to Jayson. "I'm pleased to meet you. I've admired your work for years."

"Thank you," he said with a smile just for her. "And I've been admiring yours."

A tinge of red crept up her cheeks and into her forehead. It astonished me to see my poised friend Shelley blush. I hoped it was his reputation as a major artist and not Jayson's bad-boy smile that was causing it.

"Thank you," Shelley said. "It's my first real showing in Vancouver, and I'm finding it a bit overwhelming. It's my hometown, you know. I went to university with Barbara."

"No, I did not know," he said, giving me speculative look and a wink.

I watched in amazement as Shelley babbled like a teenager. I'd almost forgotten this side of her. I hoped Shelley's husband was here somewhere. For all his lack of real interest in others, Jayson is a charmer when he wants to be, as I know all too well.

I suddenly wished that Nick were here, too. I could use his solid, very masculine presence, if only to give Jayson something to think about. I grinned at the idea of holding Nick's arm while he towered over Jayson. At a hair over five-ten, Jayson is sensitive about his lack of inches, the only weakness I've ever seen him display.

Well, at least I could distract Shelley.

"Shelley, I'd just begun to look at your work," I said. "I like what I'm seeing. You've really changed your technique."

"Yes, I have. Does it work?"

"From what I've seen, extremely well."

"I agree," said Jayson, his voice at its mellowest.

And I know his mellow when I hear it. It usually means he has new prey in sight.

"So Barbara," he said, turning to me. "Why have I never met Shelley before?"

Funny, he'd stopped calling me *cara*.

"Shelley lives in Seattle now. With her husband." I took great satisfaction in adding that last tidbit of information. It didn't seem to faze him.

"I predict we will see more of your work, Shelley," said Jayson. "It is truly good."

"Thank you," she said with another blush. I really hoped it was the sincerity in his voice she was responding to.

Jayson is a good judge of art as well as a good artist, I'll give him that, and he can be generous with his praise. It was the reason his disparagement of my painting hit me so hard.

I had to believe he was being honest with me—after all, we were in love. Or we were supposed to be.

And I'd seen how generous he could be with other artists. It was one of the things I liked best about him. These days, it's one of the only things I like about him.

I was beginning to think I might either have to physically drag Shelley away or see her work on my own, when our little three-some was interrupted by a scream from the other side of the room.

———

THE HIGH-PITCHED BUZZ of many conversations ceased and the abrupt silence seemed to echo in the crowded room. It was unnerving.

"That was Judy," Shelley said on a gasp.

Judy Moore was one of the three artists whose work was on display.

Shelley, Jayson and I looked at each other and without a word moved towards the scream. Everyone else had the same idea, so we were wading through a crush of art lovers.

I was pushing and shoving, trying to get as close as I could.

There had been desperation in that scream. I felt the cold trickle of fear in my chest.

Somehow we all three made it to the far corner where everyone was gathered in a tight knot, staring at the woman who lay on the floor.

"It's Deirdre," Shelley gasped, her hand to her throat.

Deirdre Brandt was the last of the three exhibitors. Her paintings hung on the opposite wall, a dance of color and emotion.

"Call 911," someone said.

A forest of cell phones appeared.

"What happened?" someone else was asking.

"She'd been feeling ill all night. Then she said her chest hurt and she was dizzy," a short brunette said.

I pushed my way forward. "Is she breathing?"

A tall man crouched down beside her, shook his head. Before I could move, he'd begun CPR.

"Someone go out front, wait for the ambulance and direct them here," I said, then turned to Shelley. "Does Deirdre have a history of heart problems?"

"No, not that I know of. Why?"

"Because this looks like a heart attack," I said.

"It can't be! She's too young!"

"Is she a heavy drug user?"

"I know she uses cocaine on occasion."

"Who doesn't?" came from someone in the crowd, breaking the

shocked silence. Someone else laughed, a high-pitched, hysterical sound, quickly silenced.

"This could be a reaction." I looked at the stunned faces surrounding Deirdre. "Does anyone have any aspirin?"

"I have some Tylenol," a woman wearing Armani offered.

I shook my head. "It has to be aspirin. If we can crush it, get some down her, it will mitigate the damage if it is a heart attack."

No one seemed to have any aspirin.

The man crouching beside Deirdre was still performing CPR.

I could hear the distant wail of an ambulance, coming closer. Thank God we were close to VGH. And Vancouver General has one of the best heart programs in the country. If this was a heart attack.

I looked at the woman lying on the floor.

Deirdre laid motionless, her face too pale and a blue tinge around her mouth. She looked to be the same age as Shelley and myself, maybe a year or two younger, though with the heavy makeup it was hard to tell. She had dark hair and high cheekbones and was wearing a dress of cherry red silk, with a deep décolletage and a thigh high slit.

Looking at her festive attire, I felt helpless, and sad.

Seconds later the ambulance pulled up outside, lights flashing and the attendants rushed in, taking over with practiced efficiency.

One took over the CPR, the other bent over Deirdre with a stethoscope.

"She's in v-tach," he said after a moment. "We have to get her in."

There was an aura of panic about him despite his smooth movements as he set up the gurney.

The first man paused long enough to help slide Deirdre on, then resumed CPR as they hastened for the door.

With a diminishing wail, they were gone.

For a long moment the gallery was silent.

Then the buzz of conversation resumed. Several patrons left, while others were eagerly discussing what had happened.

"How can this have happened to her?" asked one.

"She had a wild past," I heard the woman in Armani say.

"Well, I need a drink," Jayson said at my elbow.

"I need to go to the hospital, see how Deirdre is," Shelley said, her voice strained. "Barbara, will you come with me?"

"Of course. Shall I get my car?"

"Can we walk? I need some air."

It was perhaps ten blocks to the hospital, and the night was still clear. "Yes, we can walk."

"Then I will say goodbye for now," Jayson said, pressing Shelley's hand. "But when you know she is well, you will come back?"

"If I can," she said distractedly, not really looking at him. "Barbara, do you know where—oh, there she is."

She walked through the well-dressed throng to where the owners of the gallery, Len and Margaret Courtland, stood. Len looked gray, but Margaret looked remarkably composed. I'd always heard that she was the tougher of the two. Shelley whispered something in Margaret's ear, nodding at whatever she said in return.

"We can go now," Shelley said as she made her way back to where Jayson and I stood.

I nodded and led the way towards the door. "Is Deirdre a close friend?" I asked her as we cleared the door.

"No. To be honest, I don't even like her. But she's a fellow artist, and—I can't just go on with my evening as if nothing had happened. I need to know if she's okay. Does that sound too weird?"

"I think it sounds very compassionate." And what I'd have expected from the Shelley I used to know.

We didn't talk much in the fifteen minutes or so it took to make our way to the hospital. I don't know what Shelley was thinking about, but I was wondering about the woman who'd lain at our feet less than half an hour earlier.

I hadn't had a chance to look at her work, though I'd make a point of going back later in the week to do so. Deirdre Brandt had started to make a buzz in the art world a couple of years ago, and she was selling big pieces for a lot of money. I wondered how she'd come to be included in the Courtland show.

Mostly I was wondering what had caused Deirdre's heart attack, and hoping she'd be okay.

I also felt fiercely glad it hadn't been me, and guilty with it.

Deirdre was too young and the wrong sex for heart disease, but I'd heard what the ambulance attendants had said. I'd had an aunt who'd had a heart attack in her early forties. She'd lived, but though they'd never determined the exact cause, there was some speculation it might be congenital.

I'd learned what to watch out for, and what the various terms meant.

If Deirdre went into v-fib they had about ten minutes to get her to a defibrillator and shock her heart back into a regular beat. And while most ambulances carried portable defibrillators, not all of them did. They'd have to get her to Emergency in time.

CHAPTER SEVEN

The emergency room was the usual Friday night chaos, the waiting room packed with people, some waiting for news, others in need of attention. One boy was clasping a bleeding arm, an elderly woman whose ankle was at an odd angle was quietly moaning.

It was a depressing place to be when you could do nothing to help. I looked at Shelley, whose face had taken on a gray tinge, and led her to a chair in the corner.

"You sit here. I'll go talk to the nurse."

I had to wait, but when I finally reached the desk, the dark haired woman wearing blue scrubs greeted me patiently. "Yes?"

"A patient with heart problems was brought in earlier. Deirdre Brandt?"

She consulted her computer. "Are you family?"

"No."

"I'm sorry, you'll have to wait until her family are contacted."

A quiver ran down my spine. "Can you tell me anything?"

"I'm sorry. Not until the family are notified. Do you have any information on her next of kin?"

"Let me check."

I went back to Shelley, whose clenched hands and pale face showed the strain she was feeling. I was feeling a tad unnerved myself. Sudden death is never easy, and things weren't sounding good for Deirdre. "They're not going to tell us anything. Does she have family here?"

"I'm not sure Deirdre has any family."

"Who would they need to notify?"

"Her agent would know. Maryse Stevens."

"Do you have the number?"

She pulled out a business card with a shaky hand. "Here."

I took it to the nurse. "This is the contact for Deirdre Brandt. She's in Seattle. Is there anything we can do by waiting here?"

"Thank you, but I'm afraid not."

I nodded, turned back to Shelley. "We can't do anything here tonight. We should probably go."

"Is Deirdre going to be all right?"

There was no point sharing my fears with Shelley. "They can't tell us anything yet. I think we should go."

"I guess so. If you're sure there's nothing we can do?"

"I'm sure. Do you want to go back to the gallery?"

"I don't think I can face all those people, the questions. What I really need is a drink."

"I know just the place."

———

GUIDO MET us at the restaurant door, took one look at Shelley's face and was quick with a glass of Barolo, probably hoping the rich wine would put some color back in her face. Grabbing a stool at the bar, Shelley half-propped herself on the counter and took a grateful sip.

Something was nagging at me about the scene at the gallery. "Look, Shelley," I said. "I'd like to go back to the gallery. I don't want to leave you alone, though. Is your husband in town?"

She nodded. "He was at the opening, but he had to leave for a meeting just before you arrived. I'll see him back at the hotel later. But I'm fine, really."

She seemed better, and Guido was hovering solicitously. "If you're sure? Will you be okay here for half an hour or so?"

She nodded. "I think so. Thanks, Barbara. I'm glad to be here, it's quieter than the gallery."

Which was ironic given that the restaurant was its usual raucous Friday night self.

Guido assured me that he would look after my friend until I got back, at which Shelley gave a watery grin and held up her glass.

"Keep these coming, and I'll be fine," she said.

Guido beamed, ready to take her at her word. Copious amounts of good wine weren't such a bad idea at that—probably as good a treatment for shock as any.

I gave her a quick hug, smiled my thanks at Guido, and headed back to the gallery.

———

WALKING north along Granville Street towards the Courtland Gallery, the noise and rush of traffic hit me like a blow. My brain was already in overdrive, and the congested streets seem to press against me.

Vancouver gets busier and busier. Watching the cars whoosh by me, I was forcibly reminded how many people now live here, bringing with them all the problems of a major city, from over-crowding and gridlock to drugs, gang wars and murder.

When I got to the gallery, people were milling around, and the noise level had risen to an unbearable level. There was a sharpness to the sound that hadn't been there before, an edge I heard as panic and fear.

When someone we know has a heart attack, it brings the sense of our own mortality home in a way most of us would rather not accept or admit. When someone Deirdre's age has a heart attack, we're confronted with the randomness of life and death.

Somehow the elegant formality of this affair made it worse.

The room was hot, it was crowded, and I could see at a glance that Deirdre was the main topic of discussion. I saw Jayson in the far corner, in earnest discussion with his agent and another man I didn't recognize.

Now I was here, I wasn't sure what I was looking for or why I'd felt driven to return. Nothing looked wrong. Maybe I've simply seen too much evil—every death is suspect.

And if it was? Then it wouldn't be my problem anyway—it would be a police issue. With a shrug, I turned to go.

———

BACK AT GUIDO'S, Shelley was looking more relaxed. In fact, she was so relaxed she was practically sliding off her chair. She never could handle her wine.

"We'd better get you home," I told her. "Do you want to stay at my place, or go back to your hotel?"

She smiled happily. "Hotel, please."

"You don't want to talk about Deirdre?"

She shook her head vehemently. "Tomorrow. I've just managed to forget. I don't want to remember."

Made sense to me. I didn't feel much like talking either. I called her a cab, and saw her off, making a mental note to call her in the morning. Not early, though. Shelley was going to need quite a few cups of coffee before she'd be up to talking to anyone.

CHAPTER EIGHT

I woke far too early the following morning, the events of the previous evening running in an endless loop through my brain. I was tired and wanted to slide back into sleep, but I couldn't stop thinking about Deirdre and how random life can be.

My mind hung onto the image of her being bundled onto a gurney. Lying there in my queen-size, extra cushy bed, I felt oddly vulnerable. The cost of being human, I guess.

Finally I got up and went for a run.

The air was fresh and cool, with a hint of threatening rain. I ran for nearly an hour, down along Hemlock, with only the occasional car whizzing by, across Fourth and down to Granville Island, where even the Market was dark and shuttered. Heading west, I circled Kits Point, past the Planetarium and the Maritime Museum.

Across the dark bay, the lights of the West End looked like a mosaic against the darkness of mountains and sky. I ran along Kits Beach, circled the salt-water pool, which wouldn't open for the season until May, past the entertainment stage, and up Yew to 8th Avenue. Because 8th is a designated bike route, I find it makes a good running route, and the big houses with their old gardens give me fodder for speculating about their owners lives.

By the time I got back I was feeling better. Winded, but better. A hot shower improved my mood even further. At least until I half-tripped over the furry body planted square in the middle of my bath mat. I grabbed for a towel.

"Cat. What are you doing here?"

Cat appeared in my apartment a while ago, and seemed to like it. He visits pretty much whenever he feels like it. One of these days I was going to have to figure out whom he belongs to. And how he get in.

Cat was looking from me to the shower and back to me, as if questioning why anyone would get that wet by choice.

"Would you move please? You're in my way."

"Mmmmrrrowwr."

"Oh all right. If you move, you can have tuna for breakfast."

He moved. Cat always knows a good deal when he hears one.

I explained last night's debacle to him as I dried myself. He didn't say much, but he watched every move. And he padded behind me when I headed for the kitchen.

Of course, if it weren't for the tuna, he'd still be sitting in the middle of the bathmat, ignoring me. I knew that, but I fed him his tuna anyway.

"Mrrrrrrtt."

"You're welcome."

Watching the orange head go down, the tail wrapped around his front toes, pink tongue flicking in and out at incredible speed, I found myself smiling. Annoying as he is, I enjoy Cat's company. And he knows it, the furry devil.

But I'd never admit it to anyone else.

———

IT WAS seven when I got to the office. Too early for the jackhammers. Bonus.

I was glad to have all those reports to finalize, anything rather than think about death. But by eight-thirty I was having trouble focusing. The events of the night before kept intruding into my paperwork.

I needed to be doing something active, and Kathleen's case wasn't at that stage yet.

I called Shelley's room, but got no answer, so I left a message at the desk for her to call me. I thought about calling the hospital, but there didn't seem much point. I wasn't family, I'd never even met the woman.

I stared at the mess on my desk, hoping Deirdre was okay, sure that she wasn't. The phone rang, and I grabbed for it.

"Barbara, I want you to do something about Kathleen," Andrea said.

"Hi, Andrea. Fine, thanks. How are you?"

"Not funny. This is serious, Barbara. I'm really worried about her and I want to you talk to her."

"Why?"

"Because I hired you, that's why."

She hadn't, actually. "No, why are you worried about her?"

"Oh. Kathleen phoned in sick. And she doesn't answer my calls. She's never done that before. And her latest supervisor says there are problems."

Great. Still, it was a welcome distraction. "Kathleen seemed fine yesterday."

"Not at work she didn't. And she never phones in sick. I'm afraid something is seriously wrong with her."

"So why are you calling me? I'm no counselor."

Andrea chortled. "Not hardly."

"Thanks a lot."

"Well, you have to admit that caring concern is hardly your strong point."

Which was why I wasn't in that field. "So I have a problem with stupidity. May I remind you that you called me?"

"I know, I know. Look, Kathleen's been a mess since Bill's death. She hired you, so you should be the one to talk to her. Besides, she won't even return my calls."

I couldn't argue with Andrea's logic. Or rather, I could have tried, but it wouldn't have done me any good. I gave in to the inevitable. "What did the supervisor tell you?"

"What?"

I grinned. Andrea had been bracing for an argument and had lost sight of her original question. "Kathleen's supervisor, something wrong? Remember?"

"Oh, right. She said Kathleen's been distracted, making mistakes. She even complained about Kathleen's style of dress."

"So?"

"So if you'd ever met Kathleen before this whole mess started, you'd know she's always perfectly groomed."

I thought about the Kathleen who had presented herself in my office after the fiasco at Brady's. I could see what Andrea meant—I almost hadn't believed the two Kathleens were the same person. "I'll go talk to her."

"Today?"

Was it even worth arguing? Plus there was the distraction factor. "Sure."

"And you'll let me know how she is?"

"Yes, I'll let you know how she is. Okay?"

There was a small silence. "I do appreciate this, Barbara. You know that."

"Yeah, yeah. I'll talk to you later."

"Thanks, Barbara."

"Bye, Andrea," I said, and hung up before she could think of anything else for me to do.

———

HALF AN HOUR later I was on my way to Kathleen's apartment. It was still cool, but the sun was peering through a light cloud cover, and I enjoyed the twenty-minute drive. Except for the traffic snarls.

The morning rush was winding down, but even though I was going against traffic, it was pretty heavy going until I got over the

Burrard Street Bridge. Normally I'm frustrated by the delays, but this morning for some reason I just rolled down the window and enjoyed the freshness of early spring air.

Kathleen lived in one of the older four story walk-ups in a nicely treed area just off Forty-first Street. I've always been amused by the contradiction those apartments represented. Kerrisdale is an upscale neighborhood and the walk-ups, while well built and spacious, with the hardwood floors and real plaster of their era, are downscale. Mostly thirties era square boxes of no particular architectural merit, they showed their age. But then, the rents were almost equally antique, so you didn't often see vacancy signs.

Kathleen's apartment was on the third floor, facing the alley. It wouldn't have been my choice, I prefer the top floor, facing the street, but it would be quiet and undoubtedly the rent was cheaper.

I remember my own temping days, when I'd seriously considered going vegetarian, because tofu is cheaper than beef. Now that I think about it, I mostly ate beans. What can I say? Money was tight, I had to make choices, and I refused to give up good coffee.

So I recognized that Kathleen's choice of apartments probably reflected her priorities. I wondered what she'd chosen to spend money on instead of high rent. And how those priorities fit with her determination to pay my fees.

Pride can be expensive—I hoped her credit was good.

I walked up three flights of stairs covered in worn brown carpet, down a long, equally shabby hallway, until I found 307. I paused, considering the plain, brown-painted door. It was steel, with multiple locks and a long, re-enforced pry-bar. Someone was security conscious.

I knocked, not sure what I was expecting. After a long moment, I could sense someone looking at me through the peephole, though I couldn't see anything. Another long moment, then there was a clicking of all those locks being opened. The door swung open and Kathleen stood back, inviting me in.

The foyer was small, painted a fresh white, and the hardwood floor gleamed. The place smelled of sour milk and garbage that needed to be taken out.

I looked at Kathleen. She wore a pair of frayed jeans and a sweatshirt that needed washing. Her long hair hung in lank strands around a pale face. There was a smudge of what looked like chocolate on her chin. Her eyes were bloodshot and seemed to have trouble focusing.

This was a far cry from Andrea's perfectly groomed employee. She'd been right. Something was very wrong here.

Kathleen gestured me into the living room, which was spacious, with solid dark, antique-looking furniture. I stared at the bright paintings studded here and there against the white walls, stunned.

A Tom Thompson, a Lawren Harris, an E.J. Hughes, an early Jackson Pollock, a Gathie Falk. They didn't look like copies. And was that an Emily Carr drawing?

I'd never be able to afford even one of these. Now I understood the steel door with all the locks.

What was art like that doing in a four-story walk-up? These weren't the results of setting priorities. Was there money somewhere in Kathleen's background?

I glanced at my contradictory client, then around the room. Spotless walls and gleaming floors were contradicted by a mess of papers, newspapers, used dishes and coffee strewn over every available surface. This was not the apartment of a woman in control of her life.

"Would you like a cup of coffee?" Kathleen offered.

"Sure," I said, more to get her out of the room than anything. I really just wanted to sit and stare at the art on the walls, but I needed to take a closer look at the debris that had washed up on the sofa first.

"I'll be right back," she said, disappearing into the kitchen.

It had no pass-through, unlike most newer apartments, so she couldn't see what I was up to. Of course, I couldn't see what she was up to, either. And I was a little concerned about that coffee, given the state of her apartment. Still, as long as I avoided the cream, I figured I'd be okay.

"Would you like anything to eat?" Kathleen called out.

"No, thanks," I said quickly. The way this place smelled, I wasn't touching the food.

Looking for anything that might explain some of the contradictions my new client kept displaying, I walked over to the carved walnut coffee table. I glanced quickly through the bills stacked there, all unpaid—phone, hydro, water, newspaper, cable. Nothing out of the ordinary, nothing extravagant.

She subscribed to basic cable, for heaven's sake. Who did that in these days of two hundred channels and streaming video?

Of course, with art like this on the walls, who needed TV? I'd happily spend my evenings in the company of these works.

I was hoping for correspondence, unpaid Visa bills, an appointment calendar, even a journal, but no such luck. It seemed Kathleen did not keep her life on display, even in her current state.

"Milk or sugar?" she called.

"Just black, thanks."

I glanced around. She had good taste. White walls, earth-toned furnishings, dramatic art.

I moved closer. Yes, all originals. And these weren't just any paintings. If I remembered my art history classes correctly, each work represented a turning point in the artist's career.

They were mind-boggling.

I couldn't begin to imagine what they were worth. How had she afforded them?

And what would it be like to live surrounded by art like this?

I drank in the sheer talent displayed on the walls. If I lived with these paintings, I'd be painting again for real. I wouldn't be able to help myself.

And I found myself envying Kathleen, no matter how messed up her life might be, that she shared her life with these amazing works. But why did she have them?

The contrast between the modest apartment, the frugal bills and these pieces was staggering. I just hoped she had really, really good security.

I glanced around. If she did, it was high end and well disguised.

I was standing in front of the Carr, salivating, when Kathleen returned. "You like it?" she asked.

"Who wouldn't? You have wonderful taste."

"Thank-you."

I'd hoped for something more.

Usually collectors love to talk about their pieces—where they got them, why, sometimes even what they're worth now. I tried again. "Have you owned them long?"

"Quite a while. Why don't we sit here," she said, indicating two tweedy armchairs at one end of the sofa and setting two mugs of coffee on the end table between them. "You can ask me whatever you came here to ask."

So much for finding out about my client's contradictions. "Thanks," I said, managing not to grit my teeth as I reached for a mug and took a sip. "This is good."

"You sound surprised."

"Not at all." Yes, I was. I'd been bracing myself for something that tasted the way the apartment smelled.

"So, Barbara, why are you here? And how did you know where I was?" Kathleen asked, giving me a challenging look.

"I've come to give you an update. And I have a few more questions for you. Andrea told me you were here."

"So now you're checking up on me?"

"Kathleen, what is going on? You hired me, remember? Because of Bill's death."

Her eyes filled with tears. "I'm sorry. I'm not myself."

I'd have said that was fairly evident. "What's wrong?"

She shook her head. "Why don't we start over? Hello Barbara, it's lovely to see you. How have you been?"

Her cheery words rang empty.

I'd play along for the moment. But I wasn't leaving until I figured out what was going on. "I wanted to let you know I'd talked to the RCMP sergeant in charge of the investigation. And to Bill's former boss."

"You have? That's wonderful. What did you find out?"

"Not a lot yet, I'm afraid. The police are definitely considering it a suspicious death, but they're not naming suspects."

"Did they mention me?"

"No." Not directly in relation to the investigation, anyway. It worried me that she was so afraid she'd be implicated. There was still something she wasn't telling me, and that made me nervous.

"You're sure?"

"Yes, I'm sure. Kathleen, what aren't you telling me?"

"Me? Nothing? Like what?"

"Like why you're so upset. Why would the police connect you with Bill at all?"

"Because we were friends."

"And?"

"And because well, we were sleeping together."

"Yes, you'd already told me that." I stopped, looked at her expression, a combination of defiance and guilt. "But you don't mean three years ago, do you? You mean you were sleeping with him recently?"

She nodded.

"When? Not the night he died?"

"Yes."

Oh boy. I was going to get even with Andrea for guilting me into taking this case. "So did you go to his room or did he come to yours?"

"I went to his."

"At what time?"

"I guess around midnight. Maybe twelve-thirty."

"So you found the body when you woke up?"

"No, I went up before breakfast like I told you. I'd gone back to my own room."

"You didn't stay the whole night?"

"No. No, of course not. I left around two."

Of course not? Why of course not? The more I heard about this relationship, the more warped it seemed. "And he was alive when you left?"

Kathleen's eyes grew so large and dark I wondered if she could still see. "Yes, he was alive. He was fine."

"He didn't seem to be feeling ill? Complaining of a stomach ache, or nausea?"

She shook her head. "Bill always said he never felt better than after making love with me. He said it again that night. Then he fell asleep."

Of course he did. "Was he asleep long?"

"I don't know. I slipped out, quietly, so I wouldn't disturb him."

"So you were the last person to see Bill Rampage alive?"

Her hands fidgeted in her lap. "I—I guess so."

No wonder she thought she might be a suspect. Why do I get all the fun cases? "But the police haven't contacted you since? That's a good sign. They're not focused on you."

Kathleen's eyes darted off to one side.

Now what? "They haven't contacted you, have they?"

"No," she said, peering at me from beneath downcast lashes.

"Kathleen, what aren't you telling me?"

"Nothing."

"Nothing?"

"No. Nothing."

"You're sure?"

"Why would I lie?"

That's what I wanted to know. "You might have any number of reasons. Keep in mind that you hired me. If you want me to do the job you hired me to do, you have to tell me the truth."

"I am telling you the truth. And if you don't believe me, then maybe you aren't the right person to handle my case."

"Maybe not." Oddly enough, I wasn't ready to give up this case. Now I wanted to know what had happened to Bill Rampage. And I'd get the truth out of her, sooner or later. "But a P. I.—any P. I.— has to ask the hard questions."

"I guess."

Time to try another angle. "So tell me about Terri, the woman who was with Bill that weekend. Do you know where she works? I have a few questions I'd like to ask her."

"I don't see why you need to ask her anything. She wasn't even there when Bill died."

"She might know if Bill was worried about anything, if he had any enemies."

"I know that—and he didn't. Bill was the kindest, gentlest man. He never had an enemy in his life."

I bit my tongue to keep from reminding her that her kind, gentle man had been murdered. Someone hadn't liked him. "I'd still like to talk to Terri. Do you have any idea where I'd start looking for her?"

Kathleen gave me a stubborn look. "No idea."

Okay, then. "Is there anything else you can think of?"

"No, nothing. What do you plan to do next?"

"I think it's time I went to Hornby and looked around." After I tracked down Terri, and the receptionist at Willis and Murphy.

Kathleen's expression lightened. "Oh, that's good."

"Why?"

"Well, because that's where it happened."

Nice grasp of the obvious. Still, I'd cut her some slack. She didn't look like she was having an easy time of it. "Kathleen, are you all right?"

She cast me a swift look, then nodded. "I'm okay. And if you mean the state of this place," she gestured to the mess, "my cleaning lady was sick. She'll be in tomorrow."

Uh huh. Well, at least Kathleen was alive, coherent, and still capable of making a good cup of coffee. That should reassure Andrea.

"I'll be in touch," I said, and took my leave.

As I walked to the car, I thought about the conversation. Kathleen was a mess. It's amazing what love can do to normally logical, sensible people. According to Andrea, Kathleen was usually very neat, organized and in control. Yet since the Bill's death, her life seemed to have fallen apart.

And when it came to Bill, her actions and reasoning had been completely illogical.

I shook my head and my thoughts slid to Nick. Who was nothing like Bill. Or Jayson.

I wished he'd call. I wouldn't mind discussing this case with him. Even just hearing his voice. So maybe we did have a relationship, after all.

CHAPTER NINE

Since my mother also lives in Kerrisdale, I swung by her wrought-iron-balconied apartment building after I left Kathleen's. I could see my mother's ten-year old beige Camry parked down the block, so it was possible I'd caught her home. I buzzed her apartment.

"Yes?"

"Mother, it's Barbara."

"Barbara? Come up."

I waited for the tone, then swung the heavy door open. Unlike Kathleen, my mother lives in one of the newer complexes, a ten-story brick structure that boasts two elevators. She's only on the fifth floor, though, so I took the stairs, which were softly carpeted and well lit.

My mother was waiting for me at her apartment door. The white walls and hardwood flooring reminded me of Kathleen's place, but the air was fresh and smelt faintly of daffodils. There were paintings on the wall here too, but unlike at Kathleen's, these were prints. Impressionists, nicely framed. And there wasn't a cushion out of place.

So why did my heart rate start climbing immediately?

My mother ushered me into her faux terra-cotta kitchen, just big enough for a bistro table and two chairs, and put on the kettle. "Tea, Barbara?"

I nodded. I don't usually drink tea, but I knew if I asked for coffee, I'd get instant. And to my mind instant coffee is a waste of everyone's time.

"Thanks." I watched as she bustled around, arranging tea things on a tray with a bright homespun napkin.

With a pot of tea and a plate of homemade gingersnaps in front of us, she turned an expectant face to me. "What can I do for you, dear?"

I shrugged, feeling awkward, wishing I'd had more sleep. I'm never at my best when I'm short of sleep. "I thought I'd drop in. I was visiting a client a few blocks away."

"I see. Tea?"

"Please." I watched her pour, her motions smooth, practiced, wondering how often through the years I'd seen this ritual. "Susanna mentioned you'd signed up for skydiving lessons."

"Ah." She looked up at me. The twinkle in her eyes took me by surprise. "No wonder you're here. Is she giving you a hard time?"

For a second I didn't know what to say.

"No," I said after a beat, then grinned at her. "But I think it would help if I can tell her we talked about it. So tell me about your lessons."

Her face seemed to glow. "Barbara, you'd never believe how good it feels to come so close to something you've always dreamed of doing."

"Are you really going to go through with it?"

A small frown touched her brows and I felt like an idiot. "You don't approve either?"

"Of course I approve. I think it's a very gutsy move."

"Language, Barbara." She smiled at me. "I think it's pretty gutsy, myself."

"So who doesn't approve?" As if I didn't know.

"Susanna. She doesn't understand. I think she thinks I'm past it." Then she winked at me.

While I was still struggling to believe what I'd seen, she'd leaned forward, put her hand on mine. "You understand how important it is not to feel limited, don't you, Barbara? Tell me I'm doing the right thing."

"If it's right for you, it's the right thing," I said, feeling like a hypocrite.

If I was honest with myself, had I really pushed against my limits as an artist? Or had I given up, accepted the rejections, gone for the steady paycheck? "And Susanna's worried about you."

My mother snorted. Snorted! "Probably thinks I'll break my fool legs. Well, if I do, serves me right." She gave me a look I'd never seen before. "And it would be worth it."

"So when is your first jump?"

"I have three more lessons."

The relief I felt surprised me. Seems I wasn't quite ready to picture my mother leaping out of plane at ten thousand feet. Who knew?

"Let me know when the big day comes. I'd like to be there, cheer you on."

Her face lit up. "Really, Barbara?"

"Really. You'll let me know?"

"I'll let you know."

DRIVING BACK TO MY OFFICE, my brain kept playing checkers, leaping from one thought to another. Kathleen's messy apartment. My mother, jumping out of a plane. Things Kathleen had said.

My mind flipped back to tea with my mother, and the fact that I'd actually enjoyed myself. It used to be that visiting her left me feeling defeated and defiant. No matter what I did, she'd always seemed disappointed in me.

Not that anything was ever said. There was always this faint air of "how could you let me down like this" that hung in the air, like some kind of mist. Today was different.

I wasn't used to being in sympathy with anything my mother says, much less having her look to me for support. It had left me feeling keyed up, restless. The last thing I felt like doing was going back to the office and trying to sort out the maze of facts that was Kathleen's case.

Making a sudden decision, I flipped on a turn signal. Willis and Murphy was a few blocks away. I'd go see if that receptionist was willing to talk.

She was.

Before I could introduce myself, her eyes teared up. "You're—you're here about Bill, aren't you?"

"Yes."

"And about why he was killed?"

She hadn't bothered to moderate her voice. I glanced around me. The stylish waiting room was empty. It looked like my timing was perfect. "Yes. And I'd like to ask you a few questions, if that's all right?"

"For Bill, anything." She teared up again. "I feel so guilty."

"Guilty?"

She nodded, dabbing at her eyes. "I was pretty upset with him for being out of town that weekend. It was our anniversary."

"Oh?" I said. Kathleen had told me he was dating someone named Terri, but this couldn't be Terri—Terri had been with him on Hornby. "What number?"

"It was our third week of dating," she said, hiding her face in a pale pink handkerchief.

She was tiny, with delicate features and a most impressive figure. Her manner was warm and polished, but her intellect seemed a little lacking. Even if Bill Rampage had lived, I doubted there would have been many more anniversaries for them.

And I questioned his judgment in getting involved with someone he'd have to keep seeing literally every day. Luckily she was too caught up in her own feelings to notice mine. I was having trouble keeping my expression blank.

"Can you tell me if he was worried about anything? Before that weekend, I mean."

"Oh, no. He was always in a good mood. Nothing worried Bill."

"He didn't seem upset about anything?"

"Not Bill."

Right. "And did he have any enemies that you knew of?"

"Oh, not Bill. Everyone loved him."

Too much, maybe? And he was still dead.

"One more question. I'm trying to get in touch with as many of Bill's friends as I can. Do you know a woman named Terri?"

She tapped a finger against her lips for a moment. "Terri? No—no, I don't think so. Bill had so many friends. He was such a wonderful man."

And apparently contact with him induced stupidity and blindness in the women around him. On an impulse I asked, "What about a woman named Kathleen?"

"Kathleen? Oh, that name I know. She used to call here all the time. Bill told me to always tell her he was out."

"Always?"

"Always."

"He never took her calls?"

"Never once."

"Do you know why?"

"He didn't say."

And of course she didn't ask. "Don't you think that was a little out of character for Bill? I mean, him being such a nice man and all?"

"Oh, no, the way he asked, as a personal favor, you knew he had a good reason. And he'd give me a wink and a grin when I told him she'd called, and thank me so nicely."

So Bill wouldn't take Kathleen's calls. What was that about? I'd have to ask next time I saw her, see how she spun that one. "Did he ask you to hold calls from anyone else?"

"No, just Kathleen. And lots of his friends called here, too."

"How many is lots?"

"Oh—I don't know. Four, five. Maybe more. I couldn't keep track."

"All women?"

"Yes. At least mostly."

And she thought she was dating him? Yikes. "One more question, if you can."

"Sure."

"Were things going well for Bill here, at work?"

"Always. Bill was so smart."

Right. I played a hunch. "And how were Bill and Mr. Murphy getting along?"

Her eyes got big. "Oh. I'd forgotten. Tad—Mr. Murphy—was yelling at Bill the day before he left. And, and I think it had something to do with me."

"With you?"

She nodded, her expressions halfway between embarrassment and pride. I knew that look. I'd worn it myself once, when I was about fifteen. "Did you date Tad before you dated Bill?"

She nodded again. "But don't tell anyone, okay? It's supposed to be a secret."

"That's how you got the job, isn't it."

"Yes. But I'm good at what I do. Honest."

"And how long have you been here?"

"Six months."

And four weeks ago she'd started dating Bill. And dumped Tad? Not a smart career move, I was guessing. "Did you hear what Bill and Tad were saying?"

"No. They weren't happy with each other, though."

No, probably not. "Were they both yelling?"

She thought about it for a moment. "Mostly Tad. Bill was trying to calm him down, I think."

Probably telling him she wasn't worth it, I thought. "Are you still seeing Tad?"

She glanced down at her fingers, then shot a sideways look at me. "No. Not since—well, you know."

"Not since you started dating Bill."

She nodded.

"Even now, when Bill is—gone?"

Her glossy lips set. "Especially now. No one could replace him. No-one."

Of course not. "Do you happen to know where Mr. Murphy was that weekend?"

She looked puzzled. "Tad? Not specifically, but he often spends the weekend on Salt Spring. He has a home there, right on the water. It's gorgeous."

And you could catch a ferry from Salt Spring Island to Victoria, drive up island and catch the two ferries to Hornby, all in less than two hours. "But you don't know if he was there last weekend?"

"No, but Janet would know. His secretary."

I remembered Janet. She wasn't likely to tell me anything. "Do you think you could find out for me? And call me?"

"Sure. Janet's easy to talk to. Why do you want to know?"

Oh brother. Talk about innocents. "Trust me. It's to help Bill."

"For Bill." She beamed at me.

"When did you last talk to Bill? Before he left on Thursday?"

"Oh, no. He called from the lodge, like he promised."

"He called from Hornby?"

"Uh huh."

Was I finally going to get a break in this case? "And what did he say?"

"That he missed me. Stuff like that."

I hung onto my patience with both hands and kept my voice even. "Can you remember exactly what he said? It could be important."

Her brow crinkled, then she shook her head. "Sorry. It made me feel better, that's all I remember."

"Nothing more specific? You're sure?"

"Oh. He did say one thing a bit odd. I don't know if it means anything, but he said he wished he'd stayed with me. Then he said next time he chose a getaway, he'd be more careful about who'd be there. Something like that."

How close was her version was to what Bill had actually said? In her words, it didn't sound good for Kathleen.

But the words themselves could mean almost anything. What if Tad had showed up? "Did Bill ever say who else was there that weekend?"

"No, sorry. But I will find out about Tad, if that would help?"

I'd take what I could get. "Thanks, it would," I said, giving her my card.

———

BACK IN MY OFFICE, I called Shelley again. Still no answer. Where was she?

I called the gallery, and they hadn't seen her. Nor could they give me any information on Deirdre. Back to Kathleen's case. I looked at my notes, trying to find some common thread. Nothing.

I picked up the phone, called Andrea. "It's me," I said when she answered.

"How's Kathleen doing?"

"Not great, but okay."

"What does that mean?"

"It means she's better off not at work in the mood she's in, but she seems capable of looking after herself."

"Barbara, you're hopeless. I should have gone myself."

Now she suggests it. "Hey, I nearly got thrown out, and I'm the one she hired. I somehow don't think she wants visitors."

"She's upset about Bill's death?"

"You could say that."

"Poor thing. And how is the case going?"

"I think it's too early to talk about it."

"Which means you're not liking what you're finding out."

She knew me too well. "Andrea, one question. Bill Rampage was on Hornby with a woman named Terri. Any idea who she might be?"

"Terri? Terri. No, doesn't ring any bells. Why don't you ask Kathleen?"

"She says she doesn't know."

"And you don't believe her, do you? Oh, that isn't a good sign, when you start doubting your clients this early in a case. What's Kathleen done, anyway?"

"Don't get me started."

"You don't think she's guilty of something, do you?"

"Andrea, at this point I'm not sure what I think. Except that I'd better get back to my notes while things are still fresh in my mind."

"I won't keep you. Good luck, Barbara."

"Thanks. I have a feeling I'm going to need it."

———

THREE HOURS LATER, I was back at my apartment, staring into my mostly empty fridge, trying to decide if I was going to cook something or head for Guido's.

I was still stalled on Kathleen's case, though I'd got the paperwork on a couple of other cases finalized and the bills sent out. I needed a distraction, but I also needed an early night.

Before I'd decided, the phone rang. It turned out to be a distraction all right, but not exactly the kind I was looking for.

"Hello?"

"Barbara, it's me, Shelley. Deirdre's dead. She died earlier today."

I felt as if my stomach had suddenly turned hollow. I'd been half expecting the news, but I still hadn't been ready to hear it. I suddenly felt mortal, and way too vulnerable.

We live in a world that worships youth and ignores death, making the sudden death of someone young much harder to cope with. My own potential genetic tendency towards a similar sudden death made it worse.

I shoved that morbid thought away. "I am so sorry to hear that. Shelley, are you all right?"

"No, no I'm not. She's dead and—and the cops are saying it was murder. They're asking me some very direct questions. I think they suspect I killed her. I really need to talk to you. Can I come see you?"

"Of course. Come right over," I said and gave her the address. So much for my peaceful evening.

CHAPTER TEN

Half an hour later, Shelley was seated straight-backed on my leather sofa, clutching a glass of red wine and a brie-topped cracker. Her face was strained, and she looked like she might break into tears at any moment. I sat down opposite her, took a sip of my own wine, and waited.

"They—they think Deirdre was poisoned, Barbara."

I had to lean forward to hear her. "The police do?"

She nodded.

"Why? How did she die?"

"You were right—she had a massive heart attack and never recovered."

"And?"

"She didn't have a heart condition."

"So?"

"I think they found nitroglycerin in her blood."

Too much nitro could definitely trigger a heart attack. "Why are they questioning you?"

"I always carry nitro pills, Barbara. I have a form of unstable angina."

Shades of my aunt. "Prinzmetal's angina by any chance?"

"Yes, but how did you know that? Most people have never even heard of it."

I explained about my Aunt Cindy.

She was nodding. "I'm glad you understand. It makes it easier."

"But you didn't have a heart attack?"

"No. I was having these odd pains, and luckily I have a very astute doctor."

"Good thing."

"Yes."

She paused for a long moment. While I waited for her to go on, I cut a thick slice of old cheddar, put it on a cracker, and dug in. I wanted to ask "why" questions, but recognized her need to tell the story in her own way.

"I was jealous of her, Barbara," she burst out. "God help me, I was jealous of Deirdre."

I could understand it. I'd been having to work very hard not to be jealous of Shelley for having the show I'd never have. But Deirdre was dead.

Was Shelley somehow implying she'd had something to do with her death?

Shelley seemed to be finding it difficult to continue. She took a mouthful of wine and collapsed back against the sofa. When she did speak her voice was mournful.

"So beautiful," she said. "So very beautiful. You couldn't help but look. Your eye was caught, enthralled."

What was I hearing? Shelley had been jealous of Deirdre's looks? That I hadn't expected.

"I gave up portraits before I met her. Just as well. If I hadn't, I might never have painted again," Shelley added.

I was having trouble following her mental leaps. How much had she already had to drink?

"But to paint like she did—to command those sweeps of color, those subtle blendings, and still to portray such feeling, such depth of character—I would have given anything to paint like that."

Oh.

"I would have given anything to paint like that, Barbara. I was so jealous. It seemed so effortless for her. She didn't even seem to take it seriously. How could she be so casual about it? That's what I didn't understand." Shelley paused and took another mouthful of wine.

"When they offered me a showing, I was so pleased. Then I found out it was to be a joint showing, and with Deirdre of all people. It seemed so ironic. My big chance, and there she was, overshadowing everything."

"What are you telling me, Shelley?" I asked her. "Are you saying you killed Deirdre?"

She looked at me over the rim of her wineglass and began to laugh, the sound climbing towards hysteria before she abruptly broke it off.

"I suppose it would sound like that, wouldn't it?" she said, as if to herself. Then she looked directly at me. "Haven't you ever seen someone's work that is so good that you look at your own and wonder why you even bother?"

Oh, yes, I thought. I knew that feeling well. Poor Shelley.

But she hadn't answered my question, and as her friend I couldn't let her leave it there. "Shelley, what happened with Deirdre?"

"You mean aside from her having an affair with my husband?"

Oh no.

Shelley put her wineglass on the coffee table and leaned forward. "I didn't kill Deirdre, Barbara. I have no idea who did. But what is tearing me apart is that I'm glad she's dead, glad. And not because she was an awful person, and not even because she had an affair with my husband. It's because she was a better artist than I am."

She laughed harshly. "God. What does that say about me? To be glad someone is dead! And because they could put paint on canvas better than I can."

She shook her head, then met my eyes again. "I'm here because I think you're one of the few people I still know in town that might have a hope of understanding how I feel. And I really need to talk about it."

I did understand, and that scared me. I hadn't ever admitted, even to myself, how much it hurt when my paintings didn't measure up. Sure, I'd wished Jayson would fall off the face of the planet a few times, but I'd attributed that to our deteriorating relationship, not to his blighting comments on my work.

"So who do you think did kill her?" I asked, but whether I was hoping to distract her or myself I'm not sure. In any case, it didn't work.

"I don't think I care right now. It wasn't me, that's all I know. The thing I'm trying to deal with is that I'm capable of that kind of jealousy. And it's not something I ever wanted to know." She lifted the glass and swallowed the rest of her wine, then held out the empty glass with a twisted smile.

I refilled it, and my own. It was going to be a long night.

———

IN THE END, Shelley surprised me. She stayed a couple of hours, talking the whole time, then called a cab. She thanked me as she left, said she felt better. I felt worse, but I wasn't going to think about why.

At least I was fairly certain Shelley wasn't responsible for Deirdre's death. No matter what the police might think.

After she'd gone, I stood looking out the window, following the taillights of her cab as it disappeared. Then I tried calling Jerry, who often works late. No answer.

Frustrated, I pulled on my runners, went out for a long walk. I needed to clear my head after three glasses of wine, and the clear cold air should do it.

On an impulse, I turned down Andrea's tree-lined street. The lights of her three-story restored Victorian were on. Hoping she didn't have company, I knocked. She looked startled to see me standing there, then she got a good look at my face.

"Barbara, what's wrong? Come in."

I followed her through the cozy living room into her newly vintage kitchen. Andrea had spent months planning the renovation, and it showed. She'd stripped away the dreadful 70's cupboards and counter, taken up carpeting to reveal a beautiful pine floor, painted the walls a warm red, with maple cabinets, tin ceiling tiles and wide white crown molding and baseboards. It was gorgeous, and it felt like we'd stepped back in time to when the house was first built.

Andrea took down a wineglass, lifted the bottle of Shiraz already open on the creamy granite countertop and raised an eyebrow at me. "You look like you could use this."

"Yeah, but I think I've had enough wine. Got any coffee?"

She got the coffee out of the freezer, began measuring. "So what's wrong?"

"I'm worried Shelley is about to be arrested."

"Shelley Masters? I don't believe it!"

"Me neither."

"For what? I thought she painted landscapes."

For some reason that struck me as hilarious.

"It's not her paintings that are the problem," I said when I stopped laughing. "It's a little more serious than that. From what she says, the police think she might have poisoned a painter named Deirdre Brandt."

"She what? This is the Shelley that dyed her hair purple and refused to wear leather or eat meat?"

"That's the one."

"But she's a pacifist!"

"They seem to have overlooked that."

"What does Jerry say about all this?"

"Jerry's off duty."

"How inconvenient of him."

"I certainly thought so."

"So what are you going to do about it?"

"Nothing. She just wanted someone to talk to." Which brought me back to the feeling of intense relief and resultant guilt I'd been trying to ignore since Shelley left. Probably why I was here talking to Andrea.

"And you're going to leave it like that? Not try to help her? Come on, Barbara. This is your friend Shelley."

"You know I don't work for friends."

"Yeah, right."

"Someone else, someone with more emotional distance, will be able to help her more."

"No they won't. You're the best there is."

"You're biased."

"Look who got me out of jail."

"I'm trying to forget that." But she was right.

If Shelley really was in that kind of jam, I was going to do everything I could to help her. I really hoped it wouldn't come to that, but if it did, I'd be there. I knew it, and Andrea knew I knew it, judging by the satisfied expression on her face.

"Come on, it won't be that bad," Andrea said. "Hey, I've ordered a pizza. Why don't you stay and have some with me?"

"Andrea's pizza cure, good for what ails you?"

"Works every time."

"What kind of pizza?"

"That is so typical. A Chef's Special, of course."

"Well, if you'd ordered something with pineapple on it, I'd have to leave. Pineapple on pizza is a desecration."

"Only to you, Barbara, only to you. So tell me, how is Kathleen's case going?"

The coffeepot was making gurgling sounds. I snagged a cup out of the cupboard and held it out.

"Oh. That bad?" She poured the coffee, handed me the cream.

Sometimes I think Andrea knows me too well. "Worse."

"What?"

Normally I wouldn't reveal any details of a case, but Andrea was already part of this one. "She slept with him the night of the murder."

"Kathleen? She slept with—not the dead guy? The victim?"

I nodded. It almost helped, seeing Andrea's reaction.

"Kathleen slept with the victim the night before he was murdered."

"That's it."

"My Kathleen? My best employee?"

"Uh huh."

"I thought they weren't dating anymore."

"She was waiting for him, remember?"

"Oh. And the occasional romp was part of this waiting, I take it?"

"Apparently so. After the current girlfriend had departed in a huff."

"That's Terri? No wonder you want to talk to her."

"Exactly."

"So what about other suspects?"

"So far, I've got a couple of possibles, but quite frankly, none of them look as good for it as Super Secretary."

"That sounds bad. I'm sorry if I got you into the middle of something."

"Again."

"Come on, that's not fair. It's not as if I got arrested on purpose. And it wasn't my fault I got charged with killing Jake."

I grinned at her. "Not your fault you got charged? Who was found standing over his body holding a gun? In a locked suite? In the middle of the night?"

She waved her hand airily. "It could happen to anyone."

"Yeah, right. Well, with any luck, Kathleen won't be charged with Bill Rampage's death. I do have some possibilities. And I've only begun talking to his current and former girlfriends."

"Somehow that isn't reassuring," Andrea said. "What is it about love? Making normally sane women do irrational things?"

I grinned at her, hummed a few bars of 'Crazy Little Thing Called Love.' "Though I don't think Kathleen's problems started with Bill. Or love."

"No, I guess not." She cocked her head on one side and looked at me like a judgmental canary. "So, what about you and Nick?"

From Kathleen and her disastrous relationship to Nick and me. It was a leap I didn't want to make. I was saved from making a response by the doorbell. The pizza had arrived.

Even food wouldn't distract my tenacious friend for long, though. Andrea loves nothing better than to interfere in someone's love life, particularly when it's mine. We demolished the pizza in short order, then I made a hasty exit before she could start in on me again.

CHAPTER ELEVEN

Pizza at midnight is a really bad idea. So it was only eleven p.m.. Tell that to my nightmares.

I woke late and hard, then tripped over Cat, who had draped himself across the entrance to the bathroom. "Stupid cat. Why do you have to lie there, of all places?"

Cat blinked at me. Muttering to myself about stubborn felines, I stepped carefully over him, and closed the door in his indignant face.

When I opened the door again, Cat was sitting up, tail curled around his paws, gaze fixed on me. I'd seen that look before. Heading for the kitchen, I took the opened tuna can out of the fridge, put a generous portion on his plate. "Here. Eat this and get over it."

"Mmmmrrrt."

I switched on the coffee maker. We'd probably have the same battle tomorrow. And as soon as this case was over, I was finding Cat's owner, and telling them in no uncertain terms to keep him out of my apartment. Right now, I needed to go for a run.

An hour later I was climbing the dingy stairwell leading to my office, still thinking about Kathleen's case. I wanted to know exactly who had been on Hornby that weekend, and what if any connections they'd had to Bill Rampage. And I really needed to visit the island.

I went on-line and checked the sailings, then looked at my schedule dubiously. It would take an entire day, and that was assuming I left early and returned late. I didn't want to spend that kind of time in the middle of this case.

But I needed to see the layout of the Inn where Bill had died, find out who else had been there. If I scheduled it right, I could also meet with Brad Bramwell.

Resigned, I reserved spots at six-thirty a.m. and nine p.m. sailings the following day. I rather enjoy traveling by ferry, except for the time it takes, but I absolutely refuse to waste time sitting on the tarmac waiting for four hours because the ferry you wanted was full.

The reservation system BC Ferries instituted a few years back is an absolute godsend. Except of course, that then I was committed to a particular ferry. Oh well, you can't have everything.

I called the Sunshine Inn and spoke to John Grussman, the owner. He was distant at first, but when I explained I'd got the okay from the RCMP, he warmed a little. I also made a reservation for lunch in their dining room, which I suspect helped.

After I'd hung up, I poured a cup of Viennese Roast, then dialed the number Andrea had given me for Dianne Klassen. She was in, and happy to meet me for lunch. We agreed on Mary's, a small coffee shop a block away from VU's downtown campus, at noon.

I was staring at the mess on my desk, thinking about who might have hated Bill Rampage enough to kill him when the phone rang. Or did I have it backwards? Was it someone who loved Bill Rampage so much they'd killed him out of jealousy?

I didn't like that scenario. It was too close to Kathleen's. The phone rang again and I grabbed it.

It was Nick. "Where are you?" I asked.

"I'm back in town. Are you free for lunch?"

I couldn't reschedule Dianne—I was leaving for Hornby the next day. Dammit. "I wish I were. I'm meeting a source."

"Duty before pleasure."

"You're a fine one to talk. How did things go, anyway?"

"It wasn't a waste of time. Sometimes that's the most you can ask for."

"True." I knew not to ask for details—I wouldn't get them.

"On to more important matters. If you're not free for lunch, how about dinner?"

I felt a smile spread itself across my face. I do like this man. Too much for my peace of mind. "I'd love to."

"How about I pick you up. Seven-thirty or so?"

"Make it eight at my place. I don't know how long I'll be this afternoon."

"Must be some lunch you're planning."

"It's not lunch. It's what happens after lunch," I said, pitching my voice deliberately low.

There was a silence, then Nick's deep laugh. "Should I be worried?"

"Well, if you insist on going out of town for long periods of time, you can't expect me to sit around," I said, my tone as matter of fact as I could make it.

"So what you're telling me here is that I'd better make it a pretty special dinner."

"Now you're talking," I said, the laughter I'd been squelching breaking through in my voice. "I'm glad you're back, Nick."

"Yeah, me too. I've missed you, Barbara."

I didn't answer that. I'd missed him too, but actually saying the words felt like it might jinx a relationship that was actually working. "So, I'll see you tonight," I said instead, and hung up a bit too quickly.

Then realized I'd forgotten to ask him about the Rampage case. Damn! I thought about calling back, but I didn't even know where he was calling from.

Stupid, Barbara. Really stupid. I gulped down another mouthful of coffee and turning back to my notes.

————

BY NOON, I was heartily sick of reviewing the meager facts on the Rampage case. They weren't getting me anywhere, and there were too many contradictions.

I needed a fresh point of view, and a change of scene. It didn't help that it was raining again, the light gray and flat enough that I needed my headlights.

Walking into Mary's Diner, I was hit by the combined aromas of coffee, frying burgers, and overused cooking oil. The décor was typical student—brightly painted concrete block walls, faux distressed and mismatched tables and chairs. A couple of students sprawled in one corner, deep in discussion, open textbooks in front of them. One of them had purple hair, the other had no hair at all.

At the counter to my left sat a bearded professor type. A bunch of jocks—football players judging by the shoulders—were laughing uproariously in another corner. Even the waitress, pierced eyebrow and all, looked like she was a student.

When Dianne arrived, breathless, apologetic and fifteen minutes late, I did a double take. I didn't know what I'd been expecting, but it wasn't been this sprite with spiky, bright red hair and a pierced eyebrow. I think I expect all of Andrea's temps to sport a professional look that was current ten years ago. Which is why I'm constantly taken aback by them.

Dianne looked to be in her mid-twenties, with sharp hazel eyes, a bright grin and an energy that told me what had attracted Bill Rampage.

"Thanks for agreeing to see me," I said.

"No problem. I owe Andrea—big time."

"Andrea tells me you knew Bill Rampage. Tell me about him."

Before Dianne could say anything, the waitress came by.

"Mushroom burger with fries and a Coke," Dianne said to the waitress. "They're good here," she said to me.

All right! I consider myself a connoisseur of mushroom burgers, having tried them at nearly every burger joint in Vancouver. Hadn't tried this one, though. "Make that two," I said. "Except I'll have coffee."

The waitress, a twenty-something brunette with five earrings in one ear and eight in the other and a snake's tail winding down her forearm, nodded, scribbling down the order.

Dianne turned back to me. "I first met Bill Rampage when I was temping at Willis and Murphy. He was friendly, flirting, from the first—always laughing, always teasing. I didn't take him up on his offers 'til my last week there. Wouldn't have been professional. But he was too cute to resist so I went to lunch with him."

The waitress put our drinks in front of us, and Dianne downed a gulp of Coke. "Bill was funny, attentive, interested in what I had to say. He was a great guy, but he didn't know the meaning of faithful. We lasted four months, until I figured that out."

"When was this?"

"Couple of years ago. But he really was fun, so when I ran into him, we'd go out. Or he'd call me if he had tickets to something I'd like."

I was watching her face. Her eyes seemed to be focused on something only she could see. She looked like she was remembering good times, but there was sadness there, too.

Bill Rampage had meant more to her than she was letting on, but I didn't see any anger. "What was Bill like?"

Her eyes re-focused on me. "You never met him?"

"No."

"Bill was the life of the party, but he could be quiet too. He really liked women, I think that's the part that stays with you. He liked being around women, and he'd treat you like you were a princess. And of course, women responded to him." A sad note crept into her voice, and she picked up her Coke again, half hiding behind it.

"He was cute, and really fit, but a bit of a fanatic. He ran every morning, worked out at the gym three or four times a week."

She thought that was fanatical? I thought it was normal.

Dianne paused, put the Coke down, grinned at me. "But it was the diet thing that defined him. He'd take a handful of vitamins and stuff every morning and every night. He swore by wheatgrass juice —grew his own and juiced it. Sugar was the enemy to be avoided at all costs. Though personally, I don't know how he could do without chocolate."

Me neither. "Did he have enemies?"

"Enemies? Bill? I can't imagine it. Hell, even I couldn't stay mad at him, and believe me, I tried. The thing about Bill was, you were the most important thing in his life when he was with you. And that's a wonderful feeling, let me tell you."

I thought about my conversation with Nick, and how it felt to be with him. I knew what she meant. But isn't that true of the first few months of any new relationship?

"Trouble was," Dianne said, "For Bill that kind of focus applied to everyone he spent time with."

Oh. I could see where that could be a problem, if you were one of the people he was spending time with. I began to appreciate Kathleen's reaction to him a bit more. "And yet you kept seeing him?"

She grimaced. "Between you and me, he was a great lay. But he'd sleep with anyone. Anytime."

The waitress reappeared with our burger platters, and for a few moments we busied ourselves with utensils and passing the ketchup. Dianne had been right about the mushroom burger. My taste buds thought they'd reached nirvana.

"But Bill was really genuine," Dianne was saying. "When you were with him, talking to him, you forgot all your grievances."

"Do you think a former girlfriend with a grievance could have killed him?"

"A girlfriend, someone he'd dated? No way. Anyone I've ever

met who spent time with Bill had a soft spot for him that never went away."

"What about a boyfriend or a former boyfriend, if that's the effect Bill had on women?"

"I can see someone being upset, but Bill had a way of making friends with everyone."

"Even the exes?" I took a big bite of my burger, angling it over the plate to catch the juices and runaway mushrooms.

"Hey, Bill won over the weightlifter I'd been seeing. And that was one jealous dude."

"So you have no idea who might have wanted Bill dead?"

"Honestly, no. I can't quite believe he is dead. Are you sure it couldn't have been a mistake?"

"He was poisoned."

"Oh." She waved at the waitress, ordered another Coke. "Was it painful?"

"Most likely."

"Oh, poor Bill."

"You know he died on Hornby?"

She nodded.

"He'd gone there with a woman named Terri. Do you know her?"

"Terri? No. But I do know someone you could talk to, who could probably tell you more about anyone he might have been seeing."

"Oh?"

She nodded, pointing a ketchup-laden fry at me for emphasis. "Yeah. Her name's Cassandra Stone. She's on staff in Fine Arts, and she knew Bill."

"Cassandra is on faculty at VU?" We'd studied together, but I'd never much liked her. After graduation, I'd lost touch with her.

"Yeah. You know her?"

"Slightly."

"Then you should definitely call her. She's been there two years, maybe three. And she's a maestro of gossip."

Now that I thought about it, the reason I couldn't stand Cassandra back then was because she was so fond of gossip. In my current profession, I'm inclined to view that as an asset rather than a character flaw.

"Thanks, I'll give her a call."

———

BACK IN MY OFFICE, I shook the rain off my jacket, hung it on the hook behind the door and put on a pot of Italian Roast. Then I grabbed the phone, dialed.

Cassandra answered on the second ring.

"Cassandra, it's Barbara O'Grady calling. I don't know if you remember me, but..."

"Barbara. How are you? It's been years."

From the lilt in her voice, life in the academic art world suited Cassandra. I held that thought for a moment, checking for signs of jealousy.

There was a time when I thought that was the life I wanted. Now I think it would stifle me. "I'm good. And you?"

"Fabulous! And I can't get over how nice it is to hear from you."

I wondered why she was so pleased. I don't remember us being at all fond of each other.

"And what are you doing these days, Barbara? I heard rumors that you weren't painting any more, that you'd become an investigator?"

Ah, yes. The quest for gossip never sleeps. "Yes, actually, Cassandra. I've been an investigator for nearly five years now. I run my own firm these days." No need to tell her that my "firm" consisted of me and my research assistant, otherwise known as my trusty Mac.

She wasn't listening anyway. "I'm so impressed, Barbara. That must be so fascinating. You'd learn so many things about so many people!"

Right.

"So tell me, Barbara, what can I do for you? Oh, do tell me it's because of an investigation you're involved in."

She was making this far too easy. I reached for my notebook, grabbed a pen from the cluster in the beer mug commemorating a long ago Oktoberfest. "Well, actually, Cassandra, I am working on a case. Had you heard that Bill Rampage had died?"

"That was so awful. Yes, I'd heard he'd been murdered."

Funny, her tone didn't match her words. It was all coming back to me now. Cassandra is one of those people who need very little excuse to talk about others, and once she gets rolling, she'll go on forever. It used to drive me nuts. This morning I was finding it a refreshing change from the usual process of extracting information.

Cassandra was still talking. "It was such a shock. Everyone's reeling. He'd done a fair bit of work here, you know?"

"Oh?"

"Oh yes. And of course, he was such a charmer, everyone he'd ever met was a friend. If you know what I mean."

I was beginning to figure it out. "Was there anyone in particular?"

"Short term or long term?"

"Anyone who might have had a lot of emotion around Bill, either positive or negative."

"No-one comes to mind, but let me ask around. I'll call you and let you know, if you like?"

"That would be great." Cassandra could turn out to be one of the best contacts I'd made on this case. Who would have believed it?

"Let me give you my number." Then, on impulse, I asked, "Cassandra, do you know Deirdre Brandt?"

"Oh, poor Deirdre."

I took that as a yes. "I know. I really hoped she'd make it."

"You were at the gallery?"

It never took Cassandra long to put pieces together. "Yes. Shelley Masters is a friend of mine."

"Oh, yes, I remember her. Paints derivative landscapes, doesn't she? Still, it must have been so amazing for you, to have been there I mean. Part of a life and death drama. I can't imagine it."

It sounded to me like she could imagine it only too well.

"Deirdre was such a talented artist," Cassandra said. "Even if she wasn't particularly well reviewed at first."

A touch of the cat, there. The Cassandra I remembered had been very sensitive about her art and very competitive. If she was on faculty, that had paid off. Which, come to think of it, explained the other reason she was being so cordial to me—I was no longer a threat.

Not that I'd ever been much of a threat, except in her mind. "I don't know much about her, I'm afraid."

"She came out of nowhere, but in the last few years she's been getting bigger and bigger shows. It's a good thing she died of natural causes, though."

What an odd thing to say. "Oh? Why?"

"Well, if she hadn't, there would have been quite a few suspects. Including your friend Shelley."

"What do you mean?"

"Well, Deirdre had more than a few enemies, you know."

"Oh?"

"Oh, yes. She had a tendency to steal other people's men. Just last month I overheard Jan McElroy in the ladies room. She was being very nasty about poor Deirdre. I won't say she was making veiled threats, but she certainly didn't wish her well. Of course, there were rumors that Deirdre and Jan's husband had an affair that Deirdre broke off rather suddenly. And then of course, poor Shelley..."

"What about Shelley?"

"Oh, you didn't know? Shelley and her husband were having some problems, and Deirdre and Blake Masters were involved for a time."

"For how long?" I asked. I hadn't wanted to ask Shelley.

"Several months, I think."

"And was it common knowledge?"

"Everyone knew. Deirdre made sure of it. Deirdre always made sure everyone knew about her affairs, in the most public way possible. Poor Shelley. I don't know how she survived it. It was so humiliating for her."

And gave her such a terrific reason for hating Deirdre, not to mention a potential motive for murdering her. I could only hope the police got the story from someone a little less opinionated than Cassandra. "Thanks, Cassandra. You've been very helpful."

"Don't mention it. I am so glad you called me, Barbara. And I'll call you as soon as I've done a little research on Bill Rampage."

"Sounds good."

"Well, bye-bye for now."

I looked at the dead receiver in my hand for a moment, then slowly hung up. I'd got more than I bargained for when I'd called Cassandra.

CHAPTER TWELVE

eep in thought, I didn't hear the door open. When my sister spoke from the other side of the desk, I started so hard I banged my knee on the desk.

"Hello, Barbara," Susanna said, shaking out a red and tan plaid umbrella.

Some P. I. Letting my sister sneak up on me in my own office. "Susanna? What are you doing here?"

"I have to talk to you."

"I'm listening."

She chose the chair opposite me, perched on the edge of it. "I'm so worried about Mom."

Oh, good. This was going to be a fun conversation. "Coffee?"

"No thanks. I don't share your addiction."

I poured my coffee as loudly as I could, refraining from comment. I had my own opinions about where things like cleaning house fell on the addiction scale.

"You look good, Susanna." I said. "As always. New hairstyle?"

My sister and I had been born with the same straight, dark hair. Mine was still dark and straight, worn long enough to almost touch my shoulders. Susanna had been blond for years, or nearly so. Her hairdresser had layered in enough shades of blonde streaks that the impression was blond, and now she'd had it cut short and curled to frame her face. I'd have looked like a giraffe, but it suited her piquant face and smaller features.

"Thanks. I just came from my hairdresser, and thought I'd swing by and talk to you. I figured you'd be here on a Saturday."

"It's what I do," I said. It was her turn to make no comment, which was just as well.

"I did go and see Mom," I added. "She said she was fine."

"I know, she told me. And she always says that. It doesn't mean she is. Not when she's planning on jumping out of a plane"

"It also doesn't mean she wants help," I countered. "She's an adult, Susanna. She's entitled to make her own mistakes."

"Not if she's injuring herself," Susanna shot back. "And she's looking so frail."

"She's always been tiny. You know that, you take after her."

Susanna waved that off. "But doesn't she seem more frail?"

I shrugged. "Not really. But she is getting older."

Susanna had been sitting stiffly upright in the vintage burgundy leather guest chair opposite the desk. It's not easy to sit upright in those chairs—that's why I bought them. Well, that and the price. You can't beat auction prices, especially when you wait 'til the end, when most of the bidders have gone home for the evening.

Now Susanna leaned back in her chair, as though trying to get away from my words. "She's not old."

"No, she's not," I agreed. "But she seems to think she is. And sometimes that's what matters. So if skydiving is something she feels good about doing, then we shouldn't stand in her way."

"We certainly should! What if she's killed? Then how would you feel? Surely there's something we can do."

I hadn't seen my normally composed sister this agitated in years, and it worried me.

Susanna prides herself on her poise. It's what makes her such a good hostess for dear Godfrey. Probably one of the reasons he's doing so well. Much as I dislike the man, I do have to admit he's a successful businessman, even if his ethics make me cringe. Susanna seems oblivious, however, and as long as she's happy, who am I to complain?

Susanna was still talking. "It's so hard, Barb. I feel helpless, like there's nothing I can do. And there must be something. There must be something we can do."

My sister has always liked to be in control. She also likes to keep things tidy, unlike me. I thrive on creative disarray.

"Come on, Suze. This isn't so bad. At least she's not sitting there depressed."

Susanna nodded, but she didn't look very happy.

Was this really about our mother, or was something else going on? "Is something bothering you? Aside from the skydiving, I mean?"

"Yes. We haven't seen much of you lately, Barbara. We are family, you know."

I shrugged, uncomfortable. "I've been pretty busy."

"You always say that."

"Because it's true."

She gave me that look. "I'm giving a dinner party a week Sunday, and I'd like you there. No excuses this time."

I flinched. Susanna's dinner parties were stilted formal affairs, not my idea of fun. But it looked like I was out of excuses. Acceptable ones, anyway. "I'll have to get back to you."

"And bring that guy you've been seeing," Susanna added, taking me by surprise.

Oh no. "What guy?"

"The one you've been seeing. Nick Markham."

"How did you know about him?" I asked before I thought.

"I have my little ways," said my sister with a smug smile. "You're not the only one in this family who can find things out, you know."

Obviously not. But how had she found out? If Andrea had told her, I'd never forgive her. "I'll have to check about next Sunday. He may be busy."

"Well, be persuasive. Now that you're finally seeing someone again, we want to meet him."

I groaned. "Who's going to be there?"

"Just one or two couples," she said airily.

I know my sister too well—I didn't trust that answer for a minute. "I'll have to get back to you."

"Fine. Don't leave it too late," she said, standing and gathering up her purse. "I've a menu to plan."

I tried for a joke. "Menus have to be planned? I thought you just looked in the fridge and pulled out anything that wasn't wilted."

She gave me a skeptical look, shaking her head as she opened the door. "I don't know how you survive," she said, closing the door gently behind her.

I was left staring after her, torn between anger and amusement. Susanna and I are so predictable. I got up and poured myself another cup of coffee, tasted it and poured it down the sink. There's nothing worse than stale coffee.

I picked up my notes, put them down again. Stared at my calendar. It hadn't really registered that I had to be on the six-thirty a.m. ferry tomorrow for Nanaimo and Hornby Island. And tonight I'd be seeing Nick for the first time in weeks.

"Good planning, Barbara. Really good," I said to the walls.

So did I cancel Hornby? I glared at my schedule. Clearing a full day was hard. I didn't see another opening until the following week. And I really needed to get moving with Kathleen's case.

But there was no way I was postponing my time with Nick, even if I'd had a number to call him at. Which I didn't. And no way was I shortening our time together, no matter what. So I'd nap on the ferry. It would work.

The phone rang. "O'Grady Investigations, Barbara O'Grady speaking."

"Oh thank God!" It was Shelley's voice. "Barbara, I really need to talk to you. I may need to hire you. Can I come and see you?"

Oh no. Not again. "Yes. I'll be in the office for another hour at least."

Good thing I'd told Nick to pick me up at eight.

"I'll be right there," Shelley said.

———

WHEN SHELLEY BURST through the door, she looked pretty good for someone under the kind of stress she was under. She was wearing a straight, slim black skirt with black boots and a deep red wool cape thrown carelessly over one shoulder. Fine drops of rain misted her face and hair. Her lipstick matched the cape, dramatic against her thick dark hair and that smooth olive skin.

She was striking. I wondered, not for the first time, what was wrong with her husband, whom I'd still not met.

"I don't know what to do, Barbara," she said before she'd even closed the door. "The cops are always around, with a question here and a question there, I feel sick half the time, and now Blake is telling me he'll have to get back to his practice. I need someone on my side, and I'd like to hire you."

I didn't like what I was hearing about Shelley's husband. How had such a strong woman ended up with someone who treated her so badly? Then my mind flashed an image of Jayson Ho, who hadn't exactly been considerate in our time together.

Oh. Sometimes it's all about the charm.

I was willing to wager Blake Masters was as smooth and charming as they came.

"Would you like some coffee first?" I asked Shelley when she paused for breath.

She smiled a little. "I'm sorry. It's been getting to me. I'm all wound up. I can't sleep, I can't paint, I can't even think straight."

"Have a seat," I said as I went to pour the coffee. She perched in one of my vintage guest chairs, didn't say another word while I got our coffees ready. Which meant it was my turn to talk.

"First off," I told her as I handed her a cup, "you don't need to hire me to have me on your side."

Her eyes started to glisten.

"You still take cream and sugar?" I asked quickly.

"Boy, it has been a long time" she said, her voice husky. "No, these days I drink it black. I inherited my momma's hips, and I really have to avoid the sugar."

"Well, you must do a pretty good job. You look great."

"Thanks. And so I should," she added with a laugh. "One of the ways I deal with life's little ups and downs is to go shopping. Blake hates it. Some months he rants for an hour when the Visa bills come in. The best part about being a successful artist is now I can pay for my own binges."

Binges was an interesting word for her to choose, with connotations of something spun out of control. I wondered if Shelley was aware of the uncertainty she was expressing, an uncertainty at total odds with the appearance she projected.

As I sat opposite her, wearing my favorite jeans and a fitted black shirt, I was willing to bet I was the one more comfortable in my clothes. And it was beginning to sound like I was the one more comfortable in my life, too. Despite the fact that she was painting and I wasn't.

I hadn't expected that, didn't really want to know it. "So tell me about Deirdre."

"Deirdre. Where should I start?"

"Start with why you're here."

"You know Deirdre was poisoned. With nitroglycerin?"

I nodded.

"Well, we'd gone to dinner, the twelve of us…"

"Who was there? And where did you go?"

"It was Blake and I, Judy and Bob, Deirdre, the Courtlands and some investors. We went to Directions."

Directions is one of Vancouver's trendiest restaurants, located across the street and down the block from the Courtland. "Who is Bob?"

"Bob Wong, Judy Moore's husband."

"Deirdre didn't have a date?"

"No. She'd come solo."

"Did the investors know Deirdre?"

"I think one of them had bought some of her stuff, but I don't think the others knew her."

"So there were plenty of suspects. Other than you, I mean."

"I guess."

"What did you eat?"

"Everyone had something different."

"Was the nitro in the food?"

She sat forward in her chair, agitation sounding in her voice. "I don't know—the police haven't released that information."

"And was Deirdre seated near you?"

"No, she was on the other side at the far end of the table from me."

"So what makes you think you're a suspect?"

"I have the motive. And the means."

"You've been watching too many TV crime shows. But okay, what about the opportunity? Did you have that?"

She tilted her head to one side, and sat silent for a moment, obviously replaying the scene. "No," she said slowly. "No, I didn't. There wasn't a single time I could have put anything in her food."

"You're positive?"

She nodded.

"What about in her drinks? Any opportunity there?"

"No. Nothing there either."

I felt a surge of relief. "Then you may be in for a few questions, but you don't have anything to worry about."

"Thank you, Barbara."

"You're very welcome." And I meant it. For my sake as much as Shelley's—I really hate cases where the suspected killer is a friend of mine.

Shelley finished her coffee and left. I made a couple of notes from the visit, put them in a new file that I hoped I'd never need, and went back to my notes on Kathleen's case, looking for something—anything—in what I'd learned so far that might give me a direction.

Neither Dianne nor Cassandra had told me anything new, just confirmed exactly how much of a philanderer, and a charmer, Bill Rampage had been. Which didn't get me very far.

I could only hope I'd learn more on Hornby. I began to make a list of the things I needed to make sure I asked or looked into when I was there.

When I looked up again, it was pitch black outside, and just past seven o'clock. Oops.

———

I HURRIED home and had a shorter-than-planned soak in the tub with a handful of bath crystals scented with ylang-ylang and ginger, then stood contemplating my wardrobe. Such as it is. Shopping is not at the top of my list of fun things to do.

I'd forgotten to ask Nick where we were going, but we both seem to prefer casual places, so I put on black jeans and one of my favorite blue sweaters, a soft silk blend he says matches my eyes, shaking my head at myself even as I chose it.

The double ring of the phone announced his arrival. I felt a thrill of anticipation, and the backs of my knees tingled. I buzzed him up, then met him at my door for a long, satisfying kiss.

"Hey, there."

"Hey yourself," he said, his hand warm on my back. "Barbara, I've missed you."

"Me too."

He grinned at me. "Such soft words, music to my ears."

"Yeah, yeah. Never mind the mushy stuff, what's for dinner?"

He started to laugh, and I grinned at him. He hugged me. It felt good to be held, and I hugged him back.

We were both in the mood for curry, and the closest good place was the Heaven's Own Curry House on Fourth. I chose lamb curry, Nick the chicken vindaloo and we ordered a beer apiece. Sitting across the table from him in the candlelit warmth, surrounded by low conversation and the rich smell of spicy food, I felt oddly nervous. So I filled him in on the details of my latest case—without identifying my client, of course.

He had no information on Rampage's death, but said he'd make a couple of calls, see if he could pick up anything. By this time our dinners had arrived and we dug in. The service is always quick, which is one reason we come here, but the food is amazing.

We were pretty busy eating for the next few minutes, our conversation limiting itself to "Mmmm" and "Boy, this is good!" One thing I love about Nick is that he enjoys good food as much as I do.

We put our forks down at nearly the same moment. I smiled at him, looking at his empty plate. "I gather you were hungry."

"Look who's talking," he said, indicating my equally empty plate. "Feel like a movie?"

"Why don't we go down to the beach and go for a walk?"

"Sounds good."

It had stopped raining a couple of hours before. The air was washed clean, cold but somehow soft. You knew it was spring air, not autumn, just by the feel of it. And the smell—salt, turned earth and growing things all tumbled together. Far out against the ocean's darkness the moon reflected off small waves. Farther still, thick clouds massed behind the North Shore mountains, their edges moonlit in silver.

My fingers suddenly itched for a paintbrush. I ignored the feeling.

We strolled along the hard packed sand of Kits Beach, right at the edge of the surf, my hand in Nick's warm one. It felt odd to be holding hands. Wonderful, but odd.

Maybe I have been alone too long. I took in a long, deep breath. "Smell the salt in the air."

"Careful," Nick said, pulling on my hand to keep me clear of a particularly energetic wave. "Don't let the sea air go too much to your head or you'll end up with wet toes."

"Details," I said airily. "Who cares about wet toes when there's all that to look at," waving in the general direction of the city. With the dark, wave-spattered sea in the foreground, the lights of Vancouver glowed against a silhouette of craggy mountains.

Nick looked for a long moment. "It's pretty spectacular, all right."

He paused for effect, then with a sideways look, continued, "It's also pretty cold out, and if you get wet feet you'll be frozen, and probably miserable, in no time."

"Miserable? Miserable?" I said in mock offense. "Are you implying that at any time I could be less than fun to be with?"

"Mmm—think I'll take the fifth on that one," he said, grinning.

"Thanks a lot!"

"I'm merely saying that if you get your feet wet, I don't want to be around you."

"Oh, that's different, then. I get my feet wet, you leave. What happens if I get wet to the knees?"

Nick shook his head slowly. "To the knees?" he repeated. "That would be bad. Very bad indeed. Drastic measures would be called for."

"Drastic measures."

"Hmmm. We'd have to get you warm, you know. Immediately. There could be permanent damage done to the personality if you weren't warmed up immediately."

"Permanent damage you say? And you would propose to warm me exactly how?" I asked, struggling to keep a straight face.

Nick pulled me to him and kissed me long and deep. I forgot all about my toes. Then before I got my breath back, he took off across the damp grass, still holding my hand, his long strides eating up the ground.

"Wait a minute," I hollered as I matched his stride. Good thing I knew he knew I was a runner, or I'd have tripped him. As it was, I was too curious about what he was up to.

Nick finally slowed down as we reached the door of the Chocolate Shoppe. With a laugh and a flourish, he pulled the door open and ushered me in. "Your hot chocolate awaits you," he said.

"Hot chocolate?" I repeated, shaking my head in disbelief. "In the spring? You're nuts, Markham, you know that?"

Actually, it was a pretty good idea—it was cold enough to make hot chocolate welcome. Though come to think of it, really good hot chocolate is amazing all by itself—it doesn't need an excuse.

I headed for a booth in the far corner, and Nick joined me, followed in short order by two steaming cups of rich, decadently thick, spicy dark chocolate, with homemade marshmallows. It took chocolate to a whole new level. I was in heaven.

CHAPTER THIRTEEN

It was pitch black, decidedly chilly and raining lightly as I headed for the ferry, stopping on the way to pick up an extra strong coffee and a cranberry oatmeal muffin, which slightly mollified my angst at being on the road at five-thirty in the morning. Still, I was feeling pretty good.

After the cocoa Nick had come back to my place, and reminded me exactly why I'd missed him. Then I'd reminded him. And so on.

Even Cat had been chipper. I think he likes Nick. Either that, or he was happy to get his tuna a lot earlier than usual.

Nick and I started the morning with a shower for two, which, if not the long, leisurely affair I'd have liked, was still pretty damn fine. Even if I did have to be on the six-thirty a.m. ferry.

I was glad I'd reserved, since it gave me an extra half hour or so. Though as it turned out, there was no lineup at the terminal, so I wouldn't have needed to be early in any case.

But I didn't know that, and the shower would have suffered. Best twenty bucks I ever spent.

As I watched the other cars being waved aboard, I wondered why each of them was catching this particular ferry. Were they commuting? Visiting? Salesmen and women on a regular route?

We were due to dock in Nanaimo just after eight—way too early in my books, but I'd still have to hustle to make the nine o'clock sailing to Denman and Hornby.

It's a trip I usually enjoy—I stay out on deck and make the most of the spectacular coastal scenery and the fresh sea air, but this time it was too dark to see anything. I pulled my jacket around me and did a couple of fast laps of the deck to wake myself up. Then I gave up, went inside and closed my eyes for a catnap.

We reached Nanaimo much too quickly, then it was a quick run up the Island Highway to Buckley Bay, and the Denman Island ferry dock. Traffic was light so I made it in less than the usual hour, the view nothing but rain-drenched green. On the second ferry, the clouds were hanging low on the water, creating a not very interesting study in shades of gray. I sat back, closed my eyes.

My mind kept re-running the evening with Nick, how much fun we'd had. My body ached pleasurably from the night we'd spent together. I'd missed him when I hadn't seen him for three weeks, but now I really missed him.

And it wasn't just physical—I couldn't fool myself about that any longer. But I had a case to worry about. I bought another cup of coffee and buried my face in the newspaper.

Once I reached Hornby, finding the Sunshine Inn was no problem. From the size of the signage I gathered it was one of the island's main tourist destinations. The inn itself was beautiful, fitting into the landscape in a way that takes real money to achieve, all weathered cedar and rustic stone. Inside a fire blazed cheerily in the stone fireplace and thick burgundy velvet curtains were drawn against the morning chill.

"Ms. O'Grady? It is a pleasure to meet you. Please, come in, come in. And how was your trip? Pleasant, I hope." John Grussman came forward to greet me, hand outstretched.

A tall, distinguished looking man with graying hair and a hint of an accent, his greeting was warmer than I'd expected. The suspicious part of my mind wondered what he had to hide. Of course, it was always possible he'd taken one too many SuperHost courses.

"Good morning, Mr. Grussman. The trip was fine, thank you. And please call me Barbara."

"And I am John. Be welcome to the Sunshine Inn. Is there anything we can get you?"

The smell of something wonderful cooking distracted me. I'd considered eating a second breakfast on the ferry but the mass-processed eggs and cardboard bacon they were offering had changed my mind. I'd settled for a cup of coffee, which wasn't actually too bad, especially compared to the diesel oil they used to pass off as coffee. But that muffin had been a long time ago.

"Is there any chance that the dining room is open? I'm starved."

"Yes, indeed. We'd be happy to serve you breakfast," he said, waving me ahead of him.

They served me what turned out to be the best BC Benedict I'd ever eaten, the light buttery hollandaise melting over perfectly poached eggs and succulent smoked salmon. And the coffee. Strong, fragrant and rich, it was what coffee should be and seldom is.

———

AFTERWARD, I went looking for John Grussman, and asked him to show me over the place, especially the room Bill had died in. He was happy to oblige, once he'd been assured that it wouldn't result in bad publicity for his inn

John was another of that odd group who are repulsed by the reality of violent death, but fascinated by a murder case. Like the crowd that gathers at a car accident, they can't resist finding out what happened.

The inn wasn't a big place, two floors with maybe eight rooms on each floor. The bedrooms were on the second floor, half along one wing and half along the other. The room that had been Rampage's was second from the end, at the far end of the west wing. Kathleen's room was next to his, just as she'd told me.

Each room opened off the hallway and faced the gardens. There was no other entrance or exit. The murderer must have entered and exited via the shared hallway. How had they avoided being seen?

The bedrooms were cozy, wood paneled, with bright flowered chintz quilts, rag rugs on the floor and a small crystal vase of fresh spring flowers on each bedside table. The flowers were a nice touch, and had obviously come from the extensive gardens that circled the inn.

On the main floor were a large gathering room with an enormous stone fireplace, the dining room where meals were held and several smaller rooms that were used for meetings. I turned to my host.

"Do all of your guests dine together?"

He shook his head. "No, they make plans independently. Breakfast is included, and is served from six until nine. Lunch and dinner must be ordered at least a day before. Lunch is available from noon until two, dinner from six until ten."

"And do you have lunch and dinner guests that are not staying here?"

"Oh yes, frequently."

"And for breakfast?"

"No, we have only our registered guests for breakfast."

"Though you do make exceptions, I gather. My breakfast was delicious, by the way."

"I am glad to hear it. And yes, we make exceptions on occasion."

"And the day Bill Rampage died?"

"Let me check my book." He led me to a polished antique desk off the entry hall and consulted the thick blue ledger that lay atop it. "Hmmm. That would have been the eleventh, yes?"

"That's right."

"Yes. For breakfast that morning, there would have been only our guests."

"And how many is that?"

He ran a finger down the page. "I am showing six, including Mr.

Rampage. That is after Mr. Rampage's companion had left the previous day, of course."

"Terri?"

"Yes."

"Do you have her last name listed there?"

"Yes, but I am afraid I cannot give out that information. We value the privacy of our guests."

"What about the rights of your murdered guests?"

He winced, but didn't budge. "That is the responsibility of the police. It is why we have cooperated fully with them."

"I gather that applies to the names of the other guests, as well?"

"I am afraid it does."

"But the police have their names?"

"Of course."

It figured. I hoped Brad Bramwell was in an expansive mood when I visited him. "Can you tell me what time Terri left the previous day?"

"Yes, that I can tell you. I drove her to the ferry, I believe it was the two o'clock."

I made a note. "Did Bill Rampage seem at all upset or uneasy to you while he was here?"

He shook his head. "He seemed to be fine."

"What about when Terri left?"

"He seemed more resigned than upset."

"And the night of the murder?" I asked him. "Did you or your staff notice anything unusual?"

"No, we noted nothing unusual at all. But there is only my wife and myself, and two local girls who come to help with the cooking and the beds and such. And Mrs. Smith, who cleans. The girls had gone home after the dinner clear-up, and Mrs. Smith is only here during the daytime hours."

"Who was here for dinner that night? The night before the body was found."

He consulted his book. "Hmmm. There were six of our guests,

and no non-registrants. No, wait. We did have one. So we had seven guests for dinner."

No point asking him who the non-registrant had been. I'd have to find out some other way. "How many can you seat for dinner?"

"Sixteen easily. We have seated as many as twenty when the demand was high."

"And that night you had only seven?"

He nodded.

"Is it unusual to have so few non-registrants for dinner."

"Yes, it is, rather."

"Can you tell me what was served?"

"That you would have to ask my wife."

"I'll do that." I made another note. "The morning of the murder. What time was the body found?"

"Shortly after eight. I think someone went up to wake him."

"Do you know who?" I asked.

"No, I am sorry. I think it was one of the women. My wife might know."

"But you're sure it was a woman?"

"The person who screamed was female," he said, his voice certain.

"Did you see the body?" I asked him.

"Unfortunately, yes. It was not a pleasant sight."

"Oh?"

"The face was twisted, very pale, and blotched with red. He'd been quite ill. Death had not come easily to him."

I swallowed, picturing it all too vividly. John appeared to be doing the same. Despite his old-world politeness, I didn't think I'd get much more information from him, so I asked if I could speak with his wife.

"Try not to upset her," he cautioned as he led the way.

CHAPTER FOURTEEN

The kitchen was large, well equipped and very neat. It smelled warm and homey with the scents of baking bread and roasting garlic. Stainless steel appliances gleamed, while yellow walls and white cabinets kept the room bright despite the gray weather. Braids of garlic and dried herbs hung from high ceilings.

Two slim girls, both in their late teens, were working at a long granite counter on the far side of the kitchen. An older woman was stirring something on the stove.

"Mrs. Grussman?"

"Elena, please." Her accent was strong, musical. Greek perhaps? She came towards me wiping floury hands on her apron, then held out a hand for me to shake.

"Barbara O'Grady. I have a few questions, if you don't mind?"

She nodded. A small, round woman with masses of graying black hair pulled up in a loose chignon, she seemed less tense about talking to me than her husband had been.

"You know I'm looking into the death of Bill Rampage?"

She nodded again.

"Do you know who found him that morning?"

"Yes. I believe it was his woman friend. A Miss Marshall?"

"Not the woman friend he arrived with? Terri?"

"Miss Winters? No, Miss Winters had left the previous day. Some bad feeling with Miss Marshall, yes?"

So Terri was Terri Winters. "Oh? What was the problem?"

"Miss Winters, she was most unhappy that Miss Marshall was present. Most unhappy. She asked Mr. Rampage to have her leave. This was over afternoon tea, you understand."

I nodded. I could picture it. "And what did Mr. Rampage say?"

"Ah, such a charming man. He laughed, and kissed her and called her beautiful. Told her she had not a worry."

This was fascinating. "And what did Miss Winters say?"

"Oh, she was in a temper. And too beautiful, too cold, that one. She would not bend. Could not, I think."

"And?"

"And so she left, and her man, he ended up with Miss Marshall after all."

"He did?"

She gave me a look that said I wasn't fooling her for a moment. "We both know where Miss Marshall spent the night, do we not?"

Caught. Elena was sharper than I'd anticipated. Time to change tactics. "Yes. But is it enough to make you think she killed him?"

I seemed to have surprised her. "Miss Marshall? Ah, no, not Miss Marshall. She would have done anything for Mr. Rampage, that one."

"And if he avoided her? Chose other women?"

"Still she would be devoted. Women like Miss Marshall, they believe in the possible. What is, it matters not. What might be, ah, that is everything."

She was describing a woman who reacted to love exactly opposite to the way I reacted. The very idea made my skin itch. Of course, Andrea would say it was the idea of love that made me nervous, but then Andrea exaggerates. I was cautious, that's all.

But if I found out Nick was cheating on me, I wouldn't be taking the high road, waiting for him to see the error of his ways.

We would be over. Not that I thought Nick was cheating—the man I knew had too much honor to cheat.

When our relationship had run its course, he'd tell me.

Or I'd tell him. The thought depressed me, especially after the night we'd just spent.

I wrenched my thoughts back to the case. How deeply had Elena seen into the relationship between Kathleen and Bill? Her observations matched the way Kathleen had presented herself to me, but what lay underneath all that devotion?

Jealousy can be a powerful and devious emotion, and Bill had definitely given Kathleen plenty of cause for it.

"What about the other guests? How did they interact with Bill? With Mr. Rampage?" I asked.

"Ah, he flirted with all of them, but that was his nature, was it not?"

It certainly seemed to have been. "What about with a woman named Lois? Kathleen told me she was very upset at Bill's death."

"Lois? Ah, Mrs. Michaels. She is very sensitive, that one. She comes often. Once she needed rest for half a day after she saw me kill a chicken."

Mrs. Lois Michaels. I made another mental note. "Did you notice anything unusual about that weekend? Except the death, I mean. And Miss Winters' departure."

"When you run an inn, after a time you find very little is surprising."

I'd just bet. "But surely murder is not usual."

Her generous mouth tightened. "No. No, murder is not usual."

I watched her for a moment, but she wasn't about to volunteer anything.

"There was one non-registrant for dinner the previous night," I said. "Do you remember anything about him or her?"

She thought for a moment, head cocked to one side. "I think no. The guests come and go and we are always busy."

"Can you tell me what was served for dinner that evening? The night before Mr. Rampage died?"

She looked horrified. "You are saying my food has killed him?"

Oops. "No, of course not. This is a standard question, no reflection at all on the Inn or the food that is served here. But you publish the menus for your dinners in advance, don't you?" I said. Recalling with gratitude a flyer I'd noticed while waiting for the Hornby ferry.

"Oh." She looked calmer. "Oh, yes. Of course. Come with me, we will check."

I followed her to a small office off the kitchen. There was a clean white desktop, a series of shelves with neatly labeled binders. No mess, no clutter anywhere. I wondered how she did it. My office always has a dusting of paper on every surface. Elena opened a thick binder filled with neatly lettered menus and recipes.

"Here, we keep everything, you see. So there is no duplication. If a dish is well received, we may use it again, but each time the menu is different."

"This is impressive." And it was.

'Planked Filet of Wild Salmon with Organic Red Pepper Puree.' 'Wild Mushroom Risotto.' 'Grilled Salt Spring Island Lamb with Lemon and Mint-Basil Sauce.' 'Chocolate Hazelnut Mousse.' Just looking at the menus made me hungry.

"Here it is." She turned the book so I could see it better.

No wonder they'd had only one outside guests. 'Wild Mushroom Soup,' followed by a 'Salad of Mixed Greens with Citrus-Herb Dressing' sounded fine. 'Lemon Cheesecake with Raspberry Coulis' I'd sign up for. But 'Pan-Fried Organic Liver with Balsamic Roasted Onions and Yams'? Yuck.

Of course, I'm not a fan of liver. Some are. But I could see why there might not have been a rush to sign up for this dinner.

"Thank you. That is very helpful."

"Perhaps you would like to try this meal yourself? We could perhaps make it specially, for your lunch. Or better yet, I could make the liver but preceded by our nettle soup. A specialty of the house, you understand."

Oh no. Anything but liver. Though the nettle soup sounded pretty bad, too.

"Ah, no, thank you, Elena. I don't think that will be necessary. I just needed to see what was served. And this book is so complete I have all the information I need. Whatever you're making for lunch will be fine."

"If you are sure?"

Was that a twinkle I saw? "I'm sure."

She looked sideways at me, smiled. "Is there anything else?"

I'd just been paid back for implying, even for a moment, that her food might have caused Bill's death.

"No, I think that's all," I said. "Oh, I would like to talk to the rest of the staff, if that's okay?"

"Yes, that is fine. Brandy and Tiffany can talk to you while they prepare lunch. Do you wish me to introduce you?"

"No, I won't take up any more of your time. But I do have one last question."

"Yes?"

"Do all of the guests eat the same meal?"

"Oh yes. Unlike some, we do not offer several selections, only what is best and freshest."

"Would anyone have had a different meal that night?"

She shook her head. "The kitchen prepares one meal for all dinner guests. It is part of what draws people here. They exchange choice for quality."

No one else had been poisoned, which made it unlikely that Bill had eaten whatever killed him at dinner. That made my job easier.

Plus it was good to know you could eat liver and survive. "Thank you for everything, Elena."

"You are most welcome."

———

I STROLLED BACK into the kitchen and watched the two teens working for a moment. One was chopping chicken while the other peeled carrots destined for the soup of the day. If they'd been listening in on my discussion with Elena, they didn't let on. Other than the occasional glance, they ignored me.

"My name is Barbara O'Grady," I said to both of them. "I'm here looking into the death of Bill Rampage," I said when I'd had enough of the silence.

All movement stopped. The blonder one looked up, eyes sad. "It's so awful. I can't believe he's gone."

"Me neither," the other one chimed in. "I'm Tiffany, by the way, and she's Brandy."

"Can either of you tell me anything about Mr. Rampage's death?"

Both heads shook. Both faces looked sad. There was a strained silence.

Finally Brandy broke it. "It doesn't seem fair. He was so cute."

"And didn't he just know it?" the other one, Tiffany, said with a giggle.

"He had an eye, that's all," Brandy said, deftly breaking the back of a chicken carcass with a cleaver. "And he noticed what was around him, too," she added, casting me a quick look between heavily mascaraed lashes and reaching for another chicken.

I didn't comment, waiting to see what would emerge.

"Well, you'd know," said Tiffany with another giggle, and a piece of carrot peel went flying. "Oops!"

Brandy shot me another look, then deftly boned a chicken breast. "All those women were after him. All desperately trying to look younger than they were, too. But he had eyes. He knew who was real and who wasn't."

I looked at the two of them, so carefully made up, and wondered what it must have been like to grow up on this small island, when a place like the Sunshine Inn is the celebrity hotspot. "Were you at work when they found him?" I asked as delicately as I could.

Brandy's big dark eyes grew teary. "Yes, I got here about six-thirty and was helping Elena make breakfast. He really liked his eggs the way I make them."

"When was the last time you saw him?" I asked her.

"The night before," she said on a sob. "I got off shift around four. Bill was tied up until after dinner, so I came back."

Bill? What was I hearing here? "You met him the night he died?"

She nodded, lashes fluttering over brimming eyes.

"They met most nights," Tiffany contributed.

Brandy shot her a look I couldn't read, then sniffed delicately.

I was developing a decidedly negative opinion of the late Mr. Rampage. Womanizing was one thing. These girls were barely legal, though I'm sure they'd have disputed that. "What time did you meet with him that night?"

"It must have been after seven. It was a nice evening. We went for a walk."

Tiffany seemed about to speak, and Brandy shot her another look. Correctly interpreting that look, I asked if it had been a dry evening.

Brandy nodded. "Uh huh. We'd had that sunny period, you know, it lasted a few days. It was pretty warm for this time of year, too."

Somehow I'd figured that.

Bill had been a busy boy. I wondered if Kathleen had known about his trysts with this pretty but overdone teenager. Who was still speaking.

"Bill and me, we had something special," she said.

"And what was that something?"

"He—he loved me. And he wanted to be with me. Always."

Of course he did. The bastard. "Did he tell you so?"

She gave me a look as if to ask how I could be so heartless. "I just knew, the way you do when it's special, when it's right. That's how it was between us. He was always telling me how wonderful I was, how unique."

This was making me sick to my stomach. I wasn't sure how

much more I could listen to. "When did you see him last? What time?"

She shrugged. "I had to be home by eleven thirty, or my mom would create. So I guess it was just after eleven."

"Where?"

"Out back." She waved an arm vaguely in the direction of the gardens. "There's a path. It's the quickest route to my place."

"Did you see him again after that?" I asked.

She shook her head, seeming to be groping to find words. "The next thing I knew was the next morning and there was all the screaming and then they were saying he was dead," she said, and sniffed.

"You?" I said to Tiffany.

She shrugged and looked at her friend, then back at me. "No, I went straight home after my shift," she said, her eyes not quite meeting mine.

She was lying. But she wasn't likely to tell me the truth with her friend in the room. I'd have to find a way to talk to her alone.

"So what did happen that morning?" I asked.

"Like Brandy said, we were helping with the cooking. It's always hectic in the morning, and we were too busy to notice what any of Them were doing. Well, most of us were," she cast another look at Brandy, and this time it was malicious.

"I'd just put the jugs of orange juice on the sideboard," Brandy volunteered.

"Did you look for Bill?"

She nodded. "But he wasn't there." Her voice was bleak.

"Then what?"

"It wasn't but a moment till the scream."

"Who screamed?" I asked.

They looked at each other, as if for confirmation. Tiffany spoke first. "It was the haughty one," she said. "Kathleen."

"You're sure?"

Both of them nodded. I asked a few more questions, but there didn't seem to be much else they could tell me.

———

IT WASN'T LUNCHTIME YET, so I decided to check out the grounds. I went back to my Civic and changed into my hiking boots, which I'd thrown in that morning for just such an opportunity. It was still raining lightly. The grass was wet, and the air was cool and damp.

The gardens were laid out English country style, and the beds were a glorious mass of spring bulbs. A week of sunshine and unseasonably warm weather earlier in the month had everything into bloom early. Purple, mauve and pink hyacinths scented the rain-fresh air.

Manicured paths wound here and there, disappearing into a grove of trees off to the east of the grounds, and down to a tool shed and the small lake, currently covered in mist, below and to the west. I spent a good three quarters of an hour tromping around, relishing the views, the freshness of the air and the sweet spiciness of the flowers. The beauty of the garden almost offset the ugliness of murder and the bad taste Brandy's tale had left.

I found no shortage of private places to loiter, but judging by the two blankets folded in one corner of the tool shed, I was willing to bet that was Bill and Brandy's trysting spot. If the girl's story was true. I didn't see anything else that struck me as important, though I did make a rough sketch of the layout of the grounds, as well as noting how far I had to walk before I was out of sight of the house.

Then I went in for lunch, which was a spiced carrot soup, followed by chicken and mushroom crepes, both of which were delicious. I was a little chilled from my walk, so the hot food was doubly welcome.

There was no sign of the nettle soup and liver Elena had threatened. I'd lucked out. From the glint of mischief I'd seen, I'd half-expected her to change the lunch menu.

When Tiffany brought out a raspberry trifle rich with custard, my contentment was complete. Sipping a perfect cappuccino, I contemplated my surroundings.

In other circumstances, this would be a very romantic place to bring Nick. The combination of a European level of service and attention to comfort with that rustic touch was very relaxing. I looked around and tried to imagine how it had been for Kathleen and Bill.

It seemed warm and welcoming enough, but emotional undercurrents can ruin even the most idyllic spot. Just ask the staff at any honeymoon resort.

Which reminded me that the only person I hadn't talked to was Mrs. Smith. Taking my coffee cup back to the kitchen, I asked Elena where I'd find her, but all I got was an odd look and a vague wave of the hand.

I went searching and found Mrs. Smith in one of the upstairs bathrooms, on her knees, scrubbing the toilet. Then I understood the reason for the look. Mrs. Smith spoke no English.

She seemed friendly enough, nodding in my direction, her tawny face creasing with smiles, but there was no getting past the language barrier. I wondered what nationality Mr. Smith was. When I tried pantomiming a death in a last ditch effort to communicate, she gave me a puzzled look.

I gave up. Checking my watch, I saw I had about twenty minutes before I had to set out for the Nanaimo ferry. If I wanted to talk to Brad Bramwell today, that is.

After quite a bit of poking around, I found my host in the wine cellar. I cleared my throat gently to announce my presence, and he nearly dropped a bottle of vintage port.

"I have one more question," I said. "Had any of the guests from that weekend been here before?"

He nodded, his expression professionally blank. "Yes, one of the couples is one of our regulars. And Bill Rampage and Kathleen Marshall had been here before."

"They had?"

"Yes, perhaps three years ago."

It was time to have another chat with my client. After I talked to the police. I thanked him and hurried upstairs, leaving him to his wine selection.

As I raced through the lobby, I realized it was empty, the guest book unattended. And I really needed to know the names of all the guests that weekend. With a quick glance towards the staircase, I flipped the blue covers open, paged through the guest book.

The registration page for the eleventh was easy to find—John Grussman kept meticulous records. And there were the names: Kathleen Marshall, Bill Rampage, Terri Winters, Mr. & Mrs. Edward Michaels.

And Mr. & Mrs. Blake Masters.

CHAPTER FIFTEEN

I had no time to talk to anyone about Shelley and Blake being on the island the weekend Bill was murdered. Not if I wanted to catch the ferry back to Nanaimo. As I drove, my mind was churning with the information I'd uncovered.

What had Shelley been doing on Hornby the week before her show? Why hadn't she mentioned anything? Granted, she didn't know I was working on the case, but surely the murder of one of your fellow guests was worth mentioning. Maybe she hadn't wanted to talk about it.

But talk about it she would, as soon as I got back to Vancouver.

The ferry docked and I drove the hour into Nanaimo, half-noting the greenness of it all—low hills and stands of evergreens with spectacular views of the water whenever the road rose a bit. In Nanaimo, I went looking for the RCMP detachment, which I found just off the main street. The building was low, gray and weathered. The main lobby matched it. I asked for Brad Bramwell.

"He's out," said the guy on the desk. He wasn't bad looking, tall and lanky with a weathered face, but the surly look spoiled it. "Who's looking for him?"

"Barbara O'Grady," I replied.

The guy on the desk gave me a big smile. I nearly fell over. I wasn't used to this.

"He's been expecting you, asked me to call when you arrived. Hang on."

Within five minutes I was seated with a cup of steaming coffee, and Brad was on his way. I should have turned down the coffee. It was awful, especially after the amazing cappuccino I'd had at lunch. Before I'd drunk half of it, a medium height man with the build of a weightlifter and cropped dark hair that made no attempt to disguise an incipient bald spot strode up to me.

"Barbara O'Grady?"

I nodded and stood up, abandoning my coffee on the side table. We shook hands.

"Brad Bramwell. Good to meet you," he said, and turned to lead the way down a narrow hallway to a small office stacked with paper. He scooped a pile of files off of a battered wooden guest chair and gestured for me to sit down. "Want some coffee?"

I'd already learned that lesson. "No, thanks."

"So," he said, seating himself. "What can I do for you, Barbara?"

"I'm looking for any information you can give me on the Rampage death."

"You know we're considering it murder?"

I nodded.

"We haven't made an arrest yet, so there's very little I can tell you."

I'd expected that. "But he was poisoned?" I asked, anticipating the answer.

Brad didn't surprise me. "Yes."

"Have you identified the poison?"

"No. It's not one of the common ones, and the lab is backed up."

"Figures. I'd like to talk to some of the people who were staying at the inn. Can you tell me anything about them?"

"In an ongoing investigation? And with the privacy legislation that's now in place? Are you kidding?"

That's what I'd expected. I gave him a grin. "It was worth a try.

Can you at least confirm some of the details that I've learned so far?"

"Depends. What are they?"

"Rampage's face was pale but splotched with red."

"Accurate so far."

"He'd been ill. Very ill."

"You got that right."

"There were seven other people staying at the Inn, including my client. I've been told that in addition to the guests, there had been one visitor for dinner, but no-one other than the guests and the staff were at the Inn that morning."

"Right again."

"In addition to a girlfriend who left early the previous day and a previous relationship with my client, the deceased had a liaison with one of the help—Brandy."

"You are good."

"Thanks. Anything I'm missing? That you can tell me?"

"Nothing I can tell you, but you might want to have another chat with your client."

Oh no. What else hadn't Kathleen told me? "Thanks, I will. Oh, can you tell me how was the poison administered, or is that classified?"

He paused for a moment, as if considering it. I held my breath. Then he grinned.

"Can't hurt, I guess. But keep it to yourself, at least for now."

"I'll do that."

"There were traces of the poison in the water glass on his bedside table," Brad said. "Seems he used to take a whole handful of vitamins and food supplements every night. Guess he tossed the water down without even tasting it."

I winced at the irony. "So it definitely wasn't in something he ate."

"Not unless he was poisoned twice."

"Any idea when he died?"

He gave me a long, measuring look. "You'll keep it confidential?"

"Of course."

He grinned. "Of course, you would. Doesn't make much difference anyway. Based on what the doc says, he died between five and seven that morning."

Brad Bramwell's very obvious admiration made me uncomfortable. I decided to ignore it, brought to mind what little I knew of forensics. "Rigor was fully established, then?"

Brad nodded.

I thought about it. "It took him that long to die?"

"Doc says anywhere from half an hour to three or four hours. Depending on the poison."

I didn't like much of what I'd learned about Bill Rampage so far, but no one deserves to die like that. "Poor man. Couldn't he have called out for help?"

"He was probably in a coma."

Which was probably a blessing, unless the poison had an antidote. "Can you tell me how long before you expect to make an arrest?"

"'Fraid not. But we're taking a lot of pressure to close this one."

I nodded. "I'll bet. Well, thanks for your help."

He waved off my thanks. "I haven't done anything. Wish I could be more help."

"No, you've been great. Thanks," I said, standing up and shaking his hand.

He held mine a moment too long. "It was a pleasure to finally meet you, Barbara."

His sincerity was flattering, but unsettling. I made my exit as quickly as I could. He gave me his card, and said feel free to call. I thanked him, said I would.

By the time I caught my ferry home, it was dark. The clouds still hadn't lifted, though, so even the lights of Nanaimo were hidden. It was a long and dreary journey. I kept trying to call Shelley, but it went straight to the hotel's voice mail. Where was she?

CHAPTER SIXTEEN

The next morning I was up early again, and headed out for a run. It wasn't raining, and the cool air felt good. For three-quarters of an hour I didn't have to think.

By the time I got to the office, it was still too early to be called a civilized hour, so I took my time putting on a pot of French Roast coffee. The extra-dark roast. I'd just taken a couple of sips when the phone rang. I eyed it warily.

"Hello?"

"Barbara, you are in early. I'm so pleased."

I wasn't so pleased to hear Cassandra's gushing tones. "Oh?"

"I had lunch with several people and everyone is discussing who killed poor Bill."

Oh, don't tell me she'd dated him too. "Uh, Cassandra. Did you know Bill Rampage?"

"Oh, sure. We were an item for a time."

Was there anyone in the city the man hadn't dated?

"It was ages ago," she continued. "Eight months at least."

Uh huh. I swallowed more coffee. "Do you happen to know who else he'd dated?"

Cassandra reeled off a list of half a dozen other women, none of whom I recognized. "Anyone else at VU?"

"Not that I know of, and I think I'd know."

Maybe. Maybe not. She obviously didn't know about Dianne Klassen. "So you were saying?"

"Oh, yes," she said, instantly drawn back into the drama. "Because everyone knew Bill personally, everyone has a theory. Rumors are flying and fingers are being pointed."

She paused dramatically, her voice lowering. "It's as though they're expecting the murderer to strike again."

Now that was a cheerful thought.

Cassandra wasn't done. She'd apparently dissected the current mental state of each and every person who'd known Bill. After she finally stopped talking, I hung up the phone and sat staring very thoughtfully into space.

The problem with Bill Rampage's death was that there were too many people with a potential motive, and they weren't limited to the people known to have been on Hornby when he died.

Of course, there was also the fact that my client was lying to me.

And the fact that Shelley had also known Bill Rampage. And been on the island when he died. Please tell me she hadn't had an affair with him, as well. Then I'd probably have to add her husband to my list of suspects.

I grinned at the thought, hauled out my case notes. Bill Rampage had been involved with Kathleen by her own admission, with Dianne, with Terri, with Brandy at the inn as well as with the half-dozen women Cassandra had listed, not to mention with Cassandra herself. There had also been the "hot date" Murphy had mentioned, probably the receptionist.

I wondered how much each knew about the others, and how they felt about it. Cassandra didn't seem to care, but then Cassandra's never been typical about anything.

The person I really wanted to talk to was Kathleen again. Followed by Shelley, and then Terri Winter and Lois Michaels. I hauled out the phone book, and let my fingers do the walking.

Kathleen wasn't answering her phone.

And there was still no answer from Shelley. I left another message, but I was beginning to worry. Had something gone wrong?

————

I LUCKED out on my third call. Terri Winters agreed to meet me for coffee at ten.

Since she worked in an upscale clothing shop on South Granville, we agreed to meet at Beans & More on the corner of Twelfth and Granville. I was early, but I spotted her sunk into one of the deep leather armchairs by the window.

She'd told me she'd be wearing a pink suit, but I'd have recognized her even without that. A sleek platinum blond with dark brows, lashes and roots, she looked expensive.

The smile she gave me seemed genuine enough, though it did display perfect teeth and a complete absence of smile lines. How did she do that? For about half a second I was tempted to ask her what moisturizer she used.

"Barbara O'Grady?"

She already had an espresso in front of her. I'd been expecting a flavored latte. Maybe I was judging her too quickly.

I nodded. "I'll grab a coffee," I said.

Two minutes later I was sinking down with my large Italian Roast and taking out my notepad. "I hope you don't mind if I take notes?"

"No, that's fine. I'm not sure what I can tell you, though."

"Well, you could start by telling me why you left Hornby so abruptly."

"I left because That Woman was there, and she wouldn't leave." The venom in Terri Winter's voice didn't match her expression, which hadn't changed. That explained the lack of smile lines. It wasn't some miracle moisturizer, it was Botox.

"That Woman?" Not that there was any real doubt.

"Kathleen Marshall."

Here was one woman who apparently couldn't handle Bill's other liaisons. "Why do you call her That Woman?"

"Because she had a thing for Bill, and she wouldn't let him alone. Everywhere we went, there she was. On the Seawall, out for dinner. Even on Hornby, for heaven's sake."

Okay, maybe this was specific venom, not general venom. And maybe she had reason. I could hear Kathleen's voice in my head—"I made a point of knowing where he was."

"And you don't think that was a coincidence?"

"Ha." In a less deliberately elegant woman, I'd have said she snorted. "Tell that to the judge."

"Judge?"

"The one who issued the restraining order against her."

"There was a restraining order against Kathleen Marshall?"

Terri nodded. "She wouldn't leave us—him—alone. Finally I talked, I mean finally Bill decided to get a restraining order. She wasn't allowed to be within fifty meters of him."

Oh boy. So that was what Brad Bramwell had been referring to. No wonder he'd guessed my client's name. And Kathleen had kept this from me? Just wait till I got my hands on her!

"And did that solve it?"

"Solve it?" I thought I saw the shadow of a frown line. This was one frustrated lady. "It made things worse."

"Worse? How?"

"She kept showing up, wherever we were. And Bill wouldn't do anything about it."

So Bill Rampage hadn't been too serious about that restraining order. "What did you do?"

An elegant shrug. "What could I do? I endured."

Right. "So what happened on Hornby?"

Her very blue eyes narrowed. "When she showed up yet again, I finally reached the end of my patience. I told Bill either That Woman went or I would." Her hands clenched around her espresso cup. "He just laughed."

"So you left."

"Yes, I did. I had no choice."

"What was Kathleen doing?"

"Doing? She was doing what she always did—hovering. We'd run into her out walking. She sat beside us at dinner. Her room was next to ours, for God's sake!"

"She didn't say or do anything—threatening?"

"She didn't have to. Her very presence was a threat. She was not going away, and she was making very sure I knew it."

Ah. They'd been engaged in a female version of a pissing contest, and Terri Winters had lost. No wonder she was choked. "Did you feel that Kathleen Marshall posed any physical threat to Bill or to you?"

"Who knows? That Woman is capable of anything."

I took a sip of my coffee. "Is she capable of murdering Bill Rampage?"

"If she finally realized she couldn't have Bill, sure. As far as I'm concerned, That Woman is quite capable of murder."

Uh huh. No bias in that statement. "Can you tell me if Bill had any enemies? Anyone that might have been really unhappy with him?"

"Other than That Woman? No. Bill was a great guy, made friends with everyone he met. I still can't believe he's gone." She flicked at her eyes with a manicured finger.

"I'm sorry for your loss. Just for the record, can you tell me where you were last Saturday night?"

She stared at me. "You can't think that I—? As if I ever could! I cared about Bill."

I left the question hanging in the air between us.

"Oh, very well. I was here, in Vancouver. I'd gone out to dinner with friends. I got in late, after midnight. And the last ferry leaves Hornby at six p.m. You can check that if you like."

"No need." But ferries were not the only way to get to Hornby Island.

Terri stood up, her face a polite mask, her eyes hard and cold. "I have to get back to work. I'm late as it is."

I stood up too, held out my hand. "Thank you for meeting with me."

Terri gave a curt nod, ignored my outstretched hand and strode out.

Witch. But now I really needed to talk to Kathleen.

———

AS I STROLLED up Granville Street, I pulled out my cell phone, tried Kathleen's number. No answer.

I called Andrea, who didn't know where Kathleen was, except that she wasn't working.

"You're sure you haven't heard from her?"

"I think I'd remember."

"Andrea, I really need to talk to her. I have a few small questions for her."

"Uh oh. I know that tone. You don't sound very happy with your client."

Catching a curious look from a passerby, I walked a little way down fourteenth, sat on a wooden bench in front of Meinhardt's. I was less than a block from my place, but there was no point in going home to make the calls. I'd have to come back this way anyway. "That's putting it mildly," I told Andrea.

"Should I ask?"

I considered telling her, decided I couldn't afford the time. "You don't want to know."

"I was afraid of that. Well, let me know how it goes," Andrea said. Then she made one of those irritating split-second conversational shifts. "Have you heard from Nick?"

"What is this?" I muttered. "First my sister, now you. Can't I even have a relationship in peace?"

"What's this about your sister?"

"Susanna stopped by the office day before yesterday. You didn't tell Susanna about Nick, did you?"

"Me? Talk to Susanna? Would I do that?"

"Not usually. But in this case I don't know. Did you?"

"Nope. I'm innocent. Why? What did she say?"

"She wants me to come for dinner a week Sunday, and bring Nick."

"So, you're taking him home to meet the family, huh? This should be interesting."

"I don't know if I'll ask him or not."

"Come on, Barbara. You've been seeing him for nearly four months now. Don't you think it's about time?"

"No, I don't."

"Stop being such a chicken. I mean, I've barely met the man, and I'm your best friend."

Maybe if I didn't answer she'd give up?

Andrea sighed. "You can't keep Nick under wraps forever, you know. At some point you're going to have to introduce him to the rest of your life. And vice versa."

"You keep telling me I don't have a life."

A kid who looked about twelve was skateboarding by, caught that one and grinned. Always nice to know my life is so amusing. Sometimes I hate cell phones.

"You haven't had," Andrea was saying, "But I think you're in the process of creating one. Just don't screw it up!"

"Thanks, Mom."

"I'm right and you know it."

"He's away a lot." Even I could tell this was a less than convincing comeback.

Andrea's silence was eloquent. She knows me too well. Maybe I was being a little slow in expanding my relationship with Nick beyond the two of us. But it was working, and I'm always reluctant to mess with success.

So exactly why had I told Susanna I'd bring Nick to dinner with my mother, my sister and her family?

"What does Nick say about Sunday dinner?" Andrea asked.

I wasn't going to tell her. I knew how she'd react. And I was right.

"You haven't even told him yet, have you? You can't keep separating the pieces of your life like that," Andrea said.

"Like what?"

"Like the way you focus so hard on each and every case you take on that you have no time or energy for a private life. Are you denying it?"

I wasn't denying anything. I just wasn't having this conversation.

"And don't think this conversation will go away if you ignore it."

"How about if I hang up?"

"Just try it!"

So I did. Picturing Andrea's face, I grinned all the way back to the office.

CHAPTER SEVENTEEN

Striding into my office fifteen minutes later, the first thing I saw was the flashing light on my phone. Obviously not urgent, or they would have called my cell phone. Wrong again.

The message was from Blake Masters, Shelley's husband, and his cultured tones were strained. He wanted to meet with me as soon as possible. Shelley was in jail.

I felt anxiety tightening in my chest. Why had they arrested Shelley? Surely there couldn't be solid evidence against her. And why did Blake want to meet with me?

Half an hour later, I was sitting opposite Blake in the Asian-influenced bar of his upscale hotel. I'd come prepared to dislike the man, but I could see what had attracted Shelley. He was tall, an inch or so over six feet, boyishly handsome. A blond Viking, wearing Armani. Polished was the word that sprang to mind.

He wasn't my type—I've never gone for blond men—but he was extremely attractive in a stylish, power broker way. Think Brad Pitt in *Ocean's Eleven* with a few more years on him. He was also distraught. The martini he was halfway through didn't seem to be helping.

I took a sip of my Merlot. "Why don't you start by telling me why Shelley was arrested."

"I wish I knew why they arrested her. It makes no sense."

"What did the police say?"

"Besides charging her with first degree murder, you mean? Not much."

"Do you have a lawyer in town?"

"Yes, we've retained Ian Craig."

Obviously money was no object. Good. Shelley deserved the best. "He'll find out in short order what the police think they have on Shelley."

He drained his martini, slammed the glass down. Signaled for another.

Uh oh. I waited for the other shoe to drop.

"Barbara, I have to go back to Seattle. Tomorrow."

"Tomorrow? Can't you put it off?"

He shook his head. "I've got surgery scheduled the following day."

"Surely you can reschedule?"

"I'm afraid not. Timing is critical for these patients, and there isn't anyone else I trust to work on them"

I knew that Blake did a lot of reconstructive work for burn victims, as well as the more lucrative cosmetic surgery, so I was prepared to give him the benefit of the doubt, but still. This was no time to be abandoning his wife.

Surely there were other surgeons practicing in Seattle. I said as much.

"But none I trust," he repeated.

"What about Shelley?"

He looked down, stroked a finger down the stem of the Martini glass that had just been placed in front of him.

"You know, the fact that you two have reconnected is important to Shelley," he said. "And it means so much to her that you've been so supportive through all this."

"I'm glad." I said. Surely he didn't think my presence could make up for his absence?

"I'd like to hire you to work with Craig on clearing Shelley's name."

Oh no. "Are you sure that's necessary?"

"It's probably not strictly necessary, but I'm hoping it will give Shelley the feeling of how much support there is for her. Especially now."

"I really think she needs you here."

"I know. Unfortunately, that isn't going to be possible. I'll fly back on the weekend."

Terrific. Five days from now. "You don't need to hire me. I'd visit Shelley every day anyway."

"She thinks very highly of you. She'll derive comfort from knowing you're working on getting her out of this. So, will you take the case?"

What could I say? Shelley is a friend. Much as I hate working for friends, especially on murder cases, I couldn't ignore her plight. Especially when her husband wouldn't even be there.

"Yes, I'll take the case."

"Good." He pulled out an embossed leather checkbook. "How much?"

———

AS I LEFT THE HOTEL, it started to rain, a relentless drizzle that seemed appropriate to the mood I was in. I put up my hood and dashed to the car, swearing under my breath. Grabbing that rare on-street parking spot had seemed such a coup at the time. Now I wished I'd been underground, paying exorbitant rates, but at least dry.

When I got back to my office this time, my feet wet and my jeans soaked to the knees, I wanted to kick something. Luckily the filing cabinet is tough. Unfortunately, I'm not as tough as I think I am.

I limped to my desk and unpacked sushi from the bento box I'd picked up on Robson. I read somewhere that at last count, Vancouver had something like a thousand sushi shops, but this one was my favorite because it was always fresh, cheap and delicious. Today's sushi had better be up to standard—my wet feet were due to an unexpectedly full gutter outside the sushi shop.

The only positive in the entire outing was that Blake hadn't even flinched when I'd told him what my retainer would be.

I'd have taken the job for nothing for Shelley's sake, but Blake had annoyed me. And my negative impression of him hadn't been improved by meeting him. I had no hesitation in taking Blake's check. At least I'd be well paid.

As I took a bite of *ebi*, sweet raw shrimp on sushi rice with wasabi paste, I realized I hadn't even asked Blake about being on Hornby Island the weekend Bill Rampage had been murdered. I'd been so shocked to hear that Shelley had been arrested, it had gone right out of my head.

Which annoyed me still further. It didn't really matter, as I was likely to get more answers from Shelley than Blake, but it meant another delay.

We had to get Shelley out of jail before I could ask her anything.

Turning on the computer, I tasted the excellent salmon *sashimi*, then stared moodily at the screen. This was not how things were supposed to be turning out. With a sigh I loaded Shelley's file and brought it up to date, adding a few comments about Blake, which made me feel better.

Then I picked up the phone and called Kathleen, my lying client. I got the answering machine. Again. That did it—if she wouldn't answer the phone, she'd have to deal with me in person.

On the way to Kathleen's, windshield wipers swicking furiously back and forth, I swung by my bank and deposited Blake's check. Sometimes I need to be reminded that this is a job, and that I work in order to eat and to pay my mortgage. And to keep Cat in tuna, I thought with a half-grin.

The grin vanished as I pulled up in front of Kathleen's building. It was confrontation time.

————

WHEN KATHLEEN OPENED THE DOOR, she looked, if anything, worse than the last time I'd seen her. But the apartment smelled fresh, so she couldn't have degenerated too much. Or maybe there really was a cleaning lady.

She looked at me blankly for a moment. "Barbara?"

Then her face lit up. "Have you found her? Have you found the one who killed my Bill?"

Kathleen thought a woman had killed Bill? "No, I'm still working on the case. But I do have some questions for you. May I come in?"

She stepped aside, gesturing me into the living room. Without the mess, the full impact of the room hit me. It was stunning. That incredible artwork leapt off the walls, demanding my attention.

I forced myself to concentrate on why I was here.

I sat in the armchair, Kathleen on the sofa kitty-corner from me. I half turned so I could watch her face. "Kathleen, I know Bill Rampage had a restraining order against you. Why didn't you tell me about it?"

Her face seemed to fold in on itself. "I couldn't talk about it. If I told you, it made it more real. And it wasn't. He didn't really mean it, not my Bill. He didn't really want me to keep away from him. He couldn't. We meant too much to each other. It was all her."

I was beginning to worry about my client's mental stability. "Her?"

"The bimbo. Terri Winter."

So she did know Terri's last name. Nice of her to tell me. "Why would she have anything to do with the restraining order?"

"Please don't say those words. I can't bear it. It's so humiliating."

And her behavior towards Bill wasn't? "About Terri?"

"She talked him into it. She must have. She always hated me."

"Why did she hate you, Kathleen?"

"She knew I was the one who really mattered to Bill. She never had a chance, and she knew it. She was just—just—arm candy."

Arm candy? "Kathleen, the receptionist at Willis and Murphy says Bill wouldn't take your calls. He told her to tell you he was out. Always. If you two were so close, why would he do that?"

"Because I was too distracting to him. He couldn't concentrate on work after a conversation with me."

Oh boy. She had it all figured out. Hearing the depth of her self-delusion, I didn't know whether to pity her or worry about her.

I couldn't imagine being physically afraid of my client, but obsessions can make people do things way beyond their normal characters. "Kathleen, did you kill Bill Rampage?"

She glared at me. "Of course not. I loved him. How could you ask me such a thing?"

"Kathleen, you were the last person to see him alive. He died of poisoning not long after you left him. And by court order, you were forbidden to be within fifty meters of him. I'm not surprised you're worried about being charged with his murder. What I don't understand is what you expect me to do for you."

You can never tell how people are going to react. Somehow my words shocked Kathleen out of her emotional state.

"I didn't kill Bill. I loved him," she said again. "Why would I kill him? I wanted to be with him always. That's why I hired you. Someone else wanted him dead. Your job is to find out who."

This time I really did believe her. Or at least I believed that's what Kathleen believed.

Which didn't mean my client was innocent. "I'm going to need more help than I've been getting from you to this point."

She nodded.

"Let's start with why you asked if I'd found her."

She looked blank.

"When you answered the door. You asked if I'd found her, the one who killed Bill. Kathleen, do you know who killed him?"

"No."

"Do you suspect someone?"

She hesitated.

"If you aren't honest with me now, I'm off this case."

"All right. All right. It's just—well, I don't want to be wrong."

"I understand. Accusing someone of murder is a very serious…"

"No, you don't understand. I don't want to look—like I'm imagining things. Paranoid."

What? After everything she'd just told me, she didn't want to look paranoid? I did not understand this woman.

"What do you mean?" I managed to ask in a level voice.

She was watching my face. "Not what you've obviously assumed. Look, I have my reasons. I want Bill's killer to pay, I want that more than anything. But in order for that to happen, you have to find them. You have to prove they did it. It can't rest on anything I tell you."

"Are you saying you won't testify in court?" I asked, half-joking.

"That is exactly what I'm saying," she said, hands folded primly in her lap.

I stared at her. For a moment there I'd been talking to Andrea's efficient, organized employee. Now I didn't know whom I was talking to.

It was as if she'd read my mind. "You don't need to understand me. Just find Bill's killer."

A slight smile sat oddly on her tense face.

"If I promise you I'll use whatever you tell me as a starting point only, that no-one will ever know I got the lead from you? Is that enough for you to tell me who you suspect?"

She watched me steadily, lips slightly pursed. After long moments of tense silence, she nodded. "Yes. I know you're a good detective, Andrea told me that. It's why I hired you. If anyone can find the killer, you can."

"Thanks for the vote of confidence."

I'd expected her to be annoyed, but she smiled a little. "You don't have to like me. You just have to find Bill's killer."

"And you think that is…?"

"One of the girls."

Kathleen thought one of the girls had killed Bill Rampage? Which girls? My mind flashed back to the kitchen of the Sunshine Inn, where Brandy and Tiffany had calmly and methodically severed chicken parts. Those girls?

She thought one of those giddy teenagers had killed her former lover? "Which girls?" I asked her.

"The ones at the Inn," Kathleen said. "The teenage helpers."

"Tiffany and Brandy?"

"Are those their names?" Kathleen put her hand against her mouth, as if to hold back a sob.

"Yes. But why them? What makes you think one of them killed him?"

"Bill had a soft spot for women, all women," Kathleen said softly. "He'd laugh, he'd flirt, and he'd tease. But he was never serious. Women understood that, but those girls? No. They didn't have the experience, the maturity. They saw what they wanted to believe. And when that belief proved not to be true? Then they were angry. Sometimes very angry."

Could Kathleen be talking about herself? Was there some twist in her personality, some hidden aspect that took revenge on Bill Rampage for an insult the rest of her personality refused to admit? "Did you see something that makes you accuse them? Hear something?"

"They both hovered around him like butterflies around a particularly sweet flower. But it was the blonde one who pursued him."

I didn't point out that Kathleen herself had done that and more. I was afraid my client would disintegrate completely if I did. "Pursued him?"

"She kept turning up, blushing and giggling. Bill joked that he kept tripping over her."

Apparently that wasn't all he'd done. "That's hardly sufficient for an accusation of murder."

"No. But there's more."

Was she blushing? She was. What was this?

"What else?" I prompted.

"This is hard for me. Hard to admit that Bill wasn't always… wise in his choices."

No kidding. "Go on."

"He—he may have encouraged her more than he should. Even led her on, a little."

Oh, I'd say he'd led her on more than a little. "Led her on?"

"Kissed her. More than once, too."

And when Kathleen found out? Had it been one insult too many? "How do you know?"

"I saw them. In the gardens. They didn't know I was there."

"Were you following Bill?"

She nodded. "I'd hoped for a private conversation with him."

A tryst, more like. And she'd seen another tryst. One that didn't include her. "How did you feel, seeing that?"

Kathleen looked startled. "Me? Oh, it didn't bother me. I'm used to it. I know he doesn't mean anything by it. He just needs to sow his wild oats before he settles down. I know I'm his choice, that we'll end up…" Her eyes widened, then tired up. "I mean, I always knew we'd end up together."

She was used to it? My client's talent for self-deception didn't seem to have any limits. Which worried me more with every word I heard. Exactly how far did her obsession with Bill Rampage go?

"But after seeing this interlude, you think the blonde girl might have poisoned Bill?" I asked.

She nodded.

"Why?"

"The very young are sometimes violent in their passions. And I heard her declaring undying love to Bill."

"What did he say?"

"He laughed and kissed her again. He'd never lie to them."

Of course not. "You think that this teenager, finding out about you and Bill, might have poisoned him?"

"It's the only thing that makes sense."

Nothing made sense. "How would she have known about you and Bill?"

"Maybe she saw us go to his room."

"On the Saturday night?"

Kathleen wouldn't meet my eyes.

Oh no. "You were with him on Friday night as well?"

She nodded without looking up. "Friday afternoon, actually."

"I thought Terri didn't leave until Saturday."

"She didn't."

Oh, great. No wonder Terri had left. Except she hadn't mentioned it. "Did Terri find out?"

She shook her head.

"Were you and Bill together on Thursday night as well?"

"Of course not."

Well, at least she'd had that much sense.

"Bill didn't get there until Friday."

Okay. Moving right along. "So if it was this blonde girl, how would she have killed Bill? I don't imagine there's much access to poisons in the kitchen."

"She probably got it from the old bat."

"Mrs. Smith?"

"No, not her. Elena. She's supposed to be the local herb witch, and I suspect she knows a lot about things she's not supposed to know."

Thinking back on my conversation with Elena, it wouldn't surprise me a bit. "It sounds like I need to make another trip to Hornby."

"Probably."

And why hadn't she told me all this before I went to Hornby the first time?

I reined in my temper, which wanted very badly to fire my client. Or at least tell her what I thought of her actions. Not a professional move.

"Is there anything else I should know before I go?" I said. "Anything else you haven't told me?"

"No, nothing. I swear."

I mostly believed her this time. Or at least, I believed there was nothing important her conscious mind hadn't told me. Her subconscious I didn't even want to think about.

But I was going to have to, if I wanted to solve this case.

CHAPTER EIGHTEEN

Back in my office again, I transcribed my notes, thinking about what I'd learned, what I still had to learn. Did Kathleen have some kind of mental disorder, or was she just completely obsessed with the idea of Bill being her soul mate?

And how was I going to find out?

Would a mental disorder be a solid defense, if she really had killed her philandering lover? And why did women put up with some men, anyway?

Shaking my head, I put in a call to Jerry, who wasn't in. I left a message.

Then I tried Nick's number. To my surprise, he was in.

"Hey, babe" he said, his voice warm.

I grinned. Okay, other men are definitely worth it. Except what was he doing back in town? Why hadn't he called? "Don't call me that."

He chuckled. "How did I know you'd say that?"

"What? Are you calling me predictable?"

"Not me. I never said a word. Now, what can I do for you?" he continued, his tone suddenly businesslike.

"Someone just walked in, didn't they?"

"Yes. That's correct."

"You know that Shelley Masters is a friend of mine?"

He started to groan, caught himself. "I believe an arrest has been made in that case."

"Yeah, that's what I'm worried about. They arrested Shelley."

"It's a Vancouver police matter, I'm afraid. The incident happened in their jurisdiction."

"I know. I wondered if you'd picked up anything."

"No, I'm afraid not. But I'll check into it, and call you back."

"Sounds like a plan" I said. "How about dinner tonight?"

"Certainly," he said, and rung off.

Well, at least he'd sounded enthusiastic. And it gave me something to look forward to. Which, given the way the rest of my life was going, might mean the difference between sanity and me yanking the phone out of the wall and running screaming from my office. Or not.

I sighed, put in a call to Lois Michaels. Left yet another message.

Staring at my notes, I realized Cassandra might be able to answer some of my questions. And it was time we actually met in person. Or re-met, if there's such a word.

Cassandra was more than happy to meet for coffee. Big surprise. Unless she's changed out of all recognition, Cassandra's as big a coffee fiend as I am.

Even thinking about that fact made me uneasy. One of these days, I might actually have to start watching the amount of coffee I drink.

Just not anytime soon.

———

THROWING BACK MY HOOD, I walked into the small, trendy coffee shop. I had no trouble spotting Cassandra, despite the fact that I'd not seen her in more than ten years. Her style was still dramatic, very much the artist.

Long, dark hair swept casually back from a high forehead,

bright red lipstick and her trademark spectacular earrings, with just a hint of the professor in the tailoring of her scarlet jacket. An umbrella covered in scarlet poppies dripped beside her.

"Barbara," she practically squealed when she caught sight of me. "You haven't changed a bit."

Shows how much she knows. "Nice to see you too, Cassandra. How are you?"

"Me? Oh, fantastic, as always. And I'm dying to know what you wanted to meet about."

"Why don't I grab a coffee, and I'll fill you in. Are the lattes good here?" I asked, glancing at the distinctively oversized cup in front of her.

"This is a caramel almond latte, and it's fantastic. Try one."

"I think I'll stick with a cappuccino," I said, shuddering at the thought of all that sugar. "I'll be right back."

"So, what's up?" she asked as I sank into the nubby gray chair next to hers.

"Deirdre Brandt," I said. "I'm looking into her death, so I need to know as much about her life as possible."

"Barbara, how exciting! Does this mean Shelley hired you?"

I couldn't think of any reason not to tell her that much. She'd guessed anyway. "Shelley's husband, actually. And it's confidential for the time being."

"Of course. You know I love keeping secrets."

I didn't know any such thing.

"Does that mean things are good again between Shelley and her husband?" Cassandra was asking.

"They seem to be." Except for the fact that he'd left town, of course.

"But I heard she's in jail."

Of course she had. "She is. I still can't believe it. I don't know what the police are thinking."

"So you don't think she did it?"

"No, I definitely don't think she did it."

Cassandra flicked her dark hair behind her and leaned forward.

"Despite the affair? Jealousy is a powerful emotion," she said in a half-whisper.

"Speaking of jealousy, did you ever feel jealous of Bill Rampage?"

"Me? Of Bill?" She threw back her head, braying with laughter. "You have to love someone to be jealous of them. Bill was great fun, but love him? You'd have to be self-destructive to do that."

I thought about my conversation with Kathleen. Cassandra had a point. But then I'd always wondered if Cassandra was too self-involved to love anyone. Sometimes I wondered the same about myself. "About Deirdre, then. Do you know anything about her background?"

"Oh, my dear. Yes. She was an exotic dancer for quite a number of years, and an artist's model on the side. Somewhere along the line she started painting—I think one of her men must have given her pointers. Deirdre always had men, plural, and plenty of them."

She gave that laugh, gulped down some of her caramel latte. "Anyway, she launched her career at a small, very avant-garde gallery in Seattle. She had a few showings and there were a couple of positive notices of her work, but she could easily have disappeared without a ripple."

Cassandra leaned towards me a little. "Deirdre's work was good, but there was nothing gripping about it. It didn't have that edge. You know, Barbara."

Indeed I did know.

For an artist to achieve any degree of recognition, his or her work had to have a quality that lifted it out of the ordinary, from the merely pretty or decorative to the emotionally compelling. It was the downfall of many an art student. I knew—it had been mine.

And there are few feelings more devastating than when you finally realize you will never be quite good enough, no matter how much you love it or how hard you work.

I still couldn't think about the day I'd looked at my latest work and realized Jayson was right. It might be technically good, but it didn't breathe.

"I'm not sure what happened," Cassandra was saying. "But Deirdre's next show was totally different, more like the work she's showing here. Suddenly her women were grittier, harder edged, looking back at the viewer as if challenging them. The reviews began to speak of "this brave new voice in women's art". Deirdre stopped dancing, devoted herself full time to her art."

Cassandra's eyes met mine. "It might be interesting to know how she survived. She couldn't have been making much at the start."

I wondered again about Cassandra's sources.

"Anyway," she continued. "Deirdre was on her way. Now she is, or rather she was, selling paintings for five and six figures. Must be nice."

Except for being dead, of course. Kind of hard to enjoy your success when you've been murdered. "Did Deirdre have enemies?"

"Other than various wronged wives, I've never heard of any."

"What about close friends?"

"Funny, I never thought of Deirdre as having friends," she said.

"No?"

"She was too competitive, especially with other women. With men, I doubt she ever got beyond sex."

We've all known women like Deirdre. But I found myself wondering if she was really as one dimensional as the woman Cassandra was describing. Few of us are. "Was she in town just for this show?"

"I think so."

"Did she know anyone here?"

"Just the Courtlands. Oh, and Shelley and her husband of course."

This wasn't going to be easy. "What about the third artist?"

"Judy Moore? She's from Seattle too, but I don't know how well Deirdre knew her."

I'd have to ask Shelley. "Have you heard any speculation on why someone might have killed Deirdre?"

Cassandra took a sip of her latte, flipped back her hair. "Well…"

"Whatever it is, I need to know."

"You're not going to like it. Most people think Shelley killed her."

"Why?"

"Well, there's the history between Deirdre and Blake, of course. And then Deirdre beat Shelley out for a couple of commissions. But it certainly didn't help that Deirdre and Blake Masters were seen having drinks together the first evening they were in town."

She was right. I didn't like it. And it didn't fit.

Why would Blake go from a weekend getaway on Hornby with Shelley to an illicit tryst in Vancouver with Deirdre? Did the man think he wouldn't get found out? Or did he not care?

"Deirdre and Blake were seen together? Where?"

"The Marathon. Deirdre was staying there."

"You're sure?" I asked her.

"Oh yes."

I'd check anyway, but my gut said Cassandra was right. This was not good news for Shelley. It just deepened what was already seen as her motive.

I wondered why Blake hadn't said anything when he hired me. Maybe he thought no one knew. Maybe he was just a total jerk. "Anything else?"

"No." She shook her head and her chandelier earrings swung, glinting red as they caught the light.

I'd heard enough, anyway. There was something about Cassandra's delight in knowing all the grimy details that nauseated me.

I drained my coffee. "Thanks, Cassandra. For the information, and for meeting with me. I hate to run, but I'm on a tight schedule with this one."

"Oh, I understand. I'm happy to help. And I'll call you if I hear anything else, shall I?"

"Good idea," I said, and escaped.

I headed back to the office. The earlier downpour had down-graded to a light mist. As I drove past trendy boutiques shoulder to shoulder with the fresh vegetable markets on West Broadway, I speculated on what I'd just heard.

Something told me I didn't yet know enough about Deirdre Brandt. Who was she? Where had she come from? What made her tick? Why she had been killed and who had killed her might flow from that.

I could only hope that it would.

———

WHEN I GOT BACK to my office, there were two messages waiting. One from Lois Michaels, the other from a Tiffany Arthur.

Tiffany? The only Tiffany I'd met recently had been the teenager on Hornby.

I looked at the area code. 604. Vancouver. And the number looked familiar. I did a search on my contacts list and came up with Willis and Murphy.

Of course. The blonde receptionist mourning her three week anniversary with Bill.

I called Mrs. Michaels first—she'd been the hardest to reach. She answered on the first ring.

"Lois Michaels?"

"Yes?"

"My name is Barbara O'Grady. I'm a private investigator looking into the death of Bill Rampage. I'd like to ask you a few questions."

"Oh. Oh, that was a dreadful business. What can I tell you?"

"I was hoping we could meet, perhaps for coffee? I'll try not to take too much of your time."

"I have a very busy schedule, but...," I could hear pages turning. "Yes, I believe I could squeeze in a meeting tomorrow morning. Say around eleven?"

"Eleven is good. Where would you like to meet?"

"I don't have much time, so I would appreciate it if you came to my home. Is that possible?"

"Of course."

"It is on West Forty-fifth," she said. And gave met the address.

"Terrific. I'll see you tomorrow at eleven. And thank you, Mrs. Michaels."

"You're welcome, dear."

I made a note in my calendar, picked up the phone again. For a change, my luck was holding.

"Willis and Murphy."

"Is this Tiffany Arthur?"

"Yes, this is she."

"It's Barbara O'Grady calling. You left me a message?"

"Oh, oh I'm so glad you called back. But I can't talk now. I don't want to be overheard. Can we meet?"

I really didn't want to go out again, especially into rush hour traffic, but I wanted whatever information Tiffany might have for me. "Sure. What time do you get off? I'll buy you a drink."

"You will? Oh, that's wonderful. I get off at five-thirty, but why don't I meet you at the Garden Lounge? In the Four Seasons?"

It was too far to walk in the time I had available, but at least there'd be parking in the nearby Pacific Centre Mall. "I'll meet you there."

"Okay. Bye."

———

TIFFANY ARTHUR SAT by one of the rain-splattered windows, under a large palm tree. She looked nervous and pleased to see me at the same time. The room was busy, humming with the chatter and pick-up lines of the after-work-and-cocktails crowd. Tiffany ordered a peach bellini. I heroically refrained from comment and ordered a glass of the Burrowing Owl Cabernet Sauvignon. "What did you want to tell me, Tiffany?"

"Well…," she paused and downed a good part of her bellini, as if for courage. "I talked to Janet. You know, William's—Mr. Murphy's —assistant?"

"Go on."

"Well, she—Janet, that is—she told me that Mr. Murphy had been away that weekend. And she thought he'd gone to Saltspring, but that she wasn't sure, because he might have changed plans?"

Always nice to have conclusive evidence. "Did she say anything else?"

"Oh, I haven't even gotten to the good part yet. But I need to tell you how, I mean the way that I found out. Or it won't make sense."

It might not make sense anyway, judging by what I'd heard so far. "Go on."

"Well, a little later, this was yesterday, she came back to me and said that Mr. Murphy had been on Saltspring, because he'd asked her to file the materials he'd got from the real estate agent there," Tiffany said.

She took a swig of her bellini. "And the notes he'd made on the places he'd seen? She told me he was looking for a better place, and that some of the places he was considering were worth a couple million dollars! She showed me pictures."

Tiffany took another swig of her drink, watching my face to see if I was suitably impressed.

"Really? But why would she show them to you?"

She blushed, hid her face in her drink. "Well, I think she might know, about Tad, Mr. Murphy and me, you know? And I think maybe she's trying to impress me, to help him impress me, so we'll get back together. Him and me, I mean, not me and Janet."

She giggled. "It did impress me, but not enough to get back with Tad. Nothing could do that."

"But you're pretty sure he was on Saltspring that weekend?"

"Sure. And I haven't told you the good part yet."

"Oh?"

"Uh huh. This morning, guess what happened? Janet came back, all in a tizzy, and told me to forget what she'd said. She said she'd been confused, that Tad, Mr. Murphy hadn't been to Saltspring this month at all."

Tiffany waved at the waitress for another bellini, then leaned towards me a lowered her voice. "And Janet said that she was sorry she'd misled me, and could I please forget we'd ever talked about it? So I said of course, that I never remembered half of what people told me anyway. And she thanked me and went away. But you know what I did then?"

I played along. "No, what?"

"You'll never guess."

Probably not. "Go on."

"I called the real estate agent myself. The one on the stuff she showed me? I'd remembered the name, and I looked her up, and asked her and she checked for me. She confirmed that Tad had met with her that weekend! Both days!! And she'd showed him three places on Saturday, two in the morning and one in the early afternoon."

Leaving him plenty of time to get to Hornby in time for dinner. Finally. A lead that didn't go straight back to my client. "Do you have the name of the agent?"

She nodded, handed me a half sheet of paper with tiny, cramped printing on it. "I thought you might need it."

"That's good work, Tiffany. Thank you."

"It is good, isn't it? So, will it help Bill? I mean, help find whoever did that to him?"

"Yes, I think it might."

"Good. 'Cause I think they deserve the worst. Not that it'll ever make up for Bill being gone, but at least they'll pay." She raised her second bellini in a mock-toast, and downed half of it.

She sounded like Kathleen. And she was drinking like she was Zelda Fitzgerald. "Tiffany, are you driving?"

She looked at me blankly. "No, I'm sitting here—oh, you mean will I be driving later? No, I took the bus. I know better than to drink and drive."

Well, that was something. "Is there anything else you wanted to tell me?"

"No. But that's enough, isn't it?"

At least it gave me another suspect, and possibly a strong one. And I didn't mind at all if Tad Murphy turned out to be the killer. "Yes, that's enough."

———

I'D FINALLY GOTTEN HOME, made it halfway down the hall when the phone rang. I nearly didn't answer it. I was tired and fed-up with people whose motives and actions made no sense to me. On the fourth ring I caved.

"Barbara, do you feel like catching a bite at Guido's?" Andrea asked.

It sounded like a plan to me. Talking to Andrea was the one thing likely to improve my current outlook. Well, that or an evening with Nick—OMG! "Andrea, I'm supposed to be having dinner with Nick."

"Why don't you sound like that's a good thing? And what do you mean, supposed to be?"

"It's just that I forgot about it."

"He's finally back in town and you forgot about a date with him." She let the pause stretch out. "Okay, what did he do wrong?"

"What? He didn't do anything wrong. Why?"

"Because when you start forgetting dates with your men, it's the beginning of the end."

"No, it isn't. Nick and I are fine." I glared at the phone. "And what do you mean, my men? There haven't exactly been that many of them."

"So how are you and Nick, then?"

"We're good. I keep telling you that."

"Yes, you do. You'd probably better call him then, don't you think?"

Oops. Either I was more tired than I knew, or Andrea had a point about my relationship with Nick. "I'll call you tomorrow."

"Sure thing, Barbara. Say hi to Nick for me."

"Yeah, yeah. Bye, Andrea."

Before I punched in Nick's number, I noticed the "message waiting" blinking at me. I must be tired. I'd missed that when I came in. I punched in the required sequence, and got Nick's warm voice.

"Barbara, I'm so sorry, but I'm going to have to take a rain check on dinner. Something's come up here. But I'll make it up to you this weekend. We'll paint the town. I'll call to make arrangements as soon as I'm free."

On top of the day I'd had, this was too much. I picked up the phone. "Andrea, it's me. Nick's just cancelled dinner. Are you still free?"

"Barbara? You must be having a bad day. I can hear that 'I need wine and I need it now' note in your voice from here."

"Trust me, you don't want to know."

"But you'll tell me about it anyway, won't you?"

"Probably. The stuff I can repeat, at least."

"Then I'll have to tell you about my day in return, and we can both weep in our wine."

"Half an hour?"

"See you there."

CHAPTER NINETEEN

The next morning, I opened my eyes reluctantly. I wasn't looking forward to the day. The cool nose that immediately pressed itself against mine didn't help any.

"Cat!" I yelled, sitting bolt upright. "Dogs are supposed to be the ones with wet noses. Not you."

Cat grinned at me. Or at least, that's what it looked like.

"Why me?" I muttered as I headed for the coffee. "Why out of all the people in this building did you choose me to harass? I don't even like cats."

Cat must have snuck through the living room, because he was sitting in the kitchen, tail wrapped around his legs, eyes fixed on his dish, when I got there. Or maybe he really does walk through walls.

"You're a pain. You know that, don't you?" I asked him as I dished out his tuna.

Cat purred. Somehow the sound made my day a little brighter. But I wasn't going to tell him that.

I put on coffee and made the slice of toast that was all I felt like having after making a pig of myself on some truly amazing lasagna at Guido's the previous evening.

Ordering that second bottle of wine had been a mistake, even if we did get Guido to join us. At least I didn't have a hangover.

Still, it had been fun—Andrea and I hadn't had the chance to catch up like that in months. But this morning I felt like the python that ate the pig. Time for a run.

———

"LEGS, DO YOUR THING." And I was off.

I deliberately stretched my stride so I could feel every muscle work, tasting the salt in the air. It was overcast and damp, but at least it wasn't raining. Yet.

I was running the Seawall that snakes around Stanley Park, counting the freighters at anchor off English Bay as I went. Ten of them, more than usual. Otherwise the bay was empty.

If there'd been a wind, I'd have seen a few sailboats, even this early on a damp, chilly day. On a clear day, the bay is overrun with dots of sail. Give them wind and sun, and Vancouver's sailors tend to take the day off, if only to make up for all the other days.

The Seawall too was almost deserted. There was an old lady walking her dog, a couple of other runners, and that was pretty much it. I was glad, because it meant I didn't have to keep a part of my mind alert for collisions—I could just run.

And I needed to run, to let my mind click off as my body counted the miles. Needed to work off last night's dinner, and work the confusion stemming from my two newest cases out of my pores.

———

BY NINE I was at my desk and in the middle of reviewing up my notes from the previous day when the phone rang. I answered warily.

It was Ian Craig, Shelley's lawyer, asking if I were free for a nine-thirty meeting. I checked my watch. If I went straight there, I'd make it.

Less than half an hour later, I was sitting in a very posh office, across a highly polished expanse of rosewood from Ian Craig. Though I knew his reputation, we'd not met before. In his late fifties, Ian Craig was tall, impeccably turned out, calm and confident. It seemed odd to me that neither of his clients were there—Shelley was still in jail and Blake was back in Seattle. It didn't seem to faze him in the least.

He considered me coolly, then said, "You come highly recommended, Ms. O'Grady."

"Good to hear. And please, call me Barbara."

"Then I am Ian," he responded, though I detected a slight hesitation. This was a man who preferred formality. "I understand Blake Masters has already hired you."

"That's right. But it wasn't clear exactly what he hired me to do. Nor was he clear on the details of the police case. I'm hoping you can fill me in."

"That is why you are here." He paused, spun the gold pen that was the only item resting on all that beautiful wood. "How well do you know Mrs. Masters?"

"Shelley? We were friends in university, but until very recently I'd lost touch with her."

"I see. Are you aware of the difficulties in her marriage?"

"If you mean the affair between Blake Masters and Deirdre Brandt, yes I am."

He nodded. "Good. That makes it simpler, as that appears to be the main motive in this case. Although the affair apparently ended some time ago."

"It did?"

"That is what my clients tell me."

"Hmmm. That isn't what my sources tell me. And I'm assuming you'd like me to verify whether your client's statement is true."

His lips turned down slightly. "Indeed. Particularly if it is not true."

I nodded. "So that's motive. What about means and opportunity?"

"Deirdre Brandt appears to have died of nitroglycerin poisoning."

Which confirmed what Shelley had told me. "Appears to have?"

"That is what I've been told."

"I see. And of course, Shelley carries nitroglycerin tablets."

"Unfortunately, yes, she does. And it seems that the Courtlands took all of the artists, Blake, Judy's husband Bob and several key collectors were taken to Destinations for dinner. There were twelve of them, in all. The dinner ended perhaps half an hour before the show opened."

Which matched what Shelley had told me. "I'm surprised the Courtlands had time to go out for dinner before a show opening. Usually gallery owners are too busy dealing with last minute crises."

"I gather it's normal practice for them."

They'd have to be hyper-organized. No wonder Courtland's had such a terrific reputation. "I gather we're assuming the nitro was in something served at the restaurant?"

"That seems to be the operative assumption, given the time frame," he said.

"I suppose it's too much to hope they found traces of anything at the restaurant?"

"Everything had gone through the dishwasher well before the police were aware the circumstances were suspicious."

"Which makes things more difficult," I said.

"Quite. Well, Barbara?"

His expression was—skeptical? What was this?

"Well?"

"Where do you intend to start?"

That was easy. But why the skepticism? "I'll start by digging up anything I can on the affair between Blake and Deirdre. I'll look into any relationships Deirdre may have had with the people at this dinner. I'll also check into the cause of death, and if there was any other opportunity for the nitro to be given. Have I missed anything?"

"Not yet."

Was he being sarcastic? "I'll need to speak with Shelley, and as soon as possible."

"I will have my secretary arrange something for tomorrow and advise you."

"I'd appreciate it. Is there anything else?"

"Not at the moment. Thank you for coming in. I'm sure we'll work well together."

He was? That wasn't the impression he'd given so far. "Likewise. Should my formal reports go to you, or to Blake?"

"You had better send them to me. In case there is anything I can use in preparing my defense."

Wasn't that the whole point? "I'll be sure to do so. Good day, Ian."

———

I WALKED out of Ian Craig's office feeling stunned. Not just by the fact that he clearly wasn't impressed that I'd be working with him. It was the case itself.

When Blake had hired me, it hadn't really sunk in what I was taking on. I'd felt more like I'd be providing moral support to Shelley than anything else.

But Ian Craig was dead serious. In his formal office, the evidence seemed to weigh more heavily.

Shelley was really in trouble. I'd never expected her to be a serious suspect, despite her concerns.

I'd been wrong.

And now it was up to me to get her out of that trouble. And I had no clue where I was going to start.

Now I was really worried for Shelley.

Canada doesn't have the death penalty, so at least she wasn't facing that, but life in prison is no picnic. And there wouldn't be much question the crime was premeditated.

Presumably you'd have to grind up quite a number of nitroglycerin pills to produce a fatal dose. It wasn't the kind of thing you could dash off to the washroom and do in between courses at dinner.

I didn't believe she was guilty, but the evidence must have been pretty solid before they'd arrested her.

Which was where I'd start, with the evidence. Not with whatever the police had, but with the poison itself. How potent was it? How had it been administered? I didn't have the answers, but I knew who did.

CHAPTER TWENTY

The small drugstore on Davie Street in the West End was deserted, despite the busy foot traffic outside. That didn't happen often. I headed for the back.

"Hey, Patrick. Since you've nothing better to do, I thought I'd come in and ask annoying questions."

Patrick Carmichael stood up from the stool he'd been lounging on, a grin creasing his lean face and leaned across the counter. "Ah, my favorite customer. Not that you ever buy anything. How do you stay so disgustingly healthy, anyway?"

"Clean living?"

"You? Not a chance. So, why are you here? Tell me you've developed some unmentionable disease, and you'll need multiple prescriptions."

"Nope, sorry. I just came in to entertain you."

He sighed theatrically, held a hand to his forehead. "What is it this time?"

"I've got a case where a woman died of a nitroglycerin overdose."

"She died from an overdose of nitro? Now that's one I don't

usually hear. People overdose on the stuff all the time, but it doesn't usually kill them."

"They do? Why?"

"Nitro's mostly prescribed to heart patients with angina. Most of those patients are older, and sometimes their memories—well, you can imagine."

"They forget how much they've taken and take more than they should."

"Exactly."

"But it isn't fatal?"

"No. Oh, it can be. Nitro is a class six poison, which most people don't realize."

"Nitro is poisonous?"

"Yup."

I hadn't known that, and I found it unsettling to think of Aunt Cindy swallowing poison to stay alive. "So why don't they die?"

"Because they usually recognize the symptoms in time, and get themselves to a hospital."

"So if Deirdre had been taken to the hospital in time, she'd have lived."

"Deirdre?"

"The woman who died."

He ran a hand through bright red hair, leaving it standing more on end than usual. "Somehow it's worse when you name them."

"And worse still if you actually see them."

"You were there when she died?"

"No, when she collapsed."

"What were the symptoms? How long was this after she'd ingested the nitro?"

"Whoa. One question at a time. This was at an art opening. She'd apparently had a headache for quite a while, been nauseous…"

"Art opening? Are we talking about Deirdre Brandt?"

"Yes."

"My God! Her work was amazing. I thought about buying a piece myself. Have you seen it?"

"Not yet."

"You've never seen Deirdre Brandt's work? I thought you were an art aficionado?"

"Only sometimes, Patrick, only sometimes. So tell me about her work."

"I ran into it in a gallery in Seattle maybe four years ago. She captures the pain of being on the outside in a way I've never seen equaled. Those portraits don't just speak, they yell. I've never forgotten them. And I've been kicking myself ever since that I didn't buy a piece then, when they were still almost affordable."

"What does almost affordable mean?" I asked, thinking of Cassandra's comments.

"Most pieces ranged between ten and twenty thousand."

"Ouch. What does her stuff go for now?"

"Oh, somewhere between eighty and four hundred thousand. And that was before she died. I'd hate to think what they're asking now."

"I can imagine." Too bad you had to be dead to make it really big in the art world.

"I'd heard Deirdre Brandt had died, but I'd had no idea of the circumstances." He played with a pen lying on the spotless white counter, his expression more somber than I'd ever seen it, then looked up. "You say she'd been headachy, nauseous. Then what?"

"She collapsed. Pale, sweaty. Blue tinge around the lips. By the time the ambulance arrived, she was already in v-tach."

"God! How awful. You were right, though."

"About?"

"Her death was totally preventable. If she'd gone to hospital when she first started feeling nauseous, she'd have been okay. She was probably feeling short of breath and faint, too. I wonder why she didn't go to emergency, with those symptoms."

"Probably because it was the opening night of her show. There were some very important collectors there."

"Still, she should have recognized the symptoms as dangerous."

"Not necessarily. Deirdre Brandt didn't have a heart condition."

"Didn't have a heart condition? Then how did she overdose on nitroglycerin tablets?"

"She didn't. Somebody did it for her."

"Murder? You're sure it wasn't accidental? A nitro high?"

"There's already an arrest in the case."

He shook his head. "Unbelievable. I'm guessing you have a client who is involved somehow."

Involved wasn't the word. "You could say that."

"Too bad. What other questions did you have?"

I'd been thinking about the timing. "If getting Deirdre to a hospital earlier would have saved her, then nitro isn't a very reliable drug for killing someone."

"Very unreliable, I'd say."

"So maybe someone was wanting to scare her, not kill her."

"Or someone was using whatever was easily to hand."

"And gambling that she'd be too professional to leave her opening? What kind of mind could devise stakes like that?—Will she leave in time to save herself? That is truly cold."

"Well, murderers generally aren't nice people."

"Ever the pragmatist." I'd seen a few nasty deaths over the past few years, but this one gave me shivers. "So how quickly would nitro have acted?"

"Well, if she was already in tachycardia when the ambulance came, she'd most likely have taken, or been given, the drug two to five hours earlier. When did the ambulance come?"

"Around nine-thirty."

"So she probably ingested it between four-thirty and seven-thirty. Maybe earlier, maybe later, it would depend on her metabolism. When do the police suspect she was poisoned? I assume they've connected that to a suspect?"

"You assume correctly." Unfortunately for Shelley. "A group of people had dinner at Destinations before the opening. They would have been eating around six-thirty."

"That would fit. Any evidence as to how the drug was administered?"

"That would be too easy. Can you tell me how it might have been administered, and what effect that could have had on the reaction time?"

"Not a question I'm normally asked about nitro. Most people just dissolve it under their tongue. But you could crush it, dissolve it in liquid. That would be the fastest acting, especially on an empty stomach. Or you could mix the crushed powder into food, which would slow it down."

"Can it be absorbed through the skin?"

"Yes, but probably not in a concentration that would do much harm."

"So, the likelihood is that she swallowed it in some form?"

"I can't think of any other method that would cause death," Patrick said.

Which didn't help Shelley much.

———

I GLANCED AROUND ME. The store was still quiet. There were no impatient customers lining up, prescriptions in hand. Patrick was watching me with a quizzical look on his face.

"If you have another few minutes free? I've got another case that I could use your input on."

"Not another death by poison?"

"Well, yes."

"You're kidding me!"

I shook my head.

He let out a soft whistle. "I didn't think anybody used poison any more. Too easy to trace these days. Which poison?"

"That's the problem, I don't know."

"It hasn't been identified? With all the gizmos they've got these days?"

"Apparently not."

"Hmmmm. Means it's something they wouldn't normally test for. What were the symptoms?"

I grinned. I'd known he wouldn't be able to resist the challenge.

I thought about everything I'd learned about Bill Rampage's unpleasant death, organized it in my mind. "The victim's skin was blotchy and he'd been very ill."

"Whoa. That covers a lot of territory," Patrick said. "It could be one of the heart drugs, any number of synthetics or botanicals, even cyanide. Which is a botanical, strictly speaking."

"Cyanide?"

He laughed. "Funny how that always catches everyone's attention. We've all been raised on too many classic mysteries. Scent of bitter almonds and all that. Cyanide doesn't get used much any more—it's too easy to spot. And it's usually the first thing the police test for."

"I'd think that would only apply if someone was trying to cover up the murder."

"And in this case?"

"If they'd been hoping to cover it up, they picked the wrong poison. There didn't seem to be any doubt in anyone's mind that he'd been poisoned."

"Going by the state of the room and the state of the body, I gather?"

I nodded.

"What if the murderer hadn't had a chance to tidy up after himself? Who found the body?"

"My client."

"Ouch. So I guess it wouldn't help you to prove that she'd been interrupted before she could set the room to rights."

"Not particularly."

"You really do seem to get the challenging cases, don't you Barbara?"

He had that right. "Your theory doesn't work, though. The first thing K—my client did when she saw the body was to let out a shriek they could hear in the kitchen. Hardly the reaction of a killer."

"Unless there was someone right behind her, and she had no choice but the scream."

Uh oh. He was making sense. And it wasn't a question I'd asked when I'd been at the Inn. Between my conversation with Kathleen and this little chat, I wasn't feeling any better about this case.

"Do you know how this poison was administered?" Patrick was asking.

"That I know. It was in his water glass."

"Any idea of how long it took him to die?"

"Apparently he'd swallow down a handful of vitamins right before he turned in, which seems to have been about two a.m. He was dead by eight a.m., and by the state of the bed linens, it doesn't sound like he died right away. Does that tell you anything?"

"It doesn't narrow the field any, I'm afraid."

"You mentioned botanicals earlier. What did you mean?"

"There are any numbers of common plants that are a class six poison, which most people don't realize."

"Like what?"

"*Datura*, for one."

"*Datura?*"

"It's a close relative of deadly nightshade. All parts of the plant are poisonous, and even handling the leaves can induce mild hallucinations."

"I gather it's pretty hard to get your hands on, though. Right?"

He grinned at me. "Have you seen the new plant the local nurseries have started carrying? It's a tree, about five feet tall, with really large yellow or orange trumpet shaped flowers. Angel's Trumpet is one name for it."

"Sure. In fact, Andrea was thinking about getting one..." I broke off, stared at him. "That's *datura*? You're kidding, right?"

"'Fraid not."

"That can't be legal."

"Sure is. It's not the only one, either."

"Surely the others are rarer."

"Got any rhododendrons growing around your apartment?"

"Two or three. In Vancouver, who doesn't? But that can't be…"

He nodded. "Class six poison. If you floated the flowers in water for a few hours, then drank the water, you'd be making a quick trip to the hospital."

My mind flashed to the tour I'd taken of the Inn's grounds. It was too early for rhododendrons to bloom, wasn't it? I suddenly wished I had more interest in gardening. "What are the symptoms?"

"Nausea, vomiting, coma."

It could be. "But I'm pretty sure rhodos aren't in bloom yet."

"Don't need to be. The whole plant is poisonous."

I pictured the Sunshine Inn's extensive and varied gardens, thought about that poisoned water glass. "If it was a botanical poison that killed this guy, it would probably take the labs a while to identify, wouldn't it?"

"Probably. Of course, the same could be true of almost any obscure poison."

"You're a lot of help."

He grinned at me, hazel eyes twinkling. "I try."

"Bear with me on this. Hornby is pretty isolated. Once you're there, it would be hard to get your hands on poison, and if you did, the trail would lead to you pretty quickly."

"I'm with you so far."

I thought about what I'd learnt about Bill to date, thought about the people who'd been on Hornby that weekend.

"What if this were a crime of passion, what if the victim did or said something that pushed the killer over the edge." I wasn't necessarily helping Kathleen's case any here, but I ignored that inconvenient fact. "What if, for whatever reason, whoever it was decided to kill Bill on the spot. And they knew enough to recognize which plants were poisonous, knew how to administer the dose."

"Go on. I'm with you so far."

"You said rhododendron flowers could poison the water they sat in for a few hours. Is that true of other plants?"

"I think so."

"What about leaves and stems? Can you soak the rhododendron stems in water and get the same effect?"

"Not as easily. And it takes longer. You're better to make a salad of some of the more tender varieties."

I shuddered. "Patrick, you sound entirely too cheerful about the whole idea. And our killer didn't make a salad. They poisoned some water."

"Hmmm. Why don't I do some research on the easiest way to distill a plant poison at this time of year, match it against your guy's symptoms. Would that help?"

"That would be great. And Patrick? Thanks."

"Any time, Barbara. You have no idea how boring being a pharmacist can be. These little discussions of ours spice up my life immensely."

From comments he'd let fall in the past, I had a feeling that Patrick's social life was spicy enough to provide any excitement he might require, but I'd vowed never to ask. Some things you're better off not knowing.

I walked back to the car, then glanced at my watch. Yikes! I'd nearly forgotten my appointment with Lois Michaels. At least I wasn't too far away. I started the car.

As I drove towards Kerrisdale, I kept noticing bright plantings of rhododendrons in full bloom. They were everywhere.

CHAPTER TWENTY-ONE

Lois Michaels was a sweet-faced woman in her late seventies, well dressed, well groomed. The beautifully cut powder-blue suit she wore flattered a still-trim figure and emphasized her pale blue eyes.

The Michaels lived in one of those beautiful Victorian houses that these days were worth several million. Or so. The house was immaculately kept and beautifully furnished, but I was amused to note that Kathleen had the better art collection.

She ushered me into a brightly lit room off the kitchen that looked out over extensive, rain-washed gardens. There was a roll-top desk paired somewhat incongruously with a blue ergonomic desk chair, and a couple of deep chairs, upholstered in supple navy leather, drawn up near a small fireplace. The walls were pale cream with white accents, and the overall effect was welcoming. The yeasty smell of baking bread added to the effect.

"I thought we'd talk in here, dear," Lois said. "It's much less formal than the drawing room. It's quite my favorite room."

I could see why. Looking about me I realized that I'd love to have a house with a room like this one, positioned to catch the morning sun. I'd keep the chairs, but instead of a desk, I'd have an easel. "Thank you for agreeing to meet with me," I said.

"I gather you have some questions about that dreadful murder."

"Yes, I do."

"Go ahead, dear."

I found myself oddly reluctant to begin, to ask this sweet-faced old lady about murder. She reminded me of my mother's mother, who had died when I was only six, and of whom I remembered only a sweet face and sweeter voice. We were never supposed to bother her or upset her.

I remember playing too loudly one afternoon, upsetting my grandmother's nap, and being firmly punished for it.

"Do you visit the Sunshine Inn often?" I asked.

"Oh, yes. It is one of Henry and my favorite places. Has been for years."

"So you know the Grussmans well?"

"Well, they are not friends, but we do have a long-standing acquaintance, yes. Elena has such a magic hand with the herbs."

Which reminded me of Kathleen's comments. "I gather she's quite an expert on their non-culinary uses as well."

Lois smiled gently. "So they say. Personally I've never discussed it with her."

"Oh? Who has told you about it, then?"

She gave me a sharp look. "No-one in particular. One hears things, over time."

That was helpful. Not. "Tell me about the weekend of the murder. When did you arrive?"

"On the Saturday morning."

"Had you met any of the other guests before?"

"No. One of the things we've always liked about the Inn was that we never ran into anyone we knew."

"Did you get to know any of them?"

"Heavens, no. Our weekends at the Inn were about resting, not socializing."

She was beginning to sound like a first class snob. I resisted the urge to needle her, which I tend to succumb to in the presence of snobs, particularly of the well-heeled variety. But in this case, I needed information more than I needed to give in to my darker side.

"And did you? Rest, I mean?"

"Yes, indeed. We'd sleep in, read, walk, and eat. It was a perfect break."

Okay, maybe she wasn't a snob. It sounded pretty good to me, too. "Did you happen to notice Bill Rampage? Before the murder, I mean."

"Notice him?" She gave a little laugh. "My dear, the man was charming, impossible to ignore. He even flirted with me."

And she hadn't minded a bit, had she? "What about Terri Winter?"

"Ah, yes. A woman of style but no class."

Harsh, but I hadn't liked Terri either. "I gather she left early."

Lois Michaels nodded. "Yes, on the Saturday. I believe there was some tension with one of the other women over Bill."

"Kathleen Marshall?"

"Yes, that was the one. Now she had neither class nor style."

Maybe she was a snob. "And what about the Masters'?"

"He was quite lovely, but she was nothing but a tramp. Too much paint on her face and hands, even if she was an artist."

Shelley? A tramp?

"And now that you have reminded me, there was some tension there, between Mr. Masters—Blake, and Bill Rampage. Blake Masters seemed to be jealous of the attention his wife was giving to Bill."

Shelley was flirting with Bill Rampage? I couldn't picture it. "Are you sure that Shelley, Mrs. Masters, was flirting with him? Not Bill flirting with Shelley?"

"Oh, yes, I'm very sure who was doing the flirting. Though I don't think flirting quite captures the nature of the attention Mrs. Masters was giving. If you take my meaning."

Oh, yeah, I'd got it. I just didn't believe it. This was Shelley we were talking about? Had she changed that much? Or was she getting even with Blake for his past flirtations?

Lois Michaels had a small frown between carefully penciled-in brows. "Mrs. Masters—I think you have the name wrong, my dear."

Now I was really confused. "It wasn't Mrs. Masters?"

"No, no. It was Mrs. Masters. But I don't think it was Mrs. Shelley Masters."

"Not..."

"I think the name Blake Masters called her was Deirdre. Deirdre Masters."

I stared at her for a moment while my brain struggled to put together pieces from two very different puzzles.

Deirdre had been on Hornby Island with Blake Masters, the weekend Bill Rampage was killed?

Deirdre, whose affair with Blake had just resumed?

Deirdre, who had since been poisoned?

That Deirdre?

"Can you describe Mrs. Masters?"

"Oh, well. She was a brunette, wore too much makeup, very red lipstick. Her clothes were all too tight and too low-cut. She seemed to spend most of her time taunting Mr. Masters, without ever saying anything. And she liked to have the attention of every man in the room."

Well, that certainly sounded like everything I'd heard about Deirdre Brandt. But what was she doing on Hornby with Blake? Where was Shelley?

And how did Bill Rampage's murder relate to Deirdre Brandt's murder? Or was it a huge coincidence that they'd been poisoned within a week of each other?

I don't believe in coincidences.

I had to talk to Shelley. Even if I did have to talk to her in a jail cell.

And then there was Blake. Now him I really wanted to talk to.

———

LOIS MICHAELS WAS WATCHING ME, a look of concern on her face. She had no idea of the revelation she'd just given me. And the questions it had raised.

I took a deep breath, focused on Bill Rampage's death. "You said that Blake Masters seemed jealous of Bill Rampage. What did he do to make you think so?"

"He glowered at him from the other side of the dining room. And he tried to take Deirdre Masters out of a room whenever Bill Rampage entered. She usually refused to go, of course."

"And did Deirdre Masters and Bill Rampage ever get beyond a —flirtation?"

"Oh, I don't think they had time, dear. Besides, Bill had better taste than that. And of course, Mr. Masters was always there."

Of course he was. "Always?"

"Always."

"That must have made for an interesting weekend."

"It might have been a difficult one, except that Bill was so charming. He cut through the tension and put everyone at ease. Well, everyone except Mr. Masters."

I wrenched my mind back to the so-charming Bill Rampage and his other conquests. "And what did you think of the girls who worked at the Inn? Brandy and Tiffany?"

She crossed one delicate ankle over the other. "They were completely classless, even trashy. Both of them. And both panting over Bill Rampage. As if he'd ever give them the time of day."

"Were you aware of any tension or animosity between Bill and anyone else who was there?"

"There was the tension between Bill and Blake Masters. Though I don't know if it was strong enough to be called animosity. And between Terri and that Kathleen. That was definitely strong enough. No-one else."

"What about the two teenagers? I understand one of them had a fling with Bill. One of the other guests thought she might, if rejected, have been angry enough to kill him."

The look of distaste on her face was almost funny. She looked as if she'd bitten into something bitter. "A fling? Bill and that—that underdressed child? Oh, I hardly think so, my dear. Someone has been setting you up. Or perhaps trying to distract you."

If I'd had the story from anyone except Brandy herself and her friend Tiffany, I might have thought she was right. "So you didn't see anything that would make you suspect either Brandy or Tiffany of wanting to kill Bill."

"No, not at all. Aside from Blake Masters, everyone loved Bill. The poor man was virtually smothered with affection from all sides. Why, it made me want to rescue him."

Of course it had. This case was really beginning to get to me. Was there anyone Bill hadn't won over? Other than Blake Masters and Tad Murphy, that is?

Which reminded me. "Do you happen to know Tad Murphy?"

"Why yes. His mother is a dear friend of mine. Such a lovely boy."

So much for Lois Michael's judgment. "Did you see him that weekend?"

"Why yes. I believe he came looking for Bill. And now that you mention it, I don't believe he was too happy with him."

She frowned a little. "He was even rather abrupt with me, and that is not like Tad. Not like him at all."

"When did Tad arrive?"

"It was the Saturday. In the afternoon."

"And do you know what time?"

"Yes, we'd come in from a walk. I believe it was around four."

"You say he wasn't too happy with Bill. What makes you say that?"

"His tone when he spoke to him."

"What did they talk about?"

"I couldn't hear much. Tad demanded that they go for a walk, which they did."

"How long were they gone?"

"Perhaps half an hour later Bill returned, and chatted with us by the fire for a bit."

"And Tad?"

"Originally I thought he'd gone, but then I saw him at dinner, dining by himself. He kept glaring at Bill, which is not like Tad at all. And he even declined my invitation to join us for dinner, most rudely."

So, now I knew Tad Murphy had been the outside guest that night. "Do you know when he left?"

"I would assume after dinner. I did not see him again."

"Was there anything else unusual about that evening?"

"No, nothing."

"And the following morning? Was anyone acting oddly? For the situation, I mean?"

"I believe we all behaved with the shock appropriate when one of our company had been brutally murdered in his bed."

Whoa. She sounded like she'd read too many Victorian melodramas. "So you didn't notice the behavior of anyone in particular."

"No."

"What about Kathleen Marshall? How did she seem?"

"Thoroughly shocked and deeply grieved. Inappropriately hysterical, of course, but one must forgive her. After all, she did find the body, which cannot have been easy for her."

"And Deirdre Br—Masters?" Whom I still couldn't believe had been there.

"That one. Well, she was very pale, of course. But would you believe, I saw her with her sketchbook, not an hour after poor Bill's body was found. Then she had the poor taste to make a fuss over a canvas, later that day. Can you imagine?"

The image stopped me cold. "Who was Mrs. Masters sketching? Do you know?"

"Why, that Kathleen Marshall. She even followed her around. And I can't think why. Kathleen looked absolutely dreadful—white, her hair every which way, her eyes—well, her eyes looked as empty as the sea after a nor'easter."

Deirdre was sketching a grief-ridden Kathleen? Why? "You're sure it was Kathleen Marshall that Deirdre was sketching?" I asked.

Lois Michaels didn't seem to hear me. Her lips pursed, she seemed to be looking into space, and focusing on something only she could see.

"Perhaps I was wrong," she said softly. "Perhaps she really did care for Bill after all."

"Who cared for him, Mrs. Michaels?"

She started, and looked at me. "Oh. Did I say that out loud?"

"Yes."

She shook her head. "Must be getting old. Kathleen Marshall. When I think about how she looked afterwards, I realize she must really have cared for him, for Bill Rampage. What else could have affected her so deeply?"

I wished I could believe that—it would make working for Kathleen so much easier. But that cynical little voice kept telling me that guilt can look as devastated as love.

"Well, thank you for your time, Mrs. Michaels. And if you think of anything else, please give me a call," I said, handing her my card.

"I will be certain to do so."

I wasn't holding my breath. I had the feeling Lois had told me all she had to tell. Still, now I knew that Tad Murphy had been at the inn that night. Despite what he'd told me.

CHAPTER TWENTY-TWO

When I got back to my office, I was finishing off a grilled bratwurst and still trying to figure out how Blake and Deirdre fit into Kathleen's case. The bratwurst was from a little stand on West Broadway. They always have a lineup, but I stop whenever I'm in the neighborhood. The food is too good to pass up.

Blake and Deirdre, on the other hand, I wanted to dismiss. Their being on Hornby, and Deirdre flirting with Bill, just didn't fit.

It was pretty hard to ignore that two people had been poisoned within a week of each other, though. Two people who'd been staying at the same inn the weekend the first one had died. I wondered if Brad Bramwell was following up that thread, and wished I'd known enough at the time to have asked him.

He must know about Deirdre's death though, mustn't he? So surely he'd be following it up.

Unless, like me, he'd assumed that Mrs. Blake Masters really was Mrs. Blake Masters? No, he'd have checked Shelley's movements, found out she was still in Seattle.

Or was she?

I really needed to talk to Shelley, find out what her part in this was.

It did look as though Cassandra's information that Blake and Deirdre were back together had been right. And they'd resumed their affair before Blake's arrival in Vancouver.

Had Shelley known? And why had Blake denied it to his lawyer? Shelley's lawyer, that is.

Was Blake afraid Shelley really had killed Deirdre and he was covering for her? Or was he so arrogant that he thought he could get away with anything he chose, simply by denying it? I was leaning towards the latter, but that probably had more to do with my distaste for Blake than with the facts.

And what about Deirdre? What had she been doing restarting an affair that, according to Cassandra, Deirdre herself had ended? And why had she been sketching Kathleen?

If Lois was right and Deirdre had been flirting with Bill, why? To make Blake jealous? It seemed to have worked, given Lois' description of Blake glowering across the room. But why make him jealous? And would Blake have acted on it?

Could Blake have killed Bill, then killed Deirdre?

I thought about Blake Masters. Polished, urbane. You could argue he was callous, heading back to Seattle when his wife was in jail.

You could also argue he'd made sure she'd have legal and moral support before going.

I hadn't liked Blake, but I didn't see him as a murderer. And I didn't see him succumbing to a jealous rage. He seemed like the careful, plan-it-all-out type to me. Still, I'd been wrong before.

And I was reaching too hard, stretching the few facts I had to places they didn't fit.

I didn't want to see Kathleen as a killer, but I still couldn't discount her. Same thing with Shelley. All I could do was keep asking questions, keep gathering facts.

With a sigh, I picked up the phone, punched in my code.

There were five messages. Two were from Kathleen, one was from Jerry, one from Brad Bramwell and one from Nick.

Kathleen's first message asked me to call her as soon as I got in. She really needed to talk to me. I made a note.

Then came Nick's voice. "I hoped I'd catch you in. Look, Barbara, I don't know when I'm going to be able to cash in that rain check. I'd been hoping for this weekend, but the best I can do is to call you Friday and let you know. I hope that's okay, but if you have to make other plans, go ahead." He sounded almost as discouraged as I felt hearing the words.

Then another call from Kathleen again, frantic. "Barbara, I hope you get this message. The police want to talk to me. I'm worried and I don't know what to do. Plus I think someone is following me. Can you call me?"

Why hadn't she called my cell phone, damn it? What did she think I'd given her the number for?

I pressed 5 to find out when the message had come in. Two hours ago, and she'd been calling from her home number. I dialed her number, but her voice mail picked up on the first ring. Dammit. Where was she?

The next call was from Jerry, politely asking me to call ASAP. Uh-oh. When Jerry's that polite, it means he's calling me in an official capacity. I wondered what was up.

Finally a message from Brad Bramwell, saying that he'd appreciate a call and leaving me the number. That message had come in fifteen minutes ago.

What was going on? I thought about the calls. Why was Jerry calling me? Was it about Shelley, or had Brad Bramwell recruited him?

Had Jerry called Kathleen, or had it been Brad Bramwell? I was betting on the latter. It was possible that they wanted to confirm details and she'd overreacted.

As my mind processed options, my fingers were punching in Jerry's number. Of course he wasn't there, but when I gave my name, the impersonal voice on the other end said, "Oh, Ms.

O'Grady. Just hold for a moment, please. He asked to be notified when you called."

This was decidedly out of character for Jerry, a fact that made me nervous on principle. I sat and listened to soothing music for much too long. It didn't have the desired effect. Finally Jerry came on the line.

"O'Grady. Thanks for calling back," he said.

"Never mind being polite, Jerry. What's so important?"

"You never change, Barbara."

"Neither do you. So give. Which case?"

"Rampage's death."

So I'd been right. I grabbed for a pen. "Bramwell called you?"

"Yes."

"Why?"

"Your client is missing."

"What do you mean, my client is missing? And how do you know who my client is, anyway?"

"Kathleen Marshall, right?"

I didn't want to confirm it, but my silence told him what he needed to know.

"Bramwell's been trying to contact her for the last two days. She didn't return any of his calls, and now she seems to have vanished. Do you know where she is?"

"No, but I met with her yesterday." And she hadn't mentioned any calls. What was it going to take to get Kathleen to level with me? A murder charge?

"Where?"

"Her apartment."

"Well, she's not there now."

But she had been. She'd called me from there. "How do you know that?"

"I sent a patrolman over to check on her, at Bramwell's request."

"To arrest her?"

"No. Just to bring her in for questioning."

"Why?"

"You'd have to ask him that."

I planned to. "When was this?"

"A couple of hours ago."

Had Kathleen called me while there was a policeman hammering on her door? "So how do you know she wasn't there and just not answering her door?"

"The blinds were drawn. Her car was gone. There was a note canceling her paper until further notice."

These days, that could well be normal behavior for Kathleen. "Are you sure about the timing?"

"That it was two hours ago? Let me check." I heard papers rustling. "Yeah, he was there at two fifty-seven."

Kathleen's message had come in at two fifty-eight. She'd been in her apartment then, apparently hiding. So where was she now? "Are you planning on arresting her?"

"No. We'd just like to find her. Know where she is, O'Grady?"

"Sorry, no. I can't help you there."

"Can't, or won't?"

"Can't. I have no idea where she is." Or why.

"But you'll let me know if you hear from her."

"Sure." Eventually.

"See that you do."

"Yes, sir!"

"Funny, O'Grady."

"I thought so."

"You would. Take care of yourself."

"You too, Jerry."

———

AFTER JERRY HAD HUNG UP, I stared at the crack in the far wall and listened to the rain for a few moments, contemplating what I knew of Kathleen Marshall. Not nearly enough, and way too much. I picked up the phone and dialed Brad Bramwell in Nanaimo.

"Bramwell."

"Brad, it's Barbara O'Grady."

"Barbara. Thanks for calling back. How are you?"

"I'm good, thanks. What's up?"

"Barbara, I need to talk to your client, and I'm having some trouble getting hold of her. I wondered if you might be able to put me in touch with her."

"What did you need to talk to her about?"

He hesitated.

I grinned, imagining his expression. "You'd love to tell me it's classified. But you know if you do that I'm not likely to tell you anything, right?"

He laughed. "You don't miss much, do you?"

"I try."

"I need to clarify some points in her statement of what happened the night Rampage got killed."

I pulled my notepad towards me, began doodling. "Is she a suspect?"

"Officially? No."

"Unofficially?"

"Unofficially everyone's a suspect until this thing is closed."

"How long is your list of official suspects?"

"You know I can't tell you that."

"But you're making progress."

"We'll make more progress when the lab reports come back."

I drew an exclamation mark. What was holding up those reports? "Oh?"

"Oops. Well, having given you that much, I might as well give you the rest. You'll dig it out anyway."

"You have too much faith in me."

"I don't think so."

I found his praise embarrassing. And was he flirting with me? "Thanks."

"Hey, you deserve it."

He was flirting with me. I wasn't sure how I felt about that. He was no Nick, but he was a nice guy, and kind of cute, now that I thought about it. "About those lab tests?"

"Right. Well, we still haven't definitively identified the poison that killed Rampage. It's not one of the common ones, so we've had to run further tests, and the lab is backed up. But that information is confidential."

"I'll keep it to myself."

"I know. That's why I told you. So, have you heard from your client in the last few days?"

Hmmm. Were we playing tit for tat? He told me about the lab tests, I told him where Kathleen was? Well, too bad. I wasn't playing. "I met with her yesterday."

"Yesterday? Morning or afternoon?"

"Morning."

"Did she mention I'd been trying to reach her?"

"No, she didn't. "

"Odd."

He didn't know the half of it. "One thing I wondered. During your investigation, how closely did you look at the staff of the Sunshine Inn?"

"Pretty closely. Why?"

"Well, for what it's worth, Kathleen seems to think one of the two girls may have poisoned Rampage." Or says she does.

No way I was sharing my suspicions about my client with a representative of the law.

"Does she now? Which one?"

"The blond one. Brandy."

"Huh." He was silent for a moment. I really wanted a cup of coffee, but I was out of pre-ground, and it's too noisy to grind more when I'm on the phone.

"She say why she thinks Brandy did it?"

"Jealousy. Passion. Apparently she saw Rampage and the girl together a couple of times. Sound possible?"

"With murder, anything is possible. Hell, you're the one uncovered Maria's killer. You know."

"Yeah, I do." Unfortunately. There seemed to be no limit to the things people will do to other people.

"So do you know where your client is now?"

No point in evading the question. I really didn't know. "No, I don't. All I know is she left me a couple of voice mails in the last few hours, and now she's not returning my calls."

"My information is that she seems to have taken off."

"Great."

"You don't know anything about it?"

"'Fraid not. But when I see her, if I see her, I'll pass on the message that you need to talk to her."

"The strong message."

"The strong message. Though frankly, I'm not sure how much good it will do."

"Let me worry about that."

"Fair enough. I do have one other question for you, though." Might as well ask.

"Shoot."

"The other couples that were at the inn that weekend. How closely are you looking at them?"

"We did a standard run early on, but nothing popped."

It didn't surprise me—Bill had died on the Sunday, Deirdre on the Thursday. Brad had probably already cleared Blake and companion. "And the Masters, Mr. and Mrs. Is it Shelley Masters or Deirdre Masters you were looking at?"

"How did you get those names?"

"I'm good at what I do. You said so yourself. Remember?"

He chuckled, then I heard the rustle of paper. "Mrs. Blake Masters. Shelley Masters. Why?"

He hadn't made the connection. But if he thought it was Shelley, and then found out she'd been arrested for poisoning Deirdre—it wouldn't look good for Shelley.

Still, it was Bill Rampage who'd died on Hornby, not Blake Masters. Shelley had no motive for murdering Bill. And it would be useful to have independent confirmation of what Lois Michaels had told me.

"Because I have information that the woman who was with Blake Masters answered to the name of Deirdre. From the description I got, she wasn't his wife."

"Huh. Okay, I'll look into it. Thanks, Barbara. And I look forward to talking with you again."

"Don't mention it." I hung up, looked down, and discovered I'd covered the page with drawings of flowers. Rhododendrons. Trumpet-shaped *datura*.

My subconscious is not subtle. I stared at the collection of pencil marks. What was I missing?

I thought about everything Patrick Carmichael had said and everything I didn't know. Then I picked up the phone book, flipped a few pages. It was worth a shot. I dialed.

"UBC Botanical Garden, this is the Hortline. Can I help you?"

"Can you tell me what flowers would be blooming the last week of March this year?"

"In Vancouver?"

"Well, on Hornby Island, actually."

"They'd be a week earlier. Any particular genus?"

Like I'd know. "No, just anything that will bloom then, in this climate."

"Hold on a moment."

I listened to their canned music, staring at my drawings and wondering if I was finally losing it.

She came back. "We have that information. Do you have a fax number?"

I gave it to her.

"You should get this in about half an hour."

"Thanks very much."

"You're most welcome."

I'd just hung up when the phone rang again. Kathleen?

It was Ian Craig. "I've arranged for you to see Shelley in half an hour. I assume that's convenient?"

It wasn't. I thought he'd said tomorrow. Today I wanted to go and look for Kathleen, even though I was pretty sure she wouldn't be there.

But I also needed to talk to Shelley, and I couldn't do so without Ian Craig. No point pissing him off. Not yet, anyway. "It's fine."

"Good. I'll meet you at the station. Just give them my name. They'll be expecting you."

"Thanks."

"Don't mention it." And he hung up.

I checked my watch. Not even enough time to grab a coffee. Shaking my head, I grabbed my purse, my jacket and locked up.

CHAPTER TWENTY-THREE

Ian Craig met me at the main reception area, and we were guided down a series of long halls and shown into a drab little conference room. Seating myself at the battered Formica table, I wondered which idiot had chosen to paint the room this particular shade of green.

It wasn't hospital green, exactly, more like someone had been trying for a cross between that and olive green. It was probably supposed to be soothing, and in one sense I suppose it worked. Wondering if the moron who chose the paint had any color sense at all certainly took my mind off why I was there.

Until Shelley walked in the other door, followed by a six foot four armed guard. The guard waited until she was seated across from us, eyes scanning for any threat, then went out, closing the door behind him. Normally being in the same room as someone openly bearing arms would have bothered me, but all I could focus on was Shelley.

She looked stunning and awful at the same time. With her height, her dark coloring and high cheekbones, the orange prison jumpsuit actually suited her, despite limp hair and no makeup. But it was the lines of suffering on her face and the bleakness in her eyes I couldn't look away from.

Ian had warned me beforehand that we couldn't touch, or I would have held out my hands to her.

I wanted to say something comforting, but couldn't summon the words. "Shelley, only you could make an orange monkey suit look like high fashion," I said instead.

It surprised a grin out of her. "Typical Barbara," she said. "Even in here, you've got a smart remark."

"Hey, I do what I can."

"I am so glad to see you, Barbara. And you of course, Ian."

"Of course," he said dryly.

I shot him a look. There might be more to Ian Craig than I'd thought.

"But why are you both here?"

"Ms. O'Grady has been hired to work on your case. And she had a few questions. Ms. O'Grady?"

"Thanks, and it's Barbara," I told him, then turned back to Shelley. "Shelley, are you okay with me working for you?"

"It gives me hope, Barbara."

"We will get you out of here, Mrs. Masters," Ian said.

"Call me Shelley, please, Ian. I know you will get me out. And with Barbara working with you, I can begin to believe I won't have to come back."

She gave him a slightly wobbly smile. "You see, you don't know her. I do. When Barbara takes something on, she's unbelievably determined."

"Oh, come on. I'm not that bad."

She nodded. "Yes, you are. You literally never give up. Which is why I can't understand how you could give up your painting."

I could sense Ian giving me a considering look. "Shelley, this is neither the time nor the place to talk about my painting."

"What if I refuse to answer your questions until we do talk about it?"

"They haven't given us a lot of time here," Ian said.

Shelley was still looking at me. "Well?"

"All right, I'll tell you. Just not now."

She didn't look like she believed me. "I have your promise?"

"All right, yes. Yes, you have my promise. Though I can't believe you're even thinking about my painting when you're in here charged with murder."

"I have a lot of time to think in here. And maybe there's a connection."

"Connection?" Ian asked. "What kind of connection?"

"To art. To painting, and what it means to the artist, to those who respond to art. Deirdre was an artist, a good one. She was killed at an art opening. As I've told Barbara before, Ian, I was jealous of Deirdre, but as an artist, not as a woman. I didn't kill her over it. But maybe someone else did."

She turned to me. "That's the other reason I'm glad you're here, Barbara. You may be the only investigator in the city who has the background and the sensitivity to get to the bottom of this."

She paused and looked down at her hands, which were tightly gripped on the dark green table. "I did not kill Deirdre Brandt. I don't know who did. But every instinct I possess says that she was killed because she was an artist."

"Not because of her numerous affairs?" I asked her.

Shelley shook her head. "I don't think so, but don't ask me why. She certainly hurt enough people with her affairs."

"Including you?"

"Yes. I loved my husband. I didn't want to lose him to a piranha, no matter how good a painter she is. Was."

"Piranha's a pretty strong term for someone you say you were only jealous of as a painter," Ian put in.

"No. Piranha is a good description of Deirdre's style. It didn't matter if she was after Blake or someone else—nothing got in her way, and she didn't leave much behind."

Nice woman. "Did you know Blake was seeing Deirdre while

they were both here for the show?" I asked, watching her face closely.

Shelley went white. "No, I didn't know. Are you sure?"

Unless she was a better actress than I'd ever known her to be, Shelley hadn't known.

"That's what I hear, anyway. It's something I need to look into."

"How could he? He promised me..." She broke off, pressed a clenched fist against her mouth.

I gave her a moment. "I'm sorry, Shelley. I have a few more questions I have to ask you. Okay?"

She nodded.

"What did he promise you?"

"That they were done. That he'd ended the affair and didn't plan ever to see her again."

The first was a lie, according to what Cassandra had said. The second? I didn't know. Not until I could confirm what Lois Michaels had told me. "When did you arrive in Vancouver?"

"The day before I ran into you, Barbara. The Tuesday."

"And where were you coming from?"

"Seattle. It took forever to get everything packed up for the show. Why?"

"I'll tell you later. Where had you spent the previous weekend?"

"In Seattle. I had a couple of paintings to finish, and I was scrambling to get everything ready."

"Where was Blake that weekend?"

"Blake? At a conference, in Boston. He flew back and met me here. Why?"

So it had been Blake and Deirdre on Hornby.

I glanced at Ian Craig, but his bland expression gave nothing away.

And I wasn't going to tell Shelley, not while she was still in jail. I hadn't yet decided how much to tell Ian Craig, who was looking back and forth between us, no expression at all on his face. "Trust me on this one," I told Shelley.

"It's a good thing it's you, Barbara. You know that, don't you?"

"Yeah, I know. And I will get you out of here."

She smiled, but it was wobbly. "I know you will."

———

SO I'D ESTABLISHED that Blake had continued to cheat on Shelley with Deirdre. That both Blake and Deirdre had been on Hornby the weekend Bill Rampage was killed. And that Shelley hadn't known any of it.

Leaving her without much of a motive for killing Deirdre.

Unless she was lying to me.

I looked at Shelley's wan face, and shoved back the unwelcome thought. I couldn't completely discount it though. Not if I was to do my job properly.

"Next question," I said. "Your nitro pills. Do you always carry them?"

Shelley nodded. "Always." Her voice was thick with tears.

"And do you know if any were missing?"

Shelley looked at her lawyer. "This is confidential, right? Nothing I say here can be used against me?"

I felt as though I'd been flash-frozen. Was Shelley guilty after all? She couldn't be. Could she?

Ian nodded. "That's correct. Ms. O'Grady—Barbara—is under the same rule of client privilege as I am right now."

"No, I don't know if any of my pills were missing. Not for sure," Shelley said to me.

A wave of relief washed through me. "Not for sure? You think some were missing?"

"Well, given that the police confiscated my prescription and arrested me, yes, I suspect some were missing."

"They confiscated your nitro? But what about your heart condition?"

"No fears, they provided a replacement," she said. "They couldn't have their prime suspect dying in their jail, now could they?"

"So you don't actually know if any were missing?"

"No. But when they asked for the bottle, it didn't look as full as I'd have expected."

"Nitro pills are pretty small. I'm surprised you noticed."

"Normally I wouldn't have, but this was a new prescription, and I'd dumped what was left of the previous one on top, so there were more than I was used to seeing."

"Do you know how many there should have been?"

"Yes. Normally I'd have had no idea—I used them when I needed them, and made sure I had a refill when they got low."

"And this time?"

"Because it was a new bottle, when I dumped the last of the old bottle on top, I noticed that I'd run lower than I usually do. I remember thinking I was cutting it too fine with only ten left. It was a day or so before I came up here, and I'd been too busy putting the show together to get a refill."

"So you would have had how many pills at that point?"

"A hundred and ten. If the pharmacist counted right and I remembered right."

I made a note. I noticed Ian Craig doing the same. "And how many did you use after you got the refill."

"None."

"You're sure?"

"Very sure. I make a note each time I use them."

"Can you tell how many you used each time?"

"No, I don't note that."

"But there should have been a hundred and ten?"

"Yes."

"And neither of you know how many the police actually found?"

Both shook their heads.

"Did they ask you when you last filled the prescription?"

"The date was on the bottle."

"Oh. Right. Did they ask you anything about it?"

She nodded, wouldn't meet my eyes. I had a bad feeling about this. "What did they ask?"

"If I'd taken any. And how many."

"And you said?"

"That I wanted my lawyer."

"Without answering the question?"

"Yes."

Oh boy. This didn't sound good. "Why?"

"They'd confiscated the pills. They must already have known what killed her. Mine must even have been the right brand, or dosage or something. If I told them there should be a hundred and ten, and they had less than that, it was going to confirm their belief that I did it, right?"

She had a point. "What happened when Ian arrived?"

"She answered their question," Ian said.

"And told them there should have been a hundred and ten pills?"

"Yes," Shelley said.

"And what happened after you told the police you'd had one hundred and ten nitro pills the last time you counted them?"

"Then they arrested me," Shelley said.

Ouch. "So we need to find out who might have had access to your pills. Where did you keep them?"

"In my purse, always."

"Was there ever a time when someone could have slipped pills out of your purse without your noticing?"

"I can't think of a time, but there must have been. In the restaurant, maybe? It was crowded, noisy. People were changing places to talk."

"Who was sitting where, initially?"

"If you have paper, I'll draw it for you."

Wordlessly Ian extracted a pen and a legal pad from his briefcase and pushed it across the table to Shelley. She wrote for a bit, muttering to herself, then pushed it across the table to me.

"That's how the evening started, as best I can remember."

I looked at it. Shelley had been sitting at the far end of a long table, Deirdre had been at the near end and on the other side of the table. No one had sat at the two ends. "Who was sitting nearest the door?"

"I was."

"And where were the washrooms?"

She pulled the legal pad back, wrote on it, pushed it back. I looked at it.

She'd drawn in the restaurant around them. Shelley had always been good at sketching and very accurate with proportions, which had been my bane. Her revised sketch showed Deirdre seated along the far wall, with the access to either the door or the washrooms by passing behind Shelley.

"So, no one would have had to walk behind Deirdre for any reason," I commented.

"Except the waiters, no," Shelley agreed.

"And who are the couple you were sitting with?"

It was Ian who answered me. "The Donners, both major art collectors. Shelley, had they expressed an interest in your work?"

"Yes."

"Impressive," he said.

"It seemed so at the time."

I glanced around the dreary room, thought about the vistas that had been opening for her before Deirdre's murder. No wonder she sounded depressed. "Why was Blake seated beside Deirdre?"

"I don't know."

"Were you upset about it?"

"At the time? Yes. But I was too worried about the reaction to the show to be more than mildly annoyed. I remember thinking I wished he'd shown me a little moral support. On the other hand, I was concentrating on the Donners."

"Why wasn't Deirdre schmoozing collectors too?"

"Those at the dinner had already bought several of her pieces."

Deirdre really had made it. "You said people were moving around. Who do you remember sitting beside Deirdre that evening?"

Shelley rubbed her forehead. "I think—I think Blake sat beside her all evening," she said. "I was talking, so I might not have noticed, but every time I looked for him, that's where he was."

Blake, who was so obviously not here. "And across from her?"

"Dane Courtland, I think, for most of the evening."

My newly developed Deirdre radar went off. "Dane Courtland? Were he and Deirdre close?"

"Well, I had heard rumors they were having an affair, though I never saw any sign of it."

"And did his wife know about this?"

"I'm guessing she must have."

"I don't get the impression that Margaret Courtland is a forgiving woman."

She smiled at me. "That's one way of putting it."

"Do you think she was unforgiving enough to take revenge on Deirdre?"

"That I don't know. In my dealings with her, I've found her the stronger member of that partnership. And there was no doubt that Dane was hers."

"And if someone trespassed on her territory?"

"I doubt she'd take it lightly. But murder?" She shook her head. "I doubt it. But the only thing I know for sure is that I didn't murder Deirdre."

"And if Margaret hadn't meant to kill Deirdre? What if she thought Deirdre would feel ill enough to teach her a lesson? Most people don't think of nitro as poisonous."

"Me included. Yes, I could see that happening."

"Did Margaret have access to your purse at any point during the evening?"

"She was sitting at my end of the table for awhile."

"Could she have got to your purse without anyone noticing?"

"Maybe. And if not at the restaurant, she'd have had no problem getting to it earlier, in the gallery."

"Did she know you carried nitro?"

"Oh, sure. I tell anyone I do a lot of work with, just in case there's ever problems."

I nodded, made another note. Ian Craig had been listening to our exchange with interest. "You'll follow up on that angle, Barbara?" he asked now.

"Oh, yeah," I assured him.

Shelley laughed. It was an odd sound in that cheerless place. "You can count on it," she assured him. "It's the only thing that gives me hope in this awful place."

CHAPTER TWENTY-FOUR

As we emerged from the courthouse it had stopped raining and the clouds were clearing. By the time I got to the car I was on my cell to Cassandra. She hadn't mentioned Dane Courtland when she'd talked about Deirdre. Did that mean she didn't know about him? I should have known better.

"Oh, Barbara, you are so funny," she said. "As if I'd ever tell everything I knew."

"Then you did know about them?"

"Oh, sure."

It took an effort of will to refrain from demanding why she hadn't mentioned it, but there was no point in offending her. She was too valuable as an information source. "What did you hear about the Courtlands?"

That was all it took.

"Well," she said, her voice dropping to confide. "He's been seen with her in little smoky bars, late at night. Word is he's absolutely smitten with Deirdre. Or he was, anyway. And she's furious. Present tense, I think."

"I thought you told me that Deirdre was seen having drinks

with Blake Masters." Not to mention spending the weekend with him on Hornby.

"Oh, she was."

"So which one was she seeing?"

"Both of them. At least. Deirdre liked to keep her men dangling. In multiples, wherever possible."

"And they put up with that?"

"Barbara, don't you know anything? A little healthy competition makes a woman more desirable."

There was nothing healthy about the games Deirdre had been playing. "Were there any other men that Deirdre was keeping dangling?"

"No… no, I don't think there were any others at that moment."

"Just those two."

"That I know of, anyway."

"So Deirdre and Blake had resumed their affair?"

"Resumed it? Really, Barbara, what makes you think it ever ended?"

"You said it had."

"Oh. Well, it turns out I may have been wrong."

"Oh?"

"Yes. I was talking to Amy, Amy Grant? In Seattle? I gather she'd seen Deirdre and Blake more than once in some of the dives that Deirdre used to frequent. And they were not Blake's normal stomping grounds."

"Places that Shelley would never go."

"Exactly."

"Why didn't he just divorce Shelley?"

"You'd have to ask Shelley that. And I'd love to know the answer."

I'd just bet she would. And she'd never hear it from me. "You mentioned before that Jan McIlroy had reason to hate Deirdre. Anyone else? Anyone specific?"

"No, just those three."

"Three?"

"Jan McIlroy, Margaret Courtland and Shelley Masters. The wronged spouses. Except Jan's been out of town—she and Jim have been in the Caribbean all month. I think it's an attempt at a second honeymoon. Not that it'll help, not with Jim's wandering eye."

Right. I was down to two potential suspects. "Thanks Cassandra. And if you think of anyone else…?"

"I'll be in touch. You can count on it, Barbara."

I was sure I could.

———

I SAT behind the wheel of my car and looked at my notes from my meeting with Shelley, thought about what Cassandra had said. Everything I heard about Deirdre and her relationships with men seemed uglier, more hurtful to others.

As if in contrast, it was turning into a beautiful day, still cool but sunny. Pedestrians were cutting across Smythe with an insouciance you don't see when it's raining. On a rainy day they're more likely to get hit.

On a day like today, they might get sworn at, but there won't be much heat in it. It's hard to get really angry on a sunny Vancouver day in early spring. Unless you're dealing with two murders, that is.

It seemed all wrong that the sun should be shining while Shelley, who loved painting spring sunlight, was locked up in jail. I looked back at my notes.

What I wanted to do was go shopping at Granville Island, maybe go for a long walk at Jericho, then coffee at the Kits Grind. Forget about Kathleen for a couple of hours, pretend Shelley was fine.

What I was going to do was go look for Kathleen, then head for the Courtland Gallery. I needed to talk to Margaret Courtland. And it was time I saw Deirdre Brandt's paintings for myself.

I dialed Kathleen's number. Two rings, then the answering machine. Either Kathleen hadn't come home, or she hadn't checked her machine. Damn.

I checked voice mail. Nothing. Looks like I was headed for Kerrisdale.

I punched in another number.

"Trusted Temps, Andrea speaking."

"Hi, it's me."

"Hello, you. What's up?"

"Have you heard from Kathleen?"

"No. I haven't heard a word. Why? Has something happened?"

"She appears to have vanished. Any idea where she might have gone?"

"No, I don't. Barbara, is something wrong?"

"The police want to ask her a few questions and she appears to have freaked out and taken off."

Andrea sighed. "I really want to tell you that Kathleen wouldn't behave like that, but I suspect that's exactly what the Kathleen we've been dealing with lately would do."

"Looks like it."

"She's not hiding in her apartment, refusing to answer the phone?"

"I'm on my way over there now, to check that out."

"Good. And I am sorry for getting you into this, Barbara."

"Now you're sorry"

"I know, I know. Just let me know what you find, okay?"

"Yeah, sure. Bye, Andrea."

———

I PULLED up in front of Kathleen's apartment and sat for a moment eyeing the building. It looked half-asleep in the thin sunlight, blinds drawn, no-one visible inside or outside. Red tulips marched down the walkway.

I got out of the car and strode up to the door, punched Kathleen's number. Nothing. Punched it again. Still nothing.

I checked the listing of names. To my surprise, there was a manager listed. After seeing those paintings, I'd assumed Kathleen owned her apartment, rather than renting. It was so incongruous, that incredible art collection in a rented apartment.

The thought of her tenant insurance made me cringe. Yet another contradiction in my puzzling client. I buzzed the manager.

"Yeah?"

"My name is Barbara O'Grady. I'm a friend of Kathleen Marshall's, in 307."

"So?"

"So no-one's seen her for a couple of days, and I'm worried about her."

"Well, I saw her this morning."

"You did? And she looked fine?"

"Same as ever. Was that it?"

"I rang her apartment and she wasn't answering."

"She went out."

"When?"

"This morning, not that it's any of your business."

"Did she have her bags with her?"

"And that's definitely none of your business."

"I'm concerned about her. She didn't say where she was going, or when she'd be back?"

"Look, it's not my job to be a message center for the tenants."

Now I remembered why I'd been so happy to stop renting, mortgage or no mortgage. "Of course. Sorry for disturbing you."

———

BACK IN MY car I made a note. Okay, so much for Plan A. Now, what was plan B? I dialed Andrea again, filled her in.

"So the landlord saw her this morning."

"So he says."

"And that's when she left a message for you?"

"Yes."

"Maybe she'll be back tonight."

"I have a feeling she's running. She hasn't been any too stable the last few times I've talked to her. Any idea where she'd go?"

"I don't think I even know this Kathleen Marshall," Andrea said. "I've no idea where she'd go."

"Does she have any relatives in town?"

"I think she has a sister."

"Same last name?"

"No. Just a sec, I think I might have it." I listened to canned music for a bit, then Andrea was back.

"Found it. The sister's name is Mary Roberts," and she gave me the number. "Keep in touch on this?"

"Sure. Thanks, Andrea." I rung off, dialed the sister's number. And got an answering machine. Frustrated, I left a message for her to call me as soon as possible, leaving my cell phone number.

CHAPTER TWENTY-FIVE

Half an hour later I was standing in front of one of Deirdre's paintings in the Courtland Gallery. It depicted a nude woman reclining on a couch in a posture reminiscent of Manet's *Olympia*. There the resemblance stopped.

Here was no well-fed sensuality. This woman was bone thin, and the feverish intensity of her hungry gaze seemed to pin me to the spot, demanding answers to a question I could only guess at. Deirdre had captured her subject's desperation and her humanity in a way that was impossible to ignore.

The subject of the next portrait was almost as thin, but the diamonds at wrist and throat suggested it was from choice, not necessity. This woman was beautifully coiffed, gowned in a floor-length amethyst satin gown and standing against an indistinct background with one hand on a wrought iron railing. Her expression was serene but her eyes were haunted.

She looked as if she'd paid in blood for every gem she wore.

Somehow Deirdre had captured the woman behind the façade so effectively that I felt I knew her, understood her story, and pitied her.

I looked from Deirdre's canvases to the serene landscapes

hanging on the opposite wall. The two styles were very different. Shelley's work and Deirdre's were a very effective contrast to each other and to Judy Moore's still lifes. The contrast highlighted the merits of each work.

Len and Margaret Courtland know their stuff.

All three styles were effective, but there was a gripping immediacy in Deirdre's work that the other two lacked. Looking back and forth, imagining my own work hung beside Deirdre's, I could understand Shelley's envy of Deirdre's work.

I moved on to Deirdre's next painting. A haggard blond stood behind a counter staring out with total indifference—to her surroundings, to her world, maybe to her life. The despair Deirdre had caught was startling.

I spent forty minutes wandering around the small gallery, looking closely at each painting, comparing one to another. No matter how you looked at it, these works were stunning.

Suddenly I wanted very much to see Deirdre's earlier works. These paintings were gripping, alive. What had her early works been like?

Here and there I stopped to make a note or two. The title for each work included a woman's name. The model?

I noted them down. I wanted to talk to the models, if I could find them. None of them looked as though they belonged to the white picket fence in the suburbs.

For some, of no fixed address was more likely, while others looked like they belonged on the social register. Beside each name, I noted the going price. *Polyester Lily* was selling for a hundred and fifty thousand, *Potted Angelica* for three hundred thousand dollars. No question, Deirdre had made it.

Until someone had killed her.

———

I GLANCED AROUND ME. The gallery was deserted, except for Margaret Courtland, who was working behind the big desk halfway down the gallery. It seemed as good a time as any to talk to her.

"Margaret?"

She looked up. "It's Barbara O'Grady, isn't it? You're Shelley Masters' friend. The investigator, right?"

Once I'd hoped she'd someday recognize my name as an artist. Now I was glad I wasn't still chasing that dream. Given the questions I was about ask her, I'd be worried about career-threatening consequences if I still had aspirations of being a serious artist. I didn't think Margaret Courtland was going to like me very much when we were done.

"That's right. Do you have a moment? I have a few questions."

Her mind seemed to be on something else. "Barbara O'Grady? I know that name."

"Oh?"

"Mmmm. Not recently, though. Do you paint?"

"I used to. Shelley and I studied together."

She was nodding. "I thought so. I remember seeing a couple of your pieces some years ago. At the time I thought you had something, that with a little seasoning you could be quite good."

She had? It was high praise from this woman.

I felt a little rush of pride, found myself at a loss for words. "Thank you."

"I haven't seen anything recently, though."

"No. I gave it up when I opened my own firm." It wasn't quite the truth, but it would do.

"You gave it up? You have talent. How could you give it up?"

I shrugged, not knowing what to say. Here, too late, was the confirmation I'd needed years ago.

I wasn't an artist anymore. Now my job was getting Shelley out of jail. "Do you have time to answer a few questions?"

Sharp green eyes met mine. "Yes, I'll answer your questions," said Margaret Courtland. "If you'll answer mine first."

She had me and she knew it. "Sure. Go ahead."

"Why did you stop painting?"

Why did she want to know? It's not like there's any shortage of talented artists around. "My work wasn't good enough. Not for the long haul."

"Who told you that?"

Jayson's face flashed through my mind. "No-one had to tell me."

"Do you still paint?"

"No."

She just looked at me.

"A little, once in a while. Not often."

"And what do you paint? I seem to remember landscapes, very realistic."

She had an amazing memory. "Yes. Or rather, yes, that's what I used to paint. Now, I've tightened the focus on the scenes, and loosened the detail." It was so long since I'd tried to describe what I was doing, I stumbled over it.

"Hmmm. Given what you used to paint, it sounds interesting. I'd like to see your work."

"Why?"

She laughed. "That's not the usual response from an artist whose work I want to see."

"I'm not an artist."

"Are you sure about that?"

I really didn't want to answer that question. Hell, I didn't even want to think about it. I gave up my ambitions as a painter years ago, and it wasn't easy then.

Why did everyone suddenly seem so interested in my painting now?

But this was Margaret Courtland, of the Courtland Gallery, wanting to see my work. My silence must have conveyed the ambivalence I felt.

"So, when can I see them?"

"I haven't anything ready."

"No artist ever has anything 'ready'. Funnily enough, the better the artist, the less ready they are."

Was she trying to divert me from my investigation? Maybe get me on her side? "You still haven't said why you're interested in my paintings."

"I saw something in your early work. I'd like to see where you've taken it. So, can we set a date?"

She wasn't going to give up. "Fine, but after Shelley is out of jail."

"Yes, I heard she'd been arrested. That is truly terrible. "

"Yes, it is. Which is why I wanted to ask you some questions."

"Fair enough. May I have your card?"

I pulled one out, handed it to her. "Why?"

She tucked it into her desk diary. "So I remember to contact you about seeing your work. Now, what did you want to know?"

She wasn't acting as if she'd had anything to do with Deirdre's death. On some level, I relaxed a little. I didn't want her to be guilty.

But I didn't believe she was being straight with me. Her sudden interest in my paintings was a little too convenient. Much as part of me wanted to believe in it. "Do you recall seeing or hearing anything suspicious the day Deirdre was killed?"

She shook her head. "No. It was the typical chaotic opening day, but we didn't have some of the usual traumas."

"Which are?"

"Oh, framers not delivering on time, caterers bringing champagne but not glasses, artists having fits because something wasn't hung to their satisfaction."

"How did you find the three artists to deal with?"

"Shelley, Judy and Deirdre? Deirdre was the most demanding, there's no question. But as long as her paintings were hung to her satisfaction, she was fine."

"And were they?"

"Oh yes. I made very sure of that."

I'd just bet she had. "And the other two. Any friction with them? Or amongst them?"

"No, nothing. Shelley's a dream to deal with. And as far as I could see, the three got along just fine."

"Were you aware of any tension between Deirdre and Shelley?"

"No, I didn't sense anything."

"You're sure?"

"Yes. Why, what did I miss?"

"Deirdre and Blake Masters had an affair. There's some dispute as to whether it was ongoing." I was watching her reaction closely.

Margaret Courtland's jaw muscles tightened, but she betrayed no other reaction. "Poor Shelley. I had no idea. And no, there was no sign of that."

The art world tends to be pretty small sometimes. How had she remained unaware of the gossip about Deirdre and Blake? "You hadn't heard anything about Deirdre and Blake Masters?"

"No, nothing."

"What about Deirdre and other men?"

"I try not to listen to gossip."

"Not even when it concerns your own husband?"

She glared at me. "Especially then."

"And is there any truth to the rumor that your husband and Deirdre were having an affair?"

"No. None at all."

"I'm sorry, but is it possible you were unaware of it?"

"I think I'd know if my husband was having an affair."

"Many women don't."

"Then they aren't paying attention. Exactly what did you hear?"

"That Deirdre and your husband were seen together at a number of bars in the evening."

She smiled, tightly. "And from that you assumed they were having an affair?"

"Given Deirdre's reputation, that seemed to be the general assumption. Is there another explanation?"

"My husband happens to love jazz, especially experimental jazz. Unfortunately, I abhor it. Deirdre shared Len's love for that music. When she was in town, they would go and explore the more outré of musical dives. I stayed home with a good book, quite happily. I trust my husband, Barbara."

That was her story and she was sticking to it. Fine. I'd buy it for now, but with reservations. "Do you have any idea who poisoned Deirdre Brandt?"

"So she was poisoned?"

"Yes."

"With what?"

"Shelley's nitroglycerin pills are what the police seem to think."

"Oh, poor Shelley. Is that why they arrested her?"

"Yes. Do you have any idea who might have done so?"

"It wasn't me, if that's what you are asking."

"That's always good to know. Would anyone have had the opportunity?"

"It would have been the evening of the show, then?"

I nodded.

"We had all gone out for dinner. And I suppose Shelley kept her pills in her purse? In fact, I know she did. She'd even showed me where they were, in case of an emergency."

"Who else would have known?"

"Well, I suppose her husband, I don't know who else. You would have to check with her."

"Did you ever see anyone with an opportunity to take something from Shelley's purse? Or a chance to put something in Deirdre's food or drink?"

"I don't know. I suppose any of us could have done so, either here or at the restaurant. It was a pretty confused evening."

"Can you think about it, let me know if you remember anything specific? You have my card."

Not that she'd be using it for anything else, not now I'd practically accused her of murder and her husband of infidelity. Oh, well. There went my career as an artist. Again.

"Yes, I have your card. I'll call you."

Sure she would.

I was pretty sure I'd be talking to her again, but not about my art. I ignored the twinge of regret that thought brought with it. If I hadn't let go of my desire to be a painter as completely as I'd thought, I didn't want to know.

I was prepared to consider what Margaret had told me, but I hadn't crossed her off my list of suspects. She had as much motive, means and opportunity as Shelley had. And her explanation of her husband's little outings with Deirdre was a bit too pat, given what I'd learned about the late artist.

Still, I found the combination of my conversation with Margaret Courtland and viewing the dead woman's work unsettling enough that I treated myself to a coffee at the nearby Beans café, then went for a walk.

Sauntering down Granville Street, I people watched and window shopped, distracting myself with the display of color, form and sound. Until I passed a street woman whose dark eyes looked like they belonged in one of Deirdre's works, wrenching me back to my waiting cases.

CHAPTER TWENTY-SIX

Back in my office I typed up my notes, then sat and glared at them. I needed to go to Hornby Island again. There were questions I had to ask, and I needed to do it face to face. You lose so much when you can't see someone's expression.

I also needed to go to Seattle. Same reason. Two murders, two clients accused of murder. Now the murders seemed to be connected. Both were urgent, but led me in two different directions. And I still had to track down Kathleen.

The coffee maker burbled. I grabbed my favorite oversized mug, poured, and added cream.

My gaze fell on the fax machine and its evocative nest of paper. Was I expecting a fax? Pulled it out.

Oh, right. It was the list of plants in bloom while Kathleen and Bill had been staying on Hornby. The helpful woman at the UBC Botanical Garden had been true to her word. I ran my eye down the page, recognizing only a couple. I couldn't do much with this list, but I knew someone who could.

"Belton Pharmacy."

"Patrick?"

"Speaking."

"It's Barbara. Barbara O'Grady."

"Ah, my favorite non-client. And how are you today? Not sick, I suppose."

"No, I..."

"If you're calling about the poisonous plants, I'm just getting started."

"Actually, I thought I'd narrow your search a little."

"Most considerate of you. How?"

"I have a list here of all the plants that were blooming around the time of the murder. Could you look at it and see if any of them are poisonous?"

"I can do that. But you do know that not all poisonous plants bloom, don't you? Or at least not what we'd consider blooms."

I should have known. Suddenly my little burst of energy left me. "Would you have a look at this list anyway? You never know. And I can fax it to you."

"Truer words. Will do, Barbara. And how urgent is this?"

I thought about my missing client. "I'm afraid it's getting more urgent by the hour."

"Then I will try to get an answer to you today. Yes?"

"If you could, I'll be in your debt forever."

"Just try to develop an interesting illness the next time you come in, will you? Robust health is so boring in my trade."

I laughed. "I'll see what I can do. Thanks, Patrick."

"Anytime, dear lady. Anytime."

As I sent the fax, I thought about the vast gardens at the Sunshine Inn, and how many potential poisons the grounds must conceal.

So which one had killed Bill Rampage?

Pulling one of my worn-in leather guest chairs to the window, I sank into it, stared out at the gathering clouds and sipped my coffee. Kathleen was missing. Shelley was in prison. Hell, even Nick was missing.

I had nothing but questions in every direction, I was running out of time and there was only one of me. What was I going to do?

The answers weren't leaping to mind. Various pieces swirled in my mind in some kind of chaotic dance, like a kaleidoscope of death. Bill's death. Deirdre's death. Who stood to gain, in either case?

I didn't know.

Before I'd finished brooding, my cell phone rang. I leapt to answer it, nearly dumping coffee on myself.

"Barbara O'Grady here."

"Ms. O'Grady? This is Mary Roberts. Kathleen's sister? You left me a message?"

"Mrs. Roberts. Thank you for calling back. Yes, I'm looking for Kathleen. Do you know where she is?"

Her voice was soft, hesitant. "Yes, I do know."

"I need to talk to her."

"I'm afraid that won't be possible."

"Mrs. Roberts, I'm a private investigator. Kathleen hired me to investigate a friend's death."

"Bill Rampage."

"Yes. Did you know Bill?"

"No, we'd never met, but Kathleen told me a great deal about him."

Kathleen planned to marry Bill and her family had never met him? She really had been harboring delusions about that relationship. "Then you understand why I need to speak with her."

"Maybe you could give me a little more detail?"

Damn. "The police need to talk to Kathleen, and they haven't been able to reach her. I've been asked to find her, before they are forced to make things more formal."

"More formal? What does that mean?"

"At worst, it could mean arresting her. It would be much better if Kathleen agrees to meet with the police."

"Surely you can't mean Kathleen is a suspect in this murder?" Mary Roberts sounded horrified.

"I don't think she's a serious suspect," I found myself saying, mentally crossing my fingers. "But they need to speak with her, and they are inclined to see her disappearance in the wrong light. I really do need to talk to Kathleen."

"I'm afraid that won't be possible."

Maybe I'd been too reassuring. "Why not?"

"Kathleen is—unwell."

"Unwell?"

"Yes, unwell. She can't answer questions right now."

Can't or won't? "Mrs. Roberts, I think we need to have this conversation in person. I can be there in half an hour."

"Now?"

"I don't think Kathleen can afford for us to waste time."

"Is this necessary?"

"I think so. What is your address?"

"Oh, very well." She gave me the address, which was in West Vancouver.

———

IT TOOK me a while to find the place.

Mary Roberts lived in West Vancouver all right, but at the far end, almost all the way to the ferry terminal at Horseshoe Bay. The area was all thickly wooded, angling down to the bay. The Roberts house itself was located on a thickly treed slope behind the golf course. When I finally found the house, it was a sprawling rancher with a spectacular view.

Contemplating the steep driveway, I decided to walk up rather than subject my aging Honda to the incline. Driving into this garage must be a real pain in winter, I thought as my calf muscles took the strain of the steep slope. Add a little snow and this driveway would be like a bobsled run.

Vancouver doesn't get that much snow, but what little there is all seems to fall on North and West Van.

I rang the bell and an attractive woman in her mid-thirties, with a resemblance to Kathleen around her eyes, answered. "Yes? Can I help you?"

I showed her my identification.

She read my license carefully and looked me up and down. Apparently I passed muster, because she opened the door wider to invite me in.

"Would you like a cup of tea?" she asked, ushering me into a large, homey kitchen.

Mary Roberts was about my age, which would make her several years older than Kathleen, and she seemed more stable than my client. She was tiny, even dainty, with dark hair and reserved dark eyes to go with that soft voice. She didn't seem to know quite what to do with me.

That was okay. I knew exactly why I was there.

"Mrs. Roberts, for Kathleen's sake, I need to speak with her right away. You do understand how important that is?"

"Well, yes. But Kathleen needs to a break from everything just now."

"Is she here?"

"Here?"

"In this house."

She glanced around, as if expecting to see her sister materialize. "Here? No. No, of course not."

I didn't believe her. "Look, Mary. May I call you Mary?"

"What? Oh, yes, yes, please do. Mrs. Roberts sounds like my mother-in-law. And she makes me nervous," she said with a quick grin.

There was more spark there than I'd thought. I almost felt bad about pushing her so hard. Almost. But I needed to find Kathleen, and soon. Before the cops ran out of patience.

"Hiding Kathleen isn't going to help her. Not now."

"Hiding her? I'm not hiding her."

"You do know where she is?"

She nodded, her face sad. The kettle began to boil, and Mary went off and fussed with the tea things for a moment, then brought a laden tray back to the table. She sat down and looked at her hands in her lap for a moment, then met my eyes.

"Look, Mary," I said, leaning forward. "The longer it is before the police get to talk to Kathleen, the worse it looks for her."

Mary's cheeks were flushed and she was nibbling on the edge of a fingernail. "I think I'll have to confide in you," she said after a pause that went on too long. "Kathleen trusted you enough to hire you. I'll have to trust you too."

She looked down at her hands. "Kathleen hasn't had an easy life. She's always been—delicate. Nervy."

I wasn't liking the sound of this.

"I think this situation has pushed her too far."

Which situation? The death of her fantasy lover?

Mary reached for the teapot, poured. "Cream? Sugar? A biscuit?"

Peak Freans, I noted. And not a chocolate one in the lot. "No, thanks."

Finally she ran out of distractions. "It's so sad," she said, and her eyes filled with tears.

"Where is she?" I asked, keeping my tone as gentle as I could.

"Shady Gates. It's—a private hospital."

Oh boy. Shady Gates is a private hospital specializing in psychiatric cases. I hadn't expected this, though maybe I should have, given Kathleen's recent behavior, and the odd nature of her relationship with Bill.

Suddenly I regretted every negative thought I'd had about my client. "I know it. Can you tell me why she's there?"

She sobbed quietly for a moment, but she seemed to need to talk about her sister, because she quickly pulled herself together. "Kathleen has problems—with depression," she began.

Now they tell me. "Go on."

"She's always been—sensitive," Mary said hesitating on the last word. "She expects things to work a certain way, and when they don't, she gets upset, even paranoid."

Don't we all? "Things?"

"People. Kathleen has trouble with social interactions—she couldn't ever handle a full-time job."

I didn't like the sound of this. "So why is she at Shady Gates?"

"Her friend's death was too much for her. She had a breakdown."

I nodded. "She seemed to be taking Bill's death hard."

"Yes. I gather he was a good friend."

What was this? "I understood that he and Kathleen had dated for six months and then been friends for several years. Kathleen was very serious about him."

"No, no. You must have that wrong. Kathleen has never had a relationship that lasted more than a few weeks. She's not even very good with friendship. She gets too intense, then either they run or she does."

Now I was confused. "Is it possible to see her?"

Mary shook her head. "I'm afraid she can't have visitors. Her emotional balance is too delicate."

I could hear some doctor's pompous tone through her words, so I didn't even try to argue. Instead, I said, "Forgive me for asking, but a private hospital is expensive. Can you manage the fees long enough to help her?"

"Oh, her trust fund will handle it. It's nice of you to be concerned, though."

Trust fund? Kathleen had a trust fund? Well, at least that explained the art collection. "If Kathleen has a trust fund, why does she work as a temp?"

Mary looked confused again. "Work? Kathleen doesn't work. She does a little volunteer work."

Somebody was seriously out of touch with reality, and I had a sinking feeling it was my client. As I thought about my interactions with Kathleen in light of what Mary had said, I felt pity instead of annoyance.

"Actually, she's been working as a temp for 'Trusted Temps' for the last three years. The owner is a friend of mine, which is how I met Kathleen. I understand Kathleen does very good work."

Mary looked horrified. "But the stress of an ongoing job—no wonder she's been doing so poorly lately."

"I think Bill's death had a great deal to do with it," I said. "Kathleen told me she intended to marry him."

Mary's desolate expression made me wish I'd kept my big mouth shut.

"Oh, the poor thing. If you only knew how unlikely that was. Kathleen isn't stable enough for a relationship. And she was talking marriage? Oh, I'll have to talk to Dr. Odlander about this. Immediately."

Poor Kathleen.

There was nothing left to say. Making a mental note of the doctor's name, I thanked Mary for her time. She was picking up the phone before I made it to the front door.

———

LESS THAN AN HOUR LATER, I was sitting in Dr. Charles Odlander's opulent private office at Shady Grove. The good doctor was being charming, probably because he thought I was there at the request of her family.

I can't imagine how he got that idea.

It didn't help much, though, because he wouldn't let me see Kathleen, let alone talk to her. He explained her condition in the same words that Mary had used.

"She is improving, trust me, Ms. O'Grady," he said with a smile that showed very white, strong teeth. He leaned forward to lay one large hand on my arm. "And she really is receiving the best care."

"I don't doubt that for a minute," I said with an equally false smile. Especially if Kathleen's trust fund was a large one. "Can you tell me what caused this reaction? And how long before I can talk to her?"

"It was clearly a stress reaction, coupled with depression. Though Kathleen was, shall we say, unfocused when we asked her about the cause. She is also displaying a degree of paranoia that I find most worrisome. As for the cure, she will heal in her own good time. Though the information Mrs. Roberts has just given us tells me that she needs even more time than I'd thought."

Uh huh. "It really is essential that I talk with her."

"My dear Ms. O'Grady, of course you may do so. As soon as it is safe for both you and her."

"Safe? Is Kathleen dangerous?"

"Of course she isn't. I merely meant that it would be upsetting for both of you if you were to see her in her current state."

Sure you did, I thought. You slipped there, doc. Too many years of dealing with worried and therefore gullible relatives, I'd guess. I wondered if this too-smooth doctor was capable of helping my client, or if he was too focused on his bottom line to care about the patients.

I stood up and thanked him for his time, all the while wondering whom I could bribe to tell me the real story. And how I was going to get Kathleen out of this place.

As I walked down the tree-lined drive, I was wondering how long it would take Brad Bramwell to find her here. And whether it would gain Kathleen anything if I told him where she was. At least he didn't have to worry about her leaving town…

Some instinct made me look over my shoulder. Dr. Charles was standing at his office window, staring after me. Caught, he lifted one hand in an affable wave. I waved back, smiling, hoping he'd be as annoyed by my calm as I was by his.

The light was fading rapidly, but I could see a curtain moving in one of the windows on the far end of the upper floor. Kathleen? It wasn't likely. How was I going to find her, talk to her?

This case was getting worse by the day. And I was getting nowhere. I hate that!

Half an hour later I was even more frustrated. I'd tried to call Patrick, to see if he could put a rush on my list of poisonous plants, and been told he'd left for the day. I left a message for him to call me, then looked up his home number. Nothing. Stupid unlisted numbers.

Now what? It didn't look like Kathleen was going to be much

help to me, or herself, for quite some time. And the RCMP weren't likely to get more patient. The best thing I could do for her would be to direct some of that interest elsewhere. Like to the real killer. I was starting to believe it wasn't my client, which was a relief.

So, where did I look for answers? Hornby or Seattle?

On Hornby, I could ask more questions about Brandy, Tad Murphy and Blake Masters. And follow up on Kathleen's accusation that Brandy had killed Bill. In Seattle, I could talk to Blake himself—which might well prove a waste of time. And look into Deirdre's past.

Hornby was of more immediate help to Kathleen, Seattle to Shelley. But Shelley was about to be released on bail, and her trial was unlikely to be scheduled immediately. Given Kathleen's reportedly fragile mental state, I wasn't sure how she'd deal with being arrested.

Which meant I was headed for Hornby in the morning. Thinking about my crowded schedule, I decided to wing it. Not one of my brighter ideas, as it turned out.

CHAPTER TWENTY-SEVEN

The following morning I cursed and batted at my alarm when it went off at a ridiculously early hour. Then I tripped over Cat on my way to the shower, and he left four lines of blood on my ankle in retaliation.

My day trip to Hornby was not off to a promising start.

Waiting in line for the ferry in the gray pre-dawn light, the trip began to seem a waste of time. With Shelley in jail, Kathleen locked in at Shady Groves, and so many questions leading in every direction, what was I doing taking a day to go to Hornby? There were too many things I needed to do here.

And how could I place Kathleen's needs above Shelley's?

Shelley was my friend, Kathleen was just a client. Only the memory of Mary Roberts' worried eyes kept me from turning around and heading to my office.

Kathleen *was* my client. She was in as much jeopardy as Shelley, maybe more—Kathleen's sanity could be at stake. And I hated the idea I was adding to her stress because I couldn't find the evidence to keep her out of jail.

As the long line of cars began to move, waved on by a yellow rain-slickered ferry worker, I felt calmer about my decision.

———

WHEN I ARRIVED at the Inn, after way too many delays en route, finally things began to go my way. The rain that had been threatening all morning was still holding off. Elena was in, and had time to talk to me.

I suggested a stroll through the grounds. She was happy to agree.

"It is so beautiful this time of year," Elena said as we passed a mass of striped red and white tulips in bloom. "And I don't get out nearly often enough. There is always something demanding my attention."

I made sympathetic noises.

She gave me a skeptical look. I've never done sympathetic noises well.

"Why do you not tell me why you have come, Barbara. It is not to stroll in our gardens, I think, no matter how beautiful."

I grinned, and decided to gamble on honesty. Elena struck me as a woman who didn't like dancing around issues any more than I did. "True. I have some questions about Brandy and Bill Rampage. You hinted that there was something between them the last time we talked, and since then, I have heard the same thing, in varying detail, from a number of people."

"Yes. What did you want to know?"

"If Brandy had discovered that Bill was also having sex with someone else, someone other than the girlfriend who left, what would her reaction have been?"

Elena paused, then nodded. "Yes, I do not doubt he was. Well, Brandy is young. Her response would have been emotional and extreme."

I thought of the teenager wielding a cleaver on chicken carcasses. "Would she turn violent?"

"I do not think so. I have seen no signs of violence in her. I think it more likely that she would enact a tragedy. Her life would be over, she could never trust men, she would never love again."

"Not so different from her response to Bill's death."

"Indeed."

"And her friend? Tiffany? Is she the type to defend her friend's honor if she found out Bill was 'cheating' on Brandy?"

"That one? More likely to rejoice, I think. She is the shadow, the one always somewhat jealous of what the friend has, but unwilling to lose the reflected glow."

It was a scathing, and probably very accurate, assessment. Elena didn't miss much. "Do you think she would kill?"

Elena cocked her head, looking like an inquisitive myna bird. "If she thought to go undetected, perhaps. But not Bill Rampage. He was a prize to her—and of value only because her friend wanted him."

It was an unsettling thought. In fact the whole case was unsettling, riddled with unfaithful men and desperate women. Whatever happened to lasting relationships? Not that I was one to talk.

"But if she couldn't catch his interest? Would she take it out on him?"

"I think not. To do so would admit defeat."

I'd seen people killed for less reason. And there was something in Tiffany's character, a meanness, that I didn't trust. I added her to my mental list of suspects, put a question mark beside Brandy's name.

"Do you recall a guest named Tad Murphy? He was here for dinner the night before Bill Rampage was murdered."

"Was it that night he was here? Ah. I am sorry, we have so many guests, it is difficult to remember when a particular one was here. And yes, I do remember him, because I found the relation between him and Bill so interesting. That Tad is also a shadow, another who goes through life resenting what others have."

I was with her on that one. 'Shadow' was a remarkably apt description of Murphy, who was as fake and shallow as his own smile. And how he'd hate hearing that description of himself.

"Do you know when Murphy left?"

"No, I am sorry. I did not see him after dinner. But if you ask at the ferry, I think they may know. It is a small island."

"What about one of the couples who were here, Blake and Deirdre Masters. Did you see anything of their interactions with Bill Rampage?"

Elena smiled. "It was an interesting group that weekend. Sometimes it is like that, yes?"

"I guess it must be. But the Masters?"

"She is the bird of prey—is it raptor?"

Interesting image for Deirdre. "Yes."

"Always she watches for the weak, for the small and vulnerable. She toyed with Bill Rampage, but it was toying only. She had no real interest, I think."

"He wasn't weak enough?"

"Oh, I think perhaps, but not interesting enough. He and she, they play the same game, but she was better at it. He would tear muscles only, she would tear out the heart."

This lady was scary. And I wasn't sure if I meant Deirdre, or Elena. I could see why Kathleen had called Elena a witch. But there was a fearless quality to her honesty that I respected.

I even believed most of what she said. It was too sharply cutting to be false. "And Blake Masters?"

"Oh, a victim. Bleeding but still alive. Her little game was being played out for his benefit. He was given room to run, you see, before she pounced again."

I shivered. I'd seen wild things play such games. "And his reaction? Blake's, I mean."

"He was very angry with her, and for more than this game, I think. He watched, and knew she toyed with him."

"Blake Masters was angry with Deirdre? Not with Bill?"

"Oh, some of the anger spilled over, but it was the woman he was most upset with."

"Was he angry enough with Bill to have poisoned him?"

Elena shrugged eloquent shoulders. "Perhaps. But if I were to wager, I would say no. The heat was for the woman—anger and passion, mixed together. If he had found them together, then perhaps, in the heat of the moment, a fight. But poison? No."

Hmmm. "Would it surprise you to know that the woman, Deirdre, died of poison less than a week after Bill Rampage did?"

Elena pursed full lips and shook her head. "Not that she was murdered. Such a one would make many enemies. Eventually she would misjudge a weakness, a breaking point, and a victim would fight back."

"Do you think Blake Masters could have killed her?"

"Could have—yes. There was enough anger there for that. But there will be others, too, if you look. The killer would not be obvious, unless you know their breaking point."

I had the sinking feeling she was right. Finding Deirdre's killer would not be easy. And I wasn't doing so well on Bill's killer, either. Might as well ask Elena straight out.

"If you had to choose one of the people who was here the weekend Bill died, had to point to one and say, 'I think you killed Bill Rampage', who would it be?"

She looked at me for a long moment. "It should not be a difficult question, though to confront them, that would be hard. But—I do not know. No, more, I do not feel any of them have killed him."

That was my problem too.

If I had to choose, my suspicion was falling about equally on either Tad Murphy or Blake Masters. Though Elena herself was still a contender, if only because she was pragmatic and strong enough to do it. But only if Bill had been a threat to her or her world, and I'd seen nothing to suggest that. "Then who did?"

A shrug. "I have no sense of that."

A lot of help she was. "I see. Another question, then. I understand you grow the herbs that are used to season all the dishes. It's something of a specialty of yours?"

"That is right," she said with a smile. "And before you ask, yes, I am very knowledgeable about herbs, their curative as well as their not-so-benign properties. I still practice the skills that my grandmothers knew. The use of herbs for seasoning and for healing."

Like I said, she was sharp. "But you know also of their uses as poisons."

"Of course. Though your North American varieties not so well as those of my homeland. But you are wondering what I might know about whatever poisoned Mr. Rampage."

"Yes."

"Of course. The answer, I am afraid, is very little. There are too many poisons that might have caused his symptoms."

I considered asking her to look at my list of the plants that were blooming then, and ask which of those were poisonous, but I wasn't sure I trusted her quite that far. I'd wait for Patrick's response.

Elena had a dispassionate clarity when looking at others, a trait I suspect many people think I share. It could be a survival mechanism or a personality trait. It could also be the mark of a sociopath. Not a cheery thought.

My suspects now included Tad, Blake, Elena herself and both Brandy and Tiffany, though the latter three weren't strong suspects. And I still couldn't eliminate Kathleen, Dammit.

I'd find out when Tad had left the island, but I couldn't see that it mattered. Whoever had killed Bill hadn't needed to be at the Inn when he died. They only had to have been there long enough to replace the water in his water carafe. And speaking of carafes...

———

I TRACKED down Brandy in the kitchen. She was wielding the cleaver with a little more enthusiasm than I was comfortable with on a large, bloody piece of beef.

"Brandy," I said.

"Yeah?" she said, without looking up or ceasing her chopping.

"I have a few questions, if you don't mind. About Bill's death."

It was the magic word. Down went the cleaver, up came the eyes, already filling with tears. "For Bill? Anything. What did you want to know?"

"Can you tell me who sets up the guest rooms, before the next guests check in?"

"Me and Tiffany, usually. Except she's slow, so I end up doing most of them. Especially for the guests I like."

I made an educated guess. "So you would have set up Bill's room?"

She nodded. "Yeah. It was like, an honor."

Right. "Can you show me your routine?"

"My routine?"

"How you go about setting up each room. If there are any empty rooms, that is."

"Oh." She nodded and waved for me to follow her. "We have a late check-in. C'mon, I'll show you."

I followed her up the stairs and down the hall to the room Bill had died in. Brandy paused at the doorway, gave an exaggerated shiver, and said, *sotto voce*, "I can't ever come into this room without thinking of him, y'know?"

She flung open the door. "It's made up now, but if you like, I can tell you all the stuff I do. When a guest leaves, like."

"That would be helpful."

"Okay. Well, obviously I change the bed, put the linens in a hamper I bring with me. Then I throw out the flowers, dump the water in the vase, the carafe and the glass in the bathroom sink, and put them into the hamper."

She indicated a rounded crystal water glass with matching carafe, both gleaming, and a long, narrow crystal vase that held two red and white striped tulips. The frilly kind.

"I go into the bathroom, and clear out the soaps and lotions, mop down the sink, tub and floor. Plus the toilet. Which can be really gross. You wouldn't believe the mess that people sometimes leave," she confided. "And the more money they have, the worse it can be. I really hate this part of the job."

I could imagine. I'd spent a couple of summers as a chambermaid, learning enough about the ways of the guest world that now I always leave a hefty tip when I stay at a hotel. "What happens to the vase, the carafe and the water glass when you've collected them?"

"Oh, they go to the kitchen where we do a special cycle on the dishwasher."

So they were glass, not crystal. "Then you collect them from the kitchen again and put them into the rooms?"

"No, they have to go into the linen room first. After they've been inspected by Mrs. Perfect."

"Mrs. Perfect?"

Brandy blushed, which amazed me. "Mrs. Grussman, I mean."

Ah. Elena. It didn't surprise me that her housekeeping standards were exacting. "And then?"

"I'll show you. Come on." She led the way back down the hall, threw open the door into a small room lined with shelves and smelling of lavender. One section held towels, one sheets, and one an assortment of gleaming glassware—vases, carafes and glasses.

"We get a new set of everything from here for each room, fill the carafes, arrange the flowers. Whatever."

"And where do you fill the carafes from?"

Again she blushed.

Memories of my chambermaid days resurfaced. "Let me guess. You're supposed to use the filtered water from the kitchen, but it's up and down the stairs too many times, so you use water from the bathroom sink. Right?"

She hesitated.

"Don't worry, I won't tell Mrs. Perfect."

She cast me a sly look, grinned. "Okay, then. Yeah, we use the water from the sinks."

"Ever use the filtered water?"

"Only if she's, like, standing over us."

"And the weekend Bill Rampage was last here?"

Her eyes went teary. "The sink. And I'll never forgive myself. The last drink he ever had was tap water."

It wasn't the water that was the problem. Obviously the police were still managing to keep the real cause of death a secret. "The last drink?"

"He used to tell me how much he appreciated that I gave him fresh water every day. Cause he took all these vitamins every day, right before bed. To keep—to keep healthy." And her voice broke into a wail.

"Who else knew about this? About his vitamins and the water, I mean."

"Everybody, I guess. Cause he told me, like when I was serving dinner, and everybody was there."

So much for narrowing the suspect list. "And when did you change his drinking water? On the Saturday, I mean?"

"It was the last thing I did. Probably around two."

"In the afternoon?"

She nodded.

So the murderer had to have changed the water again sometime after that, but before Kathleen went to his room. "And did you change his flowers, do you remember?"

She shook her head. "No, I changed the water. The flowers were still fresh, and smelled so sweet."

Wait a minute. "You remember what the flowers were?"

"Sure. Lily of the valley. They're my favorite. I was so happy to be giving them to Bill."

But were they poisonous? Surely not. Those small white bells, poisonous? You saw them everywhere, and they looked so innocent.

Then I thought about the rhododendrons I also saw every-where. "Do you know what flowers the other guests had?"

She looked puzzled. "They'd have the same. We have a really big bed of lilies over by the stream that gets a lot of sun or something, so they bloom, like, really early every year. And we always give all the guests the same flowers."

No help there. Assuming lily of the valley was poisonous, of course. But if it was, how simple. Pour the water from the vase into the glass and presto. One murder weapon. Or was it even simpler than that?

"Brandy, which of the vases were used for lily of the valley? In Bill's room, I mean."

"Oh, that's easy." She pulled down a small, classically shaped, faceted vase. "These ones."

There was no way that vase could be mistaken for a glass. Or a carafe. I let out a breath I'd been holding since picturing an exhausted Bill downing his vitamins with the water from the vase, not the carafe. But he hadn't died by error. That would have been too easy.

Besides, I didn't even know if those pure white bells were poisonous.

"Thanks, Brandy."

"So, that will help you, like, find the murderer."

Like, I hoped so. "It will help, Brandy. And if you think of anything else, give me a call, okay?"

"Sure thing," she said. Probably with no idea of what she'd already told me.

———

MENTALLY SHAKING my head at Brandy's combination of assumed sophistication and lack of worldliness, I drove back across the island. It was starting to rain again as I parked and strolled down to the ferry terminal. Half a dozen cars were waiting for the next ferry, which I could see leaving Denman, about ten minutes away. I was planning how I'd raise the question of Tad with the ferry workers when my cell phone rang.

"Hello?"

"Barbara? Barbara, I have to talk to you. Right away."

It was Shelley and she sounded hysterical. "I'm still on Hornby Island. Can it wait until tomorrow?"

"No, it can't wait. I don't know what I'm going to do. Barbara, I need to talk to you now. Today. What are you doing on Hornby, anyway? I thought you were working for me."

I felt a sudden stab of guilt for choosing Kathleen's problems over hers. "Long story. Look, Shelley, can you tell me what's going on?"

Her voice caught in a sob. "Not on the phone. Can't you come back to Vancouver?"

I'd never heard Shelley this upset. I made an instant decision. "Yes, I'll come back. I should be there by five, five-thirty at the latest. Did the bail hearing go well?"

"I'm out, anyway. I'm at the Hathaway."

At least she was out of jail. It was a start.

"I'll meet you there, all right?"

"Yes. I'll wait for you. And I'll order a bottle of wine and some cheese or something from room service."

Good plan. I had a feeling I was going to need it. "I'll see you then."

Hanging up, I wondered what had pushed Shelley to hysterics, when jail and her husband's semi-desertion hadn't done so.

Had the police found more evidence? Or, the unthinkable, had Shelley been lying when she'd said she hadn't killed Deirdre? Had guilt caught up with her?

I didn't even want to think about Shelley being guilty, but after her call, I couldn't stop the questions darting through my brain. I wished she could have told me what was wrong, but she'd seemed too distraught. Plus cell phone conversations are never secure.

If I was going to hear that Shelley had killed Deirdre, it needed to be in person. I really hoped that wasn't what she needed to tell me. I didn't know how I'd deal with that, let alone how I'd help Shelley deal with it.

I walked back to my car, moved it into the ferry lineup. At least Shelley's timing was good. Ten minutes later and I'd have been waiting an hour till the next ferry, which would put me on the five o'clock ferry rather than the three o'clock out of Nanaimo.

Which reminded me. I called and changed my reservation from the seven o'clock to the three. Finishing the call, I could see the low blue and white ferry coming in, barely visible now through what was becoming a downpour. I had just enough time to call Brad Bramwell.

Who wasn't in.

I debated leaving a message, but what would I say? You can't talk to my client because she's in a mental facility, and oh by the way, I think I've found five other suspects who might have wanted to kill Bill Rampage? Six if I included Elena.

And that I might also have found the poison that killed him? No, that was another conversation that needed to be held live and in person.

So who had poisoned Bill's water glass? And why? The answer seemed simple—jealousy. Unfortunately it applied equally to all the suspects, except perhaps Elena. And that included my client. The one with the tenuous grasp on reality.

To give Bill his due, he'd been an equal-opportunity philanderer. I couldn't think of anyone he'd left out of the mix, except Elena, as far as I knew. Though she had seemed fond of him.

How well had Elena known Bill? I didn't really see her as his killer, but I've learned the hard way not to make assumptions. Find the facts, check them, and re-check them—that's the key in this business.

"Oh, and intuition never comes into it?" I could hear Andrea saying in my head. "Barbara, you take the facts and make leaps with them."

Well, if I did, I still started with facts. Very solid facts.

Like the motive that Bill's philandering had given all the suspects. Kathleen and Brandy because he'd cheated on them, Tad and Blake because they'd been jealous of Bill's relationship with their women and Tiffany because he'd ignored her in favor of her friend. And Elena? I'd have to work on that one.

So much for motive. What about means? I was willing to bet that Bill had been poisoned using one of the plants that grew so abundantly around the Inn, maybe even with lily of the valley. To which all of them had access. And if Elena was the most knowl-edgeable on the subject, the information wasn't exactly hard to come by.

That brought me to opportunity. Again, any of them could gone into Bill's room, replaced the water in his glass with the deadlier variety, and left. They didn't even have to have been on the island when he died. Just at some point after two p.m.

I shook my head. It was impossible.

As far as I could see, Kathleen was no more and no less plausible a suspect than the other five. I was leaning a little towards Blake Masters, despite what Elena had said.

Probably because I didn't like the man. Of course, I didn't like Tad either, but as the only non-guest, he might have found gaining access to the guest's rooms more difficult.

So why did Brad Bramwell suddenly want to talk to Kathleen? Other than the fact that she'd been stalking Bill, of course. Before I'd finished adding up the case against my client, an orange clad deckhand waved my car onto the ferry.

CHAPTER TWENTY-EIGHT

When I knocked on Shelley's hotel room door at five-twenty, Shelley flung it open and embraced me. She didn't look as bad as I'd expected, I noted with relief. She was pale, a bit shaky, a little red around the eyes, but her hair flowed in shining waves down her back and she wore lounging pajamas in an amethyst silk that set off her complexion.

"Thank you for coming, Barbara," she said, reaching behind her to hand me a glass of red wine.

I took a sip. A full-bodied Cabernet with a hint of cherries and chocolate, it was a very good vintage. The mess my emotions were in after that interminable ferry ride, I needed every expensive mouthful.

There's nothing slower than a ferry through the Gulf Islands when you're in a hurry. And nothing more peaceful when you're not.

"Thanks—guess you knew I needed this. Now, why don't you tell me what's going on?"

She beckoned me into the sitting area, flopped bonelessly on the cream leather sofa and reached for her own glass. "I don't know where to start."

"Start with why you called," I prompted, glancing around me rather than looking at her. I was dreading what she had to tell me. The suite was spacious and tranquil in shades of ivory and gold, but it wasn't enough to calm me. Somebody hadn't spared on the costs, though.

"It's Blake. He's not coming back."

Thank God! She hadn't murdered Deirdre. "What do you mean he's not coming back?"

"He was supposed to fly in tomorrow."

And this was why she'd dragged me back from Hornby? "For the weekend?"

She nodded, seemingly unable to go on.

Okay, what was Shelley's idiot husband playing at now? "And he's not coming?"

"No." It was half-choked.

"Did he say why not?"

Shelley took a breath that caught, then another. "He said there were things he needed to take care of, problems with his practice."

"And are there?"

It took her a while to answer, but then she lifted her chin, met my eyes. "Even if something is urgent, he has coverage. He could have been here. If he'd wanted to be." And she started to cry.

What could I say? The guy was a jerk. I looked at Shelley. Now I could see the doubt and fear behind her eyes.

Despite the attention to her hair and clothes, this woman was beaten.

Where was the exuberant women who had asked me to her opening? Was it only a week ago?

Shelley's three days in jail had cost her more than I'd expected. She seemed to have lost all her confidence and any sense of personal power, and her louse husband's letting her down like this was the final straw.

My fists clenched. None of this was right. And there wasn't anything I could do about it.

No. I wouldn't accept that.

There had to be something I could do, some way to help her. My mind flipped to a bumper sticker I'd seen the other day— 'Women are like teabags, they get stronger when they're in hot water.'

It didn't seem to apply to Shelley, not now, but it had applied to the buoyant, dynamic Shelley I used to know. Where was that woman? She still had to be in there, somewhere. I couldn't let her go on like this.

"Sniffling over him isn't going to help. Why don't you start by telling me what's really wrong?"

Shelley looked at me blankly for a long moment, then her lips quirked and she started to laugh. For an interminable moment I was afraid my shock therapy had backfired and she'd exchanged one form of hysteria for another, but after a moment she stopped laughing and sat staring into her mug.

"I think I lost Blake a long time ago," she finally said in a quiet voice. "But I didn't want to admit it. Any more than I wanted to admit that I was jealous of Deirdre's artistic abilities."

"You mean you lost him to Deirdre?"

She shook her head. "That's too simple. And I meant it when I said I didn't really care when she and Blake had that fling."

This was getting confusing.

Which shouldn't surprise me—anything connected with the relationships in these two cases was confusing. Come to that, my relationship with Nick was confusing, and that had nothing to do with either case. Maybe this was just my old problem with relationships—only on steroids. "Then what do you mean?"

"There wasn't any heat left between us. We went the right places, saw the right people. We were the 'golden couple', but when we weren't in public, we didn't shine for each other. I guess we couldn't be bothered."

It was a depressing picture she was painting, and a sad one. Where does the magic between two people go? Or is it just sex, worn out with custom and 'stale with use'. Which I think is the only

Shakespeare quote that I still recall from high school. Now if I could only remember which play…

"So why did you stay?"

"It was being married I liked, the security of it. That's what I held onto, what I cared about."

"Are you talking about financial security?"

"I guess it would sound like that, wouldn't it? Especially from a starving artist. Except that I wasn't starving anymore. And maybe that was the problem, maybe the artist in the garret thing was what attracted Blake in the first place, who knows?"

She paused, staring into her wine glass, then drank another mouthful. "Sure, his money was great at first, but the last few years I've been selling pretty well. It's not Blake's money I need, it's Blake."

She drank more wine, glanced at me. "If I'm honest, maybe it isn't even him. I like being part of a couple, having someone to count on."

She gave me a crooked grin. "Listen to me—someone to count on. And when I need him the most, Blake leaves town. And I don't think he's coming back. Pretty unfair, huh?"

It sounded like Shelley hadn't had what I'd consider a relationship for some time. But then my idea of what constitutes a relationship may be slightly unrealistic, given that mine don't seem to last very long.

Still, it seemed like a good time to play devil's advocate. Maybe things weren't as bleak as Shelley was painting them.

"Well, he didn't just leave. First he hired the best lawyer in town for you. He hired me. He booked this great suite for you to come back to."

"Yeah, after I was released from jail. What kind of husband leaves town and makes excuses not to return while his wife is in jail?"

I looked at her thoughtfully for a long moment. "Can I ask you a hard question?"

"Oh, like you haven't been?" she quipped. Then more soberly, "Sure, go ahead."

"If you stayed in the marriage for the security, why did he stay?"

"Ouch," she said. "To be blunt, I'm not sure I know. It wasn't the sex—he could get that elsewhere, and was quite happy to do so."

"Not just Deirdre?"

"No. Not even close."

"And you ignored them?"

"Uh huh."

I couldn't imagine living the kind of life she was describing. Oh, I'd dated my share of cheats, but the minute I'd found out, they were gone. I didn't understand why Shelley had stayed.

But who was I to judge?

"So if it wasn't the sex, what was it?" I asked Shelley. "Why did Blake stay in the marriage?"

––––––––

SHELLEY FINISHED her wine in one long swallow, then met my eyes. "You know, it's funny, I've never asked myself why Blake chose to stay married to me. I was working too hard to avoid thinking about why I stayed with him, I guess. Queen of denial, that's me."

She gave a laugh that had no humor in it. "Looking back, I think maybe he stayed because we were the 'golden couple', because I was his entrée into the art world. I was starting to get quite a bit of recognition in Seattle, and he liked that. How cynical is that?" she said, and poured herself another glass of wine.

"What did you give him that Deirdre couldn't?" I asked, watching her expression closely.

"Or wouldn't," she said, with a wry twist to her lips. "Deirdre had no interest in acquiring a husband of her own. She liked them best when they belonged to someone else."

"Blake knew that?"

"He must have. And anyway, Blake's Grandmama liked me."

"Somehow I can't see Blake caring what a little old lady thinks, no matter how closely related. Is she really that important to him?"

Shelley grinned that quirky grin, drank some wine. "She may not be, but her money is. And whither goeth her opinion, there goeth her money."

I could see that. The man was more of a jerk than I'd thought. "How much money are we talking about?"

"No-one is exactly sure, but she's worth millions. According to Blake, it could be as much as thirty million."

"Wow. So if Blake divorced you, he might have lost some of his grandmother's good opinion? And all that lovely money?"

"She's pretty hard to read, but I'd say so. She threatens to write them out of her will every time they do anything she doesn't agree with. For all I know, she actually changes her will."

"Them? Who's them?"

"Blake and his cousin. Blake's parents were killed in a car crash twenty-four years ago. And Ron, that's the cousin, his mother never married. She died of a drug overdose more than thirty years ago."

I did some quick mental calculations. "So who raised Ron? And took on guardianship of Blake?"

"Blake's Grandmama. Sometimes it seems Ron's her favorite, sometimes Blake is. As far as I can tell, the cousins hate each other, though they're scrupulously polite in public. And in front of Grandmama."

"So Blake isn't likely to risk doing anything that might see him permanently out of favor."

"Like divorcing me, you mean?" Shelley said. "I hadn't thought of it like that, but you may have a point."

"Would that be enough for her to cut him out? Permanently?"

Shelley shrugged. "Who knows? It doesn't seem to take much to make her change her heir."

"So Blake might be afraid that's what would happen?"

She looked thoughtful, then nodded. "Yes, that's possible. Blake's a worrier."

"Then why isn't he coming back now? Surely his absence in your time of need won't sit well with Grandmama."

"Funny, Barbara."

"But true."

"Yeah. Maybe." She downed the rest of her wine, stood up to get a new bottle. "More?" she asked, holding it towards me.

"Please. This is good wine."

"A new favorite. I was pretty sure you'd like it."

"Very much. But about Blake?"

"Cheese?"

I couldn't resist the melting Camembert, or the fresh baguette. But Shelley wasn't distracting me that easily. "About Blake?"

"I really don't want to think about this."

"I know. And?"

"And—he's obviously distancing himself from me."

"You're sure you aren't being too hard on him?" I had to ask, though it pained me to give the jerk the benefit of the doubt. "Maybe he really has been held up, and he'll get here as soon as he can."

"No," Shelley said. "No, you wouldn't even ask that if you'd heard him. You've never heard such flimsy excuses. And he didn't even make the effort to sound sincere. How stupid does he think I am?"

"I doubt he thinks you're stupid at all."

It took a moment for that to sink in, then her eyes widened. "You think he did it on purpose. That he wants me to know he's not coming back?"

"Well?"

"Yes. Yes, it's possible. More than possible. The bastard! But why?"

The more she told me about her dear Blake, the less I could understand why she was still married to him. Or why she'd married him in the first place.

I pictured him in my mind. Not my type, but maybe I could

understand why she'd married him. Just not why they were still together.

"Well, if he's distancing himself, and he's letting you know it…"

"He thinks I'm guilty! He actually believes I killed his ex-lover. And he doesn't want to be contaminated by being near me. How could he know me so little? We were married, for God's sake."

I wondered if she was aware she'd used the past tense. "Maybe."

"What do you mean, maybe?" Shelley's cheeks flamed with color, her eyes sparked and her voice got louder with every word. "He thinks I committed murder, and he's run back to his safe little hole. What other explanation is there?"

"Maybe he thinks you'll be found guilty."

"But that's what I said…" she stopped abruptly.

"Oh," she said, after a long silence. "Oh. If he stayed married to me because of Grandmama's good opinion, then even she can't condemn him for ditching a convicted killer. That's it, isn't it? This gives him his out."

"If her opinion is why he's stayed married to you, it certainly fits."

"But that's so—so cold!"

Yes, it was. "And is Blake? Cold?"

"I—of course not. He's reserved. It's his upbringing."

Uh huh. Sure it was. And there was a total love bunny under all that frost. "Do you believe that? Still?"

Shelley gulped down more wine.

Placing the glass carefully on the coffee table, she looked at me. "Maybe not. But I want you to find out. Can you do that? In addition to clearing my name, I want to hire you to find out the truth about Blake, and what he's telling people about me. I'll pay you myself. Personally. I mean, I want a separate contract with you on this. Right now, you're working for Blake, because he's paying the lawyers' fees right?"

I nodded.

"For this one, I want you working directly for me."

I thought about it. Was there a conflict? There was a definitely a fine line here, and one I'd have to keep a careful eye on. I wasn't going to compromise my professional ethics.

But what Shelley was asking me to do had nothing to do with clearing her name, or finding out who had killed Deirdre. It was more like gathering background for a divorce action.

Which this might well turn into.

I looked into my old friend's tired eyes, and decided to do it.

At worst, it might overlap with Kathleen's case, but only if Blake had killed Bill, which seemed unlikely despite my earlier musings.

Unless of course Blake had killed Deirdre.

Yeah, I liked that thought. Blake was a little short on motive, but other than that it was perfect. "Yes, I can take your case. But I won't charge you, Shelley. Put this one down to friendship."

"Forget it," she said. "I'm not taking advantage of you like that, Barbara. And if you're worried about my being able to afford you, don't. The irony is I'm doing very well now."

"I'm glad to hear it." And I was. Especially given what I was probably going to find out about Blake. It would be easier for Shelley if she could support herself.

Though I suspected she'd do quite well out of their divorce if we were right about Blake. Mental cruelty made for pretty good grounds.

———

BUT BEFORE I could do any work for Shelley, I had a few things I needed her to clarify. And a few doubts of my own to lay to rest. I leaned forward. "Shelley, about that weekend when you were in Seattle and Blake had gone to Boston."

"Yes?"

"Did you know that Deirdre and Blake stayed at an inn on Hornby Island that weekend?"

Shelley's eyes widened and her fists clenched. "That—that bastard! I'm busting my butt to get ready for this show, and he's saying he wishes he could be around to help."

She stood up and started pacing the room. Just a little unsteadily. "That lying hypocrite! He was with her all weekend, then sneaking around here, too."

I was relieved. Some things about my old friend hadn't changed at all—and she really hadn't known Blake was still seeing Deirdre. There was no way she could fake this passion. Especially after all the wine she'd drunk. *In vino, veritas.* "Yes."

"Rat fink. Soulless, lying cheat!"

I wasn't arguing. The color was returning to Shelley's cheeks, the snap to her eyes. A little vituperation can be good for the soul. "There's another factor, Shelley. Someone died that weekend, another guest at the inn."

"Oh, how awful. What happened?"

"A man named Bill Rampage was poisoned. Have you ever heard of him?"

"Never. Poisoned? Like Deirdre, you mean?"

"Different poison, but..."

"Let me guess. Deirdre was flirting with this Rampage, right? And Blake was jealous?"

"My sources say he was angry."

"You don't think—No. No, Barbara. Blake isn't a murderer. He doesn't have it in him. He's a cad, a liar and a cheat, but he's not a killer. I've been married to the man for seven years—I know what he's capable of."

Not from what she'd been telling me so far, she didn't. "So I guess he's not top of your list for killing Deirdre, either?"

She looked at me.

I grinned. "Hey, it was worth a shot."

"Not funny, Barbara."

"I thought it was."

"You would. We're not at university anymore, remember? Aren't you supposed to be a professional investigator now?"

"I was investigating."

"By suggesting Blake killed Deirdre? You are remembering they were lovers?"

"Crime of passion."

Shelley laughed. "Blake? Yeah, right."

So Blake wasn't the world's most passionate lover, either. I just didn't get it. Other than nice packaging, what did the guy have going for him?

I guess some women have rotten taste in men, and it looked like my friend Shelley fell into that category. "Seriously, though, I do have a question for you."

"Sure."

"Who did kill Deirdre? If it wasn't you and it wasn't Blake?"

"How can you say it's serious when you mention murder and Blake in the same sentence."

I shrugged.

Shelley shook her head. "I don't know. I've been trying to think. I don't think many people liked Deirdre, but to hate her enough to kill her? I just don't know. But that's your area, isn't it? You'll find the killer?"

I felt like explaining to her all the myriad reasons people kill—some of them pretty stupid—but she'd had enough shocks for one day. I shook my head. "Not necessarily. I'm working to clear your name, Shelley. Whatever that takes."

"That's good enough for me. And as of now, you're also working to find out the truth about Blake. Right?"

"Right." Sleazy though I was sure it would prove to be, I'd find out the truth about Blake. Then I'd clear Shelley's name. Oh, and Kathleen's. Then I'd have lunch.

Super P. I. to the rescue.

I grinned, then sobered.

There was a murderer out there somewhere.

———

BACK IN MY OFFICE, I booted up the computer and went online. These days, personal net worth is one of those secrets that aren't so secret. I did a little sleuthing on Blake's grandmother, and what do you know? The old lady was worth closer to fifty million dollars than thirty. The stock market run-up in the late 90's had been good to her, and she must have some pretty savvy advisers, because she hadn't lost much in the crash in 2000, nor the one in 2008.

Staying in line to inherit that kind of cash would give most people a motive. But a motive for what?

If Grandmama really liked Shelley, Blake deserting her when she'd been charged with murder seemed like the worst thing the guy could do. But surely not even a rigid old lady could fault him for not wanting to be tied to a murderess. I swore softly. I could just hear his smooth voice, explaining it all.

If I was right about Blake divorcing Shelley, that is. No sign of that yet.

I checked out Deirdre Brandt. She'd been nearly destitute for a while, but things had picked up. She'd be leaving someone a rather tidy estate. As I gazed at the figures, something was nagging at me about this woman, but I couldn't pin it down. Time to track down a little more info on Deirdre.

I called Cassandra, who wasn't in. I left a message.

I tried calling Patrick, to ask him about lily of the valley, but he'd left for the day and I had no way of reaching him. Damn it. All I needed was a yes or a no.

I tried the Web, but couldn't find a site to tell me if lily of the valley was poisonous or not. How to grow them, yes, but not if they were lethal.

Then, feeling slightly guilty, as if I were betraying her, I checked Shelley's financials, and Blake's. What Shelley had told me was correct. She really didn't need Blake's money, though he had rather a lot of it. When she said she was doing quite well, she'd meant it.

I was impressed. And relieved.

It looked like a trip to Seattle was in order. I needed to know more about Blake Masters—what made him tick, why he'd treat Shelley the way he had. And I needed to talk to Blake about Bill Rampage's murder.

While I was there, I hoped to find someone who'd known

Deirdre well. I needed to know more about Shelley's supposed victim, the one who'd left so much anger in her wake.

Plus I needed to know about Deirdre's change in fortune, needed to understand the woman who'd created such powerful works while creating so much chaos around her.

CHAPTER TWENTY-NINE

Seattle was gray and overcast, the lowering skies matching my mood. Between worrying about Shelley and wondering about Kathleen, I hadn't slept well. I hadn't heard from Nick, either. And I still hadn't given Susanna an answer about her dinner party.

The only thing that had gone as expected was Cat's impatient demands for tuna. I was glad to give it to him, if only because it was a situation I actually had a solution for.

I'd left Vancouver at six, planning to hit the galleries at ten when they opened. I hadn't counted on how bad the traffic's gotten on the I5, or the road construction that had snarled things up for miles. At least when I finally arrived, I had a starting point.

When I'd talked to Cassandra the previous evening, she'd given me the names of five galleries that handled Deirdre's work, including one that had handled her early work. The galleries weren't even hard to find, though parking was a nightmare. The various owners were happy to show me her stuff.

That was the easy part. The hard part was where it would lead me.

The paintings in the first three galleries I visited were similar in style and feel to the ones I'd seen at the Courtland. I was still in awe.

It was the paintings in the fourth gallery, Deirdre's early work, that stopped me cold. Cassandra had said there'd been a shift in Deirdre's style—but I hadn't imagined anything this extreme.

The younger Deirdre had painted only portraits of the women who dwell on society's fringes. Those women were brittle, trapped inside their frames like insects pinned under glass. In the later portraits, the women were alive—the humanity and the pain of each sitter reaching out and catching at my heart.

I hit gold with the fifth gallery. A spare space with only a few of Deirdre's works, they had an early Brandt hanging beside one of her newer paintings. Looking from one to the other was shocking.

The later work held a compassion for the humanity of the stripper that was absent from the earlier. The poverty and high costs of a life lived hard were apparent in both works, yet the earlier repelled me with its ugliness while the later drew me in, sharing something of the sitter's soul. How had Deirdre grown her talent to this extent?

Whatever change she'd made, it must have been cataclysmic. The painter of the first work knew her world in all its ugliness. The painter of the second knew and accepted herself, as well as her subjects. No wonder Shelley was jealous.

Looking from one to the other, I was jealous, too. If I had known how to make this kind of leap, I'd never have given up painting, Jayson or no Jayson. Even now, I'd give almost anything to be able to make the leap in my painting abilities that Deirdre had made in hers.

My search for Deirdre's killer suddenly took on new meaning.

No matter how difficult Deirdre's personality, she had been very, very talented. And she should have had years ahead of her in which to produce even better work.

Whoever had killed her deserved to be locked away for depriving us of whatever works Deirdre might have produced.

Unable to look at the paintings any longer, I turned away.

———

THE FOXY MERMAID is a strip joint down on the bay not far from the Pike Place Market, across the tracks and just beyond the tourist area. According to the owner of the fourth gallery, the one who'd first shown her works, Deirdre had danced here at one time and continued to come by in search of models.

I wasn't entirely sure why I was here, but something was nudging me towards Deirdre's past and this place seemed as good a starting point as any.

Walking into the beer-redolent main room, blinking against the sudden dimness, I recognized one of the dancers as the subject of the painting *Polyester Lily*, which was currently hanging in the Courtland. I waited until she finished her set with a series of flourishes around the pole set in the center of the stage, then approached. She stared me up and down with dead dark eyes and a face that said 'no visitors' as I asked about Deirdre.

"Yeah, I knew her," she finally said. "So what?"

It wasn't an invitation, but I wasn't giving up. "So have you seen her since she painted your portrait?"

She shrugged as if it didn't matter. "Dunno," she said.

How helpful. "You know she's dead? Murdered."

Another shrug, but the lines around her mouth hardened. Whatever she might know, she wasn't going to give it up easily.

"Her painting of you is incredible," I said on an impulse. "It makes me sick that she'll never paint another. And I'd like to know that whoever killed her will pay."

Lily listened in stony silence, then turned away.

It was my turn to shrug. I felt like an idiot, but I'd meant every word. Then Lily looked back over her shoulder, and beckoned to me to follow her.

I was pretty sure it wasn't a bright move—I didn't know this city or its players—but I followed her anyway.

In a tiny, crowded dressing room, layered with discarded clothes and thick with the scent of too-heavy perfume, Lily closed the door behind us and turned to face me. "She shouldn't have died," she said in a brittle voice. "But she made enemies."

Her face twisted in what it took me a moment to realize was a smile. When I didn't respond, her eyes darted to the door, then she licked her lips nervously and continued. "Deirdre—came up the hard way. She was one of us, never tried to pretend she wasn't, the only one who made it out. But it wasn't enough. She never really believed it, never."

"Believed what?"

"That she was out."

Looking at the squalor around me, I couldn't blame Deirdre for not wanting to come back here. The stale, over-scented air was making me nauseous. But surely Deirdre was making enough money that she'd never have to worry? "Why not?"

Lily shrugged. It seemed to be her favored response whenever I asked the wrong question. I tried again. "Did you know Deirdre long?"

"Yeah. We grew up together."

Looking at Lily's ravaged face, thinking about the up-scale galleries where Deirdre's paintings hung, it was hard to believe. "Here in Seattle?"

"Yeah."

"Where?"

"It's not there anymore. They condemned the buildings, paved over them."

Which probably summarized Lily's life, but not Deirdre's. "You said Deirdre made it out. Out of what?"

Lily's eyes darted around the room. "Just stuff. Places like this."

"Are there others who knew Deirdre from back then?"

"Dunno."

"She was a truly amazing artist. How did she start painting?"

Another shrug. "Dunno."

It seemed Lily had a very selective memory. Either that, or the life she'd lived had burned out large portions of her brain. Looking into her empty eyes, I could easily believe either possibility. "Did Deirdre always like art?"

A spark lit those dull eyes. "She used to draw. Always had paper and pencil, even when there weren't no food."

"Did anyone teach her? To paint?"

Lily's face closed tighter than before. She didn't answer.

I wasn't giving up. "When did she stop drawing?"

The lines in Lily's face deepened. "Men always looked at her. She always had something. Always."

Maybe I was hearing the answer to how Deirdre had started painting? "Men?"

Lily shrugged.

Finally I gave her my card and left, feeling frustrated. I hadn't handled Lily well. I sensed she knew much more about Deirdre than she'd shared, but I hadn't been able to reach her. She'd seemed afraid, but I couldn't even guess of what. Or of whom.

AS I LEFT the dressing room, hurrying through the darkened building, the back of my neck prickled. I didn't like the feeling. Taking a quick look behind me, I didn't spot anyone.

I hurried out the doors and into the relative security of the street outside, only to be reminded that I was in a questionable part of town, and it was late. My neck prickled again.

Quickening my stride, I heard footsteps behind me. When I spun around, there was no one there. Walking faster still, I was wishing I'd parked closer.

A heavy hand fell on my shoulder from behind, stopping and half-turning me. I had a fleeting glimpse of a tall heavy-set man, with a nose that had been broken and a scar bisecting his eyebrow. I'd never seen him before, and I wasn't anxious to spend any time with him now. Before he could say anything, I brought my knee up sharply and left him groaning on the sidewalk.

I lit out for my car. With enough adrenaline in my blood to fuel a racehorse, I was in the car and peeling out of the parking lot in what seemed like seconds.

My mind was racing almost as fast as my heart. Who was he? What did he want with me, and what did it have to do with Deirdre Brandt?

I'd been asking questions—had I made someone nervous? I hoped I hadn't caused problems for Lily. Because I was no-where near done with my questioning.

———

NO LESS DETERMINED TO find Deirdre's killer, but feeling shakier than I wanted to admit, I drove to my next destination, Deirdre's agent's home. I'd called earlier and got no response. I was hoping to catch her at home now.

My luck was in—Maryse Stevens was home, if not particularly pleased by my visit. I had the impression of a tough, cynical lady, who knew her stuff and didn't have time to have a softer side.

Nor did she have time for me, not until I told her that I was curious about why Deirdre's work had changed so much, and watched in astonishment as her features seemed to cave in on themselves.

She stepped back and opened the door wide enough for me to enter.

Wondering what I'd triggered, I walked into a foyer that seemed to be all black marble and glass. She led me up a white-carpeted stairway into a starkly modern room with a spectacular view of the downtown skyline, and gestured me towards the white leather sofa. She didn't wait for me to sit down.

"Why should an investigator care about Deirdre Brandt's art?" It was a long-time smoker's voice, harsh and rasping.

I seated myself, took my time in replying. "I need to know everything I can about Deirdre's life, if I'm to find her killer. As an artist, her art was a key part of her life. And from what I've seen of her work, Deirdre's art grew out of her past. Something in her life or her past got her killed. Her art is one place to start."

Maryse didn't say anything, just stared at me hard, then gestured towards the bar. I took it for acceptance, and nodded.

"White wine, please." I wouldn't dare drink red wine in a décor this white.

She fetched wine for me and what smelled like bourbon for herself. "Fine, I'll talk to you. I probably shouldn't, but what the hell, Dee's already dead. How much worse can it get?

Dee was a pistol, I'll say that for her. Not the easiest of clients, but her sales made up for that. Those paintings just about walked off the walls, they sold that well."

She took a deep drag off her cigarette, pausing to blow a perfect smoke ring. "I took her on right after her first big sale. Some little nobody had been repping her, didn't do much of a job of it. Still, I had more to work with, I'll give her that."

She took another deep drag, watching my reaction carefully. "If you've seen her work, you know what I mean?"

I nodded.

"I'm considered a pretty tough cookie in my world, but I was always glad that my connections were the only thing I had that Dee wanted. If you know what I mean?"

"Not exactly."

She lifted her glass in a mock toast and drained half of it, thunking it down on the coffee table between us. "I was divorced before I met Deirdre, and it wasn't long before she was making more money than I was. Not that I minded."

She reached for her glass and drained the rest of it in one long swallow, then took a deep drag on her cigarette. "Hell, the more she made, the more I made. But I wouldn't have wanted to be anybody she considered competition. Or one of Dee's models."

"Want another?" she asked, standing.

I looked at my wineglass, still three-quarters full and shook my head. As my host headed for the bar I decided that I'd better ask my questions while she was still capable of answering them. "What happened when someone had something Dee wanted?"

"She'd take it. She'd find a way and she'd take whatever she wanted."

"Do you know an artist named Shelley Masters?"

Maryse gave me a wry smile and drained half her refill, then turned to top it up again. Her words drifted over her shoulder. "That, my dear, was one of Dee's more civilized interactions. And she even gave him back when she was done."

"You figure she was done with Blake Masters?"

"Sure, she'd moved on. Her next guy was a senator—power, money, even pretty good looking. She always kept a hold, though—never let anyone go completely. Never knew when she might need them again."

Them?

"You said Blake was one of Deirdre's more civilized interactions. What about the others? The less civilized ones?"

She shrugged, drifting back to the sofa with a full glass. "Who could keep track?"

"Do you know any of the names?"

Maryse blew smoke at me. "And why should I tell you if I do?"

"Because it might help me find Deirdre's killer."

"And it might stir up a whole mess of trouble, too. No thanks."

"So you're going to let whoever killed Deirdre walk?"

"I'm going to let you, or the police, who are supposed to be looking into this, find the killer. You don't need me."

I wasn't doing any better with Maryse than I had with Lily. Who was Deirdre, that two such different women were reacting with the same look? Was it fear?

But Maryse wasn't Lily. She might be equally brittle, but she didn't strike me as being as vulnerable. Maryse I could push. "You said you wouldn't have wanted to be one of Deirdre's models. Why not?"

Maryse drained her bourbon. "Did you see the painting called *Polyester Lily*?"

"I saw it at the Courtland show." I didn't tell her I'd also talked to Lily.

"Wonderful work, isn't it? Well, very few people know this, and if Dee were still alive I wouldn't be repeating it. The less she knew I knew, the better. Lily knew Dee from the bad old days, when they were both strippers in places far worse than the ones you'll find Lily in these days."

I thought about the Foxy Mermaid and shuddered.

"Not that Dee would ever have admitted it, but I have my sources. I have to keep ahead of my artists, y'know."

Her words were beginning to slur, and I wondered how many she'd had before I arrived.

"Dee was heavy into coke back then and she financed her habit with a little dealing on the side. She got caught in a bad spot, and she set Lily up to take the fall. That's where Lily got that scar."

I couldn't stop my next question. "How could she paint her with such depth and compassion after treating her like that?"

Maryse shrugged, and blew smoke at me. "That's the paradox of Dee Brandt. After she started to make money, she pulled Lily out of the gutter, got her the job at the Foxy Mermaid, paid her to sit for the portrait. 'Course, she'd helped put her in the gutter in the first place."

She took another deep drag. "Dee had another cute habit—she liked to take away other women's men, parade them around, then dump 'em. She never painted the men, though. Only the women."

"I noticed there were no portraits of men. Why not?"

"Deirdre was good at capturing women's emotions."

I thought about those brilliant paintings, about what Maryse was implying. Deirdre had painted the wives of her lovers? "Are you saying Deirdre liked to paint traumatized women?"

She laughed coarsely. "Did I say that? Thought I said she liked to paint women."

I thought of the pampered, elegant women I'd seen in the some of the later paintings, of the pain in their eyes and in the set of their mouths. "Did she paint the rejected wives of all her lovers?"

"Most of them."

It was an ugly thought. But it gave me a way to find Deirdre's rejected lovers—identify her bejeweled subjects. "One thing I've been wondering. What caused the change in Deirdre's work? In her later paintings, she painted with such compassion, such honesty. It's as though the paint and canvas allow the women to speak the truths of their lives."

Maryse laughed again. "Deirdre saw something, all right. She used to tell me she'd found a way to see into people's souls. Dangerous work that, looking into people's souls. Maybe even got her killed. Ask too many questions, you might find out how."

Was that a threat? "What kind of questions?"

"If I knew that, I might be the one gets killed. I think it's time you left, now. Thanks so much for coming."

Not a threat then, a warning. As I drove back to my hotel, I couldn't get Maryse's words out of my head. "She used to tell me she'd found a way to see into people's souls."

What had Deirdre meant by that?

And was Maryse right? Had Deirdre become too much of a threat to someone? Was that why she was killed?

CHAPTER THIRTY

By the time I left Maryse, it was nearly seven, and I hadn't even talked to Blake Masters. I booked into the Horizon on Fifth, dumped my suitcase and laptop in a perfectly adequate hotel room, and gave him a call.

"Barbara? What are you doing in town? Where is Shelley?"

"Shelley's in Vancouver. I'm in town on another matter." Or two. I was here for both Kathleen and Shelley.

"What can I do for you?"

"I wondered if you're free to get together for a drink? I have a few questions I'd like to ask you about Deirdre."

"About Deirdre? Aren't you supposed to be looking for her killer?"

I squashed the urge to tell him I liked wasting people's time. "I need to understand the victim to solve a murder. Do you have time for a few questions?"

"Tonight?"

"If that's possible."

He hesitated. "I have a business dinner tonight, but I could probably meet you first. Say, seven-thirty at the Grand?"

———

SITTING opposite Blake in a dimly lit bar where the sound of conversation was muted by thick carpeting, dark woods and tapestry paneled walls, I guessed that he hadn't wanted to be overheard. This wasn't the kind of trendy, up to the minute place I'd have expected him to frequent. The other patrons were either white-haired or leaning towards each other with an intensity that radiated illicit passion.

Blake was waiting for me when I arrived, a half-empty martini glass in front of him. Just like the last time I'd met him. I wondered again if he had a drinking problem.

Nodding a greeting, he waved the waitress over. "Red wine, Barbara?"

"Yes, thanks. Cabernet if you have it."

"Mondavi?"

"Perfect. Thanks."

"How does Shelley seem to you?" Blake asked as the waitress walked off. "I've been so worried about her."

Sure he had. Which is why he was still in Seattle. "She's bearing up."

"Shelley's always been a trooper. I wish I could be with her this weekend, but at least I know she has you on her team."

"Why aren't you there, Blake? Surely any business could be postponed."

"Normally, yes. And believe me, I did everything I could to change the plans."

Sorry, didn't believe a word of it.

"But there was too much happening this weekend. I can't go into it—it's confidential, and far too convoluted to discuss anyway. But it truly is critical that I'm in town this weekend."

I'd have to look into the details of his practice. "I'm sure Shelley understands."

It was hard to tell in the dimness of the bar, but it looked like he flushed slightly. Guilty conscience? "She's an amazing woman."

"Yes, she is," I said, then thanked the waitress who'd just put my wine in front of me. Turning back to Blake, I said, "Now, about Deirdre?"

"Of course. What can I tell you?"

That's what I wanted to know. "Do you own any of her paintings?"

It clearly wasn't the question he'd been expecting. "No. No, I don't, though I wish I did. They're worth a fair bit now. And she was brilliant."

"Yes, she was. And the value of her paintings has certainly gone up. It's why most art critics remind me of vultures."

"Vultures?"

"They hang around waiting for the artist to die, then they feast."

"Oh." Blake didn't look impressed.

I guess you had to be an artist, even a failed one, to get the humor. Shelley would have laughed, bless her. "What I'm wondering is why Deirdre's painting style changed so much? It would have been nearly ten years ago."

"I didn't know her then. And I didn't know her that well anyway."

"Shelley says you did."

"Shelley...?"

He hadn't known Shelley knew? That wasn't the impression I'd got from her. "Shelley says you and Deirdre were lovers."

He drained his martini in one gulp and signaled for another. "I suppose there's no point lying about it. Yes, we were. But it had ended long before Deirdre died."

"Had it?"

"Why do you say it like that?"

"Because you were seen with Deirdre in various bars in Vancouver, in the days preceding her murder."

"Well, at least I know I'm getting my money's worth in hiring you," he said with a crooked smile. I suddenly caught a glimpse of the man Shelley had fallen for. "Though why you're looking into my movements I don't know."

"I'm not. I'm looking into Deirdre's."

"Ah. Well, we were not at that time lovers."

"No?"

"No."

"You were meeting because…?"

"Because she wanted to talk to me about a commission."

"You'd commissioned a painting from her? Of Shelley?"

"No, I hadn't actually commissioned a painting. And not of Shelley."

"Then?"

"Look, it was a stupid idea, and nothing came of it, okay?"

"But if you were still meeting about it, the idea was still alive?" I winced at my choice of words.

Blake's martini arrived and he slugged down half of it. "No, but Deirdre was persistent when she wanted something."

"Oh? And what did she want?"

"It's not relevant."

"Look, the woman is dead. You hired me to clear your wife's name, remember? And sometimes the smallest detail is relevant. So what did Deirdre want?"

"If you must know, she wanted to paint me."

She did? Or was it Blake who'd wanted a portrait of himself? "Deirdre didn't paint men."

"Look, that's why I didn't want to say anything, why I've never mentioned it. She wanted to branch out, to take on a new challenge. Only she didn't know if it would be successful, so she didn't want anyone to know. Especially when it wasn't going well."

"So she'd started this painting?"

Blake looked caught, as if he'd said something he hadn't meant to. I wondered how many martinis he'd had.

"No, I don't think so—she was always vague about her paintings, but I think she was upset about the concept for the painting of me. She couldn't get the images to come together, or something. And then I decided that I didn't want her to do a portrait of me. That was the end of it."

Maybe in his mind. But if what he was saying was true, had that been the end of it for Deirdre? I wondered if Maryse knew anything about Deirdre wanting to paint men.

"That explains why you were together in Vancouver. What about why you were together at the Sunshine Inn on Hornby Island the weekend before? And sharing a room, I might add."

He went pale, then inhaled the remainder of his martini. "No-one knew we were there. How did you find out?"

"Let's just say I'm thorough. Well?"

"Deirdre was—persuasive. She was upset about our breakup. And she was both passionate and convincing that we needed to be together again."

Something wasn't ringing true. "I thought she was the one to break off the relationship."

Pride warred with caution in his face, and caution won. "She did. But Deirdre was mercurial. It was one of her charms. She could be equally passionate about whichever side of an argument she happened to be on."

That little trait would make her a royal pain to live with.

If she actually lived with any of her conquests, that is. Which I tended to doubt, given Maryse's comments. "Yet I heard she was doing some pretty heavy flirting with one of the other guests."

He picked up his empty martini glass, stared at it as if wondering what had happened to the contents, put it back down. "Oh, that was Deirdre. She flirted with everyone. It didn't mean anything," he said, attempting a laugh. It failed.

"My sources say you were angry with her."

"Angry is a little strong. I was certainly annoyed. She'd dragged me over there, when I should have been with my wife, and then she ignored me. Really, I was angry with myself for agreeing to go in the first place."

"So you were angry."

"What? No. No, not angry, guilty. I should have stayed with Shelley."

Yeah, like he'd done this time. "You sure you weren't angry with Deirdre about Bill Rampage? The guy who was murdered?"

He paled, then flushed. "I don't like what you're insinuating. That poor guy—his death was nothing to do with me."

Was that genuine emotion I heard when he spoke of Bill? He hadn't known him before—I'd checked. "Do you know something about that death?"

"No, how could I?" he said. Too quickly?

"That's what I'm asking."

"Look, he was poisoned, which means he died one of the nastiest deaths possible. I didn't know the guy, but I feel for anyone who died like that."

Strong emotion there, for sure, but I couldn't identify it. Anger? Guilt? Fear? All of those?

Had he killed Bill over Deirdre? "You didn't feel Bill and Deirdre had betrayed you?"

"No. It was just flirting. And besides, we didn't have that kind of relationship."

"What kind did you have?"

"The convenient kind."

Pretty cold, if true. But somehow I didn't think it was true.

Something had flashed in his face, gone too quickly for me to read, but there was strong emotion there.

And that didn't equate to convenience. "And did Deirdre know this?"

"Naturally. Those were her terms."

Ouch. "And you agreed to those terms?"

He raised his brows at me. "I'm a normal male, Barbara. And she was a very sexy lady."

I'd walked right into that one. "And when you arrived in Vancouver? Your relationship just continued? Conveniently?"

I'd let the sarcasm slip through, but Blake ignored it. If he even heard it through the martini insulation, that is.

"That's right," he said. "I didn't see much of her though. I had to be there for Shelley."

Yeah, right. "Did Deirdre ever mention anyone she was worried about, or afraid of?"

"I've thought about it, but no. She never mentioned anything."

"We both know Shelley didn't kill Deirdre, so do you know anyone else who might have had a motive?"

"I wish I could think of someone else." He started to say something more, then stopped.

I let the silence hang, watching his face. Finding it handsome enough, with good bones, and well-tended skin—but empty.

After a moment he said, "People said Deirdre had enemies, but all I ever saw was envy. She was a talented, sexy woman who lived life on a grand scale. There weren't many who could match her, and she didn't bother to hide that."

"So you two parted on a good note? Despite Hornby?"

"Yes. Very much so. Knowing Deirdre added immensely to my life."

"Did Shelley know how you felt about Deirdre?"

A frown appeared. "She knew I admired her. In fact, I wished Shelley could be more like Deirdre. I had no idea she knew Deirdre and I had been lovers, though. And that worries me."

Poor Shelley. I couldn't imagine being married to this pathetic excuse for a man. "Why?"

"Well, it certainly gives her motive, doesn't it?"

Only if you were worth keeping, you jerk. "You can't mean you think Shelley is guilty?"

"I don't want to think it."

Was he actively trying to frame Shelley?

The thought flashed through my mind, illuminating so many things. Maybe he didn't just want Shelley in jail. Maybe he intended to participate in the process.

And if so, he'd set her up nicely. Leaving her alone in Vancouver. Dropping hints to me.

Who else had he told?

And was this all about his grandmother's money? Or was there something else?

———

ONE THING WAS clear to me. I couldn't keep working for this jerk. Not when I was beginning to suspect Shelley's interests and his conflicted when it came to clearing her name.

But I couldn't tell him that part. My mind raced.

"Blake, I'm afraid going to have to excuse myself from this case," I said. "Consider this my official notice. I'll send you a full report to date, and reimburse you for the balance of the retainer."

Was that a look of satisfaction in his eyes? He covered it instantly, if so.

"This is rather sudden," he said. "May I ask why? I thought you and Shelley were friends."

"We are," I said. "That's the problem. Things are looking bad for her—very bad—and I'm not making any progress. Everything I've uncovered to date points directly to Shelley."

Which was telling in itself, given that she was innocent. But Blake wouldn't see that.

He didn't. Instead he gripped his glass a little tighter, shoulders slumping. "I can't persuade you to stay on?" he said heavily.

It would have been more effective if I hadn't caught the sly sideways glance he gave me.

"No. I can't bear to be the one who fails Shelley. I'm more use to her as a friend right now than I am as an investigator. Besides, Ian Craig is a damn good lawyer, and he'll have the excellent investigators on payroll. Shelley needs the best."

Blake didn't even pretend to argue. "I respect your candor. You've done good work for my wife, regardless of the outcome. I'll give Craig a call, let him know. And don't worry about the retainer. You've more than earned all of it already."

I thanked him, though it nearly choked me to do so.

"One last request," I said. "I'd like to be the one to explain this to Shelley. If it's okay with you?"

And to tell her that I was now working solely for her.

Blake gave me a sad look and a magnanimous nod.

Jerk.

———

THE "WHY" of Blake's behavior continued to escape me. Once I'd removed myself from the case, Blake, not surprisingly, had nothing further to say. He went on to his 'business meeting' and I went back to the hotel, angry and determined.

I called Shelley and told her I'd talked to Blake, and that from now on I'd be working only for her.

"I don't understand," she said. "You won't be working on my defense any more?"

"I won't be working for Blake any more," I said. "I'm still working to clear your name."

"But…"

"Meanwhile, you need to find yourself a new lawyer. An impartial one."

"Ian Craig is very good."

"Sure. But Blake hired him, not you. And I think you need someone you hired yourself."

She drew in a soft breath. "Barbara? Is there something about Blake you're not telling me?"

"I'm still unravelling Deirdre's life, and who might have hated her enough to kill her. But I'm increasingly uncomfortable about the extent of her relationship with Blake. And having your defense lawyer reporting to him seems a little too much like a conflict of interest."

"Oh," Shelley said. There was a little silence. "How bad is it?"

"I don't have enough of the picture yet," I said. "I'll brief you when I'm back in town. You focus on finding a good criminal defense lawyer. Do you know anyone local?"

"No."

I gave her Claire Chan's number. "Tell her I told you to call."

"Thanks, Barbara. And please call me as soon as you have anything."

I promised to do so, and rung off. Then I ordered room service and spent the next three hours chasing information on the internet.

It seemed Blake was a partner with three other surgeons with various specialties, and they were doing very nicely indeed. Given the little I know about the US medical system, it was possible he was in discussions with an HMO or even another partnership about a merger. Maybe he really couldn't leave town.

I wasn't buying it, though. He'd been too nervous. He was hiding something, and I was determined to find out what that something was.

In a merger, the personal reputation and history of the partners usually becomes an issue. Having a murderer for a wife would be a major business liability, yet Blake hadn't even mentioned that little problem. Which, to my way of thinking, only strengthened the possibility that he might be trying to frame Shelley.

As I stared at the financials on the screen, I thought about Blake's statement that Deirdre had wanted to paint him, had in fact already begun a portrait. Was he lying about that, too?

Somehow I didn't think so. He'd been too uncomfortable, too reluctant to give me details. So what was that all about?

Was there something odd about Deirdre's relationship with her subjects? Maryse had said Deirdre had seen into her subject's souls. Thinking about Deirdre's later works, I could believe that she had. But how had she done it?

I began a search for information on Deirdre's works. By ten-fifteen, I had a listing of a good number of her paintings, and who owned them. All were portraits, all were of women.

The ones I'd already seen, at the Courtland and the five galleries here, represented about a fifth of her work. It was a workable number. Now, who might recognize the subjects, or rather, those subjects who came from the same world as Blake and Shelley? I picked up the phone.

CHAPTER THIRTY-ONE

A t ten the following morning, I met Angie Barrett at the Fifth Avenue Gallery. Cassandra had come through for me again, not only giving me Angie's name, but also calling her and setting everything up. I might have to actually consider liking the woman if she kept this up.

Angie was a petite, vivacious redhead, wearing a fitted turquoise jacket over a black sweater, skirt and high-heeled black boots. Her outfit probably cost double what I spent on clothes in a year. Maybe two.

"Mrs. Barrett? Thank you for meeting me."

She held out a hand and dark eyes danced at me. "Oh, it's Angie, please. And don't thank me. This is so much fun. I've never helped out on an investigation before."

At least she was enthusiastic. "I'm Barbara. Are you ready?"

"Lead on."

We went from painting to painting, with Angie unfailingly identifying the sitters.

"This is Serena Witherspoon."

"Were her husband and Deirdre involved?"

"Oh, my, yes. He was one of Deirdre's more notorious

conquests. Not that the man isn't a skirt-chaser. He is, and first-class, too. But he'd been discreet before. Serena could choose to ignore what was going on. And she did."

"Not this time?"

"Deirdre had the man so tightly wrapped around her little finger he'd do anything she asked. Which included flashy jewelry that she proudly proclaimed had come from him, designer gowns and only the best restaurants. He even took Deirdre away for the weekend on Serena's birthday."

"Ouch. How did Serena take all this?"

"My dear, she was livid. Absolutely livid. Swore she'd get even with Deirdre if it was the last thing she did."

"And did she?"

"She divorced Witherspoon, took him for everything she could. But if that was supposed to be her revenge on Deirdre, it backfired. Deirdre dumped Witherspoon the following day."

"What did Serena do then?"

"As far as anyone knows, she put it behind her. Cut Deirdre cold every chance she got, of course, and made sure Deirdre was never invited to any function her circle was involved with."

"That's all?"

"That's all."

"And was it enough for Serena?"

Angie shrugged. "Who knows."

"When was this portrait painted?"

"A few months before Serena divorced Witherspoon."

"You're kidding. Why would Serena sit for it?"

"You would have to ask Serena. She's never said, and no one dared ask. Personally, I'd guess Witherspoon asked her to."

"What? Why?"

"Again, I don't know, but I'd guess a last-ditch attempt at recon-ciliation."

"Does Serena still live in Seattle?"

"Of course, as does Witherspoon."

I nodded, made a note, and we moved on to the next painting.

"Belinda Dorset," Angie said. "Pretty much the same story as Serena."

"Did she divorce her husband too?"

"Indeed she did."

"After threatening Deirdre?"

"Yes, and after she threw a glass of wine in Deirdre's face at a cocktail party that some incompetent hostess had invited both of them to."

"Was this before or after Deirdre painted Belinda's portrait?"

"Oh, after. A few weeks, maybe a month later, I think."

"And Belinda still lives in Seattle?"

"Yes."

I made another note. "And this one?"

"Janine Haughton. She was engaged to Alan Creighton."

"The industrialist?"

"Yes."

"Was engaged. Deirdre?"

"Yes, indeed. Deirdre took one look at Alan and made a play for him."

"He fell for it?"

"When Deirdre put her mind to it, the men couldn't seem to resist her."

I thought of Deirdre as I'd last seen her, stretched out on a gurney, fighting to live. "Why?"

"She was very vivid, very dramatic, with a husky voice and an intimate way of looking at a man. I've heard more than one gentleman say she dripped sex." Angie looked at me and grinned. "Personally, I suspect she'd learned more than a few sexual tricks, and she wasn't shy about using them. Anywhere."

I raised an eyebrow.

Angie giggled. "There were enough rumors that I'm sure it's true. She'd choose her next victim, then find a secluded spot at a party or function."

"She seduced them in public?"

"The next thing to it, I think. Though on a couple of occasions, she'd be seen leaving a bathroom or antechamber with one of her conquests, both of them rather mussed."

I thought about it. The element of risk probably added to the excitement for Deirdre and to the attraction for her victim. If you liked sex that way.

Me, I preferred something a little more intimate. Suddenly, I missed Nick intensely—the closeness, the heat between us. Annoyed with myself, I shook off the feeling. "What about this one?"

"Althea Carter. More of the same."

We both contemplated the portrait for a moment. "She doesn't look happy."

"No. She looks bitter, as if she's regretting every one of those diamonds she's wearing."

"Deirdre was very talented."

"But twisted, don't you think?"

I was beginning to get a sense of exactly how twisted Deirdre had been. It worried me, because it seemed to be tied directly into her brilliance as an artist. "Who's next?"

———

STANDING near the door of the fourth and final gallery, I had sore feet, a list of women and their ex-husbands to talk to, and a new respect for Angie's in-depth knowledge of her world. It wasn't a world I wanted any part of, but if I'd kept on with my painting, these people would have been my clients. I was suddenly glad I didn't have to worry about it.

I turned to Angie. "I need your advice."

"Barbara, I'm happy to help, in case you haven't already figured that out. This is too much fun."

"I need to talk to some of these women."

"About their portraits? That may not be easy. Most of them want to forget about the paintings, and about the artist."

That didn't surprise me. "I still need to talk to them."

"Why?"

"Because it may have a bearing on who killed Deirdre."

"You think one of these women killed Deirdre? You're kidding me, right?"

"I don't know who killed Deirdre. But I think her art had something to do with it."

"Which is why we've been looking at all these portraits, right?"

"Right. So can you suggest anyone who would be willing to talk to me?"

She nodded. "Sure can. And your timing is perfect, too. Annabelle will be about ready to start the cocktail hour. I'm sure she'd be happy to join us."

Before I could respond, she'd pulled out her cell phone and was talking to Annabelle, who, it appeared, was willing to meet with me.

Angie disconnected, and beamed at me. "The lounge at the Meridien, in half an hour. She'll meet us there. Okay?"

I hadn't planned on having Angie along, but what could I say? She'd been amazingly helpful so far. Even if she was enjoying herself a little more than I was comfortable with.

Murder investigations are not supposed to be fun. Death is too real for that.

"Thanks. That works," I said.

———

HALF AN HOUR LATER, I was sipping a Merlot, watching Annabelle Martins saunter towards us. She was exquisitely put together, still far too thin, but she looked less haunted than she had in her portrait. Even so, I could see that Deirdre had caught the essence of the woman on canvas—pretty, shallow and rather frightened. How had she seen her so clearly?

And how Annabelle must hate that portrait.

Angie waved her over, and pulled back a chair. Annabelle sank into it, and the waitress appeared with the cosmopolitan that Angie had pre-ordered for her.

"Glad you could make it, Annabelle," Angie said. "This is Barbara O'Grady. She's a private investigator, looking into the murder of Deirdre Brandt."

Annabelle took a swig of her pink drink, eyeing me over the top of the glass. "I hope you don't think I killed her," she said. "I'd have liked to, of course, but that opportunity never came my way."

"Why not?"

Annabelle grimaced. "Deirdre was too fond of the spotlight, surrounded herself with too many powerful people. And I don't know much about poisons and such. Besides, I'd have preferred to stab her in that rather obvious chest of hers. In front of witnesses. If that wouldn't have ended with me in jail, of course. Which it would have."

"True. Why did you want her dead?"

"She was a bitch."

Angie patted Annabelle's hand. "She's dead now, dear. I think you can tell the truth. It might even help."

Annabelle looked at Angie, then gulped down some more of her drink. "Maybe you're right."

She turned to me. "It was bad enough when she went after my husband, then paraded her conquest in front of me while the whole world watched. But Duncan has always had a roving eye. I'd have got over that."

"So what did she do that you didn't get over?"

Annabelle finished off her cosmo, signaled for another one. "Painted my portrait. Oh, it's not what she put on the canvas, though that's bad enough."

Thinking about the stark revelation that was her portrait, I could only agree. I cringed slightly even talking about to her about it. And there was something worse? "What then?"

Annabelle leaned forward, lowered her voice. "I'm only telling you this because it was like a refined form of torture. I'd have to sit there for hours, and the whole time she was pick, pick picking at me. Did I know Duncan liked to be mastered in bed? Did I know he'd asked her to have sex with both of us, at the same time? Did I know he considered me lacking in bed? Did I know he'd nearly decided to marry my sister instead of me?"

She drank down half of her fresh drink. "It was as if she was determined to strip me bare, leave me nothing that was mine."

I thought about the portraits I'd been so envious of. Was that how Deirdre had seen into her subjects' souls? By violating them, stripping them bare? I thought about Lily's face as she talked of Deirdre.

It fit. It was ugly, but it fit.

I put down my wine, not sure I could stomach another mouthful.

"Why didn't you stop, refuse to sit for her again?"

Annabelle shrugged. "I knew you'd ask that, and I don't know if I can tell you. She was very clever. She used Duncan to make me stay. He kept hinting that if I let Deirdre finish the portrait, he'd come back to me, and then everything would be back to normal. And by the end of the first session with Deirdre, I felt that I'd be lucky to have him, that no other man could ever want me."

She emptied her glass and stood up, throwing a twenty on the table. "I'm sorry, Angie. I can't talk about this any more. Give me a call next week sometime."

"I will," Angie promised. "And thanks, Annabelle."

"Sure," said Annabelle, and hurried out.

I looked at Angie.

"Well," I said. "Think they'd all be like that?"

She looked sad. "She doesn't have much depth, Annabelle, but she's a good person. She didn't deserve that."

"No. No, I suspect none of them deserved that."

"I agree. And yes, I think they'd all be like that. And I think Deirdre deserved to die. No matter how great a painter she was."

I took a deep breath, released it. Tried not to think of Deirdre as a fellow artist, or in any way related to me or to the art I still, reluctantly, cared about.

"I think I agree. But I still need to know who killed her."

Angie shrugged. "I can't help you there. I'm not sure I want to know. They should probably be rewarded for killing her, not jailed."

A large part of me agreed with her—the outraged part that apparently was still an artist, despite my protestations to the contrary. "Maybe. But unless I find the real killer, it's my friend Shelley who'll be in jail. For life."

"That's Shelley Masters, isn't it? I'd heard she'd been arrested. Which is odd when you think that Shelley is one of the few Deirdre didn't paint."

"She didn't? I wonder why not," I said, more to myself than to her.

"Maybe she couldn't find a big enough weak spot to destroy her with."

"Or maybe she had another victim in mind," I said slowly, thinking about my conversation with Blake.

"Oh?"

Maybe Deirdre had decided to paint Blake rather than Shelley. But why?

Deirdre seemed to destroy her models. Was there something she thought she could use against Blake? Was that what the flirting on Hornby had been about?

If she'd kept that up, what would Blake's reaction have been? Assuming Deirdre really had decided to paint Blake, that is. "I'll tell you about it when I can. If I can."

"I guess I'll have to be content with that. But do let me know if I can help."

"I can't thank you enough for all the help you've given me."

"Certainly you can. Tell me what happens."

"I will. And give me a call if you think of anything else that might be pertinent," I said, giving her my card.

CHAPTER THIRTY-TWO

Back in my hotel room, I poured a glass of Merlot from the mini-bar to take away the bad taste of the day's efforts. Then I ran a hot bath and sank back to contemplate the list of names I'd compiled.

I thought about what Annabelle and Angie had said. Deirdre had painted every one of the spurned wives or fiancées of her lovers.

Every one of them except for Shelley, that is. Why not Shelley? And why the interest in Blake instead? Deirdre had never painted men.

Just stolen them.

I reached for my cell phone, punched in the number.

"Hello?"

"Shelley? It's Barbara."

"Where are you?"

"Still in Seattle."

"Why does it sound like you're in an echo chamber?"

"I'm in the bath."

"Nice. Hard day?"

"Don't even ask."

"Okay, I won't. What do you need to know?"

"How did you guess I needed to know something?"

"Why else would you be calling me from Seattle?"

"True enough. So, I've been looking at a lot of Deirdre's paintings, especially the wives of her ex-lovers."

"Why are you—never mind. You're the detective. And you want to know why she never painted me, right?"

"Yup."

"Truth is, I don't know."

"She never asked you."

"No. Never."

"Do you know of any other wives or girlfriends of lovers she didn't paint?"

There was a short silence. "I'm not sure I've seen all of her work, but I can only think of a couple. Serena Witherspoon, for one."

"She's hanging in the Fifth Avenue Gallery."

"Marcia Feldman."

I checked my list. "Eastside Gallery."

"Then no, I can't think of any of them she didn't paint. Except me. I wonder why?"

"I think I might know. Apparently she was considering doing a portrait of Blake."

"Deirdre was? But she doesn't—or rather she didn't—paint men."

"Exactly what I said. So you didn't know about it?"

"No. And I hadn't heard a whisper, either. It would have been the story of the year if anyone had known about it."

"It was that big a deal?"

"Deirdre was hyped as a woman's artist, a woman capable of seeing into the soul of another woman." She paused. "It was true, too. Which hardly seems fair when she was such an awful person."

I now fully agreed with that assessment. "So if Deirdre had started painting men?"

"She'd probably have become an even bigger artist. If she could pull it off. You know, I had the impression that all that hype about her being a woman's artist had begun to grate on her."

"Grate on her? How?"

"Well, a definition is limiting, isn't it? And Deirdre was always competitive, always lusting after the next rung on the ladder."

Maryse had said she'd never want to be between Deirdre and something she wanted. I wondered how badly Deirdre had wanted to break out of that definition. And exactly what she'd have to do.

"I'm curious. Would you have posed for her?"

"I like to think not, but I know that for some of the others, the men promised to end things with Deirdre if their wives would sit for a portrait. If Blake had asked, I might have done it. And Deirdre is, was, an increasingly renowned artist. Having her do your portrait was an honor. Of sorts."

"Some honor."

"Yeah."

I was still thinking about Deirdre lusting after that next level. "So if Deirdre had started a painting of Blake, who would know about it?"

"Well, Blake, of course. What does he say?"

"He got very evasive on the subject. Who else?"

"Maryse, I guess. Her agent. I can't think of anyone else. Deirdre didn't trust people. Her past life, I guess."

"Or she was judging others by herself. I think you're being too easy on her, Shelley."

"Well, the woman is dead."

"Yes, and if we're to find out why, we have to know who she antagonized, and how."

"You're right." She sighed. "This is so hard. You talked to Blake, though?"

"Yes, and I'll probably talk to him again before I come back. For what it's worth, he was on his way to a 'business meeting' last night."

"You didn't believe him?"

"I'm not sure. Do you know if there's been any discussion about selling out his partnership? Or expanding it?"

She gave a bitter little laugh. "That's the kind of thing Blake never discussed with me. Why?"

"His financials allow for the possibility, anyway. So his excuse for staying in Seattle might be legitimate."

"I wish I could believe that changed things. But it doesn't, does it Barbara?"

I thought about Blake's leap to incriminate Shelley. "I wish I could tell you it did, but I can't. I don't know, Shelley. One thing I did wonder, though. Does Blake have a drinking problem?"

There was a silence.

"Shelley?"

"Sorry, you took me by surprise. Normally he's fairly abstemious. Likes to think of himself as a connoisseur."

"Connoisseur of what?"

"Red wine and single malt scotch. And probably women, too."

I ignored the bitter aside. "Both times I've met with him he's been drinking martinis. Plural."

"That isn't like him. The only time I've ever seen Blake drink like that was when the market fell and he lost a lot of money."

"So he tends to drink if he's stressed?"

"I guess. I've never seen him order a martini, though."

I made a mental leap. "What was Deirdre's drink of choice, do you know?"

"Deirdre? She liked martinis, why?" Then, slowly, "Oh, you don't think he's—mourning her?"

Was he mourning her? Or celebrating her demise? "At this point, I'm not sure what I think. Look, wait till I get back, and I'll give you my full report."

"I guess. Did you want to ask me anything else?"

"Not tonight. I'll call if anything comes up." But now I needed to talk to Maryse Stevens again.

"Okay. See you in a few days. And Barbara? Thanks."

"All part of the service, Shelley."

My bath was getting cold, so I got out, wrapped myself in one of the hotel's plush robes and put on a pot of coffee. Ensconcing myself in the overstuffed chair by the window, I dialed Maryse's number.

"Hello?"

"Ms. Stevens? It's Barbara O'Grady calling. I have a couple of questions about Deirdre Brandt's work, and I wondered if you'd meet me for a drink."

"Ms. O'Grady? I thought I made it clear that I'd told you everything I'm going to."

Well, that was pleasant. "I may have some new information since we last talked."

"I don't know why you think I'd care."

"Perhaps because I've found out that Deirdre had started painting men."

"Nonsense. Deirdre painted women."

"Yes, so you told me. However, I've had confirmation from several sources that she was working on a portrait of Blake Masters at the time of her death."

Okay, so I was stretching the truth a little. But Blake's evasions had been a kind of confirmation.

I heard a harshly indrawn breath. "So that's why she never painted Shelley Masters."

"It seems so."

"If what you're saying is true, Ms. O'Grady, and it seems quite a stretch, then where is this famous painting?"

What I heard in her voice this time wasn't disbelief, it was greed. "If you haven't seen it, then I'm betting it's at her studio. Her private studio."

From what I'd learned of Deirdre, she had to have a private studio.

"What makes you think it's there?"

So I was right. "You haven't been there since she died?"

"I couldn't face it."

"Too many memories?"

"Too many bad vibes."

It wasn't what I'd expected from a woman as artificial as Maryse. "You do have a key, don't you?"

"I'm her executor. Of course I have a key. But you haven't told me why you think the painting is there."

"Why don't you meet me there, and I'll show you."

"Fine, if only to get rid of you. It's on eighteenth." And she gave me the number. "I'll meet you outside the building in half an hour."

—————

I WAS PACING outside Deirdre's ultramodern loft when Maryse showed up, fifteen minutes late. She didn't apologize, just brushed past me and fumbled with the keys. "I hope you're not wasting my time, Ms. O'Grady," she threw over her shoulder as the door opened.

But it was fine for her to waste my time? Grimacing behind her back, I followed the agent into the elaborate apartment. Thick white rugs covered dark wood floors, huge windows showed a glittering cityscape framed by pure white walls. It was beautiful, though too stark for my taste.

Maryse didn't slow down, heading for a wrought iron spiral stairway at the end of the entry hall. We climbed to a large room with a spectacular view of the city lights.

Maryse didn't pause to take in the view, just flipped on the overhead lights and stood still, gaze searching the room. We both spotted the paintings at the same time. Three of them—two completed, one foggy and incomplete. The completed paintings were of women. The incomplete one depicted a man. Blake Masters.

Without a word, we moved forward. It was Blake's portrait that held our attention.

"Why is it so foggy?" I asked Maryse. "Was this a stage all her paintings went through?"

"No. Typically, Deirdre's work was decisive. She'd do a basic sketch, then from there it was all bold strokes."

I looked closer. The face was recognizably Blake, but it was as if he was out of focus. No, that wasn't right. Viewed in isolation, the portrait was adequate, but compared to the portraits beside it, Blake's face just didn't come alive. She'd softened the background as if the contrast might make him stronger, but it hadn't worked.

"Too bad she never finished it," Maryse said. "It would have been worth a fortune.

"If it was any good."

"Oh, it would have been good. You didn't know Dee. She would have done whatever she had to do, no matter the cost, to make sure it was good."

"She didn't do any bad paintings?" Everyone does bad paintings occasionally—that canvas that you eventually abandon because it will never reflect the vision you were trying to capture.

"Not Deirdre. Not ever."

Looking back at the unfinished canvas, suddenly I could see what was wrong. Deirdre hadn't found her vision. She'd thought she had, but when she started to paint, it wouldn't come together. "So she wouldn't have abandoned this?

"Never."

"Not even if it never came together for her?"

"You didn't know Dee. She would never back down from a challenge."

"So how would she have faced this particular challenge?"

Maryse shrugged, and waved her cigarette towards the canvas. "You'd have to ask him."

"Why?" Did Maryse know how Deirdre captured her victim's souls on canvas?

"Dee worked very closely with her subjects," Maryse said, sauntering towards the painting, then looking at it with her head cocked to one side. "I'm sure she'd have got real close to this one. He's a looker, isn't he? Poor sod."

So Maryse did know about Deirdre's methods. And Deirdre had

begun seeing Blake again. Was that after she'd tried and failed to capture him in paint?

What was it he'd said—Deirdre had wanted to talk about his portrait? Talking wouldn't have been all she wanted. But how badly did she want to break free of the label "woman's painter"?

And what price would she pay for that freedom? Goosebumps rose along my spine at the thought.

"Why not go back to painting women, when that came so easily to her, and this one was coming hard?"

"I've seen Dee go out of her way to find new challenges to defeat, and the harder they were, the better she liked them. She was a woman who always had to win."

Or one who couldn't afford to lose. I thought about Lily at the Foxy Mermaid. Lily had said Deirdre never believed she'd made it out.

"Maybe she felt she had something to prove," I said. "But how far would she go to prove it?"

"What do you mean?"

"Never mind." Maryse wasn't the one who could answer the questions that were running through my brain. And I somehow didn't think Blake Masters, who probably could answer them, would be willing to.

Back at the Horizon, I ordered steak and a salad from room service and poured a large glass of wine. Flipping through my notes, I went from Maryse to Lily, from Angie to Annabelle, and back again. They were all telling me the same thing.

Deirdre had used her subject's pain to see into the depth of their souls. She'd captured those souls on canvas, earning herself a career and an international reputation. And Deirdre had caused the pain she painted so evocatively.

Had that been the price of her genius?

Because Deirdre had painted with genius—it was there on the canvas, bold and clear. But what about Deirdre herself? What had those brilliant paintings cost her, what had lust for success turned her into?

It was a frightening thought for any artist. How far would I be willing to go to paint the paintings I knew I could do?

I knew I wasn't willing to do what Deirdre had done, not even for that career I used to dream about. Hell, I hadn't even been willing to suspend my own self-judgment. I'd allowed myself to be driven away from something that mattered to me. Then.

If I allowed myself to be drawn back to painting, what would I be prepared to do in order to succeed at this second chance? What would I be prepared to stake? My own soul? Others?

It was an unsettling thought, and one I didn't have time to dwell on now.

The state of Deirdre's soul wasn't my business, but the cause of her death was. And there was no doubt in my mind that her paintings had led to her murder.

Let's face it, anyone Deirdre had painted had a motive to kill her. And part of me didn't blame them.

I don't believe anyone has the right to take the life of another human being, except in self-defense. But Deirdre had tried to destroy her subjects, and she had perverted her art. It didn't excuse murder, but perhaps it explained it.

But Deirdre hadn't painted Shelley. She'd painted all the other dumped wives, but not Shelley.

Instead, Deirdre had painted Blake, or tried to. Only his portrait had failed. And according to Maryse, who should know, Deirdre wasn't a woman to give up. To succeed, Deirdre probably had to paint Blake in pain.

Yet breaking off their relationship hadn't caused him enough pain, judging by the portrait I'd seen. Had Deirdre thought it would?

And how would she have reacted to that failure? Not well, I was guessing. How would she then have gone about creating the degree of pain she needed in Blake?

And how far was she prepared to go?

What would Blake value so deeply that stripping it away would leave his soul naked to her brush? Had Deirdre known him well enough to know? And had Blake known what she was up to?

He must eventually have figured it out, but when?

Too many questions, with no facts. Except that Deirdre had never painted Shelley, and Blake was trying to cast doubts on her innocence.

I made a last note and rolled my shoulders back to release the tension they were holding. I needed a break from the ugliness of this case.

I brushed out my hair, added some lipstick and headed for the hotel bar.

CHAPTER THIRTY-THREE

The following morning I grabbed a coffee then went out for a run. More wine, empty chatter and a couple of lame pickup attempts the night before hadn't improved my mood. Nor had it dispelled the lingering bleakness caused by thinking about Deirdre's choices. Where was Nick when I needed him?

I hadn't slept well. The conversations I'd had over the previous two days played in an endless loop in my mind. The things I'd learned about Deirdre and her painting style made the muscles behind my eyes ache.

I kept seeing Blake's face as he said Deirdre had wanted to paint his portrait.

I needed to run. I needed the release, the feel-good endorphins. I also needed to process some of the questions I'd been asking the previous night, and the conclusions they seemed to lead to.

Any further questions could wait until I figured out what my intuition was trying to tell me. And running is the only thing I've found that shuts shut off the logical side of my brain long enough to do that. Except for sex, that is.

As my feet pounded along the path, I breathed deeply, concentrating on the rhythm of my breath and the looseness that gradually flowed into my muscles. Despite lowering gray clouds and a light drizzle, I'd driven to Volunteer Park—I love the quiet and the fresh greenness of it. Plus the way I was feeling I couldn't face the urban decay or the looks I'd get if I ran downtown.

And as I ran, my unruly thoughts gradually solidified until I realized I'd only been looking at half the equation. I'd been so focused on whether Blake had killed Deirdre, I'd forgotten about Bill Rampage.

Two poisonings, two deaths. Blake present at both. He'd felt some strong emotion about Bill Rampage, and if my speculations were correct Deirdre was threatening him with something.

But did Blake have it in him to kill, not once, but twice? What kind of threat could Deirdre have made that would push him to murder?

It isn't easy for most of us to take a life, no matter what we see on TV. Even sociopaths have to work up to it. And most of us aren't sociopaths. So why do we kill?

Usually to protect someone or something we care about so deeply we see no alternative. What would that someone or something be for Blake? If he'd killed Deirdre to stop her from inflicting whatever pain she was inflicting on him, then why kill Bill? Unless it was losing Deirdre that Blake feared?

But he'd already lost her once, and survived quite nicely. Or seemed to.

What if Blake had never intended to kill Bill? What if the poison had been intended for Deirdre, and somehow ended up in Bill's room? Was that even possible?

The rooms were across from each other, but surely Blake would have known his own room. Unless Deirdre had spent the night in Bill's room?

No, Kathleen had been with Bill.

I wasn't liking that explanation anyway. It glossed over a few things, such as if Blake had killed Bill by mistake, then why wait another five days before trying to kill Deirdre?

Assuming I wasn't reaching here, and Blake really was trying to kill Deirdre.

———

I WAS TURNING those why's and wherefores over in my mind all the way back to Vancouver. The only conclusion I came to was that I really needed to talk to Shelley. When I finally made it through the customs lineup and the rain-slowed tunnel traffic and into downtown, I intended to go straight to Shelley's hotel.

I had a few questions about Blake and what made him tick.

But I made the mistake of detouring by my office to check my messages. There were ten of them, and every caller wanted to speak with me urgently.

Patrick the pharmacist had left the first message, on the Friday. "Sorry I didn't get back to you, Barbara, but I wasn't quite finished my research into that list of yours. Plus I had a date with a hot stud, and I confess it slipped my mind. But I should have it for you later today, if that helps?"

I grinned at the thought of Patrick's hot date, the details of which I was very sure I didn't want to know. As I deleted the message, I thought about the possibility that Bill had died by lethal plant, and wondered about Blake's knowledge of the local flora. Something else to ask Shelley.

The second message was from Brad Bramwell. "Barbara, I'm still trying to reach Kathleen Marshall, and I'm not having much luck. Have you heard from her? Please call me."

He didn't sound happy. I thought about Kathleen at Shady Groves and felt vaguely guilty. Should I be telling Brad about her condition?

Or keep quiet until I sorted out whether Blake Masters could have been Bill Rampage's killer?

Well, at least if they couldn't find Kathleen, they couldn't arrest her, right? And I was mostly sure she hadn't killed her former lover, so talking to her wouldn't clarify anything for Brad.

Next was a call from my mother, sounding excited. "Barbara, I have a date for my first jump. It's on the 9th, three weeks from now. You'll be there, won't you?"

I made a note of the date. I had promised to be there, so I would be, even if the idea of watching my mother fall out of a plane, parachute or no parachute, made me feel ill.

Susanna was next, sounding annoyed. "Barbara, I haven't heard back from you. I need to know if you and Nick are coming for dinner. It's this Sunday, in case you've forgotten. I have to finalize the seating plan. Call me back as soon as you get this."

As I listened, I felt guilty, then illogically, resentful. Like I had time for this? I started to hit 7 to delete the message, then reconsidered, and hit 8.

"Susanna, it's Barbara. Sorry, Nick and I won't be able to make it on Sunday, I'm in the middle of a case. Maybe another time."

I felt a flash of satisfaction. This way I hadn't actually had to talk to her, and I hadn't given her any ammunition about the state of Nick's and my relationship. Whatever that was.

As if to mock my doubts, the next message was from Nick. "Barbara, I'm still out of town, but I'm at a number where I can be reached until Sunday." He rattled off the number. "Call me."

Today was Monday. Why hadn't I thought to check my messages? But then, why hadn't he called on my cell phone?

With a grimace, I dialed his home number, left a message that I was back in town. Maybe he'd get it.

The next message was Patrick again, on Saturday. "I've got that list for you, Barbara. I find it quite amazing how many poisons we actually grow in our gardens."

I found it distressing, actually. I didn't want to look at something beautiful and wonder how hard it would be to kill someone with it.

Hard on the heels of that thought came the idea for a painting— a garden scene, all greens and jewel tones but with an undertone of danger—beautiful but deadly. There is a woman in the scene, or no, just her hat, a book left by a bench, a pitcher and half-drunk glass of lemonade, water still beaded on the glass. The hint of lurking menace heightens the appreciation of beauty, its fragility and transience.

My fingers literally ached to pick up a paintbrush instead of a pen.

I erased Patrick's message with a shiver. I'd been spending too much time looking at Deirdre's form of evil genius and it was rubbing off on me. But the sense of that painting, the possibility of it, didn't leave me. It was like nothing I'd ever done before, but somehow I knew it could be the best work I'd ever done.

Except that I wasn't really a painter anymore, and I was supposed to be working for Shelley. Not to mention Kathleen.

The next message drove all thought of paintings from my mind. It was from Kathleen. Her voice was breathy and she was talking too fast, as if afraid she wouldn't get all the words out.

"Barbara, it's Kathleen. I need to talk to you right away. There's something I have to tell you. As soon as…" her voice broke off, as if she was listening to something. Then, even faster, "I've got to go. I'll call."

And she hung up.

Okay, Kathleen's situation was now urgent. What did she want to tell me? And why the sudden disconnect? Had she somehow got to a phone at Shady Groves, then been caught? Or was she out?

I pulled up Kathleen's file, reviewed what little I had. Nothing that hinted what she might have to tell me. No mention of Blake Masters, either. I dialed her sister Mary's number, but there was no answer, so I left a message.

I dialed back into voice mail, went through that annoying sequence of levels and passwords to pick up the rest of my messages. There was, ironically, a call from Mary Roberts that said only that she needed to talk to me, and she'd call back.

Then another message from Brad Bramwell, a 'call me, not urgent,' from Andrea, and a message from Cassandra. "Barbara, I think I have some news that you'll find very interesting. It's about Bill Rampage."

I dialed Cassandra's number, got voice mail. How is it possible to hate voice mail and resent people who don't have it, at the same time? I left a message. Same thing with Patrick.

I got up and put on a pot of Italian Roast, which I'd been craving for the last two hours, and opened a window. My office felt close and stuffy and so did my brain.

I stood for a moment, looking out. It was another gray day, though it had stopped raining. And despite the fumes of the traffic roaring by, there was an elusive scent of spring in the air. I opened the window wider, hoping to capture a little more of that freshness, and the jackhammer down the block started up.

With a curse I slammed the window shut, glared at the coffeemaker, which had yet to produce coffee, and stomped back to my desk.

The phone was not ringing. I checked my e-mail, but there was nothing relating to either case, and no other matters that couldn't wait. It was already mid-afternoon. Now what?

Talking to Kathleen was my priority. I needed to assure myself that she was all right, and that she wasn't calling to confess to killing Bill Rampage. Then I had some questions for her about Blake Masters. But how to find her?

I was adding cream when the phone rang, I pounced on it. "Mary?"

"You obviously forget all about me when I'm out of town," said a deep male voice.

"Nick!" I said, my pleasure at hearing from him clear in my voice. "Well, if you're going to cancel dates, and go out of town for interminable periods, you have to expect to be forgotten."

"Hmmm. I'll have to see what I can do to remind you. Are you free for dinner?"

"You're back in town?"

"For tonight, anyway."

"So does the dinner invite qualify as an offer I can't refuse?"

"I don't know. Does it?"

Suddenly he wasn't teasing. I glanced at my watch. It was nearly three and I still needed to talk to Kathleen—if I could find her. Not to mention Shelley. But I wanted to see him. "Yes, I'm free."

"I'll pick you up around eight?"

"Works for me."

"Your place or the office?"

"As long as it's somewhere casual, make it eight and the office."

"Done. I've missed you, Barbara." And he'd hung up before I had a chance to reply.

I sat and looked at the phone for a moment. I'd missed him, too, but I wasn't ready to admit it to him yet. Maybe I never would be.

With a sigh, I called Kathleen's sister Mary again. Still no answer.

I left her an urgent message and my cell phone number. No point waiting for calls when I could be doing something useful.

CHAPTER THIRTY-FOUR

I had no reason to expect Shelley to be sitting in her hotel room in the middle of an admittedly dreary afternoon, but she was. Another sign of what being arrested—and Blake's lack of support—had done to her.

I found it infuriating. Shelley's face lit up when she opened the door and saw me.

"Barbara! You're back. What did you find out?"

I held out one of the lattes I'd picked up on the way.

She eyed me, took a careful sip. "Caramel? Okay. What am I not going to want to hear?"

"I think we should sit down."

She led me into the dimly lit living area, perched on the sofa, and met my eyes. "Well?"

Her directness is one of the things I admire most about Shelley. "I think Blake had a strong motive for killing Deirdre," I said.

And I suspected he might have killed Bill Rampage too, but I didn't think Shelley needed to hear that now.

"Blake did? How can you say such a thing? Why would he do such a thing?"

"Bear with me for a moment. How much do you know about Deirdre's painting style?"

"Barbara, you just accused my husband of murder. I do not want to talk about his lover's painting style."

I noted that this time she hadn't leapt to defend Blake. "I think the 'why' for Deirdre's murder is her painting. Specifically, because she was painting Blake. Or trying to."

"Impossible. Deirdre didn't paint men. And Blake wouldn't be interested."

"I saw the painting."

"You did? What was it like?" For a moment the artist took over.

I could relate. Lately, my artist kept trying to break out of the attic I'd relegated her to five years ago. "Mediocre. It was recognizably Blake, but it didn't come alive. It didn't measure up to her early work, never mind anything she'd done recently."

"Deirdre did a mediocre painting?"

"I don't think she was finished with it." Not by a long shot.

Shelley thought about it. "I don't think so, either. There was no way Deirdre would show a mediocre painting. And no way she would ever admit there was something she couldn't do. But what does that have to do with why she's dead?"

I lifted my latte, swallowed. "Have you seen Deirdre's early works?"

"Yes. They're a pale copy of what she's doing now. Was doing."

"Exactly. Deirdre found a way to make her art live by capturing her subject's pain. But she had to know where that pain came from."

"What do you mean?" Shelley asked.

"Deirdre's paintings changed a few years ago, went from good to brilliant. She'd always painted women in pain, but her later paintings had a depth and a compassion that the early ones lacked."

"I agree. So?"

"So at first I thought the change was because she'd grown as an artist, learned to accept herself. Then I realized that she'd found a new way to tap into her subject's pain, to keep it immediate while she was painting them."

"But—that's impossible. However did she manage it?" Shelley asked.

———

EVEN TALKING about how Deirdre had brought her paintings to life gave me cold shivers. I used to be an occasional hiker, back when I wasn't working every weekend, and there was one route that still stands out in my mind. You had to walk along a narrow, twisting footpath, with a steep drop-off on either side, knowing that one misstep and you're falling. And it's a long way down.

Deirdre's method for taking her art to the next level—and the obsessive need to improve her paintings that drove it—gave me the same feeling. I understood that obsession all too well.

But make the wrong choices as an artist—it's one misstep and you're falling. Did I really want to go back to that world?

Did I have any choice?

"Deirdre would find the psychological sore spot for each of her subjects, and attack it during each session."

"So to paint Blake…"

"She had to find a way to cause him pain if she wanted his portrait to come alive. It was probably even more important when painting him because as a man. His emotions would be more foreign to her than the women she'd painted when she first started out."

"And Deirdre couldn't resist the challenge of expanding beyond the label of 'women's painter'," Shelley said slowly, staring at me.

It was so good to be talking to another painter. We spoke the same language, a language I'd forgotten was important to me.

"Exactly. 'Women's painter, women's writer', it's all about limits. And Deirdre wasn't going to be limited. No matter what. And she definitely wasn't going to give up, even if Blake didn't want his portrait finished."

"Maybe especially if Blake didn't want his portrait finished," Shelley said thoughtfully. "I'd guess that would give her an extra thrill."

I thought about the portraits I'd seen. "Probably. But we need to figure out what she could have used to cause Blake pain."

Shelley bit her lip, finger circling her wineglass. Finally she shook her head. "I don't know. He's so self-sufficient, he doesn't seem to need anyone. What do you think it was?"

I wondered what Shelley and Blake had shared, why she'd ever married him. I find it sad, and kinda scary, the mistakes people make in relationships, and the situations they allow themselves to get caught in, all in the name of love.

"I get the impression that Blake likes to be in control," I said.

Shelley gave me a wry smile. "You could say that."

I remembered Blake's arrogant expression, his subtle put-downs of Shelley, felt again that quiver of anger. How to say this? "He's very charming, but he almost seems to be measuring the effect of his charm."

She just stared at me for a long moment, her face paling.

"You're right," she said, as if the words were dragged from somewhere inside her. "Even with me he does that, that 'watching' thing. It isn't calculation, exactly, but there's always a distance between him and everyone else. But what does that have to do with Deirdre?"

"I'm wondering if Blake's vulnerable spot might have been money."

"Money? But Blake has money. Plenty of it."

"Maybe not enough. You've told me wants to stay on his Grand-mama's good side so she'll leave him her money. Maybe it's not really about the money, maybe what he really craves is acceptance —hers, society's, whatever. Money's a symbol for that acceptance. Is that possible?"

"Well, I've never seen it."

"Never?"

Her face grew whiter, which I wouldn't have thought possible. "I—I—"

She stopped, swallowed hard and gulped down some wine. "He's always been competitive. Over the years, I've seen him furious for days when someone, anyone, appears to be doing better than he was. I've never understood it."

"You've said Blake has no family except his grandmother and the cousin he hates who might inherit in his place. Maybe he's confused money with family, with belonging."

As I spoke, Shelley's eyes slowly filled with tears. She gave a tiny inclination of her head, an admission she didn't want to make.

"I think Deirdre was blackmailing Blake by threatening to break up your marriage," I said.

"Blake wouldn't care if our marriage broke up." Shelley's voice was flat, but the pain behind it made me sad for her. Even if I did think she was well rid of the jerk.

"Blake might not have cared about your marriage, but what if Deirdre was threatening to tell his Grandmama about her affair with Blake? She might have changed her will again. This time permanently."

"I never thought of that."

"Maybe Blake did, and couldn't risk it. With Deirdre dead and you charged with her murder, Blake would be free."

"That's horrible!"

"Yes, it is. But is it possible? Given your knowledge of Blake?"

Shelley was silent for a long moment. Finally she loosed a deep sigh and nodded. "Yes, it's possible. If Blake thought Deirdre was serious, if he really thought he'd lose everything. But I still can't believe it. And all for the sake of a painting."

"Have you ever had a painting going wrong, felt you'd do anything to get it right?"

She stared at me. "Of course I have. Barbara, you have too, haven't you?"

I nodded. There was no point denying it, to her or to myself.

Getting a painting right really did mean that much, to both of us. But there were limits. Weren't there?

Maybe I hadn't stuck with painting long enough to find out where my limits really were, but I was no Deirdre, of that I was sure. But if I had another shot at my painting career, if it all rested on one painting? What would I be prepared do for that painting?

Not what Deirdre had. I knew that much. But what were my limits?

Shelley was wrestling with the same thoughts. "I wouldn't, I couldn't do that. Damage another person. No painting is worth that much."

"No. But…"

"You're right. Some paintings are worth almost anything. But not that."

"Deirdre made a different decision."

Shelley shuddered. "I knew I didn't like that woman. I didn't know how right I was."

"I agree. And Deirdre had done a bad portrait of Blake. Knowing Deirdre, do you think she'd leave it at that?"

"Never."

"That seems to be the consensus. So how would Blake have reacted to Deirdre's version of artistic inspiration?"

"I just don't know." Shelley's color was better, and the life was back in her eyes. She sat forward in her chair. "So what do we do now? How do we find out?"

I grinned in relief. The old Shelley was back. "Does Blake know anything about gardening?"

"Gardening?" Her expression was priceless. "And how did we go from Blake as a blackmailed murderer to Blake as a gardener?"

"Humor me."

Shelley quirked an eyebrow, but answered. "As far as I know, Blake knows nothing about gardening. He won't even deal with our landscaping company."

"How about flowers? Or native plants?"

"Flowers? Blake? You've got to be kidding."

Okay, not flowers. "I don't suppose Blake has an interest in poisons?"

Shelley looked surprised. "In a way. He did a refresher course on Botox not too long ago. Does that help?"

That wasn't what I'd had in mind. Though I'll bet Blake and Bill's Terri would have had a lot to talk about.

Which started me wondering if they had talked, and what she'd thought of the situation. And maybe I needed to talk to Patrick about a wider range of poisons, if lily of the valley turned out not to be poisonous. You never knew. "I don't know. Yet. But you need to get Blake to meet you here on Wednesday. And his Grandmother too."

She looked stunned, and teary again. "But Barbara…"

"Shelley, trust me, this is critical. I don't care how you get them here. Just do it."

CHAPTER THIRTY-FIVE

My next stop was the Belton Pharmacy. And I was in luck—I could see Patrick's shock of red hair behind the counter. I made my way to the back, waited while he answered questions about cough syrup for an elderly woman. Then he looked up, grinned.

"Barbara! You've come for the results of my exhaustive research."

"Actually, I just have one question for you."

"One question? After all that? After I slaved for hours? How can you?"

"Oh, the hot date cooled off, did he?"

The tips of Patrick's ears turned red, but he grinned. "Not exactly."

"So, how many hours did you slave for?"

"You're good, Barbara. You're very good. Okay, what's your one question?"

"Is lily of the valley poisonous? And if you leave the cut flowers standing in water, will they make that water poisonous? And how quickly?"

"That's three questions. Which one should I answer?"

"Patrick!"

He grinned, opened his mouth to answer, and the lady with the cough syrup came back. Ten minutes later I'd exhausted what little patience I had left, and he was still explaining. I'd run out of shampoo that morning, and I was in a drugstore—I flashed a 'back in five' sign at Patrick and went shopping.

When I came back, shampoo and conditioner in hand, he was free. And feeling impatient, judging by the look on his face.

"Well?"

"Don't you 'well' me, Miss Barbara. You come waltzing in, ask your questions, and vanish just when you've got me intrigued."

His light bantering was a relief after the intensity of my meeting with Shelley. I grinned at him. "Never mind all that. Is lily of the valley poisonous?"

He nodded. "Class six poison."

"Six? Those innocent little flowers?"

He nodded. "Innocent nothing. It's loaded with convallatoxin."

"Convalla—what?"

"Convallatoxin. It's a glycoside poison similar to digitalis. And the symptoms match what you described."

Hot damn! "And is this convallatoxin soluble in water?"

He nodded again. "Sure is. Put cut flowers in water for twenty-four hours, the water's also a class six poison. I gather someone has been cutting lily of the valley?"

I nodded. "Little bouquets on all the bedside tables."

His eyebrows went up. "Any chance your dead guy was poisoned by mistake?"

"I already thought of that, and I don't think so. The vases look nothing like the fancy water carafes and glasses. And the water in the vases was supposed to be changed every day."

"Supposed to be?"

"I don't suppose you've ever worked as a chambermaid, but let me tell you, the work is never-ending. You quickly learn to bend any rule you can get away with."

"Ah."

"Ah, indeed," I said with a grin that matched his. "Many thanks, Patrick."

"You'll tell me what happened when this is all over, right?"

"Minus the specifics. I have to protect…"

"Your client, yeah, yeah, I know. But you'll spill the juicy details, right?"

"Don't I always?"

———

AS I DROVE BACK across the bridge, thinking about tracking down Terri, my cell phone rang.

"Barbara O'Grady."

"Barbara? This is Mary, Mary Roberts. Thank God I've found you."

Which was why Dr. Odlander found me skulking around the bleak grounds at Shady Gates some forty minutes later. Actually, Mary had told me Kathleen's room looked over the gardens, and I was reconnoitering before I went in to try to talk to her.

Skulking was what Dr. Odlander's expression said he thought I was doing when he came roaring out of the building, followed by two conspicuously over-developed men in white. It had started to rain again, and it amused me to see them getting soaked. I was dressed for the weather. They weren't.

"Miss O'Grady! You have no right to be here." This was not a happy camper, and I don't think the rain was the cause of his misery. Probably a personality defect.

"Ms. O'Grady, if you please. And I'm here on behalf of the family. Kathleen's family."

His expression told me that he didn't believe me, so I pulled out the letter of authorization Mary Roberts had faxed me and handed it to him.

He half turned to shield it from the rain and read it slowly, concentrating on every word, looking, I was sure, for the detail that would prove it a fraud. Finally he looked up, a frown firmly lodged between those bushy brows.

"Why are you here?" he demanded. "And what are you doing in the back garden?"

I looked around me. A few spindly shrubs and some yellowing grass. I raised my brows. He glared at me.

"The family has asked me to look into the conditions here, then to meet with Kathleen. At length and in private," I said.

"Certainly." His tone was enough to freeze ice cubes. "If you would follow me."

He led me through the main floor to a windowless beige room where two black club chairs sat on a thick beige carpet, facing an unlit fireplace. "Please be seated," he said. "I have a call to make."

I would have been disappointed if he hadn't called Mrs. Roberts. Obviously she'd responded as coached, though, because within fifteen minutes he was back with Kathleen in tow.

This was a much-subdued Kathleen.

Her eyes were huge in a white face. Her hair lay lank against her head. She went straight to the chair opposite mine, sat down and closed her eyes. Dr. Odlander watched her for a moment, then went out, closing the door behind him.

———

AS THE DOOR snicked shut behind her psychiatrist, Kathleen sat up and opened her eyes.

I stared at her. Where had this alert, vital woman come from? She hadn't been in the room a moment ago.

"Barbara, I am so glad to see you," she said, leaning forward and placing a hand on my arm. "I need your help."

I was glad to see her seemingly well, but this new Kathleen made me even more wary than her previous incarnations. "You said you had something to tell me?"

She nodded. "Yes, I do. I'm so glad we've got a chance to talk now. I've been thinking and thinking about Bill, and what happened that weekend."

At least we were on the same wavelength. "Yes?"

"How do we know Bill is dead?"

Okay, maybe not. "Um, Kathleen. You found his body. Remember, the poison, the convulsions?"

She laughed. "Oh, Barbara, if you could see your face. That wasn't what I meant."

The absolute stillness of the room seemed to close tight around us. Mary had said Kathleen was desperate to see me, wouldn't calm down or take her medications until she did. Now I appreciated her concern.

Kathleen seemed to have lost all touch with reality. Except that, despite her dishevelment, she looked better, more focused and alive, than I'd yet seen her. What was I missing?

"What did you mean, then?"

"Humor me, Barbara. How do we know Bill is dead?"

Right. "You found him dead, and told me about it. The police in Nanaimo confirmed it for me."

She nodded, as if I'd agreed with her. Now I was really confused.

"You see, Barbara? I found him. I was the last one to see him alive. He was my lover. I was being set up."

"Set up? By whom?"

"That's what I want you to find out. Bill wasn't killed because of something he'd done. They killed him and set me up to make me suffer, to make me lose my balance and end up in here. And I want to know who did this to me?"

I was having a little difficulty buying into this conspiracy scenario. Especially given what her sister had said about Kathleen's tendency to paranoia. "Kathleen, how did you come up with this theory?"

"I've had a lot of time to think in here," she said with a wave that encompassed the bland little room and the bleak institution that surrounded it. "And I've been thinking about Bill and me, and why he had to die."

She paused, touched a hand to her slender throat. "And Bill dying like that doesn't make sense. Everyone loved Bill, he didn't even have any enemies. There has to be more, there has to be meaning. So I thought about who would gain if I ended up back in this place..." Her voice trailed off.

Was she really on to something, not just paranoid? Had I been underestimating Kathleen all along? "And?"

"I was looking to buy another painting, for my collection. I'd arranged to meet the artist there, on Hornby, that weekend. Maybe you know her? Deirdre Brandt?"

I sunk back in my chair, feeling like I'd just had the air knocked out of me.

Kathleen had arranged to meet with Deirdre on Hornby? She was the reason Deirdre and Blake had been there that weekend?

And no one had mentioned it until now?

I felt a surge of anger at my client, who'd done nothing but lie to me. And at Blake—ditto. Even at Andrea for getting me into this mess in the first place.

I took a deep breath, fighting to over-ride my frustration at all the time I'd wasted.

Kathleen had lied to me from the get go. Which I should be used to by now. Somehow I never am. I forced my voice to a professional tone. "I've heard of her. Go on."

Kathleen glanced at me, but either I was a better actress than I'd thought, or nuances were lost on her right now. I was betting on the latter.

"Well, after Bill's death, I was so devastated, I couldn't think about anything else. So I lost my chance at the painting. And I'd gone to a lot of work to set up that meeting, sworn the painter to secrecy so no other collector would have a chance to buy the painting first. But someone did hear, they must have."

I thought about Kathleen's unique collection. I had a nasty feeling I knew what was coming, but I asked anyway.

"There's no shortage of Deirdre Brandt paintings on the market. Why was this one so important?"

"Well, if you know Deirdre, you know she's known as a woman's painter. Does brilliant portraits of women."

"And?"

"And she'd offered me the chance to buy her first portrait of a man. It would have been worth a mint."

Sometimes I hate it when I'm right. "If it was any good."

"Oh, it was good. Maybe even better than her female portraits."

As she spoke, Kathleen's voice, even her posture, had changed. Speaking of Deirdre's work, she suddenly looked and sounded like a serious collector, an expert in her area of interest.

It was hard to believe this was the same person who'd slunk into the room fifteen minutes ago. Or the one who was obsessed with her late lover.

I was so fascinated with this new Kathleen that it took me too long to realize what she'd said. Then I got it. "Wait a minute. You saw this portrait? Of a man?"

She nodded.

"When? Where?"

Kathleen looked puzzled. "On Hornby, of course. That weekend. That's why she was there."

Of course Deirdre would have taken the painting with her to see a prospective buyer. But which portrait? "Deirdre showed you a painting she'd done of a man? And it was good?"

"It was brilliant. It's going to make her name bigger than ever."

Now I was confused. All my theories revolved around Deirdre trying to paint Blake and failing. Who had Deirdre painted?

"Did you recognize the subject?" I asked Kathleen.

"Sure, it was the guy who was there with her, Blake somebody. Smooth, charming type, but the portrait showed the greedy, frightened child inside. And once you'd seen it in the portrait, you couldn't unsee it in the man."

I was liking the new version of Kathleen a lot. For one thing, she had a very discerning eye. And she'd just confirmed the suspicions I'd begun to harbor about Blake. "The painting must have been good, if it caught that side of the man."

She nodded. "It was amazing work. But you had to wonder what he thought of it."

I'd clearly badly underestimated Kathleen in my earlier dealings with her. And I wasn't the only one. That was going to have to change, once I'd cleared up this mess of a case.

I'd make sure of it.

"It didn't seem to have discouraged Blake, though," Kathleen was saying. "He was all over Deirdre, all weekend long."

What? There went my timeline on the murder.

If what Kathleen was telling me was right, the portrait of Blake I'd seen in Seattle must have been an early version. Which meant that before she came north to the Sunshine Inn, Deirdre must have begun—and finished—another version. A good, no, a brilliant version, according to Kathleen.

Who apparently knew exactly what she was talking about.

Which meant that once that new version was completed, Deirdre had no reason to torture Blake further. That wasn't why she'd gone with him to Hornby, then.

So much for Blake's motive for killing Deirdre.

If Deirdre's portrait of Blake had been as accurate as Kathleen thought it was—and given Deirdre's ability to paint the ugly side of her sitters, it probably was—I'd been right about Blake's character, but wrong about everything else.

Which left me where? Nowhere, that's where.

I still didn't know who'd killed Bill Rampage, and now I didn't know who had killed Deirdre Brandt. And both my clients were running out of time.

"So you see, that explains Bill's death," Kathleen was saying with an eager look.

I didn't see anything.

Except that Bill Rampage was dead, had probably been poisoned using lilies of the valley. And I couldn't think of even one way to ask Kathleen about her knowledge of flowers—if she was guilty of killing Bill, she'd lie. If she was innocent, I had no way of proving it.

"When they killed Bill, I couldn't think, much less negotiate to buy a painting," Kathleen was saying. "Even one that good. So they killed him and framed me so they could buy the painting."

I didn't think much of her theory, but at least she had a theory. Unlike me. "And you have no idea who 'they' are?"

She shook her head, looking at me with a belief in her eyes that made me very nervous. "No. But since I came back, I keep feeling like I'm being watched, you know. They don't want me to figure it out. Except that I have. You'll find them, Barbara, won't you? And get me out of here?"

Based on my success with this case to date, I'd be lucky if I could find my socks tomorrow morning.

"Were there any other art lovers on Hornby that weekend? Collectors? Either staying there or visiting," I hastened to add, in case Kathleen was tempted to leave out any other pertinent details.

"Not really," she said. "Though I think the Michaels collect a little."

Oh great. "What about a guy named Murphy? Tad Murphy?"

"He used to collect, mostly abstracts, though I think he's got a few early works of Jayson Ho. I've heard he's mostly into sailboats now." Her tone was dismissive.

I thought about the paintings in the lobby at Willis and Murphy. So they belonged to Murphy. I still didn't like him.

And my list of suspects was growing instead of shrinking. Not good. "What about the Grussmans? John and Elena?"

"I don't think they know anything about art."

"And did you see any of the collectors talking with Deirdre Brandt?"

"All of them, I think. She's a very social woman, though I don't like her very much. She even flirted with Bill, right in front of me, if you can imagine it. Not that it did her any good."

I realized Kathleen was referring to Deirdre in the present

tense. "Kathleen, you do know that Deirdre Brandt is dead, don't you?"

She went white. "What?"

I guess she really was in a fog after Bill's death. "She died, was murdered, five days after Bill. She died here, in Vancouver."

"She was murdered? How?"

"Poisoned."

Kathleen's voice held horror and something else I couldn't name. "The same as Bill?"

"No. No, Deirdre was killed with someone's heart medication. Overdosed, and it caused a fatal heart attack."

"How awful. And did they arrest the person whose medication it was?"

"Yes, except that I don't think she did it. She's a friend of mine," I added. "And no killer."

Kathleen's eyes widened. "Are you looking into Deirdre's murder too?"

I nodded.

"Do you think they're connected? The deaths I mean?"

"I don't know." And I really didn't.

"But it seems too coincidental if they aren't," I added, as much to myself as to her.

Kathleen looked at me. "You say Deirdre was murdered in Vancouver. Did she come straight here from Hornby?"

"Yes, as far as I can tell."

"So where's the painting? Find who she sold it to and you find your murderer."

Kathleen's logic made a few too many assumptions, but she asked a good question. What had happened to the completed painting of Blake? No one I'd talked to admitted to knowing it existed.

So where was it? And with whom?

Assuming the painting existed outside Kathleen's mind, that is. Which—given her recent behavior and current diagnosis—was a definite question mark.

But if the woman I'd been talking with this afternoon was the real Kathleen… then that painting existed. And it had to connect to Deirdre's murder? Didn't it?

Unless Deirdre's last painting turned out to be yet another of the red herrings this case seemed to be rife with.

"I'll look into it, Kathleen," I said, careful not to specify what I'd be looking into. I wasn't sure I knew, anyway.

It seemed to satisfy her.

"Please hurry, Barbara," she said. "I have to get out of here. I made the mistake of telling Dr. Odlander why I was so upset. Now he's assuming I'm paranoid and delusional. Anything I say now makes it worse. His solution is to keep feeding me tranquilizers until I can't think about anything, much less talk about it. Until you find Bill's killer and prove I was set up, I'm stuck."

Oh good, more guilt. For the first time since I took on her case, I felt wholeheartedly sorry for Kathleen.

"I'll find the killer, Kathleen," I promised. "And then I'll come and get you out of here."

Her smile was wry. "I'm counting on it, Barbara," she said. "I'm counting on it."

CHAPTER THIRTY-SIX

When I reached my car, I was annoyed to see that the windows had steamed up. While I waited for the defroster to work, I checked my watch. I still had time before Nick arrived.

I called Brad Bramwell in Nanaimo and got the desk sergeant. When I identified myself, I was put through immediately.

"Barbara O'Grady," Brad said. "Finally. And do you have any idea where your client is?"

"Possibly," I hedged. "But before you talk to her, there are a few facts you should probably know."

"Such as?"

"Has the poison that killed Bill Rampage been identified yet?"

"Let me pull the file." I heard paper rustling, then pages flipping. "It's a botanical, but that's all they've got so far," he said.

"I've been doing some research," I began.

He groaned. "I've heard about the results of your research."

I wondered who he'd been talking to, then decided I'd really rather not know. "Did you know that lily of the valley was in bloom on Hornby a couple of weeks ago?"

"Huh. And you're telling me this why?"

"Well, given that it's a class six poison, I thought you might be interested."

"Lily of the valley is a class six poison?"

"Uh huh."

"So you're telling me Bill Rampage was out chewing on the flowers?"

I grinned. "Not quite. The management very helpfully provided vases full of lily of the valley for each guest. It sat on their bedside table."

"Considerate of them. But how do we get from vases of flowers to Rampage dead?"

"You might want to have your lab check Rampage's water glass and carafe for convallatoxin."

"Convalla—what?"

That's what I'd said. I spelled it for him, listened to the scratching of his pen.

"So what's convallatoxin when it's home?"

"It's the poisonous ingredient in lily of the valley."

"Hmmm. And if this stuff is what killed Rampage, how would the killer have got it into Rampage's water glass?" he asked.

"That's the beauty of it. Lily of the valley is so toxic that the water in which flowers have been sitting for twenty-four hours or more will kill."

"So someone could have brought him a glass of water, carefully poured from their flower vase."

"Or filled his carafe. And they could have filled it from the vase of flowers right on his table."

"My God! It's close to the perfect crime."

"Maybe not. It's pretty coincidental. He could so easily have dumped the water and refilled the decanter. I gather there were no fingerprints?"

"The glass had been wiped clean."

"What about the carafe? And the vase?"

"Nothing odd on the carafe, but I doubt we checked the vase. I'll have a look at the crime scene info and call the lab. Thanks for this, Barbara."

"Don't mention it. But you will let me know what the lab says, right?" The crime scene info I'd get out of him when he called back.

"Well, we don't normally release…"

I cleared my throat. Loudly.

"Yes, I'll get back to you, Barbara."

"Thanks. I'll look forward to hearing from you."

"Not so fast. You said you knew where your client was? This information doesn't exactly clear her, you know."

"No, but it sure makes it an equal opportunity crime. Anyone there that afternoon could have put the poisoned water in his decanter."

"True enough. So where is she?"

I told him. "I don't know if you'll be able to talk to her. Or if whatever she tells you at the moment will have any value."

"I'll consider that. Thanks for the information."

"Don't forget to call," I reminded him.

Disconnecting, I called Terri. No answer. I checked my watch. I still had a good couple of hours before I was expecting Nick, and Terri should be at work. I started the engine, flicked on my turn signal.

———

TERRI, perfectly groomed in a severe black suit, was not happy to see me. I could tell, despite the fact that her expression never changed. Probably it was the venom in her tone when she glanced up and saw me.

"You!"

"I only have a couple of questions, and then I'll be out of here."

"I can't talk here," she hissed, glancing around the deserted but very stylish store.

I doubted I could afford any of their clothing, but then I

wouldn't be caught dead in most of it. Especially the ones with little frills here and there. "Then take a coffee break."

"I'm the only one working."

So what was the problem? "I'm not leaving until we've talked."

She must have read the determination in my face. "Talk fast," she said, a gimlet stare pinned on my face.

"When you were on Hornby the weekend Bill Rampage died, did you meet Blake Masters?"

"Yes, a charming man."

He was charming, on the surface anyway. He'd probably liked her, too. "And did you get the chance to talk to him?"

"Naturally."

I needed a way to extract information from her. I took a risk. "You know he's a suspect in Bill's murder?"

"Blake? Not possible. Blake is a doctor, a healer. Did you know he does pro bono work for burn victims?"

Somehow that fact kept coming up. "What a saint. Still, Bill was flirting with the woman Blake was with, and Blake didn't take it well."

"That's not true." A hint of color showed at the top of Terri's gaunt cheekbones. "We joked about it. They were two of a kind, Bill and Deirdre—flirting was second nature to them. If you took it seriously, you'd be eaten up with jealousy."

"And you don't think Blake was? Eaten up with jealousy, I mean?"

"Blake? Never. You'd do better to look at That Woman."

"Kathleen? She says she was in love with Bill. Why would she kill him?"

Terri actually snorted. "That Woman doesn't know anything about love. She's not stable."

That was true enough, at least at the moment. But between Terri and Kathleen, I preferred my client. "And what about Tad Murphy? I gather he and Bill weren't on the best of terms."

"Another one who doesn't know anything about love. A bigger phony I've yet to come across."

I guess it took one to know one. "But did Tad have a motive for killing Bill?"

"Oh, sure. He was jealous of Bill. But Tad's too much of a coward to act on it. And he wasn't even there that weekend."

I wondered if Terri knew why Tad was jealous of Bill, and what she'd say if she did know. "Tad dropped in after you left."

"Well, he's still a coward—Tad couldn't have faced Bill."

"Bill was poisoned."

"Even so, Tad wouldn't have had the stomach for it."

"As a doctor, that wouldn't have troubled Blake Masters," I said, watching for her reaction.

"Oh, we're back to Blake again, are we?" Terri said. "Well, I was there, I talked to Blake, and I know how he was feeling. He was completely enthralled with Deirdre, couldn't keep his eyes off of her. And for all she was flirting with Bill, Deirdre was more fascinated with Blake. I watched her. She'd laugh, lean in close to say something to Bill, but out of the corner of her eye she'd be watching Blake. Everything she did, she'd check to see how Blake was taking it. And he knew it."

That sounded like Deirdre was still looking for Blake's vulnerability. According to Kathleen, Deirdre had already finished the painting, so what was she up to? "How do you know Blake knew?"

She gave me an impatient look. "I told you, we laughed about it."

"How did Kathleen react to the situation?"

"That was the odd bit. She wasn't in the least jealous, just sat back looking amused."

Amused? What was there in that situation to amuse Kathleen?

I was going to have to talk to Kathleen again. I wasn't making much progress in finding Bill's murderer, even though I knew how he'd probably been killed.

"Was anyone else upset by the situation?"

Behind me a soft chime announced a customer. I glanced around to see a very thin blond who had probably benefited from several trips to one of Blake Master's colleagues. She glanced around, then drifted towards a rack of evening wear.

"No. You'll have to go now," Terri said as she hurried around the counter and towards her customer.

———

SO MUCH FOR that little fishing expedition, I thought as I turned on the coffee machine in my office. Slumping behind my desk, I contemplated the ceiling and tried to decide what I'd accomplished that day. Not much, unfortunately.

I'd started the day convinced Blake Masters had killed both Bill and Deirdre. I was ending it with no motive for Blake to have killed Bill, and not much motive for him killing Deirdre.

Still, in both cases Blake had opportunity. That was something. And there was still the possibility that the murder on Hornby had actually been an attempt to kill Deirdre, and Bill had somehow been an unintentional victim.

I glared at the ceiling. Put like that, it sounded ridiculously unlikely. But so did the motives of most of my other suspects.

The burbling of the coffee machine saved me from my thoughts. Two cups of dark roast later, I had read through the entire file on Bill Rampage's death. I was staring at a floor plan of the inn's second floor, wondering how anyone could mistake Deirdre's room for Bill Rampage's across the hall, when a rapping on the door made me jump about a foot.

I'd been concentrating so hard I hadn't heard a thing, and the stairs creak something fierce. Putting one hand against my heart, I called out, "Yes? Who is it?"

"Barbara, it's Nick. You know, your knight in shining armor? Dinner, remember?"

It was already eight?

"Yeah, yeah. I'm coming, already. You know you'd read me the riot act if I opened the door without asking, or worse, left it unlocked," I said as I opened the door.

Nick didn't reply to my wit. He was too busy kissing me.

I didn't mind. I was too busy kissing him back.

———

NICK TOOK me to Giuseppe's. It felt so good, sitting opposite him in a warm, candlelit room, filled with the smell of fresh bread, tomato sauce and garlic, I almost forgot about the murders and my inability to solve them. We started with a shared plate of antipasto, then I ordered a wonderfully garlicky *linguine con vongole.*

Nick ordered the *fettuccine alla puttanesca,* rich with tomato, garlic and olives. I hid my anxiety behind my smile and my glass of Cabernet.

"So what are you trying so hard not to think about?"

Nick's intuitiveness always surprises me, but usually I'm not at a loss for words. I downed a gulp of my wine, which is no way to treat the vintage Nick had ordered. "I ran into some snags on the case I'm working, but I don't want to waste our time together talking about it."

His eyes met mine. He seemed to be choosing his words carefully. "I've been out of touch a lot these past weeks. And I've had to cancel on you a couple of times. You sure that's not what you don't want to talk about?"

I hated it that he was right, and that I didn't know how to admit it without putting both of us on the spot. He was supposed to be the one who didn't like to talk about feelings, wasn't he? Where did he get off being more comfortable with the subject than I was?

"No, I mean, the case is a real mess," I said, and slugged back more wine.

He smiled a little. "So tell me about it," he said.

So I told him. Keeping details out of it, I told him about Kathleen and Bill and Terri, about Tiffany and Brandy and Bill. And about Tiffany and Bill and Tad, and Shelley and Blake and Deirdre. About two poisonings and too many suspects. I changed the names, but I kept the facts.

As I told it, my frustration and confusion came through clearly, as well as the cynicism so many fake relationships had triggered.

Nick listened carefully, asking a pertinent question here and there. At the end of it he sat back and looked at me, face carefully expressionless.

"And in the middle of all this I vanish on you," he said.

I couldn't deny it hadn't crossed my mind, so I shrugged and didn't say anything.

"It wasn't my choice, you know that."

"Of course."

"My job, both our jobs, make demands on our time, and we don't have much say in the matter."

"I wouldn't have it any other way. It means you understand the demands of my job."

Those dark eyes of his were watching me closely. "But it doesn't help, knowing that, does it?" he asked.

"I don't know what you mean."

He reached out across the table and took my hand, gave it a gentle squeeze. "I missed you, Barbara. I really did."

"I should hope so," I said, trying for a light tone.

"No, I mean it. I hated having to cancel. I enjoy being with you, spending time with you. I want more of that, not less."

I met his eyes across the table. He meant it. Every word. I smiled at him, squeezed his hand.

He gave me an inquiring look, and squeezed back, his eyes warm. Somehow he must have understood what I couldn't find the words to say, because he changed the subject.

"So how do you feel about tiramisu for dessert?" he asked. "And while we're waiting, I had a few thoughts on your case, if you're interested?"

I did like this man. Even if he was better at reading my emotions than I was. Hell, maybe because of it. All I knew was I didn't want this thing between us to end. Not yet, anyway.

"Tiramisu is always good," I said. "And sure, go ahead."

"The painting, the one done by the dead artist, where is it?"

I was nodding. "Exactly what I've been wondering. I figure the murderer has to have it, but whether they've kept it, destroyed it or sold it, I don't know."

Something was niggling at the back of my mind, something I'd heard or read recently. I had the feeling it was important, but I couldn't quite grasp it.

"When was it last seen, do you know?"

"I know my client saw it on Hornby, but since she didn't bother to tell me about it 'til this afternoon, I haven't had a chance to check it out."

"Ouch," said Nick, laughing.

"Tell me about it. Not only does she not tell me the artist and her lover were on Hornby the weekend the first guy was killed, she doesn't tell me they were there so she could buy a painting from the artist. I have to wonder what else she hasn't told me." Again that little niggle.

"What is it, Barbara?"

Damn, he was perceptive. "I have a feeling there's something I've forgotten, or overlooked. And whatever it is, it's critical."

"Yeah, I know that one. Every case has one of those, and usually they show up just before you're about to crack it."

"Or blow it entirely. But thank you for the kind words."

"Those weren't kind words. They were the truth. One professional to another."

One of the things that continually amazed me about Nick was his acceptance of me as an equal. Especially after four years spent with Jayson. Who didn't accept that he had any equals.

Too bad it took me so long to figure that out.

"I wish I could figure out what I've missed," I said, talking about the case, and hearing the second meaning in my words too late. Good think Nick didn't know what I was thinking.

"Is it to do with the painting?"

"Maybe. Or with my client and the artist, or—No, it's gone again."

"It'll come to you when you're not thinking about it."

"Probably. You said you had a few thoughts on the case?"

"If the painting was finished, why was the artist killed? If it really was her lover who did it, and she'd already finished the painting, what was the point?"

"Yeah, I know. I keep tripping over that one, too. And I don't have an answer, but after all the digging I've been doing, he's the one who seems to fit, you know?"

"I know. But you'll need more than that to free your friend."

"Tell me about it. Any thoughts?"

He shook his head. "Not with the information we've got so far."

"And I'm fresh out of information sources. The two people I really need to talk to are both dead."

"No point in talking to him? The artist's lover, I mean."

"I don't think so. He's pretty skittish, and he's denying the painting was ever begun."

"So go back to Hornby. Find out who else saw the painting, who it left the Island with."

I'd been really hoping to avoid another ferry-filled day. But Nick had a point, even if it did mean another early morning start. "Hornby it is. But for tonight, here comes our tiramisu."

"By all means, let's focus on the essentials."

And after dessert, we went back to my place, where we focused on some other essentials, very effectively distracting each other from everything except ourselves.

CHAPTER THIRTY-SEVEN

The following morning found me on the six-thirty ferry to Nanaimo. Again. It was still dark, raining lightly and I could feel the chill coming off the water.

Despite that, I had a smile on my face. A night of Nick had been effective medicine for the bleakness I hadn't realized the case was engendering. My body was humming, my mind was clear and I felt good.

So good that when the question that had been niggling at me worked its way to the front of my brain, it didn't register at first. What had Lois Michaels said of Deirdre, when I'd still thought she was talking about Shelley? Too much paint on her face and hands?

The reference to paint on her face I understood—in death, Deirdre's overdone makeup had stood out like a garish mask. But too much paint on her hands?

I'd ignored the comment, assumed Lois had been disparaging Deirdre's long, red nails, but what if I was wrong?

"Even if she was an artist," Lois had said. What if Lois had meant real paint? Oil paint. No, Deirdre had used acrylics, hadn't she? But still.

Had Lois seen Deirdre with acrylic paint on her hands? And when?

Somehow I didn't see Deirdre as the ill-groomed type. If her hands had been covered in paint, she'd have got it off. Unless she wasn't finished, unless...

Had Deirdre been painting on Hornby? And if so what had she been painting?

Which led me to wonder exactly when Kathleen had seen that finished painting of Blake.

———

FOUR HOURS later I had my answer. According to Brandy, Deirdre had been painting in her room on Hornby, and she'd been painting Blake.

"She kept making a real mess of the towels," Brandy said. "I thought somebody should talk to her, but Elena said to soak them in water and any that didn't come clean we'd charge her for."

"And the painting?"

"It sat there for the longest time, kinda all blurry. Then all of a sudden there's this totally awesome painting staring at me. It was like, more alive than Dr. Masters. Creepy."

"What do you mean?"

She fingered her lip. "It wasn't a very nice painting, but it had energy, you know. But he—and I mean the man himself, not the painting—he looked totally pale and sorta sick."

"How did he look when he arrived?"

A shrug. "I didn't really notice him, y'know. Not my type." She seemed to think about it. "But I guess he looked pretty good when they got here."

"So he looked worse when the painting was done?"

"I guess."

Sounds like Deirdre had run true to form. And that Blake had a motive for murder after all, at least until they'd left the island. Once

Deirdre had finished a painting, she typically lost interest in her victims.

But what had happened to the painting? "And when was the painting finished?"

Another shrug. "No idea."

I really hate dealing with teenagers. "Was it before or after Bill died?"

Her eyes filled. "After, I guess. Maybe that's why he looked so bad, because of Bill."

She could be right. Another theory shot to hell. "And Bill was in the room across the hall from Dr. and Mrs. Masters, right?"

Brandy nodded.

"The whole time?"

"Yes."

I had to eliminate the possibility that Bill had been poisoned by mistake. "And were all the rooms kept locked?"

"Sure. Except for when we're cleaning them."

"What happens then?" I asked, keeping my voice as level as I could.

"Well, then we unlock them all. It makes things easier."

I wondered if Elena knew about this little arrangement. I'd bet she didn't. "So how does that work?"

"This won't get me in trouble, will it?"

"Why should it?"

"Oh, good. Well, I do one end of the hall and Tiffany the other. But if she's short of something for one of her rooms she borrows from one of mine. And the same back."

"Things like shampoos and soaps?"

"Yeah, like that. We always store extra in the locked cabinets under the sink."

"So you and Tiffany could both be in and out of all the rooms while you're cleaning?"

"Uh huh."

"What time do you clean?"

"We usually start after lunch is cleared, around two, and we're mostly done by four."

"And do the guests ever come up to the rooms then?"

"Sometimes, not often."

"And you'd see them when they did?"

"Mostly. Usually they come and ask us for stuff, extras, or ask when we'll be done. Like that."

"And do you remember seeing anyone that Saturday afternoon? Before Bill died?"

"The cops already asked me that. No, I didn't see anyone."

Didn't mean they weren't there. And it gave the killer open access to Bill's room.

"One more question. Did Tiffany have to borrow anything from Bill's room? Or from Dr. Masters'?"

"She didn't tell me if she did."

I wasn't sure why I wanted to know, just that little niggle again. Time to talk to Tiffany. "Thanks, Brandy."

"I'll do anything to help catch Bill's killer. Anything!"

I nodded, ignoring the dramatics, and went looking for Tiffany.

I found her in the spacious kitchen, where she was gutting salmon and Elena was chopping herbs.

"Elena, do you mind if I ask Tiffany a couple of questions?"

"Not at all. Please, feel free."

Tiffany looked up, her expression sullen. "Here?"

"Can we step outside?"

She looked at the pale sunlight falling through the windows and brightened. "Okay."

I followed her through the French doors onto a flagstone patio. "Tiffany, the day before Bill Rampage died—do you remember which rooms you cleaned?"

"Sure, the three on the east end, like always

"I know it's a while ago, but do you remember if you had to get supplies from either Bill Rampage's room or Dr. Masters?"

She looked taken aback.

"It's okay, Brandy told me. And I won't say anything to Mrs. Perfect." I gave her what I hoped looked like a conspiratorial smile.

She looked a little dubious, then smiled back. "Oh. Okay, then. Let me think. I think the Michael's room was totally out of everything. Happens every time they stay—she must fill her suitcase with stuff. And with all the money they have, too."

"So where did you refill it from? Do you remember?"

Her eyes darted to one side, then back. "Well, I went into Bill's room, but there wasn't any shampoo there. So I went into Dr. Master's room and got it there."

And what was the rest of the story? "What aren't you telling me, Tiffany?"

"I don't want to get Brandy in trouble."

"This isn't about causing trouble for either of you. It's about finding the person who killed Bill Rampage."

"I guess. Well, when I was in Bill's room, I noticed Brandy hadn't got the carafe and water glass matching. And the same thing in the Masters' suite. We have two patterns, you see. And Mrs. Perfect is death on stuff like that. So I switched them."

Don't tell me! "What did you switch, Tiffany?"

"I switched the carafe from the Masters' suite to Bill's room, and vice versa. So that they matched."

She couldn't just have moved the glasses, like a normal person? "Were the carafes full?"

She nodded. "Yeah, like I remember I had to be real careful not to spill any."

Why, oh why could she not have poured out the water and refilled them? "And does anyone know you did this, Tiffany?"

"Oh, no. I didn't even tell Brandy. See, I didn't want to embarrass her."

So the poisoned water had actually been in Deirdre's suite, and Tiffany had oh, so carefully moved it to Bill Rampage's room.

Finally this case was making sense. Blake had tried once to kill Deirdre—on Hornby—and failed. Then for some reason he'd tried again and succeeded. Even though she'd already finished his portrait.

Maybe he'd killed her so he could destroy that too-accurate portrait of himself.

I had one last question. "In suites with two guests, how many carafes are there?"

"Two, of course. One on each nightstand."

"And on whose nightstand was the carafe you put in Bill's room?" I asked, knowing the answer.

"It was on Dr. Master's nightstand."

What? "Are you sure?"

She nodded. "Yeah, cause she had perfume on hers. And paintbrushes. All he had was a book. Something about burn victims. It was gruesome."

That didn't mean the poison wasn't meant for Deirdre. Still, it did pose a possibility I hadn't considered. What if Deirdre had tried to poison Blake?

The hairs on the back of my neck stood on end as I thought about what Deirdre might have been prepared to do to achieve her breakthrough portrait. Surely she'd stop short of murder.

On the other hand, what more primal fear was there than fear for one's life? Maybe she hadn't even intended to kill him. Maybe...

I yanked my errant thoughts up short. It was still likely that the poison had been brewed by Blake and intended for Deirdre. I had a question or two for Elena on the subject of flowers.

———

"SO NOW IT is my turn, yes?" Elena looked at me with her head on one side like an inquisitive raven. "What is it you would like to know?"

We were in her small office off the kitchen, surrounded by her binders, files, recipe books and seed catalogues, and the door was closed. "The weekend Bill Rampage was killed—did any of your guests express an interest in gardening, do you remember?"

She thumbed through a large register, checked the names. "Hmmm. No, no-one that weekend, not that I recall."

"Anybody express an appreciation for flowers?"

"It's funny—yes. I remember Mrs. Masters thanked me for the flowers in her room. She said they were her favorite. I remember because it seemed out of character."

"That lily of the valley would be her favorite?"

"Yes, that, I suppose, but more that she would make the effort. She was not one to pay attention to the help, that one."

Hmmm. "And did you know that lily of the valley is poisonous?"

"No, but since you are asking about it, I guessed. Is that what killed poor Mr. Rampage?"

"It may have been."

"How sad. And such a shy little flower. I will have to tell the staff to stop picking them for the guests."

"Probably a good idea."

"So is it Mrs. Masters you suspect? I would not have thought she would have a reason to kill Mr. Rampage."

I didn't think Deirdre had a reason to kill Bill Rampage either, but the pieces were beginning to fall into a truly bizarre shape. "I don't know. One last question. After the murder, when they left, did Deirdre—Masters have any paintings with her?"

Elena nodded. "Just one, and rather large. I gather she worked on it a long time before she got it right."

"Why do you say that?"

She shrugged. "She ruined a set of towels for each night they were here."

"So she painted right up until the day they left?"

"Yes."

"Which was the day Bill Rampage's body was discovered?"

She nodded.

Had Deirdre come to meet Kathleen with a portrait that wasn't finished? She must have been totally frustrated with her inability to perfect the portrait. And determined not to fail.

So how had she managed to finish the work that Kathleen had judged brilliant?

"And did you see it?"

"No, but I gathered it was of Dr. Masters."

"Do you know anyone who did see it?"

"She kept it covered, though Brandy told me she showed it to Ms. Graham."

So only Brandy and Kathleen had seen the finished painting. And presumably Blake Masters. Interesting. "I thought Brandy had to be sent home?"

"That was later. We had her lie down first. The guests did not even know she was there. But she mentioned seeing the painting."

So Kathleen hadn't lied to me. Or not about that, at least. Exactly how much had she been willing to pay for Deirdre's breakthrough painting, anyway?

My thoughts colliding with each other, I thanked Elena and went looking for Brandy.

———

I FOUND Brandy changing the towels in one of the rooms, persuaded her to accompany me to the library. Got her seated in one of the deep leather sofas. Her eyes fixed on me, a little wide. Like a startled colt, I thought, with those ridiculously long eyelashes.

"I'm getting close to finding out who killed Bill Rampage," I said. "But I have a few more questions. Is that okay?"

"For Bill? Anything."

Good. I hoped she meant it. "Brandy, Elena tells me you were there when De—Mrs. Masters showed the painting to Ms. Graham."

"Yeah? So?"

"So where was Dr. Masters?"

"Oh, he was there too."

"And what did he say when he saw the painting?"

Brandy's glance slid around the dark paneled library, as if hoping the walls would replay the scene for her. "He didn't say a word. That Kathleen—Ms. Graham, did all the talking. She kept saying how good it was, but she was crying too. Because of Bill, y'know?"

"I know."

"She seemed to really like the painting, but then she'd stand back to look at it and be crying too hard to see it. It was odd, now that I think about it."

"What was odd?"

"Well, until Mrs. Masters showed the painting, the doctor was the one doing the talking, kidding her, like, about how he'd never seen it and finally he got to see what he really looked like. Only somehow he didn't sound like he really thought it was funny."

When I deciphered what the teenager had said, I felt a glow of triumph.

This time, I thought I had the pieces in the right places.

Blake really hadn't seen the painting until it was done, didn't even know what Deirdre's vision of him looked like. It was yet another argument that he hadn't prepared that poisoned carafe for Deirdre.

"Thanks for your help, Brandy," I said. And raced to catch the next ferry.

———

SINCE I WAS PASSING through Nanaimo, I swung by the RCMP station. Took a chance on catching Brad Bramwell in. And this time it paid off.

"Barbara! What brings you here?"

I stood, leaving a cup of station's battery acid coffee stranded on the battered table behind me. "I was on my way back from Hornby and thought I'd swing by on the off chance you had a few minutes free."

"C'mon in. Still seeing Nick?"

"You know Nick?"

"I asked around."

"Yes, we're still together." And it gave me a warm glow to realize that as of last night, I was no longer doubting that. At least for now.

"Too bad," he said with a grin. "So, what can I do for you?"

He wasn't flirting with me, was he? "Was it convallatoxin that killed Bill Rampage?"

"It was, but how did you know?"

"Were there fingerprints on the vase on Bill's nightstand?"

"We didn't keep the vase as evidence."

"What about on the water carafe?"

"We found only two sets of prints, belonging to Bill Rampage and one of the maids."

"Tiffany?"

He nodded, then read something in my face and sat forward. "Why, Barbara?"

I filled him in on what I'd learned. He listened, face impassive. "Are you sure of all this?"

I nodded.

"So your current theory is?"

"Deirdre Brandt, who was registered at the Inn as Mrs. Blake Masters, tried to poison Blake Masters so that she could finish his portrait. Only Tiffany switched the carafes, and Bill Rampage died instead."

"Why didn't Masters call us in?"

"He may not have known what happened. Not then."

"And a week later Deirdre Brandt was dead."

"Yes."

He nodded slowly. "It could fit. I'll need to verify everything you've told me. And I'll need to talk to Masters."

"You can't arrest a dead woman."

"No. But I can make sure I clear the living."

I thought about Kathleen, and what a relief this would be for her. "Can I ask you to hold off on questioning Masters for a couple of days?"

He gave me a speculative look. "I'm sure you have a reason for that?"

"I think, no, I'm sure Blake Masters killed Deirdre. And I'd like the time to prove it."

"You're that close to proving it?"

"I think so."

"And you'll share whatever you find out?"

"Of course."

"Then I can wait another day or so. Especially if he's back in Seattle. Is he?"

"If you wait until Wednesday morning, I think you'll find him in Vancouver. And in jail."

"How? He's an American citizen, right?"

"Yes, but if all goes well he'll be in Vancouver tomorrow."

CHAPTER THIRTY-EIGHT

All did go well. The following morning, Blake Masters walked into Shelley's hotel room, a scowl darkening his handsome face. "Okay, Shelley, what's all this about needing me…"

He stopped dead when he saw his grandmother sitting there. "Grand! What are you doing here? Are you all right?"

She folded her hands, looked him up and down. "We've been waiting for you," she said. "Sit down and Barbara will tell us about it."

Blake didn't look happy, but she hadn't left him an option. He sat.

"After you left town, Shelley hired me to follow you," I said, watching Blake. He darted a glance at his grandmother, who sat ramrod straight, no hint of her thoughts showing on her lined face.

"I also looked into Deirdre Brandt's background. The more I uncovered, the more people I found had reason to hate her. She was a survivor who'd come up the hard way and she didn't let anyone get in her way. Art was her ticket out."

I paused, sipped my coffee and watched the tension build in Blake Master's eyes.

"Deirdre painted her subject's souls. You have only to look at her later work to see it. I wanted to know how she'd grown beyond her earlier mediocrity. I expected a life changing event or a pivotal influence."

"I hope you weren't billing me for the time you spent on this nonsense," Blake broke in.

"Don't worry, it was Shelley's tab. And it wasn't a waste."

Blake glared at Shelley.

I watched the byplay, noted Blake's grandmother watching it too, and then resumed.

"It took me a while to figure out how Deirdre could suddenly have had such insight in her art. I began to understand that she'd needed to bare those souls before she could paint them, and the more painful the baring, the more powerful the painting. That was the secret behind her phenomenal success, you see—she finally understood her own creativity, and she was prepared to pay any price to create."

I paused. I'd been watching Blake, but it was Shelley's pale face that drew my gaze. She understood only too well.

"Deirdre had to paint, had to create the best she was capable of," I said. "But somewhere along the way it got twisted. She produced her best work by causing pain in others."

"That poor woman," Shelley said suddenly.

"Poor, nothing!" Blake snapped, then darted a glance at his Grand and fell silent, lips pursed tightly.

"Deirdre had never painted men, though. Until Blake here decided to commission a portrait. You couldn't have known the price of that particular piece of vanity," I said to the by now ashen Blake.

"Deirdre couldn't resist the challenge, but she had to find the key that would take you apart. And she didn't stop until she had it. And surprise, surprise, it all started with money."

I turned to the senior Mrs. Masters, still sitting very erect but looking as though she'd tasted something sour.

"Specifically, your money. Blake was desperate to protect the image he thought you expected, and Deirdre knew too much. At first I thought she was blackmailing him, but that would have been easier to deal with, wouldn't it, Blake?" I asked as I turned toward him.

"You probably tried to buy her off," I said, and knew by his expression that I'd been right. "But to paint you, she needed to expose your flaws. Nothing you could offer her came close."

Blake shrugged. "So? I'd survive."

I watched the tiny muscles move in his throat as he glanced at his grandmother's frozen face, then quickly away.

"So what happened on Hornby?" I asked him. "Deirdre finished her portrait of you, and it wasn't flattering enough?"

Blake's face flushed. "You think that's what this is about? The woman was crazy," he burst out, as though words held back by some tremendous pressure had suddenly released.

"The whole night she was finishing my portrait, she had me convinced I was dying, that she'd poisoned me. It was the most hellish night of my life."

"And yet you kept posing?"

"I was in too much pain to leave. I lay there, my guts white agony, while she worked like a maniac behind that easel of hers. She'd pop her head around, ask how I was feeling, tell me how certain death by poison was. Then she'd smile at me, slowly, as if she were savoring it. God, she was smug. When I could think past the pain, I wanted to kill her."

"Why didn't you call for help?"

His face was bleak, remembering. "At first the pain was too bad. Then—what was the point? She'd made it clear there was no antidote."

I thought about what Patrick had said about convallatoxin—the poison could be reversed, if caught early enough. Had Deirdre known how suggestible Blake was? Was that why she'd chosen poison?

I shivered. What Deirdre had done to Blake was unspeakable. "What happened when you didn't die?"

He shrugged. "She'd told me I'd be dead by morning. Just before dawn, she finished the painting. She stood there, smirking at it. Then went into the bathroom and spent about half an hour cleaning her brushes. When she came out again, she walked over to the bed. I laid there, arms wrapped around my guts. Hating her.

"Not dead yet?" she asked and poked me.

I couldn't speak, so she poked me again. Then she walked over, sniffed my water glass, and held the carafe up to the light. She looked at me and started to laugh. She kept laughing while she covered up her precious painting.

"Surprise, Blake," she finally said. "I haven't poisoned you, I just needed a little something extra to finish the painting."

I was too drained to move. She rolled her eyes.

"You aren't poisoned, Blake," she said. "You just shouldn't eat liver."

She was still laughing. The next morning I found out how Bill Rampage had died and realized how ruthless she really was."

"You believe Deirdre killed Bill Rampage?" I asked him.

"I'm certain of it."

"Why didn't you tell the police?"

"No-one would have believed me. And by then I'd seen the painting. Deirdre was determined to show it everywhere. Kept calling it the best work she'd ever done. Nothing I could say would change her mind.

She was beyond impossible," he said harshly. "Kept talking about posterity—Christ! Did she really think I'd let her exhibit it? It wasn't even very good."

"You told her that?" Shelley asked.

"Of course."

"Have you learned nothing being married to me?"

"Even at her worst, Deirdre was worth ten of you," he said.

"But you killed her," I said.

He didn't flinch. "She wouldn't let that painting go. And she'd already made it clear that she had no limits. None. It wouldn't have ended until she'd destroyed me. Grand…"

He looked over at her, white haired, white lipped and steelspined, and for a moment I saw something wistful in his eyes. "I couldn't allow it," he said softly.

Shelley looked torn between pity and horror.

"But you were ready to see your wife go to jail for something you did?" I said.

"There's no evidence, so how can they convict either of us?"

His grandmother broke the ensuing silence. "That's where you're wrong, boy," she said, her voice clear. "You always were too fond of the easy solution, the lazy way out. It was your biggest fault as a child, and it's your biggest fault as a man."

This to a man who'd just confessed to murder!

"Ms. O'Grady has enough to give the police clear evidence that you had motive, means and opportunity," she said, inclining her head towards me in a regal nod. "And you have confessed."

"The police haven't heard my confession."

"I have heard it," she said, as if that were the end of the matter. And for Blake, perhaps it was.

CHAPTER THIRTY-NINE

I don't know what passed between Blake and his grandmother after Shelley and I left them, but Shelley tells me Blake made a full confession to the police.

"With Grand sitting right beside him, with that look in her eye," Shelley said when we met at Guido's for a late lunch the following day. "And she insisted I be there, too, so that there was no question of my innocence. And then Grand offered me her support. On her terms. Can you believe it?"

We were sitting at a table in the back, with no-one close enough to overhear. Good thing, too—Shelley was in no mood to be discreet. I just nodded, glad to see her back to herself again.

"I'm grateful my career is strong enough I could turn her down," Shelley said. "And I'm divorcing Blake." She paused, drank some of her wine.

Red, of course. A full-bodied Cabernet that's a favorite of mine.

Her next words came slowly. "I feel sorry for him. Blake seems lost."

Shelley, on the other hand, looked like the vibrant woman I'd met here that night before this whole mess had started. She was wearing a red dress that fitted her perfectly, with a red and black and gold scarf and her flaring black cape. But she clearly needed to talk.

I was happy to listen. And glad to have closure on this nasty case.

"You know he's claiming self-defense?" Shelley was saying. "And temporary insanity."

"He was so afraid she'd try to kill him again that he lost his grip on reality and killed her first?" I said with a grin.

Shelley smiled back at me. "Something like that."

Good luck to him with that argument. Though if anyone had ever been a candidate for a crime of passion, it was Deirdre. "Temporary insanity or not, he could probably use a lot of counseling."

She nodded slowly. "I'm ashamed of myself, all those years I was married to him and never knew how damaged he was."

"I suspect he worked very hard to hide it, from himself as much as anything."

She nodded, her face serious. "Maybe."

Then, after a pause, "Deirdre's work was powerful."

I had no problem following her train of thought. I hadn't been able to get her work or her life out of my mind, either. "She was true to her art, but she also needed help. Badly."

"I can't help wondering if I'm as true to my own work."

I took a deep drink of my wine. "Maybe that's the real reason I gave up painting. I wasn't willing to dig deep enough."

Shelley cocked her head. "No, I don't think that's it. Not for either of us. But it's hard painting from that kind of honesty. And it takes time."

We looked at each other, and Shelley's eyes began to twinkle. "Listen to the two of us. Talk about maudlin."

Guido brought our pasta primavera then, steaming plates piled high, and there was no more talking for a time. Over dessert and coffee we talked about her plans to go back to Seattle and work on her next show.

"I'll send you an announcement for the opening, Barbara."

"If I can get away."

"It will be my first solo show, which freaks me out. You have to come, provide moral support."

"Well…"

"For old times sake."

"Okay, okay. I know when I'm beaten. Send me the invite, and I'll drive down."

"Good." Shelley took a spoonful of tiramisu, tasted it, and closed her eyes in bliss. "Mmmm. Barbara, you have to try this. It's divine."

I tasted. "Hmmm. But if you think that's good, try this," pushing my *panna cotta* towards her.

"Oh, that is so good. What's it flavored with?"

"Lavender and honey. Guido's specialty."

"Wow. I may have to order one of those."

I waved Guido over, told him what we needed. He beamed, and moments later he was back with a second dessert.

"This is on the house, dear ladies. Those who truly appreciate good food should be rewarded."

Shelley watched him go. "He's a dear. So tell me, Barbara. When can I expect to come to one of your openings?"

I stopped, spoon halfway to my mouth. "I don't paint anymore. You know that."

"That's not what I hear." She gave me a meaningful look.

"What?"

"I was talking with Margaret Courtland. Apparently she actually managed to pry a recent work or two out of you?"

"She called me the minute she heard you were out of jail, insisted on seeing a couple of things, even though they're not finished. That is one very persistent lady." And I spooned up another mouthful of *panna cotta*.

"Funny, from what you've been telling me, I was under the impression you hadn't painted anything in years. And here you've been painting all along. You must be pretty good—Margaret has a very discerning eye."

Shelley was beaming at me. I hated this.

"Margaret is wrong. No-one will be interested in seeing my stuff, and I've nothing ready to show."

Shelley raised an eyebrow. "Margaret seems to think differently. What are you afraid of, Barbara?"

"I don't really have time to paint, that's all." And after seeing what her passion for her art had done to Deirdre, did I want to take those risks?

Shelley grinned at me. "Good luck telling Margaret that." She scooped up a generous mouthful of her dessert. "Mmmm. Send me an invitation, that's all I'm saying."

———

TURNS OUT SHELLEY WAS RIGHT—MARGARET Courtland was determined to see both of my recently completed paintings. And she didn't stop there. By week's end, I'd committed to a September delivery of seven more completed works for a show at her gallery.

What was I thinking?

I was frantically pulling canvases out of the closet in the spare room, looking for anything good enough to finish, when the phone rang. "Hello?"

"Barbara? It's Andrea. Listen, Kathleen and I want to take you to dinner, to thank you."

I must remember to call Brad and thank him for sorting things out for my client so promptly. "She's out? I mean—Kathleen's back at work?"

"No, she says she's not coming back—seems she's planning to open a small art gallery. Not something I pictured Kathleen doing, but she seems happy. And she's back to the Kathleen I know."

Given Kathleen's art collection—and what I'd seen of her professional side when she was talking about Deirdre's last painting—I thought it was perfect. "It makes sense to me. She has an uncanny ability to acquire unique paintings. It should be less stressful for her, too. "

"Except for paying the bills each month."

With Kathleen's trust fund, bills weren't going to be a problem. But Andrea didn't know that. "Spoken like a true entrepreneur," was all I said.

"So, dinner. You'll come?"

"Love to. But after everything I went through, it had better be somewhere expensive."

Andrea laughed. "We were thinking West."

Which just happened to be one of Vancouver's top restaurants. That was pulling out all the stops. "Works for me."

"And bring Nick."

A grin slid across my face as I pictured Nick's reaction to Kathleen. It was past time that he got to know my friends.

"Sure," I said. "Should be fun."

And was surprised to find I meant it.

ACKNOWLEDGMENTS

Many thanks to those who listened to the story and the process as it evolved, including (but not limited to) my first readers Carla Lewis, Sandy Constable, Roberta Rich, Kelly Morisseau, Bobbi Randall, Kayo Devcic, Sarah Rowse, Brad Rowse, Linda Roggeveen and Chris Petty. Thanks go to them for insightful comments on early drafts of the manuscript. Thanks also go to Linda Roggeveen for her eagle eye on the copyedit. Any errors are, of course, mine.